# VICTORIA DAHL

# BAD BOYS DO

HQN™

Recycling programs
for this product may
not exist in your area.

ISBN-13: 978-0-373-77602-3

BAD BOYS DO

Copyright © 2011 by Victoria Dahl

## ACKNOWLEDGMENTS

Thank you to Jennifer Echols
for her insight into the world of universities
and grad students. Having only been an
undergraduate, I needed the peek behind the
curtain! Thanks to Amy for trying her best to
keep me sane this time around. I'm sorry the duty
fell to you this year. And huge thanks to Tara
for her amazing support.

As usual, Twitter folk,
you are the best virtual water cooler a girl
could ask for. You did a great job of distracting
me from stress, not to mention work. But for
once you actually helped me concentrate, so a
big shout-out to all my #1k1hr writing friends!
Also, thanks to Jared for starting the kilt talk.

My husband truly helped me get through
to the end of this story, and I couldn't have
done it without him. And boys, I promise a great
vacation to make up for all the days I spent
locked in my bedroom with coffee and a laptop.

Last but definitely not least, a thank you
to my readers. Without you, I would not write.
You make all my books possible.

This story is for my wonderful agent, Amy.
Thank you for always being there.

# BAD BOYS DO

# CHAPTER ONE

THIS WASN'T A BOOK CLUB; it was a manhunt.

Olivia couldn't believe she'd fallen for it. Actually… she couldn't believe she'd thrown herself headfirst into it. She'd read the assigned book. Twice. She'd down-loaded important discussion points. Made detailed notes. Marked up the pages. And finally, before walking into the brewery, she'd sat in her car for ten minutes, pumping herself up for this first foray into a girls-only gathering.

*They're just women like me,* she'd assured herself. *No need to be intimidated. You'll fit right in because you'll all have the book in common.*

Now here she was, sitting in the barroom of Dono-van Brothers Brewery, listening to seven women dis-cuss their current dating lives and sexual adventures. And Olivia, having no dating life or adventurous sex to contribute, sat there like a bump on a log, the book club selection clutched tight in her tense fingers.

It wasn't that she'd never had girlfriends. She'd had a best friend in high school. And one in college. And then…then she'd had her husband. Her ex was as close as she'd gotten to a best friend in the past ten years, and he'd failed pretty spectacularly at that.

She needed girlfriends, and she needed them fast.

When Gwen Abbey had invited her to join her book club, Olivia had felt honored and relieved.

She should've known better. Gwen wasn't exactly the type to opine about literature. Oh, she was smart enough, but her attention flitted about like a humming-bird after a shot of espresso. She might read a book, but Olivia couldn't imagine her spending two hours talking about it afterward.

"I'm so glad you came!" Gwen whispered, putting an arm around Olivia's shoulders for a quick squeeze. "Isn't this fun?"

"Yes!" Olivia answered, feeling her fingers go numb against the slick cover of the book. She really, really wished she hadn't posted so many sticky notes in the pages. They fluttered like tiny blue banners under the breeze of the ceiling fan.

"Can you even believe how adorable he is?"

Olivia glanced automatically toward the bar, where a very young, very handsome man filled glasses at the tap. He was Jamie Donovan, she'd been informed, and his welcoming wave had set the whole table tittering a few moments ago. The tittering had been followed by promises—or threats—of what the women would do if they got Jamie Donovan alone for an hour. "Find out exactly what's under that kilt," had been a common re-frain.

"So," Olivia ventured, leaning closer to Gwen, "is he the reason you guys meet at this place?"

"Heck, yeah. No reason not to have a nice view while we hang out. Plus, Marie, Alyx and Carrie are all mar-ried, so this is a nice safe way for them to get a little flirtation in. They get to drool over Jamie, fantasize a little, and then their husbands benefit when they get home. Everyone is happy!"

"Great!" Olivia responded with fake enthusiasm.

But even she was tired of fake enthusiasm. Why couldn't she just be enthusiastic? Granted, it wasn't what she'd expected, and Olivia liked to know what she was getting into. She made plans. And lists. She believed that in life, you measured twice and cut once. But all the measuring in the world hadn't managed to make a good marriage. She needed to loosen up.

And in all honesty, she felt better knowing that some of the women were married. If it was just about having fun and not about picking up a man, she could get into it. Or she could try.

"Here he comes," Gwen whispered. "And it looks like we're in luck...."

"Jamie!" one of the women called. "You wore the kilt for us!"

The cute bartender with the messy dark gold hair winked at them. At *all* of them. "First Wednesday of the month. You ladies didn't think I'd forget book club, did you?"

If giggles could be raucous, these certainly were. As subtly as she could, Olivia tipped her head to the side to see past the other women. She finally caught a glimpse of the infamous kilt, and she couldn't deny that it looked good on him. Between the bottom edge of the dark kilt and the top of his work boots, a lovely expanse of tanned leg was revealed, dusted with the faint glint of golden hair. The kilt wasn't plaid. It looked like it was made from black canvas. His wide chest was covered by a faded brown T-shirt with a faintly visible Donovan Brothers logo stretched across it.

The man was gorgeous. Olivia couldn't deny that.

He continued past their large table to deliver beer to a group farther on. There was no hooting from that side of the room. The men there were focused on the baseball game on the wide-screen TV. They didn't even glance at Jamie Donovan's bare legs. The women of the book club table, on the other hand, craned their necks shamelessly. Olivia sank down a little in her chair.

"How long have you been meeting here?" she asked Gwen.

"About a year. Before that we used to meet at Starbucks. Frankly, the club was about to die. Nobody had the free time to read and then get together for meetings. But now we have one hundred percent attendance."

"And the reading?" Olivia pressed. But she didn't get an answer to that, because Jamie Donovan had reappeared, a wide smile already in place. His hair looked darker now, but the lights of the ceiling fan behind him limned it with gold.

"Happy Wednesday, ladies."

Gwen grinned. "Don't you mean happy hump day?"

"Aw, come on, Gwen. I'm a nice boy. You should be ashamed of yourself."

"I'd like to be. Wanna help?"

For a split second, Olivia thought Gwen had gone too far. She'd offended this man. He was just doing his job. Olivia touched Gwen's arm, trying to prompt her to apologize, but suddenly his face cracked and he burst into loud laughter.

"Good one," he chuckled. "You been saving that up for me?"

"Maybe," Gwen said.

"I'm honored. So do you want the usual? A pitcher of India Pale and a pitcher of amber?"

Everybody agreed, but as he started to turn away, Olivia cleared her throat. "Pardon me. Could I get a water?"

"Absolutely," he said, swinging back around. When his eyes lighted on her, he stood straighter. "Oh, hello. A new member of the club?"

Now that the smile was directed at her, Olivia found herself mute. Her lips parted. Nothing came out.

"This is Olivia," Gwen volunteered.

"Hello, Olivia."

Good Lord. How did he make the few syllables of her name sound like a kiss? A deep, slow kiss. Olivia actually shivered.

Jamie Donovan's eyes drifted down. His eyebrows rose. "Well, look at that."

Outrage rushed through her at his words. Where did he get off looking at her breasts like—

He gestured. "You actually know something about how a book club is supposed to work. The rest of you should take note. Or *notes*."

Heat flashed over her face as she looked down to her marked-up copy of *The Last of the Mohicans*. The other women booed and tossed crumpled napkins at Jamie, and Olivia was thankful for the distraction. Of course he hadn't been checking out her body. He didn't even look at her again before heading back to the bar. Olivia leaned over and slipped the book into her purse.

"I watched the movie," the woman next to her said. "It was amazing. A really great story."

"It was. I'm honestly glad I read it. Even if we're not going to discuss it tonight." She slid her eyes to Gwen. "So why did you tell me we were reading *The Last of the Mohicans?*"

Gwen shrugged. "Because you wouldn't have come if I'd told you we were just going to drink and hang out. Right?"

She wanted to be outraged that she'd been lied to, but Gwen was right. She wouldn't have come if it hadn't been a book club. The point of a book club was that it gave Olivia something to talk about. It helped smooth over those awkward conversations she usually had with other women. But now she was here, and this was exactly what she'd been trying to work up to.

"You're right," she said. "So thank you."

The discussion of *The Last of the Mohicans* led to talk of movies with hot men in them, and even Olivia could contribute to that. She'd been married, but she hadn't been blind. And when Jamie returned to the table with their beer, she wasn't blind then, either. His forearms alone were enough to draw her attention. They were strong and tan and undeniably male. She was still staring at his arms when a glass of water appeared in front of her.

"Your water, Miss Olivia," he said, addressing her as if she were a teacher. Which she was. Just a coincidence, or did the scent of dry-erase marker cling to her? "And a pint glass, too, I presume?" He slid an empty glass to sit next to the water.

She didn't like beer, but now she was fully invested.

"Absolutely," she answered, and his green eyes twinkled. God, could he just do that on demand? What a terrible and deadly skill. She averted her gaze in self-defense and kept her eyes down until he was gone. The man was constructed of nothing but charm and beauty. *Indiscriminate* charm. Fun to enjoy for a girls' night out, but definitely not something to feel flattered by. She knew that from painful experience.

But Olivia *was* flattered that Gwen had gone to the trouble of tricking her into this. That alone made her smile as she sipped at the lightest of the two beers. But the lightness belied its bitter taste, and she had to hide a grimace. Maybe she could talk the group into going out for martinis one time. But as the evening wore on, she felt the easiness of the brewery. This wasn't like a bar, where men swarmed like scavengers. Instead, it was safe and homey, and Olivia found herself loving it. She even managed to make it through half a glass of that awful beer, and by the time she excused herself to use the bathroom, her head buzzed pleasantly.

This was going to be part of her new life. A book club with no books. Women who wanted her company. And gorgeous men to wait on them hand and foot. Or one gorgeous man, at least.

Standing before the mirror, Olivia dabbed gloss on her lips, blinked several times to remoisten her contacts, and smoothed down her sleek new bob. She'd been tempted to try a new color, but she was glad she hadn't now. Because tonight she looked like herself, only better. Older, wiser and more self-assured. *Slightly* more self-assured. But not quite so confident that she didn't startle like a scared rabbit when she stepped out of the bathroom and straight into the path of Jamie Donovan.

"Oh, sorry!" She reached out a hand as if to help steady the keg balanced on his shoulder, but Jamie stepped smoothly around her and set the keg gently onto the floor behind the bar.

"Need a refill?" he asked.

"No!" she said too emphatically. His eyebrows rose. "I mean…I'm fine. Thanks."

"You don't like beer, do you?"

Olivia cringed. "No. I'm sorry. I don't mean to denigrate your life's work or anything.…"

"Oh, I think my self-worth will survive." This time his smile was a little more natural, though no less dazzling.

"It's just too bitter for me. I've never liked it. No matter how light I try to go…"

His eyes slid to the book club table. "Which one did you try?"

"The pale one?"

"India Pale Ale. There's your mistake. Light isn't always mild. India Pale Ale is notoriously hoppy. Extra hops were added to preserve it during shipment to India, hence the name."

"Oh, sure," she said, nodding as if she understood. But the truth was that she'd tried plenty of beer in her life and she hadn't liked any of it.

"Try the amber," he suggested.

"Okay." She started to turn away, but he raised a finger to stop her.

"Here." He filled a slim glass that appeared to be an overgrown cousin of a shot glass. She eyed the dark gold liquid with trepidation. She'd had no intention of trying the amber ale, but maybe he'd realized it. "Go ahead. I promise it's milder than the pale ale."

With a shrug of resignation, Olivia took the glass from him and tried a sip. She was already grimacing when she realized it wasn't so bad. "Oh."

"See? Told you." His eyes crinkled with pleasure, and Olivia told herself that the warmth pooling inside her was the beer. "Even our porter is pretty mild, though you're going to want to steer clear of the Blackjack Stout."

"Oh, no," she protested when she saw him drawing a glass of chocolate-brown beer. "No way."

"Don't you trust me?"

That couldn't be a serious question. Who the hell would trust this man and his sparkling green eyes? In fact, it was a little insulting that he'd flirt with her as if he meant it. Like she'd buy that this boy would be attracted to a thirty-five-year-old woman like her. Did he think she was so desperate she'd believe it?

Olivia raised her chin and took the glass from his hand, ignoring the slide of his skin over hers. "I wouldn't trust you in a million years," she answered, but she took a generous sip of the beer anyway, amazed that it didn't make her eyes water. It was actually kind of…smooth. "All right. Not bad."

"Have I ever lied to you?"

She couldn't help but laugh at that as she took her two tiny glasses and walked away. Every look from this guy was a lie, but they were pleasant lies, at least. Still, she knew better than to enjoy them too much. She'd fallen for that before. It was probably the only thing that Jamie Donovan had in common with Olivia's ex-husband, Victor. Charm.

So it was easy for her to walk back to the table and rejoin the women. Gwen, however, didn't make it easy for Olivia.

"Soooo," she drawled as soon as Olivia sat down. "You were awfully cozy with Jamie over there."

"I was not. He just gave me a new beer to try, that's all."

Gwen tapped one of the glasses. "*Two* new beers."

"Yes, *two* beers. Does that mean something? Is there a secret Donovan Brewery beer code, like the Victorian language of flowers?"

Gwen collapsed onto the table, laughing so hard she snorted.

"I hope you didn't drive."

"Nah, I only live four blocks away."

"I can drive you home," Olivia offered. She'd always liked Gwen, but they hadn't really started talking until news of Olivia's divorce had gone public. Over the past year, they'd gone out to lunch half a dozen times, and Gwen had confessed that it hadn't always been easy for her to make female friends, either. A wave of one hand down her body had said it all. Gwen was a natural blonde with long legs and playmate-style assets. She was not the kind of friend that women brought home to meet the husband. But Olivia didn't have a husband anymore. And she'd rather go to lunch with Gwen than think about dating again.

Gwen finally sat up, wiping tears from her eyes. "You should totally hit that," she said, pointing toward the bar.

"Yeah, right. I'm sure I'm exactly his type."

"I think his 'type' is female, and you've got that covered. He'd be a really nice dip back into the old sexing pool."

"I thought it was the dating pool."

Gwen shook her head. "It's a new world out there, Olivia."

"Oh, I know about the new world, and I am not interested in being a cougar, thank you very much."

"You've already been a trophy wife. Why don't you try the other side of the coin?"

Olivia finished off one of the sample glasses. "I was not a trophy wife. I didn't have the necessary qualifications." She eyed Gwen's chest with an obvious quirk of her brow.

"Yeah, but Victor was twelve years older than you, right? So go younger this time."

Even as she shook her head, she spared a glance for Jamie. "How old is he, anyway?"

"I'm not sure. Twenty-five? Twenty-six? He's in his damn prime."

"My God, he's just a baby."

But apparently Olivia was the only one who felt that way. Amidst a lot of smothered laughter, one of the women approached the pool table and made a big show of putting the quarters in for a game. Olivia looked on, confused by the merriment, until the woman—was it Marie?—stood up and aimed an exaggerated frown at the table. "Jamie?" she called. "The pool table's jammed!"

Jamie came around the bar, wiping his hands on a towel.

"It took my money, but it didn't give me any balls," she pouted.

"Well, I'd better take a look." He slung the towel over his shoulder and crouched down, and Olivia finally understood what was going on. His kilt hitched up, revealing a few inches of strong thigh, and even though Olivia thought this was a childish prank, she stared right along with everyone else. She wondered what those thighs felt like. Hard, she thought. Thick with muscle. Strong. They looked like they'd taste damn good, too.

He slammed a fist into the coin mechanism, then pulled several times. Ropes of muscle flexed and relaxed.

Good Lord.

"Ah, here's the problem," Jamie said. "You put a nickel in."

"Oh, silly me!"

He handed the coin over and started to get up, but his eyes swept the room and caught on Olivia. His brows rose at the same time his gaze fell to his bare knees.

"Busted," Gwen whispered, as they both whipped around to face the table.

"She shouldn't have done that," Olivia whispered back. "And we shouldn't have looked."

Gwen pressed her lips tight together to stifle her laughter.

"I'm serious!" Olivia insisted, but Jamie's voice from just behind her chair cut her off.

"Really, ladies? You're getting lazy. You pulled that trick four months ago. How about a little originality next time?"

"Aw, Jamie!" half the table cried in disappointment.

"And try not to break my pool table."

He really was adorable. Like a puppy. But Olivia kept her eyes on the table. "Are you ready, Gwen?"

"To leave? It's only eight."

Eight? Those two hours had flown by. She'd actually had *fun.* But she still had to go to the grocery store, do laundry and get to bed by ten-thirty. She got up every morning at six to run, no exceptions. "I know I'm pitiful, but I've got to get going. Are you sure you don't want a ride? I don't like the idea of you walking."

"I'll catch a ride with someone. Don't worry. I'll see you in the office tomorrow, all right?"

Olivia grabbed her purse and stood before she could get pulled back into the conversation. And for once, there was actually a possibility that she *could* be pulled back in. These women were all friendly and relaxed and funny. No one had brought up her divorce with a pointed look. No one had snidely asked where she was living now. They actually seemed to *like* her.

In fact, they all expressed disappointment that she was leaving. Several stood to hug her as she edged toward the door. "So what's next month's book?" Olivia asked, prompting the women into laughter.

"The *Kama Sutra!*" one of them called, and Olivia gave in to the temptation to give them all the finger. She giggled at their outraged laughter as she turned toward the door. And, of course, there stood Jamie Donovan, his fingers curled around the handle of the door.

"I highly recommend it," he said as he pulled the door open, letting in a gust of cool night air. "The *Kama Sutra.*"

"She's joking," Olivia made clear.

"I'm not."

She was caught in a strange mixture of happiness and acute embarrassment, but she didn't want to simply blush and stumble by him. So instead, she took up his challenge and let her eyes travel slowly down his body. He looked lovely with his arm outstretched, holding the door. "Big talker," she said as she breezed past him with a confident smile, trying to ignore the sticky notes on the book ruffling in the breeze.

"Good night, Miss Olivia," he called. "See you next month."

And the funny thing was…he probably would.

## CHAPTER TWO

Jamie Donovan looked warily around as he walked across the U campus. There wasn't much of a chance he'd bump into someone from his family. His brother and sister were both at work at the brewery, and they had long since finished their college careers. Jamie had earned his degree long ago, too, but now he was back and sneaking around like a girl past curfew.

He didn't know why he felt nervous. No one, not even his family, would care that he was taking courses on food and beverage management. They'd find it surprising, true, but in an admirable way. He was, after all, the grand fuckup of the family. The one who took nothing seriously and managed only the barest of achievements. That was why this felt so frightening. If you tried at something, you could fail, and Jamie had a long history of failing.

He managed to locate the classroom without any trouble at all, and he felt a touch of disappointment when he entered. He'd kind of hoped it would look like a culinary classroom, complete with commercial appliances and huge prep areas. But this wasn't a culinary class, and the room looked like any other lecture hall. Stadium seating. Plain gray walls. A whiteboard and computer screen at the front. And only a few other students so far. He glanced at the clock. Ten more minutes. In his nervousness, he'd shown up early.

He chose a seat near the back of the room and got out his phone to check his messages. But there was nothing. If things went wrong at the brewery, people turned to his older brother, Eric. And his sister, Tessa, only called when Jamie got up to trouble, which he most emphatically had not. He'd been good. Damn good. Better than anyone ever gave him credit for. Even that disaster two months earlier with the Kendall woman hadn't been his fault.

Well, technically it had been his fault, but he'd been trying to do the right thing, not that he'd bothered to explain that. No, he was too far gone for those kinds of petty explanations. He needed to change his life in a big way and this class was going to help him do that.

With another glance at the clock, he opened his laptop, ready to take notes. He hoped to God this course was as practical as its description had promised. If it started with a socioeconomic history of restaurants, he'd have to get up and leave. He hadn't rearranged his work schedule so he could get a better sense of his place in hospitality history. He had plans to develop. Big ones.

The door behind him opened, and as the new arrival walked past, Jamie glanced over. Then he glanced again.

No fucking way.

His initial surprise gave way to a pleased grin. It was the straitlaced woman from the book club. Amelia. No...Olivia. That was it. She was even more straitlaced today, in a pale gray dress topped by a blue cardigan. Her hair was still shiny and perfectly brushed, but today she wore little black glasses. She was just so…*neat*. Jamie felt an almost irrepressible urge to ruffle her hair, just as he had that night at the brewery. Compared to all the other women in the book club, she'd looked cool and sleek and removed.

Before he could give in to the urge to shake her up, she'd moved past him. Good thing, because he could just imagine her reaction to him reaching out and touching her.

He almost laughed out loud, but he was distracted by the fact that Miss Olivia didn't take a seat in the audience. Instead she walked straight up to the table at the front of the class and set her computer and papers down there.

Holy crap. Miss Straitlaced Olivia was his teacher.

He hadn't really meant anything by flirting with her last week, but he kind of wished he'd put more effort into it now. Because how hot was this?

She adjusted her glasses and tugged her sweater straight while Jamie noticed how slim she looked in the dress. She wasn't exactly petite—if he remembered correctly she'd been average in height. Five foot five maybe, but her slim hips and delicate arms made her seem smaller than she was. Not that she wasn't tough, though. Her eyes didn't give an inch.

Those eyes were currently sweeping coolly over the classroom, but they didn't seem to notice Jamie. He tried not to feel insulted.

"Welcome to Restaurant Development and Management," she said, her voice ringing clearly up the slope of the room. "I'm Olivia Bishop. It looks like we've got a good mix of students for this session, as we usually do during the summer. Some of you are current restaurant owners. Some of you are dipping your foot into the idea. Some are just passing through for the air-conditioning."

Laughter rumbled through the room and Jamie found himself grinning at her as if he were somehow responsible for her good work.

"As this is a community class with no credits, it'll be fairly laid-back. Please remember that when I give an assignment, it's not for a grade. It's an opportunity for you to increase your knowledge and maybe work toward a dream of opening a restaurant. Later, I'll invite some discussion about what each of you is looking for out of this session. But we're opening with information that applies to everyone regardless, so let's just jump into it, shall we?"

She fired up the computer screen and started with statistics about the restaurant business in the real word. Jamie relaxed. This was exactly the kind of class he'd been looking for. He had plenty of ideas, but he needed to understand the practicality of it.

It was just an added bonus that Olivia Bishop was going to be the one to teach him.

He typed notes into his computer and only occasionally took a break to let his gaze wander over her tight calves. She wore black flats, but he could just imagine those legs in spike heels and a short black dress. Did she ever dress that way? She'd worn dark slacks and a sleeveless sweater to the brewery. Tight black dresses probably weren't her thing. But there was something about her that made him itch to find out.

And when she finally looked up at him, when her eyes finally found him and widened, Jamie felt a sharp stab of interest. When she stumbled over her words and lost her place in the lecture, the interest grew into something more solid. It wasn't the first time he'd flustered her, after all.

Maybe Olivia Bishop wasn't as cool and calm as she thought she was.

HAD THAT DARK BEER he'd fed her damaged her brain? How else could she explain the vision of Jamie Donovan sitting in her classroom?

*It's not so strange,* Olivia tried to tell herself as she swallowed hard for the tenth time in a minute. *He's a partner in a brewery. Why wouldn't he be here?* But logic couldn't make her mind stop skipping like a scratched CD. It didn't help that he was smiling as if he knew how flustered she was.

She should've noticed his name on the enrollment sheet, but she'd gone over it two weeks ago, before the trip to the brewery. So here she was, facing him with no warning at all.

Olivia smoothed down her sweater. She clutched the delicate cotton of her favorite dress, then made herself let go before she creased it beyond repair. "Um, so… Yes, on to first-year failure rates. You hear a lot of numbers thrown about, but they mean nothing unless we… um, unless we take a closer look at the causes of failure."

She finally got back on track and made it through the full ninety minutes with a few shreds of dignity intact. Whenever she'd accidentally looked in his direction, he was diligently typing on his laptop, apparently taking the class seriously. That helped her relax, but that relaxation disappeared in an instant when she dismissed the class and Jamie started down the stairs instead of up.

There was no kilt for her to peek up, thank God. Today he wore ancient-looking jeans and another T-shirt. This shirt offered a faded Road Runner racing across his chest.

"Well, hello there, Miss Olivia."

"Don't call me that," she corrected.

His eyebrow quirked. "Ms. Bishop, then. I kind of like that. Makes me want to bring you an apple."

She couldn't stop the blush climbing up her cheeks, so she shuffled papers around and let her hair fall forward. "This is a community outreach class. It's just Olivia."

"All right. Olivia."

Just like last time, he made her name sound like something naughty. She cleared her throat. "Are you taking the class for the brewery?"

"Yes, just trying to brush up a little."

"And the first session? Was it useful?"

"It was great. Honestly, I was worried I'd be wasting my time. That it would be too esoteric for my needs, but… You were really amazing."

That brought her head up. "I was?"

"Yes. You're in charge, yet you're warm. You give the information without being dry."

"Thank you."

"And…" he leaned closer "…you're by far the prettiest teacher I've ever had."

Olivia dropped the papers she'd been straightening and stepped back. "Mr. Donovan."

"Yes?"

"This isn't appropriate."

"I know." His smile became a wicked endearment.

Olivia pretended she didn't feel the shiver work through her. That smile had nothing to do with her. He'd likely trotted it out ten times today already. It was a tool, though she wasn't exactly sure what he meant to fix with it.

"Flirtation is extremely inappropriate."

"Extremely? Come on now. You're just barely my teacher. You're not even giving me a grade, so I think 'extremely inappropriate' is a stretch. But if you're interested in being in a position of power…"

Olivia gasped and drew her chin in.

"Go out with me."

"What? No! Didn't you even hear what I said?"

"Didn't you hear what *I* said? Give me one good reason we shouldn't go on a date."

"You're…" She waved a hand toward his body. "You're just barely legal. What are you, twenty-five?"

"I'm twenty-nine. What about you? Thirty-one?"

"Thirty-five," she bit out, her teeth threatening to break under the pressure when he gave a low whistle.

"Thirty-five, huh? I'd get a note from my dad, but he died a while ago. I think he'd be okay with it though."

Olivia heard a soft growl and realized it was coming from her own throat. "No, thank you. But I appreciate the offer. Now if you don't mind, I need to get to my next class." That was an out-and-out lie, but desperate times called for desperate measures.

He shrugged, his body still perfectly loose and relaxed. "Let me know if you change your mind. You know where I sit."

He'd done that on purpose. She could see the mischief in his eyes as he turned to walk up the stairs.

Olivia had thought she was safe from the temptation to ogle since he wasn't wearing the kilt, but his ass was on a perfect eye level as he ascended the stairs. And what a prize-winning ass it was. Round and tight and lovely.

If only she were a little bit younger. Or a little less careful. But she wasn't.

She was just Olivia Bishop, but…she was learning to be happy with exactly that. She didn't need to be someone different. And Olivia Bishop would never sleep with a young man in her class. Even if he did leave her body buzzing with excitement.

"Not in a million years," she murmured as the door closed behind him.

# CHAPTER THREE

OLIVIA SPENT THE REST of her day doing the responsible things she expected of herself. She cleaned her tiny office and filed away all the papers and notes from the spring semester. She called her dentist and rescheduled an appointment that conflicted with her summer class. Then she walked across campus to the library, her arms full of books and bound reports. It was a beautiful day, so this was one responsibility she didn't mind. She was smiling by the time she dropped off the books, and instead of heading toward the nonfiction area, Olivia browsed the recent bestseller rack and paged through the fiction. Book club or not, she'd like to do more casual reading.

But her little bubble of relaxation was interrupted by the ding of her text message alert.

Hi, sweetheart. Are you going to Rashid's farewell party tonight?

Sweetheart? Her ex-husband sure had a lot of nerve. He'd cheated on her. She'd divorced him. And he still thought he could manipulate her with his little hints and endearments.

Yes, she typed, assuming he'd ask her to pass along some message. Victor always left town as soon as his last spring class finished. Olivia was actually enjoying the quiet sunshine of the campus in summertime now that she wasn't obliged to travel with Victor.

Her phone dinged again. Do you have the directions?

Olivia dropped the book she was holding and stared at her phone as the loud thunk echoed through the room. What the hell did he mean by that? The only reason she'd said yes to this party was because she was sure Victor wouldn't be there with one of his recent graduates on his arm.

No, she typed, hitting Send as if she were pulling the trigger in a game of Russian roulette. She held her breath until the phone dinged softly again.

No problem. I'll call Rashid. See you there, O.

That bastard. What right did he have to hang around when he was supposed to be gone? Had he stayed just for this? She didn't think she was that important in his life, but he certainly seemed to relish any opportunity to strike up a conversation with her while his arm was draped around another woman.

She wondered which one he'd bring this time. Allison? Or was there a new one? It didn't matter. Olivia could barely tell them apart anymore.

He'd been the one to cheat. She couldn't understand why he was having so much trouble letting go. He'd lashed out as if it had been her fault. *You're no fun,* he'd said. *You're boring! What did you expect?* But the girls he dated now…they were like trips to the circus, apparently. Nonstop entertainment and wild-animal acts.

Olivia closed the text window without replying. She picked up the book she'd dropped and left the library in a much different mood than when she'd entered. The walk across the campus now seemed an impossible distance.

She didn't want to go to the party if Victor was going. She could handle seeing him. She saw him four or five times a week at school, after all. But it wasn't fair that she had to watch him parade his toys in front of her. She wasn't even jealous anymore, she was just pissed as hell that he was so damn rude.

But Olivia never lost her temper. She didn't cause scenes. She didn't do anything emotionally impulsive. She was boring, just as he'd said. No fun. And the nice thing about having a boring ex-wife was that she never caused any trouble.

Screw him for taking advantage of that.

Jaw clenched in anger, she stomped across the green expanse of the lawn and thought of the last faculty party. Victor had brought a beautiful young woman and flaunted her with false modesty. He was a show-off, and sometimes Olivia couldn't believe she'd been married to him. What she'd thought of as a generous, outgoing spirit…that was just a need to be the center of attention.

The center of attention. Like Jamie Donovan. *He* would give Victor a run for his money.

Olivia stumbled to a stop, one of her shoes slipping off in the rough grass. She kicked off her other shoe and stared at her scarlet toenails peeping through the blades of emerald.

She couldn't, could she?

It would be wrong. Outrageous. Emotionally immature.

And she'd enjoy the hell out of it, at least for one petty moment. Victor deserved to be taught a lesson.

"No," she told herself, picking up her shoes and continuing on. The grass was a cool contrast to the hot sun. She wondered why she hadn't kicked off her shoes earlier. Sometimes loosening up brought good things.

"He did ask me out," she whispered to herself. But he hadn't asked to be used.

Anyway, she had no way of getting in touch with him. Well, she had the class lists, but that would be slimy. Way over the line. Using a student list to call for a date would reach Victor-levels of inappropriate behavior.

So there was nothing to be done, really. It wasn't as if she knew where he worked. Ha.

When she finally reached her car, Olivia slid in and laid her forehead on the steering wheel. She stared at the specks of dust on the dark speedometer.

On one hand, she'd never do something like that: walk into a man's workplace and ask him out. On the other hand, she was looking for new experiences. New adventures. New daring.

But daring didn't mean foolish. And adventurous didn't mean sneaky.

Decision made, she drove toward home, but for the first time, she noticed that her normal route took her within a block of Donovan Brothers Brewery. She couldn't see it from this side of the block, but it was there, pulsing like a terrible beacon. Luring her in.

Cursing, she turned right and drove in the opposite direction of her house. This direction took her toward the brewery, and Jamie, and the really bad decision that called to her so loudly she couldn't ignore it.

Pulling into the parking lot, she looked around as if she would recognize his car. Stupid. As stupid as getting out of the car and walking through the door, but there she was doing it, spite pushing her on.

After the bright sunlight, she couldn't see anything for a moment. This world was dark and cool and smelled strongly of icy beer and wood polish. She blinked rapidly, worried that Jamie was standing there watching her founder.

Finally, her eyes adjusted, and she was both relieved and disappointed to see that Jamie wasn't behind the bar. A blond woman with a perky ponytail stood at the tap. She slipped a lemon onto the edge of a glass, added it to a tray with three other beers and went to serve the only table that was occupied. "Hi!" she said as she passed Olivia.

"Hi," Olivia replied weakly. A quick glance showed that Jamie wasn't lurking in one of the corners of the room. Olivia eyed the swinging doors at the back, but if he was behind those doors, he may as well have been a hundred miles away. This was a sign that she wasn't meant to be here. She'd been saved from ruin and embarrassment.

Olivia slid her foot back and started to turn.

"Can I help you?"

The woman again, with her tray tucked under her arm now. She smiled widely, and Olivia felt a jolt of recognition. This girl was definitely related to Jamie.

"Did you want a beer?"

"Oh. No. I was looking for someone. Sorry, I'll just—"

"Jamie? He's not working the bar today."

Olivia blinked. Did women come in looking for Jamie all the time? Yes, of course they did.

Her chest filled with horror as she slid her left foot back to join the right. "Okay. Thanks."

"You should follow our Twitter account! He always lets everyone know when he's behind the bar."

"Oh, sure. Thanks. I'll do that." She coughed, then repeated. "Thanks."

Just as Olivia was reaching back for the door handle, the swinging doors opened and Jamie walked through.

Oh, God. *Oh, God.*

His smile froze and his eyes widened in surprise. "Ms. Ol—" His gaze slid to the female bartender and then back to Olivia. "Olivia. Hi. What are you doing here?"

The woman winked at Olivia and said, "Look who was hiding in the back," before she retreated to the bar. "Hey, Jamie," she said lightly as she passed him.

Jamie ignored her and walked toward Olivia, and her heart sped to a frightening pace. She couldn't back down now. Because what other reason could she have for being here? She hadn't even thought to bring class handouts or a book or anything that would offer an excuse for her presence. This was the kind of disaster that descended when you didn't make lists.

"Hi," she croaked.

"Hi." He put his hands in his pockets and waited, his mouth curved in a puzzled smile.

"Are you working?" she asked.

"Not really. I'm off today."

"Oh." She nodded, and kept nodding until Jamie cocked his head.

"Did I forget something in class, or...?"

Olivia took a deep breath. "Are you busy tonight?"

That popped his chin straight. "What?"

"You asked, and I said no, but...there's a party I have to go to tonight. One of the professors is leaving...."

The wide smile spreading across his face distracted her.

"What?" she snapped, irritated by the way her pulse sped.

"I'm just...surprised."

She felt a sudden fear that he'd only been kidding. It had all been a flirtatious joke. She couldn't possibly be his type. "If you don't want to—"

"Of course I want to. What time should I pick you up?"

"We can just meet there. There's no need—"

"Right. What time should I pick you up?"

For the first time, Olivia caught a glimpse of steel beneath his velvet exterior. Her pulse enjoyed it very much. "Seven-thirty?"

"Great. Seven-thirty. I'll be there. Do you want a beer or a glass of water or...?"

"No. No, thank you. I'd better just..." Guilt was turning her stomach, so she gave him her address and phone number, then stammered out a goodbye while he smiled sympathetically.

"I'll see you tonight," he said, making it sound like a promise.

She left with an awkward lurch for the door. The

heavy wood nearly closed on her leg, but thankfully Jamie caught it just before it got her. She hurried to her car and then collapsed inside.

What the hell had she just done? Why was she going on a date with a man who inspired women to regularly come into a bar to ask for him? It was madness. She must look like a fool.

"I'm not into him," she whispered to herself. "I'm doing this for *me*." And she was. But she couldn't pretend that Jamie Donovan's charm wasn't part of what she wanted. That charm felt like magic dust being sprinkled over her skin, and she wanted everyone to see the glow. Including her ex-husband.

She'd wash the magic off later and everything would be fine. But her heart was still racing when she made it home, and it didn't have anything to do with nerves.

# CHAPTER FOUR

SHE WASN'T THE TYPE OF WOMAN he normally dated. Tessa had pointed that out immediately, but Jamie had ignored her. After not dating at all for over a year, he didn't have a type anymore. He'd hit the reset button.

He stole a glance at Olivia, who stared straight out the windshield of his car as if she were the one driving. She looked different tonight, though no less uptight. Her glasses were off again and her lips glinted with shiny color. Instead of a demure dress, she wore a little black number. Not short or low cut, as he'd hoped, but it draped over her body like skimming hands.

And she smelled good. She made him think of a crisp summer night. Flowers that were cooling in the dark.

Nice.

Jamie had sworn off women for a while, but he'd make an exception for her. She was different. Calm and mature. Responsible and sharp. Maybe she'd be good for him. A positive step on the new path he was taking. Tessa had certainly been surprised.

Jamie still couldn't believe Olivia had come by the brewery. That *she'd* asked him out. Her earlier rejection had been fairly firm. It hadn't stung; asking her out had been a long shot, after all. But he must have really gotten under her skin. He smiled at the thought of being inside her head.

"Just to the right," Olivia said, pointing toward a very large house set among cliffs and pine trees. The city of Boulder sat five hundred feet below them.

"You've got friends in high places."

"Oh, these people aren't my friends. They're just colleagues."

He edged the truck onto a narrow shoulder lined with a dozen other cars. "Don't you have friends at work?"

"A few. Gwen, for one. But she won't be at this party. It'll be almost all faculty and spouses. And dates." She shot him a look, but he couldn't read it. "Not as much fun as most parties you go to, I'm sure."

"You mean like the biweekly kegger in my basement?"

"Um… Yeah. Sure."

"That was a joke, Olivia. I'm way past my kegger days."

"Way past?" she asked, her gaze dropping down his body. "I don't think that's chronologically possible."

She seemed to think of herself as much older than him, which was funny. She was only thirty-five, after all, and looked closer to thirty. Jamie got out and circled around to her side to open the door. "Careful. It's rocky here."

She set one black heel on the ground, and Jamie's mouth watered. She looked as good in heels as he'd imagined. God, he loved heels.

"Thank you," she murmured, and he forced his eyes up. He took her hand, holding tighter when she wobbled.

He felt her little gasp of surprise and she leaned into him, one foot slipping from a shoe. "I think I'm stuck."

"Here." He leaned down and Olivia's fingers spread over his back as she held herself up. Jamie tugged the shoe out from its rocky vise and brushed dust off the heel. Then he curled his hand around her foot. Her skin was soft and her foot twitched as he dragged his thumb along the curve of her arch. He slipped her shoe on her foot and let his hand slide up to her ankle, smiling at the way her breath hitched when his fingers wrapped all the way around the delicate bones. "You didn't hurt your ankle, did you?"

"No," she whispered.

He set her foot down, still holding her ankle as if she needed support. "You're sure?" He edged his hand up until his fingers opened over her calf.

"I'm sure." She cleared her throat as if she was aware of how husky she sounded. "Thank you."

"Then let's go in."

He offered his arm for the walk up the steep drive, and she accepted with a grateful smile. "We don't have to stay long. I just need to make an appearance."

"I'm sure it'll be fun."

"You're wrong about that."

"Is there anyone I need to watch out for?"

She stumbled a little, and he had to brace her. "What do you mean?" she demanded.

"Remind me to come pick you up at the front door when we leave. This hill isn't safe in heels."

"Okay. Sure. It's not safe for *me* in heels, anyway." Her laugh was tight and embarrassed, which he found damn cute on a woman like her.

"I just meant that I've heard these university functions can be tense. Who has tenure, who doesn't. Someone got the government grant another person was going for. I hear a lot of bitching about it at the bar. Is there anyone you want me to kiss up to?"

"Oh, that. No, I don't have any budget enemies. Or tenure tensions. I'm only an instructor."

"What does that mean?"

"No PhD. No tenured position. No research. I teach—that's all." Her tone was neutral, and she didn't look self-conscious about it, just matter-of-fact.

"That sounds nicer, actually."

She flashed him a smile. "I think so, too."

"All right. So no underlying tensions."

"Right. Yes. I mean no." Now she looked worried.

"Don't worry," he assured her. "I'll have a good time."

She swallowed hard enough that he heard it. "I bet you're the kind of person who has fun no matter what you're doing."

He shrugged. "I try."

"That's really nice." She stopped before the enormous wood door and took a deep breath. "But this is a university party, so I hope you're up for a challenge tonight."

Jamie let his eyes travel down her body while she was distracted by ringing the bell. "Oh, I am," he murmured.

When the door opened and they stepped in, Jamie was damn glad he'd decided on a pair of black pants and a button-down shirt tonight. Jeans would not have fit in here, and even though he'd amped it up a notch, Jamie definitely felt slightly out of place among the sculptures and polished wood. Olivia, on the other hand, fit right in. She was elegant and cool and said all the right things as she made the introductions. The notes from the piano music seemed to float around her.

But she'd been right about the party. It was boring, starting with the languid piano music that sounded as if it'd been designed to coax insomniacs to sleep. Time passed slowly. He answered the occasional question about his name and job—there never seemed to be a follow-up—and fantasized about putting his hands to her waist and pulling her in for a kiss. A long, deep kiss. He imagined that she would thaw slowly that first time. He'd have to coax it from her.

Jamie hadn't practiced his coaxing skills in a while, and he had to fight off the urge to stretch hard and crack his knuckles in anticipation.

"The brewery, right?" someone was saying to him.

Jamie blinked from his stupor to find a hulking man standing there with his wineglass held out like a pointer. An ex-football player if Jamie had ever seen one.

"I'm sorry?"

"You're with the brewery, right? Donovan Brothers? I'm Todd. Been in there a few times. Good beer."

"Thank you." Jamie introduced himself and found that, just as he'd suspected, the guy had been a power halfback at the U twenty years earlier. Jamie wasn't much of an athlete. He'd played baseball for a couple of years in high school, but he'd never taken it too seriously. Still, knowing sports was part of his job, and he settled into a conversation about last year's football season. He often wondered why these guys never got tired of the same subject. Surely Todd had already discussed last year's season a thousand times over. Then again, Jamie never got tired of talking about beer. Maybe it was comforting to know you were an expert in something.

They soon moved on to next year's lineup, and Jamie's mind wandered. How long had they been at the party? An hour? He searched the room for Olivia, trying to find her among the crowd, as he agreed with everything Todd said about the up-and-coming starting quarterback.

When he finally found Olivia, she seemed to be in the same predicament. A tiny, ancient man had her cornered, and she nodded every few seconds even as her eyes glazed over.

Jamie was just settling into listening to the story of Todd's last big game when he noticed Olivia's gaze sharpen. Her body stiffened. She shifted to the other foot. Jamie followed her gaze—straight over the top of her companion's head. It took Jamie a moment to pick anyone out of the crowd, but he finally figured out who she was staring at.

A couple had just stepped through the door. The man was tall and good-looking and enthusiastically shaking hands with everyone within his radius. The woman was blond, tan and very, very young.

Olivia had turned away from them as if she was pretending to ignore them, but as Jamie watched, the man spotted Olivia, raised his eyebrows and headed toward her. He very purposefully took his date's hand and guided her through the crowd, though he stopped every few feet to exchange words with other guests.

When he got to Olivia, he pulled her into a hug as soon as she turned toward him. Olivia cringed.

Interesting.

Todd seemed to have wrapped up his story, so Jamie said, "Those were the glory days, huh?" then slapped Todd on the back. "Come by the brewery this weekend and I'll buy you a beer."

He left Todd grinning with pride and headed toward one of the servers. Olivia's wineglass was empty and she looked like she could use another. Just as he started toward her, she looked up and said something to the man as she gestured in Jamie's direction. Surprise flickered briefly across the man's face as he turned.

"Victor," she was saying when Jamie walked up. "This is Jamie Donovan. Jamie, this is Victor. And Allison."

"Great to meet you," Jamie said, holding out his hand to Allison first, then Victor. Victor's grip was tight as a vise.

"Victor Bishop," the man said very clearly, hitting Jamie with the exact amount of shock he'd hoped for.

Bishop.

Jamie made his face stay neutral and pleasant. He didn't aim an alarmed look at Olivia, even though everything inside him wanted to pull her aside and ask for some quick clarification.

"So…" Victor said, giving Jamie's hand one last ridiculous squeeze. "How did you come to know Olivia?"

"I served her a few beers," he said dryly.

"Beers?" Victor shot Olivia an incredulous look. "You don't drink beer."

"She drinks my beer," Jamie offered with a smile.

He finally dared a glance at Olivia. Her cheeks were flushed. Her hand white-knuckled around the stem of the empty wineglass. "I gave her a few lessons."

She met his gaze and tried to smile, but the result was a tense grimace. "Jamie is part of the Donovan Brothers Brewery family," she said.

"But I've got nothing against wine. Here, Olivia." He plucked the empty from her hand and handed her a new one. He was tempted to ask Victor how *he'd* come to know Olivia, but Jamie figured he already knew. They had the same last name and the guy definitely wasn't giving off a sibling vibe.

"Well," Victor said. "It's nice to see you dating again, Olivia." His words didn't quite sound genuine. In fact, they sounded pretty damned forced, not to mention patronizing as hell.

Jamie looked him over a little more thoroughly. Victor Bishop was older than Olivia by at least ten years, and he dressed as if he were trying out for the part of "stereotypical college professor" in a local theater production. Pressed slacks, gray button-down shirt, houndstooth sport coat, brown suede shoes. But everything looked very expensive.

"So, Victor," Jamie said into the uncomfortable silence. "I haven't heard much about you." He thought he detected a faint wheeze from Olivia. "I'm guessing you work at the U?"

"Absolutely. I'm a professor of economics."

Jamie smiled. "And you, Allison? Do you work at the U or are you an innocent bystander like me?"

"Oh," the girl said, looking up at Victor as if checking on the answer. "I guess I'm an innocent bystander now. I was a teaching assistant last semester."

*Victor's* teaching assistant, Jamie would guess. He didn't need to rely on his years of bartending psychology to pick up on these undercurrents. He wondered exactly how long Olivia had been divorced. As if he'd attracted her attention with his thoughts, Olivia tucked her arm around his. Victor's gaze darted down.

"We'd better go find Rashid," she said with false cheer. "I haven't congratulated him on his new position at Stanford."

They strolled away as if they were searching for Rashid, but Jamie led her into the kitchen. There were some catering staff around, but no guests. As soon as they were out of sight of the party, Jamie let her go and stepped back. When he crossed his arms, she looked at the floor. "So," he said.

She didn't look up.

"You want to tell me what's going on?"

Her hands twisted together, but she said nothing.

"I'm guessing that Victor is your ex-husband?" She looked more than a little ashamed as she nodded, so he was confident he'd figured out the rest of it. "And he's the reason you invited me along?"

Olivia swallowed. "I wouldn't say that. I mean…it's not…"

Right. Jamie felt more pissed off than he would've expected. His first real date in nearly a year and she was faking it. Shit. This was a new experience. "Well, I'm flattered, I guess."

"Jamie—"

"Your ex-husband is playing the field with younger women. You thought you'd show off with a younger man—"

"It's not that!" she interrupted. "Or…not only that. It's more about me than you."

"Is that supposed to make me feel better?"

She crumpled a little, her shoulders dropping, and Jamie realized it was the first time he'd seen her without perfect posture. "I'm sorry," she said. "He wasn't supposed to be here."

He was a little embarrassed about how much that cheered him up. "You didn't know he'd be here? Really?"

"No, not that. It was wrong. I know it was. I wasn't playing a game, or I didn't mean to, anyway. I only agreed to come to the party because he was supposed to be gone. I've got a new life now. I didn't want to see him. When I found out he was coming… I'm so sorry. I shouldn't have brought you."

He didn't bother to disagree.

Olivia took a gulp from her wineglass, then set her shoulders back as if she'd realized she was slouching. "I apologize. I just wanted to loosen up a little."

"In front of your ex?"

"Yes, in front of my ex! He…"

Jamie saw the way she swallowed hard, her jaw clenching, and he worried she was about to cry. "Listen—"

"That girl he's with. Allison. She's not the first girl like that he's dated. And marriage didn't keep him from indulging."

"Ah."

"Predictable, isn't it? But I'm not bitter anymore. I

don't hate him. I swear it's not like that. I want to have a life that has nothing to do with him."

"Except when it does?"

Olivia shrugged and finished her wine before setting the glass carefully on the counter. While she was still turned away from him, she murmured, "He told me I wasn't any fun."

Jamie ran a hand through his hair, wondering if it would be rude to leave right at this moment. He was probably justified. Surely she wouldn't object. He'd be kind enough to drop her off at her place first. "What?"

She turned to face him. "When I caught him cheating, he told me it was because I wasn't any fun."

Jamie grimaced. "Jesus Christ."

"And you know what? I'm not fun. But that doesn't mean I can't try to be."

"You want him back?" Jamie asked, his voice so loud that she blinked in shock.

"No! That's not it at all! I'm just trying to enjoy my life. Figure out who I am. I was only twenty-two when I met him. I'm not that girl anymore. So who am I?" She met his gaze head-on and, for the first time, she let him see something of herself. Something warm and vulnerable. "Am I the kind of woman who goes on a date with someone like you?"

"Someone like me?" Jamie ordered himself not to feel primal satisfaction at the way her eyes warmed.

"You're young. Handsome. Purposefully charming."

"I like to think of it as naturally charming."

"Oh, it's natural," she said, her mouth quirking wryly. "But you use it to great effect."

"I *like* people."

She smiled then, chasing the sadness from her face. "I know you do. And you're the definition of fun. So I thought…" Color climbed up her cheeks.

Whether he was angry or not, Jamie couldn't help his interest in this woman, and the color in her cheeks intrigued him. "You thought what?"

"I'm trying new things. Like the book club. So I thought…"

"You thought you'd try me out, too?"

She flashed a surprisingly wicked smile. "I thought I'd try a *date* with you. And, unfortunately, I thought I'd do it in front of Victor. I shouldn't have. I'm sorry. It was a momentary impulse. I'd already changed my mind when you weren't at the brewery, but then you walked in.…"

He shrugged. "I'm not saying you shouldn't have shown him up. But I would've appreciated a warning."

She touched his arm. "I really am sorry. Let's leave."

"I don't know. You're already using me. I'm all dressed up. We may as well make the most of it."

"Jamie—"

"Hey." He took the hand she was gesturing with and curled it against his chest. "Just answer one question. Are you interested in me or not?"

Her fingers squeezed his. "I'm interested in you. But I think—"

"That's all I need to know right now." He eased a little closer as she brushed her hair behind her ear. A nervous gesture. "Exactly how jealous do you want to make him?"

"I don't want to make him jealous. I just want him to stop flaunting his girls in front of me. It's rude."

"Rude," he said with a smile. "You know what? You're right. It's definitely not polite. So how deep do you want to drive the point?"

Her eyes narrowed. "What do you mean?"

"A kiss? Just to teach him a lesson in etiquette?"

"Etiquette, huh?" She laughed and the sound danced over his skin. But when she was done laughing, the question still hung between them, and she eyed him with a different sort of nervousness. "You mean out there in front of everyone?"

"No. Right here."

"But…how will he know?"

He watched as she licked her lips, her tongue flashing just quickly enough to make him want more of it. "Oh," Jamie said. "He'll know."

"Well, if you think it'll work…"

"I know it'll work," he said softly, easing closer. She looked like she'd be easy to startle, and he didn't want to do that. Just as he'd expected, she shifted a little, drawing her head back a fraction of an inch.

He smiled. "Where are you going?"

"I don't know. I just…"

But her words died when he touched his mouth to hers, a careful touch, barely a kiss at all.

"Okay," she sighed, her eyes closing. "Just a kiss."

Jamie closed his own and kissed her again. A longer taste, but still soft. But this time when he drew away, she closed the space between them, and this was a real kiss. Her lips parted just enough that he could feel her breath and the warmth of her mouth. He kissed her top lip, then her bottom, touching his tongue to that plump, pink flesh.

She sighed again, whispering the sound against his skin, and Jamie couldn't wait another moment to taste her. When he slipped his tongue into her, she was hot and sweet with wine. But he still held back, barely rubbing his tongue over hers, allowing himself time to enjoy it. They were in a kitchen at a stranger's party. There'd be nothing more than kissing, and he wanted to feel every moment of it.

A few endless heartbeats later, Jamie drew back, slightly dazed as he opened his eyes to the glaring lights of the modern kitchen. Olivia looked dazed, too, blinking as if she was waking up. Her pupils were dilated, her cheeks flushed, and her lips were red as cherries. Her ex wouldn't be able to miss that, even if he wanted to.

"Wow," she whispered. "You're good at that."

"I like kissing."

"I think I do, too," she said, and he couldn't help but laugh.

"Come on. We'd better get in there before it wears off."

"What wears off?" she asked, but Jamie shook his head. She couldn't know how beautiful she looked like this. Warm and blushing and—for once—not the least bit rigid. It was almost like seeing her naked. Almost.

He took her hand and led her out to the party and all the stiff, bored people pretending to enjoy themselves. "You come to a lot of parties like this?"

"Not a lot. Not anymore. Now I get to choose which ones I go to, but unfortunately, they're all like this. Everyone trying to impress each other. Everyone on their best behavior. What kind of parties do you go to?"

"I don't go to parties. I work."

"Not as glamorous as it seems?"

"Oh, it's glamorous as all hell, Ms. Bishop, but the hours are long."

"Don't call me that," she said, smacking his arm.

"Come on. It's totally hot that you're my teacher."

"Just barely your teacher," she said, throwing his own words back at him.

"Just enough," he corrected.

Olivia laughed, bumping her elbow into his ribs as they walked toward a wall of doors that opened onto a deck. Jamie had already scoped out Victor Bishop's location, and the guy was definitely looking tense. Jamie offered him a smile.

"So why are you taking the class?" Olivia asked as they stepped onto the deck.

Jamie felt so relaxed that he almost answered honestly. Then he remembered that he was keeping a secret and snapped his mouth shut.

Olivia tilted her head. "What?"

"Nothing. I'm just brushing up on business basics."

"No, you're hiding something." They'd reached a railing that overlooked a spectacular view, but Olivia propped her back against it and faced him. "Why are you really taking the class? Seems like you've got the brewery thing down pat."

He looked past her. "What a gorgeous view from here."

"Spill it."

Shit. "I don't want to talk about it."

"Why not?"

"It's too early. I'm just starting to think it through."

"Are you going to start your own business?"

"No!"

Her eyebrows rose.

"That's not it. Honestly. It's just that… I don't know. I'm thinking more of expanding the current business."

Her face remained neutral for a moment, then her mouth made a pretty O of surprise. "You're going to add a restaurant!"

"Shh." Jamie glanced around to be sure no one heard. "Not quite. And maybe not anything at all. I'm taking your class to explore the possibilities. That's all."

"Well, I think that's great. What responsibilities do you cover at the brewery?" She turned to face the view, now that she'd wrung his secret from him.

"I manage the front room and we all have input into the brewing side." Some more than others.

"Food service would be a lot more involved, you know."

His neck burned with self-consciousness. Was she implying he couldn't handle it? "Yeah, I know."

"Well, let me know if you need help with anything."

"I'll be fine."

She bumped her hip against him. "You're right."

Maybe she did think he could handle it. Maybe she saw something in him. "Am I?"

"Yes," she said softly. "It is an amazing view."

Ah. Of course. He leaned against the railing and took it in, aware of her arm only a millimeter away from his. When goose bumps swept up her skin, he had the perfect excuse to hook her arm into his and ease her closer. A whisper of a breeze swept her hair from her neck.

"I'm glad you brought me out here," she whispered. "But we forgot to search out Victor."

"He saw us."

"He did? Do you think he could tell?"

He slid his thumb along her wrist. "Oh, he could tell."

"But how?"

Jamie met her questioning eyes. She looked absolutely puzzled, and he felt simultaneously amused and dumbfounded. "Your mouth," he said, letting his gaze fall to her lips. "Your eyes."

She shook her head as if she didn't understand.

Jamie smiled. "You looked aroused," he clarified.

The muscles of her arm jumped as a blush washed over her face. "I don't know... I'm sure that..." When she started to pull away, Jamie wrapped his fingers into hers and held her still.

"There's nothing wrong with arousal, Olivia. Is there?"

"I just—" She shook her head again, and when she pulled away, he let her go. "I don't even know you."

Alarm sparked in her wide eyes. She didn't seem to know that it was part of the excitement. Part of what had made her cheeks flush and her lips soften when he'd kissed her. "It's chemistry," he murmured. "Nothing to do with common sense. The opposite of it, in fact."

"Chemistry," she murmured. Her eyes flickered, traveling down his body, and Jamie felt those chemical reactions begin to burn again. Her mouth curved up on one side, before she shook her head and banished her smile. "Well, thank you."

"For the chemistry?"

"For playing along."

He was playing, all right, but it wasn't a part. Still, if that helped her feel better about it, Jamie could let it go.

"Can I get you another glass of wine?"

"No, I think we can go now." She winked. "Your work here is done."

"Olivia—"

"Thank you again. For everything. But I think you should just take me home."

Jamie sighed. That didn't sound like an invitation. But at least he'd gotten a kiss. He'd bring her an apple on Thursday and see where it went from there.

## CHAPTER FIVE

He hadn't called.

Olivia lay in her bed, staring at the ceiling and feeling stupid for even thinking it. She'd known he wouldn't call. She'd told herself she didn't want him to. But now that she was faced with seeing him in class in a few hours, it felt awkward. On her part, at least. Jamie would probably just laugh.

At least she hadn't invited him in when he'd walked her to her door. She'd left him with just one more kiss. One more slow, hot, body-tingling kiss.

She smiled. Maybe it was worth the awkwardness. She didn't feel like a new woman or anything, but she definitely felt a few degrees brighter.

It was a good start.

Still, even if he was interested, she didn't think she could keep walking down this road with Jamie. That man was potent. Hell, he'd been potent before he'd put his mouth on her, and then he'd gone from intoxicating to deadly. Olivia had no doubt she'd have a very good time with Jamie Donovan, but she'd be just one on a long list of women. She didn't want to think what it would be like to watch as he walked away, taking his good time with him.

Whatever her intentions, it came as no surprise to her

that when the phone rang, Olivia immediately thought of Jamie. More proof that she was already in over her head. She made herself walk slowly to the phone, then answered it without checking the ID, pretending she didn't care who it was. "Olivia Bishop."

"Oooolivia Bishop," a friendly female voice crooned.

"Gwen?" she asked, just as she realized what was about to happen.

"So I talked to Marcie last night...."

"Oh, God." Olivia put her hand to her eyes. Marcie was friends with one of Victor's fellow professors.

"You naughty little witch," Gwen drawled, obviously enjoying her secret. "You're totally getting it on with Jamie Donovan. I don't know whether to hate you or put you on a pedestal."

"I am not getting it on with Jamie Donovan."

"Liar."

Olivia smiled as she shook her head. "I'm not lying."

"Look, I admire that you're trying to protect his modesty. It's cute."

"Gwen," Olivia said, laughing. "Okay, I admit that I went to the party with him, but that is *all* that happened."

"That's all?" Gwen squealed. "Where the heck did this come from? You met him *once*. One time!"

"I know—"

"And you said you were trying to *ease* back into the dating world. This is like shooting yourself out of a cannon."

Olivia collapsed onto her bed, laughing so hard she couldn't catch her breath.

"I need all the details," Gwen said. "Please God, give me some details!"

"I'm sorry, Gwen, but I don't have any!"

"Just any level of story then. Put me out of my misery."

Olivia sighed. She wasn't going to tell Gwen everything, but if she refused to speak it would look even worse. "Jamie asked me out, and I—"

"Now, hold on. Back it up, sister."

This part wasn't easy, and she wished she could get away with leaving it out entirely. Instead, she decided to fudge the details. "I saw him. On campus. He asked me out and I said no, but then I remembered the party...."

Gwen squealed.

"We went to the party, and that was it. End of story."

"Oh, not by a long shot. What was he like? Did you make out? Did you see Victor? Oh, my God, please tell me you saw Victor."

"Jamie was nice. No, we didn't make out, but we definitely saw Victor. More importantly, Victor saw us."

"Oh, my God, I wish you were here right now so I could high-five you." Gwen had been an administrative assistant for Victor's department for two years. She wasn't a fan.

"I'll admit, it was satisfying."

"Oh, yeah? Just how satisfying?"

"Gwen. It didn't happen. And it's not going to happen. I had a great time, but that's that."

"He turned you down?"

Olivia rolled her eyes. "Boy, I wish you were here right now too. I'd high-five your head."

"Come on, Olivia. Why aren't you going to see him again?"

"It's complicated."

"It doesn't have to be."

"Well, it is. And I have to go. I'm late for my run." Really late, actually. Not only had she overslept, but she hadn't thought once about running until that moment. That was a first. She'd even gone for her run right on time the morning after she'd found out her husband was cheating.

"This isn't the end of this!" Gwen called as Olivia's thumb hovered over the end call button. "Not by far!"

Olivia stuck out her tongue and hung up.

As late as it was, she didn't immediately rise to change into her running gear. For a moment, she simply sat and savored this feeling. This strange new feeling of having a close female friend. It was almost as exhilarating as kissing Jamie, though the happiness confined itself to less interesting parts of her body. It was really...*nice.* And Olivia felt stupid for having ignored this need for so long. She would've been happier married to Victor if she hadn't dedicated herself so completely to him.

And maybe she would've seen the truth about him before she'd wasted so many years.

Regret tried to rear its ugly head, but she slapped it down. She'd spent a year wallowing, and she was done. This year was going to be *hers.* The year of Olivia. And this summer would be the kickoff.

She was teaching two classes this summer to bring in a little money, but both were light on prep and time commitment. She'd taught both before and they were noncredit classes. Even the group of students she'd agreed to mentor this summer were pretty self-sufficient, so aside from office hours and class time, she was free to do as she pleased. But what did she please?

As she brushed her teeth and pulled on shorts and a top, Olivia considered the day's options. Class only lasted until two. Afterward, she could go through the unpacked boxes still lurking at the back of her bedroom closet. Or she could go through the financial planning package she'd been meaning to review. But neither of those sounded like the actions of a woman jumping into life. Neither sounded like a day for the kind of woman who'd take a younger man to a work party and then make out with him among the kitchen staff.

Smirking as she tied her shoes, Olivia made her decision. Today she'd drive to Denver. She'd have dinner downtown by herself. She'd have a glass of wine with her meal. Or two glasses. And then she'd go to the art museum and take as many hours as she wanted to stroll through the galleries.

In addition to being fun, irresponsible and exactly what she needed, this trip would distract her from thoughts of Jamie. She'd had a great time with him, but she hadn't been fair. She'd used him, and he wasn't going to call her again. That was fine. She had a whole life to build. And now that she knew she had chemistry... Well, that opened up a whole world of possibilities, didn't it?

But four hours later, her little pep talk had worn off and she was standing in front of him in the classroom, feeling as awkward as she'd expected. Jamie just smiled down at her.

She gave him one subtle nod and then tried not to look at him again as she began her lecture on start-up costs, financing and insurance. Dry stuff, certainly, and it likely didn't apply to his plans, but he seemed to be taking detailed notes, if his flying fingers were any guide. Or else he was deeply involved in an online conversation. Hard to tell these days.

By the time she'd taken the last questions from the class and sent the students on their way, she wasn't the least bit surprised when Jamie started down the stairs instead of up. But her heart still tumbled as if she'd just received the shock of her life. Ridiculous.

He set an apple on the corner of the table. "Good afternoon, Ms. Bishop. You look pretty today."

Her face felt tight with self-consciousness. She'd thought of him when she'd chosen this dress. It was red. Too red for class, but the tiny white daisies gave her the excuse that it was perfect for summer. And she loved the way the fabric gathered along the bodice to make it look as if she had nearly average-size breasts. The padded bra helped too, but Jamie would never get her clothes off to prove any different.

"Do you want to get some lunch?"

She looked up sharply, tearing her eyes away from his ridiculous little gift. "It's two o'clock."

"All right. Do you want to get some coffee? A beer? Ice cream?"

"It was wrong of me to drag you into that situation. I do thank you for going, and I appreciate your not holding it against me. But...this isn't a good idea."

"That sounds like an awfully solemn declaration over an innocent little ice cream cone."

The man made "innocent little ice cream cone" into a filthy promise. His green eyes danced.

She wanted to shrink into herself, so Olivia set her shoulders back and made herself stand taller. But her gaze still fell to rest on the apple. "That's because it doesn't feel innocent. Not to me."

He shifted and her eyes rose, and now his face didn't look amused at all. "Doesn't that make it important then?"

It did. Too important. But she'd be damned if she'd say that. "I'm not an eighteen-year-old girl out spreading her wings. I need to be reasonable."

"I'd say you've got more than enough reasonable. You said you wanted to be fun."

"I do, but—"

"Try it, then." She had no idea how his gaze could get any warmer, but it did. "I can make anything fun, Olivia...even you."

Excitement leapt through her. She should've felt insulted, but she only felt the anticipation. The possibility. "You're just a kid. You don't understand—"

"I'm nothing like a kid," he said, his voice suddenly low and quiet. And she knew he was right. She knew it. But there was something so bright and pure about him. Something that said he still enjoyed being in the world, unlike the rest of the miserable population just making their way through. That was what drew women like moths. It was certainly drawing her.

Olivia crossed her arms and looked to the side, sweeping her gaze over the empty chairs, the dark carpet, the sickly gray of the walls that glowed under fluorescent lights. This place was the biggest part of her life and the thing was…she'd never even wanted it. How sad was that?

"Coffee," she said.

He raised one eyebrow. "Coffee? All right. Coffee's pretty fun, but…"

"Just coffee. I have plans later."

He conceded with a gracious wink. He didn't even complain when she told him she'd meet him at the café. In fact, his smile implied that he knew exactly why she'd said it. Not because she was going to drive straight to the Denver art museum afterward, but because she was afraid of what would happen if he drove her home again.

In the end, she had a surprisingly nice time. Jamie was easier to talk to than she'd expected. Oh, sure, talking to strangers was part of his job, but when they dared to step into political waters, he was thoughtful and informed. And he made her laugh. They sat on a shady patio. Olivia had a skinny latte. Jamie had an iced caramel macchiato with extra whipped cream.

When he walked her to her car, she felt as nervous as a teenage girl. With good reason, because when she opened her car door, she was caught between the door frame and the car, and Jamie leaned close.

"Can I call you?" he asked.

"Jamie…" She couldn't keep this up, but she couldn't resist forever.

"Just say yes," he whispered. And then he kissed her, and her mouth was too busy to say anything at all.

HE'D LEFT HER WITH A KISS. One damn kiss and nothing more. But even that made him smile. He'd never tell Olivia this in a million years, but dating her definitely felt more…grown-up than he was used to. Less like a hookup and more like time with an interesting woman. Not that he wouldn't hook the hell out of her given the opportunity. That one kiss had left him hard as a rock. Granted, it had been a long, deep, wet kiss.

"Hell, yeah," he murmured as he pulled into the brewery parking lot. He walked around the whole building before going in, to be sure all the doors and windows were secure and the sidewalks were clean, but when he walked through the front door, he was still lost in thoughts of Olivia.

"Where the hell have you been?" his brother, Eric, asked before Jamie's foot was even across the threshold.

All the pleasant warmth suffusing Jamie's muscles snapped to ice. "I told you I'd be in later on Thursdays from now on."

"You said you'd be in at four. It's almost 4:30."

Jamie felt his blood swell. Heat rose to his skin. He wanted to snap back. He wanted to yell that he'd put in sixty-two hours last week and he'd fucking come in thirty minutes late if he felt like it. There wasn't even one customer in the front room, for God's sake.

But he couldn't say that, because the last thing he wanted was for Eric to start asking questions about where Jamie had been, or why he'd suddenly decided to take Tuesdays off instead of Mondays, or why he needed to come in late on Thursdays. So Jamie used all his strength to hold those words in and simply muttered, "Sorry."

Eric looked surprised. Maybe he'd been angling for

a fight. But he gave in gracefully and said, "All right. Sorry I snapped at you."

Was it really that easy? They fought like cats and dogs most of the time, which was why Jamie was keeping his ideas secret until he had them fully fleshed out. If he didn't have everything in perfect order, Eric would shoot the plan down before the first words left Jamie's mouth. In fact, he'd already shot this particular plan down once, but Jamie wasn't giving up.

"Anything going on today?" he asked Eric.

"Wallace finally got in that Mexican chocolate he was waiting for. He's going to try another round of the spicy chocolate stout."

"Great."

"He wants to call it Devil's Cock."

Jamie's eyebrows flew up. "Devil's Cock?"

"Yeah. With a rooster on the label."

"And what did you say to that?"

Eric smirked. "I told him I'd think about it. After that Santa Fe show, I decided we could dare a bit more edginess. There's not a lot of subtlety out there right now."

"Well, consider me surprised. I think it could be a fantastic label. Maybe you could have it mocked up before you decide."

"Huh. That's actually a good idea. Maybe I will."

Jamie ground his teeth at the shock in Eric's voice.

"And the new menus are in." Eric handed him a pristine laminated copy of the midsummer bar menu.

"Wow, this is a nice layout."

"The new marketing company," Eric said. "I guess it's working out."

"Where's Tessa?" Jamie asked. His sister was a

much more relaxed presence and Jamie would rather get his daily update from her, but she was off today, it seemed. That explained Eric's mood. Tessa simultaneously calmed her brothers down and cheered them up.

"So." Jamie checked the time. "Are you clocking out soon?"

Apparently, he was less than subtle. Eric actually threw back his head and laughed. "I'll leave you alone. Chester prepped the bar. It's all ready for you. Knock yourself out."

"Thanks."

"Oh, and Tessa said something about a special."

Jamie groaned as Eric brushed past him. "Wait, what *kind* of special?"

His brother's laughter was the only answer. It faded as he walked into the back and the doors swung closed behind him.

"Jesus." Now Jamie was the one muttering. As much as he loved Tessa, she was driving him crazy with her Twitter mischief. She was in charge of social networking for the brewery. Unfortunately, Jamie knew nothing about the internet beyond Google and email. Even more unfortunately, Tessa used Twitter under Jamie's name, and she enjoyed putting him in awkward positions. Two weeks ago, she'd organized a "Where's Jamie?" campaign, wherein customers took a picture with him whenever they spotted him. That had been fine at the brewery, though it had slowed down his service. It had been less comfortable when he'd been at the grocery store or out for a bike ride.

He'd tried to go with the flow, but now he was feeling paranoid. He stuck his head in back. "Chester!"

he called to the part-time bartender. "Can you check Twitter on your phone? When you're finished with the washer, see what Tessa is up to tonight."

"Got it!" Chester called.

Jamie hurried back to ready the front room before the post-workday rush. Sure, Chester had already prepped, but no one else had quite the standards that Jamie did. He started with the tables so they'd be ready for the customers. He wiped down the tabletops, the chair seats and backs, and even the menus. He swept the whole room, then moved to the bar itself to get it ready.

"Hey," Chester finally popped in to say. "Tessa offered half-price pints from five to six for anyone who tells you a joke. Doesn't have to be funny."

Jamie smiled as he polished the bar to a shine. He could handle a few jokes. Or so he thought. By six o'clock, his throat hurt from laughing. It also hurt from groaning in horror. He hadn't thought so many bad jokes existed in the world, much less that he could hear them all in one hour. But he had to give it to Tessa, it had been a pretty great hour. He blazed through the whole evening in a good mood until he finally started shutting down at 8:45. At nine o'clock, he saw the last customer out with a friendly wave, locked the door and immediately pulled out his phone to call Olivia.

"Hello, Ms. Bishop."

"Jamie?" She sounded sleepy. And soft.

"I'm sorry, were you sleeping?" He glanced at the clock in confusion. Did people go to sleep at nine?

"No, not yet. I'm reading in bed."

"I was hoping you might come over for a game of pool."

"Right now?" She laughed as if he were being outrageous.

"Maybe?"

"I'm already in bed in my pajamas!"

"Oh, yeah?" He dropped into a chair and propped his feet on a table. "What kind of pajamas?" She laughed again as if he were joking. Fine. Jamie decided to imagine her in a little silk button-down shirt and her black glasses. Hot.

"How was your night?" she asked.

"Well, you made me late."

"You made yourself late."

"No," he corrected, "that hand up my shirt was definitely yours." Jamie decided right then and there that he'd never get tired of hearing her laugh. He especially liked the crack in her voice when she got embarrassed.

"I'm sorry. I'm not normally so forward. Especially not in the parking lot of a coffee place."

"You were overcome," he said. "It happens to all of us. I promise not to report you to the dean."

"Stop!" Her laughter was getting sleepier.

"What are you reading?" he asked, trying to keep her on the phone. She named a book he'd never heard of. Something that sounded dire and difficult. "My mom used to read a lot. She didn't really pass that love on to me," he admitted.

"Used to? She passed away?"

"She did. A long time ago." Jamie didn't like to talk about it. He *really* didn't like to talk about. So he kept his mouth shut and made it clear that he had nothing more to say. Olivia didn't take the hint.

"How long ago?"

"Thirteen years."

"Oh, my God. You were just a teenager."

"Yeah." He cleared his throat and tried to tell himself to be glad she hadn't asked about his dad, because then he'd have to give the whole tragic story. Leaving out the details of his own involvement.

"Were you close to her?" she asked quietly.

"I was." They'd all been close back then. His siblings and his mom and dad. He and his brother and sister were each distinct personalities, but they'd all been loved equally. It turned out that Jamie had been the one who didn't deserve it. Big shock.

"I'm not close to my mom," Olivia admitted. He heard the click of a light on her end and imagined her settling more deeply into bed. "She's cold. Exacting. And…no fun."

He smiled at the wry irony in her voice. "You're not cold," he said.

"No?"

"No. You're lying in bed in your very short pajamas, having an inappropriate conversation with one of your students, right?"

Her laughter chased his sadness away. "You don't know anything about my pajamas."

"Shh."

"And there's nothing inappropriate about this conversation."

"There could be," he insisted, "if you stopped trying to correct me."

"Jamie…" She sighed. "You're…really amazing. You know that?"

"I love it when you whisper that in bed." But her

voice was getting quieter, so Jamie gallantly offered to let her go. He thought of his schedule tomorrow and winced. He had a full day in the office plus the bar at night, and on Fridays they were open until ten. Thank God it was only a tasting room, and not a regular bar open until the wee hours. "If you can stay up an hour later, I'll tuck you in tomorrow, too."

"I'd like that," she whispered, and Jamie could practically feel her fingers drag down his neck.

"I'd like that, too." What a strange affair this was. No sex. Plenty of pillow talk. And damned if he didn't love it.

## CHAPTER SIX

"WHY AREN'T YOU RETURNING my texts?"

Olivia couldn't believe she'd answered the phone. She'd avoided talking to Victor all week, but getting out of the shower, she hadn't been able to see the phone display, and now here she was with his disapproval in her ear.

"Victor, one of the reasons I divorced you was so I wouldn't have to return your texts or phone calls or emails unless I wanted to. And I don't."

"Come on, O. What's gotten into you lately?"

She wrapped her towel tighter around her. "What are you talking about?"

"You're acting strange."

Strange. Like dating-a-younger-man strange. For three nights in a row, Jamie had talked her to sleep. She could no longer deny, even to herself, that she was getting involved with him. Talking to a man for hours while in bed was apparently an effective tool for breaking down resistance.

"Olivia?" Victor's voice sang with irritation.

"Yes?"

"Who was that guy?"

Well, the curiosity must have been eating him alive if he'd just blurted it out like that. Victor normally liked to weave in and out of difficult topics until she was too confused to remember her point. Olivia smiled. "What guy?"

"Damn it. If you want to play games—"

"Victor," she interrupted. "I'm not playing any games. My life has nothing to do with you now. Everything's final. It's done. Utterly and completely over."

"That's not true. We're still friends."

"We most certainly are not! Where do you get this stuff?"

"O, just listen—"

"No. I have to go. We'll talk another time. Or not. It really doesn't matter. Goodbye."

For the first time in months, she wasn't the least bit stressed after a phone call with Victor. She simply, honestly, didn't care. She had other things to worry about. Bigger things, hopefully.

Jamie had invited her to his place for brunch. Brunch, the most innocent-sounding of all the meals, but surely this brunch was just code for sex. They could just as easily go *out* to brunch, after all, but she was going to his place, alone, for an intimate meal.

She was terrified, yet one hundred percent ready. At least in theory.

Something had changed for her in the past few days. Dating Jamie was still dangerous and irresponsible and it would never lead anywhere. But screw it. She'd only been divorced for a year. Now was not the time for a long-term relationship. Now was the time for a sizzling-hot affair with a younger man who made her toes curl with the just the sound of his voice.

She'd been up for hours already, thinking about it.

With Jamie's job, he wasn't exactly a morning person. He'd invited her over at noon, explaining that it would have to be brunch because breakfast was the only meal he could cook well. She'd occupied herself with running and showering and drying her hair. But now she was faced with the impossible task of picking an outfit. Standing in her closet, she stared helplessly at her clothes.

She would know what to wear if they were going out. A cute sleeveless dress, no question about it. But what if he lived in a dorm-style dump? What if he had a roommate?

Brunch sounded a little elegant, but was it possible that he considered breakfast foods to be nothing more than Toaster Strudels and Slim Jims? She imagined herself sitting at a tiny table in a dress, eating powdered donuts out of a box.

"No," she scolded herself. He was twenty-nine, not nineteen. He had a real apartment with a real table and maybe even a stove he knew how to use. So she picked out a pretty yellow dress and laid it out on the bed, then turned to her dresser to face the more difficult task of choosing undergarments.

Boy, she was regretting that generously padded bra now. False advertising and potential daylight nudity did not mix. She looked down at the towel that lay flat against her chest, then back to the drawer full of pretty, delicate, unnecessary bras. Then Olivia sat down hard on her bed and faced a problem she'd been ignoring. A problem she'd tried hard to forget.

She wasn't just inexperienced at irresponsible fun. She was inexperienced, period.

Victor was the only lover she'd ever had. Ever. If she slept with Jamie, he'd be her second. Not that she would ever, ever let him know.

She was, after all, a modern, educated woman. A divorced thirty-five-year-old with no moral objections to a healthy love life. As a young woman, she hadn't been specifically saving herself for love or marriage or a soul mate. She'd just been a skinny girl in glasses who was too shy to willingly look beyond her books. And like so many quiet girls before her, she'd been struck with an awful crush on the smart teacher who'd tried to draw her out. He'd seemed so interested. In *her*, of all things. She hadn't stood a chance.

That was all well and good. She'd been inexperienced. Victor had liked that. But being inexperienced with Jamie was a whole different issue. She'd just have to fake it. Which shouldn't be too hard, really. She'd been having sex for over a decade now. One man couldn't be so radically different from another. Same parts. Same process. And she had the same body. Which was her current worry.

When she'd asked, Victor had said he didn't mind her small breasts. He didn't *mind* them. But it had been impossible to miss the way he'd looked at other women's cleavage. And of the three women she knew about, all of them had been fairly impressive in the size department.

But she was silly to worry. They were just breasts. Only one small part of what Jamie was interested in, hopefully. As for the other…she might be inexperienced, but he'd never know. She'd fake her way through it.

As pep talks went, it was lacking in enthusiasm, but

Olivia had always been a logical kind of girl. She felt better as she made herself pick out her favorite bra. It was pretty lilac cotton edged in white lace. She pulled on matching underwear and tied on the bright yellow wrap dress, then put in her contacts and did her makeup.

The clock told her she had half an hour left, and she wasn't sure what to do with herself, so Olivia simply sat on the couch with her hands folded in her lap. If she wanted to, she could just go to Jamie's house and share a meal. She knew that. But that wasn't what she wanted. She wanted to have him. She wanted to feel him on her and in her. So, scary as it was, she wouldn't back down. Someone had to be the first after Victor, and it was going to be Jamie.

After thirty quiet, calm minutes, Olivia stood, put on her heeled sandals and left for Jamie's place. She'd approach fun the way she approached everything: with logic and calm.

Logic, calm and a crazed, thundering heart. It seemed that fun wasn't easy to trick, because by the time she reached Jamie's place, she couldn't hear anything past her rushing pulse.

She vaguely noticed that he lived in a beautiful neighborhood of large houses, and his place was no exception. The porch was split into two entrances, and she walked up to the left one and knocked. When she started getting dizzy, she made herself breathe, even when she saw a figure approach behind the frosted glass.

"Ms. Bishop," he said, a smile spreading across his face like a warm, melting treat. "Thanks for coming."

Hopefully he'd be repeating that same phrase later. She fought back a nervous laugh as he opened the door wider and motioned her to step inside. She started to walk past him, then stuttered when he moved to kiss her. At the exact moment she realized he'd meant to kiss her cheek, she turned in to kiss his lips. It was too late then. Their mouths bumped awkwardly before she stepped away.

*Damn it.*

The door clicked closed.

"It smells good in here!" she said brightly.

"Thank you."

"And…" She finally registered her surroundings and turned in a slow, awed circle. "It's so pretty!" This was no dingy apartment. It wasn't even a man cave. The tall windows were open to the breeze, letting sunlight fall across wood floors. The baseboards and doors were warm, polished wood against almond-colored walls. "How long have you lived here?"

"About eighteen months." He led her toward the back, to a small kitchen done in dark granite and stainless steel.

"Beautiful. I didn't expect this."

"Oh, yeah?" he opened the oven and pulled out a pan. "What did you expect?"

She cleared her throat and didn't answer.

"Neon beer signs? Posters taped to the walls?"

"No. I—"

"I save those for my bedroom. Then I know I'll start the day off right."

"Stop," she said, slapping his arm.

Jamie snagged her wrist and pulled her into him. "I've been waiting to do this."

His arms curved around her, his mouth touched hers,

and the world crashed into them. She parted her lips and his tongue slid in, and though it started warm and slow, she was soon pushed against the kitchen counter while Jamie's tongue worked her mouth and his hands clutched her hips. She clutched him right back, loving the way he smelled and tasted and felt. For three nights, she'd fallen asleep with his voice winding around her. She'd been waiting for this.

They'd shared kisses before, but this was something different. His whole body was pressed to her. She shifted, and his hips nudged her, and lust turned inside her like a screw tightening.

Maybe he'd take her right here. Maybe he'd just set her up on the counter, and push her skirt up and her panties down. She'd never had it like that before, hot and desperate in the kitchen, cold granite against her back. She was wet already. So wet she could feel it.

Something buzzed loudly, and Olivia jerked back.

"Sorry," he said, his voice rough. "Excuse me for just a moment."

When he moved away, her nipples peaked at the sudden coolness he left behind. She felt like she was about to burst, but Jamie still moved easy and calm as he leaned over to pull another pan from the oven. "Baked omelette," he explained, as he set it down. "I hope you don't have anything against bacon."

"No, I tried being a vegetarian a few years ago. I was embarrassingly unsuccessful."

"Oh, yeah?"

"On the fourth day, I was so desperate for meat that I stopped at a convenience store on my way home from lunch and bought a taquito. I ate it at the cash register while I was still paying."

"That's pretty bad," Jamie said. "And here I thought you were so straitlaced."

She smiled even though her laces had been measured with a level. "I can get pretty crazy, I guess. Whatever you do, don't get between me and a tray of taquitos."

"I wouldn't dream of it."

Despite her intense hope, Jamie didn't return to her. Apparently there'd be no sex on the counter. The man was determined to feed her. He moved to the fridge and pulled out a bowl, and Olivia's eyes trailed down to his bare feet. Everything about him made her mouth water, even his feet. He looked young and adorable in his ancient jeans and T-shirt. When he reached back into the fridge, his shirt rose, and Olivia caught a glimpse of his tight back, the curve of his hip bone standing out in mouthwatering relief.

She was going to do this. She really was. She was going to see him naked. Touch him. Wrap herself around him. What a damn strange idea. She almost felt like she was watching herself in a movie, acting out a part.

"Olivia, can you grab this?"

This? She'd grab anything he wanted. But in the end it was just a bowl of cut fruit, and she sadly followed him through the kitchen and past the table toward the back door.

He was being very sweet, making an effort, but she didn't really need any of this. Did he always go to this much trouble for a simple round of sex? No wonder he was so popular. Service with a smile.

Her eyes on his ass, it took her a moment to notice where he'd led her. He set a carton of orange juice and a bottle of champagne on a round table. "Mimosa?"

"You have to ask? Does anyone ever say no to that?"

He frowned, but she was too distracted by her surroundings to worry. "What a great place, Jamie." They sat on a wide deck outfitted with the table and chairs and one lounge chair. That deck dropped one step down to a smaller area that included a Jacuzzi half-hidden behind a trellis. But the rest of the yard was the amazing part. A stone path wound through gardens and rock formations. At the very back of the long yard, a little waterfall fell in a perpetual tumble over a six-foot-tall rise of boulders. "It's so beautiful. Peaceful."

"Thank you." He gestured for her to sit down, handed her a mimosa, then disappeared back inside. He'd already set the table, and she found herself smiling down at her plate and the silverware, laid out with perfect neatness on a folded paper towel. Her coffee cup read, "My other mug is a pint glass."

"Do you want help?" she called.

"Nope." He stepped out, balancing two baking dishes, some serving spoons and one coffeepot. "If there's one thing I can do, it's serve a table."

He stuck the spoons smack into the middle of each dish, which reminded Olivia of the folded paper towels. His attention to detail didn't reach Martha Stewart levels. He was kind of adorable. Again.

She served herself some eggs and some coffee cake, and the combined smells were heavenly. Her stomach rumbled, but as she reached for her fork, Jamie reached for the champagne. She made herself wait politely while he poured champagne, and then the orange juice. Then he raised his glass. "To fun," he said.

"And new things," she added.

Five minutes later, Olivia was embarrassed to realize she'd already cleaned her plate. And emptied her glass. "Oh, my God, that was amazing."

"Have more," he said, already tilting the bottle. Golden liquid bubbled and sloshed. Olivia giggled and wondered if she was tipsy. Then she stole another dollop of cake.

"So did you always want to be a teacher?" he asked as he took another huge serving of bacon omelette.

"No, not really."

"You just fell into it?"

"Yes." She'd fallen into it, all right. Helped by the steady push of her husband's hand. She tried not to sigh. "But it's a subject I love. My parents were investors and entrepreneurs. There's a lot of specialized knowledge that goes into the business side of food service. Stuff a restaurateur wouldn't necessarily know. I like helping with that."

He stared intently at her. "Yeah?"

"It's a tough field. Starting a restaurant is risky and stressful and time-consuming. I like the idea of helping people with it." In fact, she'd meant to become a consultant, not a teacher. She opened her mouth to say that, but then let the words fade away, unable to form them in a way that didn't sound pitiful. She'd fallen in love with Victor. He'd wanted her time and energy invested in his career. And so that's what she'd done. She'd taken a low-paying job at the university, because his career was important. Of course it was. Who could've argued with that?

Jamie stared at her, his eyes narrowed as if he were trying to puzzle something out. Olivia wanted to shrink down and protest that she'd done what she'd thought best at the time. Yes, she'd been an idiotic twenty-three-year-old, marrying a man who'd played her perfectly, but she'd meant well. He'd been recently tenured, after all. He'd had a career to build.

"It's not a bad job," she said quietly.

"I have an idea." He didn't sound disapproving. He sounded…excited?

Olivia had trouble adjusting to this unexpected turn. "What kind of idea?"

"Maybe we could help each other."

She cocked her head in question.

"You want to learn how to have fun…."

"Yes…?"

He smiled, but it didn't hold quite his normal level of confidence. "And I want to learn how to turn the tasting room into a real brewpub."

His plan wasn't exactly a shock. She'd assumed he was heading in that direction. But it was a shock to hear him present their problems as an equal exchange. Was he proposing that she work for him in exchange for sex?

"Jamie, I…I don't know."

"What do we have to lose?"

"If I'm going to be working with your family, I'm not sure it would be appropriate to—"

"You won't be working with my family. My family doesn't know anything about this."

"I don't understand," she murmured, reaching for her glass, grateful he'd refilled it.

Jamie leaned back and held his own glass loosely between his fingers, turning it as he stared down at the tilting liquid. "My brother doesn't have a lot of confidence in me. Hell, nobody does. I guess I've brought that on myself. Let's just say there've been some instances of questionable judgement."

"With the business?"

"No, not exactly. Years ago, I sowed my oats fairly widely. And once you've cast yourself in the role of black sheep, it's hard to shake it off."

"Were there drugs involved? Anything illegal?"

"No, nothing like that. It's just that…my brother and I are nothing alike. He's a paragon of responsibility. I could never compete with that, so I didn't bother trying." He shrugged. "It's complicated. But in the end, it comes down to this. We're equal partners in the brewery, so whatever I propose, I'll have to convince both my sister and my brother that it's a good idea. So I need help. All the help I can get."

"Well, of course I'd be happy to help. But I don't need you to—"

"No, that's not true. You need help, too. And I happen to be a lot of good at fun. I cut my teeth on it."

Her face was so hot it prickled as if she'd just fallen into a field of stinging nettle. "But sex? I can't just—"

"I didn't say anything about sex."

Oh, Jesus. She pressed a cool hand to her cheek. "I don't understand."

"I mean fun. Staying up later than ten, for instance."

"I like to—"

"Sleeping late. Getting drunk under the stars. Skinny-dipping. Going to a strip club—"

"A strip club?" she yelped.

He winked. "And maybe we could work in a little can't-wait-for-it, gotta-have-it sex against the bathroom wall while we're at it. Assuming you'd consider that fun."

"I think…" Her face still burned. Her throat turned on itself until she couldn't believe she could still draw breath. This wasn't normal. This wasn't how people went about things, not even older divorcées and younger men. Maybe she should be insulted that he wanted her to bargain for time in his bed. Or against his wall.

On the other hand, it made things easier, didn't it? No worries that it was something special. Something deep. They were just…scratching each other's backs. Exchanging services.

Now that she thought about it, maybe this *was* how it was done. Maybe she was a sugar mama, albeit a rather poor one.

Isn't that how older men did it? Men like Victor offered guidance, stability, a wise hand along the way. Younger women offered tight bodies and simple needs.

"Well?" Jamie prompted, setting his glass on the table and sitting up straight. He looked right into her eyes, not the least bit embarrassed. How did he do that?

Olivia forced herself to sit straight, too. She'd wanted him anyway, hadn't she? "All right," she said, surprised at the conviction in her own voice. "You've got a deal. But I want my first lesson today."

# CHAPTER SEVEN

"I DIDN'T BRING a swimsuit," she said, confused despite her earlier bold declaration.

Jamie tried to look serious, shaking his head as he slipped the last of the dishes into the sink. "Haven't you listened to anything I said?"

He could almost see her reviewing his list of fun. In fact, her lips moved as she repeated it to herself. Her eyes widened. "But today...I thought we'd..."

"What?" he asked, pretending he didn't know what she meant.

She stammered, her face pinkening again.

"Take it slow?" he prompted, letting her off the hook. But he knew exactly what she'd meant. She thought they'd just have sex, and apparently she welcomed it. Jamie's blood pumped faster, filling his veins until his body felt tight.

She leapt on his words and nodded enthusiastically. "Yes. Take it slow."

"But I'm trying to teach you how to jump in feetfirst. Starting with the hot tub."

Her eyes slid toward the back door as she piled silverware in the sink. "But...people will see us."

"Nope. The trellis keeps it private."

"But...the walk..."

"I have towels, Olivia. Big, fluffy ones."

She swallowed and stared hard at the bright rectangle of sunlight spilling onto the kitchen floor. "All right," she said, looking terrified.

"Hey." He walked over and nudged her chin up. "I'm teasing. Maybe we could go for staying up late as a first step."

She met his gaze, and there was that vulnerability again. Jamie felt his heart turn. But then her jaw hardened. "No. You're right. I'm not the expert here, am I? I should trust you."

Her skin felt like silk when he traced the line of her chin. "It's just a hot tub," he said, because he'd be damned if he'd make her feel she was agreeing to anything else at this point. He wasn't going to shame her into sex. "Just a swim. That's all."

"Right," she said. "Just a hot tub."

"I'll leave a towel in the bedroom for you."

He walked away casually, trying not to let her know how much he was anticipating this. If she thought he lounged naked in his hot tub with a different girl every Sunday, then so be it. He stuffed a couple of condoms into his pocket, slung a towel around his neck and laid one on the bed for Olivia. Then he walked right past her, grabbing the champagne glasses as he passed.

When she turned on the water at the sink, he paused. "Just to be clear, I'll get the dishes later."

"Oh, sure," she said. The water cut off. He chuckled as he stepped outside and headed for the tub. He had set the timer to keep the water warm on the weekends, so it was already comfortably toasty. Jamie turned on the jets, dropped his clothes on the bench and stepped in.

It would take her a little while. He knew that. He could picture her perfectly, standing in the kitchen, her fingers wound together, jaw set tight as steel. She might be careful and serious, but she was strong as hell, and he had no doubt she'd work up to it.

He laid his head back and closed his eyes, picturing her walking slowly down his hallway, her heels clicking against the wood. When she reached his bedroom, she'd stare hard at the towel. Then at his bed. Her hands would hesitate over the knot that kept that wrap dress on. God, he'd give anything to be the one to untie it. To slide the sash free and watch that bright yellow fabric open. To see that first glimpse of skin. What was she wearing under there? Something sweet and modest? Something delicate and silky?

Jamie's cock was aching by the time he opened his eyes and found her standing before him. He blinked in surprise. In his mind, she'd still been nervously undressing.

"Hey," he said, his eyes sweeping down the wide white towel she clutched to her body.

Jesus Christ, she was naked under there. No doubt about it. Her eyes were wide and her knuckles glowed as pale as the cotton she clutched, but she stood straight and met his gaze.

"You're sure no one can see in?" she asked.

"I'm sure. Too many shadows."

"Could you...?"

Jamie closed his eyes again, but his ears strained to make up for that chivalry, as if he could possibly hear a towel being unwound over the sound of the rolling jets. He counted to ten, then twenty, sure that there'd be some global shift once she was naked in the water with him. At the very least, she'd splash a little.

"Can we even count it as skinny-dipping if you keep your eyes closed the whole time?"

That would be a tragedy, so Jamie opened his eyes immediately. And there she was. The swirling bubbles hid most of her body. All of it, really. He could see much more of her skin while he was sitting in class. But the few inches of her shoulders seemed startling bare above the water. Fascinatingly bare. Her dark hair just brushed along her collarbone when she moved. Water danced and dipped just an inch below that, teasing him with her nudity each time a little trough showed more skin.

Jamie forced his eyes up to her face, then realized it didn't matter. She was too busy checking out his chest to notice. He slid up a little straighter in response.

"So," she finally said. "I did it." Her smile started small, but it didn't take long for it to spread across her face.

"You certainly did. How's it feel?"

"I don't know yet." She slid a few inches to her right, coming a little closer, though there was still two feet of tub between them. From this angle, she was looking right out into the yard. A breeze stirred her hair, and he watched her take a deep breath. "It's like a cave in here. A secret."

"Yeah. Exactly."

Beyond the trellis walls, the day exploded in brightness and light. The people out there moved through their Sunday world. And no one knew Jamie and Olivia were tucked into these shadows, nude beneath the water. Her foot brushed his. He breathed very carefully.

When he'd dared her to skinny-dip with him, Jamie had felt in control. A little superior. Just as he should, as the man tasked with teaching her how to loosen up. But this wasn't like a casual dip with a tipsy girl who'd tossed her bikini top away like an unneeded jacket. This was Olivia Bishop, whose nudity seemed a precious, guarded thing. And just the glimpse of her naked shoulders felt risqué. Now Jamie didn't feel superior and calm. He felt nervous and so aroused that he was thankful for the shroud of bubbling water. Not cool to casually lounge around with a throbbing erection.

Not cool at all.

"Look at that," she whispered, and for a moment, Jamie worried the waters had cleared. But she pointed out toward the sunlight, to the hummingbird feeder he'd hung on a small tree. Two green birds danced there, swiping at each other as they competed for the sugar water.

But Olivia was smiling, so he watched her instead.

"This is really neat," she said. "Thank you."

"Oh, you're welcome," he said with an irony she seemed to miss.

"I feel different."

"Yeah?"

She turned and aimed that smile at him, and it tilted in a naughty way he'd never seen on her. "Yeah."

Jamie shifted his leg so that it slid against hers, and there was no mistaking the excitement that sparked in her eyes. "I feel strange calling you Ms. Bishop when I'm supposed to be teaching you today."

"That's because you shouldn't be calling me that and you know it."

"Okay, I'll call you Olivia then." He reached for the champagne glasses and handed her one, taking the opportunity to slide a little closer. Now his calf rested naturally against hers. "Your name is beautiful. I don't think I've met an Olivia before, and I meet a lot of people at the brewery."

"It's old-fashioned," she sighed.

"It's pretty," he insisted, not adding that it suited her perfectly. She wouldn't appreciate it, because it was old-fashioned, and that was exactly why it fit her.

Sighing, she ducked down a little farther in her seat and sipped champagne. Her expression was soft. Dreamy. And her cheeks had turned pink in the steam.

Jamie touched her temple, sliding back a strand of hair that stuck to her dampening skin. When she turned toward him, he touched his thumb to her lower lip, loving the soft give of her flesh.

She watched him, waiting, all her nervousness floating away on the steam. And hell if he could wait a moment longer.

He kissed her, very conscious of keeping his hand on her shoulder as he slid next to her. And it was strange, here in the heat, almost as if their whole bodies were part of the kiss. Every part of her was as hot and wet as her mouth at that moment. When her hand slid over his shoulders, it was as sensual as the lick of her tongue. When her knee pressed into his thigh, it slipped over him.

He tried to take it slow, but she slanted her mouth and wound her fingers into his hair. The buoyancy alone pushed him closer, and he had to brace himself to keep from covering her completely. His hand landed on her hip. His fingers naturally curved to hold her. And then his palm was sliding up her side, exploring her body, shifting her closer.

At first he thought it was only the push of water against him, but then he realized her knee was sliding between his thighs. Jamie tried to find an impossible balance between getting her closer and keeping his distance. But a moment later, his restraint had wound so tightly that it simply shattered and floated away. Olivia was trying to deepen the kiss, and now her thigh slid along his cock as her leg fit more snugly between his.

She made a little noise into his mouth. A murmur of surprise or pleasure, he wasn't sure, because his mind was occupied with the sensation of her skin against his shaft and his hands spreading over her back. She was so very naked. Every inch of her wet and available. His hands slid up to her neck, then down...slowly down, following her spine all the way to the base, then he spread his hands out, shaping her ass, holding her hips.

This time she moaned more loudly, and he had no trouble interpreting the sound.

Jamie eased her back, loving that her breath came as hard as his. He dragged his mouth down her neck as her fingers clutched his head. He set her back and lifted her hips, forcing her to stand so that he could see her. Her eyes were closed, her lips parted, and Jamie followed the trickles of beaded water that slid from her neck to her naked breasts. He kissed her collarbone, then followed the water with his mouth. When his lips closed over her nipple, Olivia gasped so loudly that he worried

he'd hurt her. But then her fingers twisted into his hair
and held him close, and he growled with approval.

Her small breasts barely curved into his palm, but
she was incredibly sensitive. When he traced his tongue
around the dark rose of her areola, her hands shook
against him. When he scraped his teeth against her
nipple she sobbed. She was amazing. He could do this
for hours, coaxing every imaginable sound of pleasure
from her mouth. It was like a pretty game, finding the
places that pleased her. Even licking the pale skin along
the side of her breast made her whimper. He teased her
before closing his mouth over the peak again.

"I can't..." she breathed.

Jamie let her nipple slide from his mouth with such
slowness that she groaned.

"I can't stand up anymore," she whispered.

"Well, then...you'd better sit down."

She put one knee on the seat next to his hip, then
lifted the other to straddle him.

For a split second, Jamie considered just sliding into
her right then. Just easing her hips down and filling her,
because he'd never wanted anything more. Nothing. No
woman, no fantasy had ever left him so desperate.

She looked down at him, her damp hair stuck to her
neck in dark coils. Her eyes so wide he could fall right
into them. Her chest rose and fell as she panted, waiting.

"Shit," he murmured, then pulled her down for a kiss.
His cock was caught between them, pressed tight to her
belly. Every time she even breathed, she slid white-hot
pleasure into his shaft. Christ, what would it feel like

when he got inside of her? He wound her hair around his fist and kissed her harder.

She was wild, her nails biting into his biceps, her hips shifting against him. Jamie's world was one big pulsing wave of lust. He dropped one hand down her back and slid his fingers along the seam of her body. He stroked her, loving the way she writhed against him, teasing her until she nearly sobbed.

Just as he was about to plunge two fingers deep within her, the world stopped. Everything stopped. They both froze, pulling back to look at each other in shock.

Jamie had no idea how long they'd been in the hot tub together, but he'd neglected to set the timer for long enough. The new silence roared in his ears. The water settled and became a quiet pond.

Olivia's eyes got even wider. She glanced around as if remembering where she was. "Oh," she said, the word whispering cool air over his cheek.

He took a deep, quiet breath, then slipped his fingers over the tight pearl of her clitoris.

"Oh," she said again, her hips jerking against him.

He was back in control now, somehow, in the quiet water. He could think a little, and he knew he didn't want this to end in the next few minutes. So he touched her slowly, carefully, drawing out her sounds of pleasure again. He followed the folds of her sex, teased her clit, tortured her by tracing her opening without ever pushing inside. And it was torture for him, too. To have his cock pressed so tightly between their bodies when everything he wanted was inches away.

Finally she dragged his face up and kissed him hard.

"Jesus, you're good at this," she growled against his mouth.

He gave a pained laugh as she sat back.

"Do you have...protection?"

Why the fuck had he left his jeans five hundred miles away? He gestured vaguely toward them, but couldn't look away from the site of her perched on his thighs. Her breasts were lovely, her nipples still hard and dark, and now he could see all the way down to the dark triangle of hair between her legs.

"Jamie," she said, her voice urgent. "Condoms?"

"In my jeans," he managed to grumble.

She leaned forward again, her body squeezing his cock so hard he saw stars of pleasure. Her arm reached past him to snag the pile of clothes.

"Thanks," he gasped, taking the jeans from her hands to pull a condom out. Then he paused for an awkward moment, trapped by her body.

"Oh," she said, scooting back to drop off his knees.

Jamie stood, slipping the condom on, aware of the way her eyes took him in. As he sank back into the water he grabbed her hand and floated her toward him. He slid a little lower so she'd have room to put her knees on the seat and kneel above him. Then he took his cock in hand and guided her down. He could watch through the clear water. When the head notched against her opening, he heard the way she drew in a deep breath and held it.

Then she eased down, her body taking him in, closing around him. He heard every flutter of her breath, every small gasp as his cock sank deeper.

Jamie didn't breathe at all. He was too busy feeling

the tightness and the pressure. He was too busy watching as he pushed inside her.

Her hand pressed against his chest. Her fingers spread wide. "Wait," she gasped, breathing harder.

Jamie waited, his teeth clenched as he felt her muscles twitch around him, then ease slightly.

"Okay," she whispered.

Thank God. Jamie finally drew a breath, then settled her down the last couple of inches. And for a moment that was it. That was all they needed. They both held still, letting the hot water calm around them. She stared down at the place where their bodies joined, as if she were as enthralled as he.

And it was quiet. So quiet. Birds sang. A car passed on his street. Far away, a lawn mower buzzed.

Jamie swept his hands up her hips, her waist, until he cupped her breasts. He teased his thumbs over her nipples and her hips jerked. Hell, yeah. That was all that was needed to break the lethargy. She rolled her hips into him with a tortured sigh. He let her set the pace. At first she was slow and easy, but when he pinched her nipples, Olivia took him faster, slamming her hips hard into him when he teased more roughly.

His orgasm was already building at the base of his cock, so Jamie tried not to think about how hot she looked. How her lean body arched back as she rode him, thrusting her breasts more firmly into his touch. He tried not to notice that he could see his shaft slide out of her when she rose, tried not to feel the impossible tightness of her pussy when she slid back down. He tried not to hear the soft, dark sound of her holding back her cries so the neighbors wouldn't hear.

But when her whimpers grew louder and her hips worked faster, Jamie knew he couldn't hold out much more. He slid a little lower in the water, easing her farther back, then he braced one hand on her hip and slipped the other between them. He could feel the perfect contrast of his hardness and her yielding sex, but lust made him clumsy, and it took him a moment to find the right spot.

"Oh, God," she whispered when he finally stroked her clit. "Jamie. Oh, God." She kept her movements tight and quick now. He gritted his teeth against the constant pleasure. "Oh, God," she whispered over and over, while Jamie prayed for strength. Finally her whisper became a sob, and her hips spasmed against him, her sex squeezing impossibly tight. She buried her face in his neck and cried his name on a muffled scream, and he dug his fingers into her hip until the spasms stopped.

Her thighs were still shaking, but he eased her up until she sat above him again, eyes dazed.

And now he let himself notice everything as he braced her hips and surged into her. Her tousled hair and sleepy eyes. The way her flushed mouth parted on a hard gasp when he sank himself to the hilt. The jut of her nipples so dark against her pale skin.

She cried his name again, and he growled with satisfaction as he thrust into her with brutal lust. Finally, he came, grunting past his clenched teeth as he worked himself inside her until every last jolt of pleasure was done.

As soon as he loosened his hold, she collapsed against him, her body draping over his as if she were boneless.

Jamie managed a bark of strained laughter. "You okay?"

"No," she said against his shoulder.

"No?"

"No. I feel...full. And sore."

"Oh, sorry. I—"

"And that wasn't anything like fun."

"Um..." He pulled his head back, trying to read her face. "Olivia—"

"That was...metaphysical perfection."

She started to laugh and Jamie breathed a sigh of relief. "Really? Well, that blows away 'You're a great kisser.' Metaphysical perfection?"

"Don't get a big head," she said. "I was there, too."

"Yeah, you definitely were."

"And...was I fun?" She was still smiling, but when she sat back to meet his gaze, he could see in her eyes that the question was real enough. Her hands rose to cover her breasts. Jamie tugged them away.

"Hey." He wrapped his fingers around hers and held her gaze. "You were a lot like perfect yourself."

Now her smile looked real. She bit her lip, looking like a proud schoolgirl. Damned appropriate. And between that naughty smile and her naked breasts and the fact that he was still inside her, Jamie felt his cock stir.

Her smile turned into an O of surprise.

"Be careful who you show all that fun to, Olivia," he said. "It's dangerous."

"I'm going to have to learn my own strength."

He winced when she laughed, but he did it with a smile. "All right, but let's test the boundaries of your newfound powers in bed this time. I don't want to know what pruning looks like on my junk."

She stood quickly, leaving him biting back a groan. And this time, when she stood naked next to the hot tub, she didn't ask him to turn around. "Hurry up, Mr. Donovan. Class resumes in five minutes."

"Five minutes," he muttered. But he thought that with Olivia, he just might be able to pull it off.

## CHAPTER EIGHT

IT HARDLY SEEMED POSSIBLE that only a few hours had passed since Olivia had left her apartment. As she hurried up the walk that wound between the little cottage-like duplexes, her hair brushed her neck, and a few of the strands were still damp against her skin.

My word.

Olivia kept her head down, because there was no way to hide the wide smile on her face, and she wanted to keep it secret. She wanted to hold it close and never tell a soul. Not because she was ashamed, but because if she let the secret free, it might dissipate. She couldn't bear to let a moment of it go.

"Where the hell have you been?" a male voice growled from the direction of her tiny porch.

Her head snapped up as she tucked her secret smile away. Her ex-husband was pushing up from the steps, his brow drawn low with tension.

"What's wrong?" she asked. "What are you doing here?"

"I was worried sick. I've been calling all day!"

"I was busy." She brushed past him and pulled her keys from her purse.

"I called early this morning."

Olivia rolled her eyes. "I was out for my run. Don't pretend you didn't know that."

He followed her up the stairs. "It was eight-thirty, Olivia. You don't run at eight-thirty. I called your home phone *and* your cell."

Guilt turned her cheeks pink. Of all things, she felt guilty about waking up late and heading out for a run at eight instead of six.

"What is going on with you?" he pressed. "You've been acting really weird."

"No, I don't think so."

"It's him, isn't it?"

Him? Every cell in her body seemed to surge toward her skin at the thought of Jamie.

"You didn't come home last night, did you? Jesus, Olivia, that boy looks young enough to be one of your students."

She turned the knob and her door swung slowly open, revealing her home just as she'd left it. Everything normal and neat and in place. But her emotions nearly disintegrated at the sight.

It didn't make any sense. That she was standing here, looking exactly the same, surrounded by the same things. Yet she'd just done something completely ridiculous. Something dirty and delicious and irresponsible. Something that had felt better than everything that had ever come before it.

And now Victor—*Victor*—was following her in, saying nonsensical words to her. Saying the most ridiculous, hypocritical, utter *shit* to her.

She dropped her keys on the table, missing the little ceramic dish by a mile and not caring.

She set down her purse and tossed her sweater over a chair instead of hanging it up.

Then she turned to face her ex-husband. "You have got to be kidding me," she pushed past her clenched jaw.

"Olivia—"

"No. What I meant was, You have got to be *fucking* kidding me."

He cringed at the sound of that word coming from her mouth. Truthfully, she cringed a little, too, but it was a relief. Like lancing a wound.

"You're in my house, asking about my personal life? *You?* It's none of your business, in case you aren't clear on that."

"It's my business when you're flaunting your life in front of my friends and colleagues. He's a *beer slinger?* What the hell were you thinking, bringing him to a university function?"

This was so outrageous that Olivia actually laughed. "I'm sorry, but...really? *Really?* You want to know something truly delicious? He *is* one of my students, Victor. And I was probably thinking the same thing you were when you brought one of your students to a party. Allison. Rachel. Whoever that girl was two years ago."

"Those women are all pursuing—"

"I was thinking that maybe I'd like to fuck him."

Victor's face drained of color as if he were a shaken Etch A Sketch, wiped clean of detail. He rocked back on his heels. "You've gone off the deep end," he whispered. "You've finally lost it."

"The complete opposite, actually."

"A woman your age, chasing after some young stud. It's pitiful."

Pitiful. After everything he'd done. In that moment, she hated him, and she wanted to wound him as he'd wounded her. "Pitiful?" she sneered. "It wasn't pitiful a half hour ago, when he had me up against his headboard."

Victor blinked and stepped back. For a split second, she saw something broken inside him. Regret and sadness. "I can't believe you," he hissed.

Hating the bolt of regret she felt, Olivia crossed her arms in defense. "Stop calling me. And don't come over. Just live your life and leave me to mine. It has nothing to do with you anymore."

He flashed a bitter, twisted smile. "Nothing to do with me? That's rich. It obviously has everything to do with me."

"Wrong. This is about me."

"Keep telling yourself that, Olivia. If that's what gets you through this disgusting little phase, you pretend it has nothing to do with me."

"Get out," she said quietly.

Victor drew something from the pocket of his coat and set it on the counter. "I was just bringing you the transfer information from the 403-B. It finally came through. That should be the last thing, thank God."

"If you get anything else, could you please just mail it?"

"With pleasure." He left, slamming the door so hard that the keys slipped off the table and landed on the tile with a crack.

Olivia stood there, stunned, not breathing. When she finally drew a breath, she realized that Victor had ruined it. He'd ruined it, turning it into something sad and vengeful. That bastard. Aside from his flaunting of women, he'd been perfectly civil to her throughout the divorce. So civil that he'd nearly driven her mad. But the moment she started to move on, he turned vicious.

Why?

Olivia picked up her keys and put them in the dish where they belonged. Then she set her purse on the chair and hung her sweater in the hall closet. The motions helped her feel a little better, but she couldn't stop the regret from pouring through her.

She'd been right. She'd let her secret out, and now the deliciousness was gone. After all, a thing couldn't be perfect and vengeful at the same time, could it?

"Crap," she muttered, rubbing her eyes with the heels of her hands. When she opened her eyes, the living room had gone crooked. She blinked half a dozen times to get her contacts back in place, cursing herself the whole time. No, she wasn't going to let Victor take this from her.

No.

She'd been daring. She'd been brave. She'd stepped so far out of her comfort zone that she hadn't even been able to see it anymore. A younger man. A hot younger man. She'd gone to his house. She'd stripped down to nothing and skinny-dipped in his hot tub. She'd *ridden* him in his hot tub.

And suddenly a little of the deliciousness was back. Impossible not to feel it when she was remembering him pushing into her. Filling her. Stretching her. That first time, that first orgasm… My God, she'd never felt anything like it. The way her body had squeezed him as she came. The way he'd felt even bigger, even wider.

"God," she breathed, shaking her head in disbelief.

Was it him? Or was it her? Good Lord, it didn't matter. She just wanted more of it. And no way was she going to let Victor take that away from her. She wasn't going to let herself doubt that Jamie had wanted it, too. She wasn't going to wonder how many times he'd done that with other women. She wasn't going to worry that he was just using her. She was using him, too, wasn't she? And if he'd done that with other women, good for him. The practice had paid off in spades.

"Fuck Victor," she said, and even if her voice sounded a little uncertain, she was glad she'd said it. If she never said the F word again, she'd used it wisely today.

And she'd enacted it damn well, too, if she did say so herself.

JAMIE FOUND HIMSELF DRIFTING, unable to concentrate on the conversation raging around him.

As if he didn't see his siblings enough at work, his sister was enforcing the Sunday family dinner again in an effort to shove them all closer together. At the time she'd announced it, Jamie hadn't minded much. After all, it meant at least one solid home-cooked meal a week. But now he couldn't help resenting it.

He'd had to send Olivia home. It was way too early in the relationship to ask her over for Sunday dinner at the old homestead. And since he'd canceled last Sunday, his sister had threatened him with violence if he canceled again. But he hadn't been ready to end the day. Hell, he would've liked the day to keep going right through until Monday morning.

The sex had been…intense. More intense than he'd

expected. He hadn't slept with anyone in months, and the last time had been a bad experience, but it wasn't just that. For the past couple of years, whatever brief connections he'd had with women had felt empty. He'd never slept around as much as everyone suspected, although he'd had some fun in his early twenties. But fun wasn't an emotion. It was just an experience. And any experience could get boring after a while.

But today, with Olivia…that had been emotion. With plenty of fun thrown in.

"Hey!" A hand passed in front of his face.

Jamie shot his sister an irritated look. "What?"

"I said I'm planning a Fourth of July barbecue the Sunday after the Fourth. Does that work for you?"

"Sure."

"You're in charge of sparklers."

"Sparklers? What's Eric in charge of?"

"Beer," Tessa said. "I'm taking care of food. And Luke's bringing plates and stuff."

Jamie gaped at her in disbelief. "I'm in charge of *sparklers?* It's a family barbecue and your boyfriend is bringing more than I am." He pointed an accusing finger at Luke. "He's not even part of the family."

Tessa rolled her eyes. "Fine. You bring plates and cups and napkins. And sparklers. Luke can help me with the food."

"Oh, are you sure you trust me?" Jamie snapped. He turned his irritation on Tessa's boyfriend. "And I've noticed your truck is here an awful lot."

Luke smiled. "Hard to believe, but I like spending time with my girlfriend."

"Yeah. A lot of *night* time. Nearly every time I close the brewery, I drive by and see your car here."

Tessa gasped. "Are you checking up on me?"

"Please. I've been checking up on you for years."

"What?" she screeched.

"Tessa," he said impatiently. "You live alone in a big house. Of course I drive by to make sure you're okay. But I guess you've got police protection now."

Said policeman, Detective Luke Asher, smiled like an angel from the other side of the table. *Angel, my ass,* Jamie thought. He'd gone to school with Luke. The guy wasn't any more of an angel than Jamie. Which was exactly why Jamie was glaring at him.

Luke took Tessa's hand. They exchanged a meaningful look. "Actually," Tessa said, "Luke's thinking of moving in."

Jamie heard his own horror voiced in Eric's choked grunt.

Luke cleared his throat, no sign of a smile on his face now. "I wanted to speak to you two about it first. Tessa lives here, but it's still your family home. So if you're uncomfortable with the idea—"

Jamie barked, "You're damn right we're uncomfortable with the idea."

"I get that," Luke said. He glanced toward Tessa.

She nodded as if she were answering a question. "He makes me happy. Jamie, you know that. You're the one who told me not to break up with him."

Jamie felt Eric's disapproval turn in his direction. "I didn't exactly tell you to get back together with him. And if he makes you so happy, why are you only talking about moving in together?"

Eric's kick was swift and effective. Jamie shut his mouth with a snap.

"We're okay with it," Eric said simply.

"Good," Tessa said with a self-satisfied smile. "I'll get dessert." She disappeared into the kitchen, leaving tense silence between the men. She'd only been dating Luke for a few months, and neither Jamie nor Eric was comfortable with the idea of their little sister being so deeply involved with a man. Especially a man with a past like Luke's.

Silence reigned until Tessa returned with apple pie. As she put a slice on Jamie's plate, she served it up with a pointed question. "So how's your dating life going?"

"Why don't you ever ask Eric that?"

"Because Eric doesn't date. Good thing, since you date enough for all of us. So tell me about that woman."

"There's nothing to tell. And I don't date that much. In comparison to Eric, sure, I get around like a rabbit on speed. But—"

"Who is she?" Tessa demanded.

"She's nobody," Jamie said, cringing as the word left his mouth.

"Well, I only saw her for a minute, but I can already tell she's way nicer than that awful Monica Kendall. So, good job."

A boulder fell out of nowhere and landed in his stomach. Jamie swallowed hard to try to dislodge it. He didn't want to talk about Monica Kendall. Ever. Especially not in conjunction with Olivia. Thankfully, Eric managed to help Jamie out for once.

"Luke, have you heard anything about the Kendalls lately? We haven't received an update in a while."

Luke sighed. "That's because there's nothing to update. The leads coming in from Taiwan have dried up. But we're working another angle with Monica."

Jamie set his fork down.

"She's still claiming that her involvement was minimal, but we're putting the pressure on her, hoping she'll reach out to her brother. I'll keep you in the loop. Don't worry."

Monica's brother, Graham, had been the guy behind the break-in at the brewery. And Monica had played a crucial role. A crucial role involving Jamie that he wished he could forget.

"I've gotta go," Jamie said, pushing his plate away.

Tessa made her regular protests, asking him to stay, complaining that he always left too soon. But he left anyway. When she needed something, she turned to Eric, the dependable one. And now she turned to Luke. Jamie was just the brother who caused trouble, and he was sick and tired of being the whipping boy.

He couldn't carry the heavy regret of his teenage years around anymore.

He was ready to grow up. To settle down and make something of himself. *Settle down,* he thought. Hell, maybe Olivia could help him with more than just his plans for the brewery....

## CHAPTER NINE

SHE'D ONLY TALKED TO HIM ONCE since Sunday, and it had been a frightening conversation. Frightening because of the warm wave that had crashed over her at the sound of his voice. Frightening because it had been so easy to lie in bed and laugh with him, the phone pressed so tight to her ear that her head had hurt afterward.

Now as she walked down the hallway toward the classroom, her nerves jumped with adrenaline. This would be her first time seeing him since…since *then*. He wouldn't be a fantastic memory anymore, he'd be right there watching her as she moved, his eyes everywhere his hands had been on Sunday.

"Olivia," his voice said, and she nearly jumped out of her skin as she spun toward that low sound.

And there he was. His dark bronze hair a little messy as if he had run his hand through it every few minutes. His green eyes smiling at her, sharing their secret. And those narrow hips that she'd wrapped her legs around…

If she thought she'd been beset by adrenaline before, Olivia had been mistaken. It surged so hard through her now that it was almost fear. "Hey," she managed to squeak.

"I'm sorry." He glanced around. "I meant, Hello, Ms. Bishop. Can I help you with that?"

She glanced stupidly down to her laptop case and books. Get it together, she ordered herself. *Please*. Olivia finally managed a smile. "No, I think I can handle it."

"Yeah?" He ducked his head, but she could still see the smile on his face. God, she wanted to touch him.

"Did you bring everything?" Olivia asked. "For after class?"

"I did. Should we—?" He gestured toward the door, but Olivia's gaze caught the movement behind him and focused there. Another student walked past, nodding a greeting at Olivia. But that wasn't the sight that made her mouth fall open. "Oh, crap," she breathed.

"Are you avoiding me?" Gwen called from forty feet away.

"No!" Olivia said, though not to Gwen. She was calling no to Jamie, who was swinging around to look behind him. "Don't!"

But it was too late. Gwen's eyes turned into perfect circles. Her mouth opened wide enough for a dental exam. She stumbled to a halt.

"Hey, Gwen," Jamie said. "How are you doing?"

"Ohmigod," Gwen gasped. Her gaze jerked to Jamie's laptop, then his face, then back to Olivia. "Ohmigod."

Jamie straightened, the awkwardness of the situation finally overcoming his natural friendliness. "Um…I'm going to go find my seat. I'm just taking a little refresher course.…"

Gwen had finally managed to close her teeth, and now she just stood there grinning like the Cheshire cat, eyes still wide and crazed.

"Goodbye, Gwen. Ms. Bishop."

The door closed silently behind him, leaving Olivia alone with Gwen.

"Ohmigod."

"Gwen—"

"Please tell me he calls you Ms. Bishop while he licks you like a damn lollipop."

"Gwen!" Olivia rushed over to grab her arm and tug her to the side of the hall. "Hush!"

"Holy shit, Olivia. He's in your *class?* I can't take this. I swear to God, it's too perfect."

Olivia was trying to maintain her stern expression. A tiny part of her did feel stern, after all. Unfortunately, the other parts felt like putting on a dance number in the hallway, complete with high kicks and glitter confetti. "You can't tell anybody," she said, her voice halfway between an order and a squeal.

Gwen actually hopped up and down, her hands clasped together. "I should've known something was up when you didn't return my call yesterday. You did it, didn't you? You did Jamie Donovan. Oh, my God, I can see it all over you."

Olivia felt a brief flash of alarm that she'd missed something in the cleanup. "What?"

"You look…*loose.* Your hair is even bouncier. And are you wearing eyeliner? To class? Oh, you cheeky, cheeky monkey."

"Promise you won't tell?"

"I won't! I swear. No matter how many details you give me, I won't tell."

Olivia's tension gave out a little, and she leaned her

back against the wall, letting it hold her up. "He's… He's… Oh, Gwen."

Gwen clasped her hands together and tucked them under her chin, as if she were a kid waiting for a Christmas present.

"He's… Oh, damn," she groaned. "I can't tell you anything. It feels too wrong. Like we're football players bragging about some chick in the hallway."

Her friend's face fell. "Aw! Come on!"

"No, I'm sorry. And I have to go. Class starts in less than a minute."

Gwen waved a dismissive hand. "Bah. Summer class. If you won't give me details—yet—at least tell me this. Is he everything I've spent hours imagining he would be?"

"Gwen!"

"I'm serious. Have my fantasies been well spent? He can't possibly be that cute and still be good in bed, can he? The universe wouldn't give so much to one man."

Olivia shook her head in happy exasperation and pushed away from the wall. "I've got to go."

But Gwen's last mournful groan got to her. And Olivia really didn't want to keep every speck of information to herself. She was bubbling over with what she'd done. So before she walked away, she leaned in close to Gwen's ear. "The universe gave him a lot. A whole hell of a lot. Shameful amounts, really."

"No!" Gwen screamed, sending Olivia into peals of laughter as she rushed toward her class. She remembered to choke back her laughter before she opened the door, but apparently the doors weren't soundproof. Everyone in the class was looking at her when she stepped in, and Jamie looked just the slightest bit nervous. Though he mostly looked highly amused as she stumbled to a halt and straightened her sweater.

His eyes burned through her as she descended, passing within inches of his body. "Is everyone ready?" she called out.

"I sure am," said one voice over the murmurs of assent.

"All right." Olivia took her place at the table and looked out over the rows of students. But in the end, she met Jamie's eyes. "Let's do this."

SHE'D NEVER ENDED a class feeling aroused before, but there was a first time for everything. Jamie was just so very *there*. Right there, oozing charisma all over the room. Every time her eyes touched him, he made her feel aware. He was either watching her intently or typing his notes with a crooked smile on his face. Olivia was beginning to wonder if an hour and a half of blushing could cause fainting. She was certainly starting to feel light-headed.

Finally, thank God, class was over. She almost groaned when she spotted two different students leave their stuff at their desks and come forward to ask her questions. A terrible response for a teacher, so she shook it off and made a conscious effort not to hurry through the spreadsheets they needed help with.

Ten minutes later, she was done, and Jamie still sat patiently in his chair, looking too big for the small space the school expected him to fill.

He raised his eyebrows and she blushed again,

smoothing down her skirt in an effort to dry her damp palms.

"Finally ready for me?" he asked.

For a split second, she imagined climbing on top of him right there. Hiking up her skirt and re-creating their hot tub encounter right in the classroom. Maybe he'd rip open her shirt, sending buttons flying so he could put his mouth to her again.

Olivia swallowed hard and closed her computer. "Yes, I'm ready."

She led the way to her office, her whole back on fire with awareness of him following behind her. She'd never felt this way before. As if her nerves were too close to her skin. As if the merest stroke of a man's finger down her arm could make her cry out. But not just any man...

When they came to her office, Jamie reached past her to open the door, and his arm slid against hers. She sucked in a hard breath at the feel of crisp hair and hot skin brushing over her arm.

"God, you smell good," he whispered. As he pushed the door open his front pressed against her back.

She shivered hard, hoping he hadn't noticed. But when she walked around her desk, she saw that his gaze dropped to her chest. Her nipples tightened further, and she knew they must be visible even under the layers of her shirt and sweater.

Jamie wasn't smiling now.

She couldn't help but wonder what would happen if she closed and locked the door. Was he tempted? Did he want her again? He couldn't possibly need this as much as she did, but he wanted her, at least. She could see that.

But as changed as Olivia felt, she hadn't turned into an entirely new person. She couldn't have sex in her office. She just couldn't. Anyway, they were here for her part of the obligation, not his. Jamie could get sex anywhere he wanted. What he needed from her was advice.

She put her computer on the floor to leave room on her desk, then gestured toward the cleared area. "Show me what you have."

For a moment, he seemed startled.

"Your plans," she clarified.

"Oh, right. The plans. Sorry, my mind was somewhere else."

She tried hard not to be thrilled at that. He was a man. Of course he thought about sex a lot. Probably the same amount he'd thought about it before he'd met her.

Jamie ran a hand through his hair and started to sit down, before rising again to reach for the door. "Do you mind if I close this? I still feel…"

"Sure. That's fine."

Once the door was safely closed, he sat down and began pulling papers from his bag. Lots of papers. Some legal-size sheets, some scraps that looked suspiciously like Donovan Brothers Brewery napkins. She didn't realize how nervous he was until he fumbled half the stack and it spread out over the floor. "Sorry. It's just…" He picked up the last of his stray notes and set them down, pressing them flat. "I've never shown these to anyone."

Olivia flashed briefly on her worries about her flat chest, then had to go perfectly still to stifle her inappropriate laughter. Once it had passed, she nodded. "I know how personal it can be. People think of businesses as dry, money-making institutions. But they can mean just as much as any other form of expression."

"Yeah. I guess." He kept his hands flat.

She tilted her head toward the papers, and he finally relented. "Okay. Let me just say this up front. I don't want to create a whole new place. I want to work with what we've already built. It's intimate. I speak to every person who comes through the door. I don't want to build an addition that'll hold fifty more tables. In fact, if we can sell it to my family as a concept that'll fit with what we already have, I think that would go over better."

"Okay."

"So…"

"Jamie." She touched his hand. "You don't have to be so nervous."

"I know." He nodded one time, just a dip of his head, and then he slid the stack of papers forward.

"First, just tell me what you're thinking."

His hands looked lost now without something to hold on to. "I'm thinking…" After a pause, he cleared his throat and tried again. "I'm thinking every brewpub I go to has a certain kind of menu. Fries and sandwiches. Heavy dishes that feature sauces made with ale. Ice cream made with stout."

Olivia barely managed not to grimace.

"The menus are massive. Even if I wanted to do that, we don't have the kitchen space for it."

"Okay."

"So I was thinking…pizza. But not delivery kind of pizza. Artisan pizza, like Italian pizza with fresh mozzarella, basil leaves, homemade sauce. And instead of making food with beer, we could offer a pairing suggestion for each choice. Something spicy would go great with a pilsner. Something with lots of meat would pair with the porter. Feta cheese is great with India Pale Ale."

He stopped talking suddenly, as if he'd caught himself going too far. But Olivia didn't know how to fill the silence. She was shocked and couldn't think what to say.

"But that's just one idea," he said on a rush.

"No, I… Wow."

His eyes fell. He stared at his open hands.

"I think it's an amazing idea. Honestly. It's unique but approachable and comfortable. I think your current customers will love it, and it'll bring in new people looking for a place to have a meal with their beer."

"Yeah?" He smiled, and when she nodded, it spread to a happy grin. "You like it?"

"I do. And not only is it a great concept, but you wouldn't need a giant commercial kitchen to pull it off."

"Exactly!" He started sorting frantically through the papers, so Olivia tucked her hands out of the way to avoid being swept up. "Here." He pulled out a page that he seemed to have ripped from a restaurant supply catalog. There were four different pizza ovens listed.

"Do you have a commercial cooler?"

"We have a big refrigerator, but I think we'd need

something larger. And probably a small freezer as well, though I'd want the ingredients served fresh."

Olivia leaned back in her chair and smiled at him.

"What?" he asked, narrowing his eyes.

"We've got a lot of work to do, but this is really encouraging. From what you'd said before, I thought maybe you had a general idea that you'd like to serve food, but you were still in the daydream phase. This is a real vision. This is going to be easy."

"It is?"

"Well, easy for me, but still lots of work for you."

He laughed, but she thought she saw a moment of stark relief cross his face. This seemed unsteady ground for him, and it was strange to see such a confident man struck by such uncertainty. She didn't quite understand it. He was a co-owner of the brewery. He ran the front room with amazing skill. But something about this idea threw him into a tailspin.

"So where do you want to start?" she asked.

"I don't know. Where do you think we should start?"

"You've already got a concept, not to mention a location. So, next up…competitive comparisons, equipment costs, design ideas and renovation costs, menu development, a public affairs campaign, the timeline, personnel plans, a budget…" She stopped when she realized how pale he was. "Are you okay?"

"Oh, sure. Yeah. I think I have some of that stuff in there. Or at least parts of it?"

She hadn't thought Jamie Donovan could get more adorable, but here he was being vulnerable, and Olivia couldn't help the warm, fuzzy feelings glowing through her. "All right," she said softly. "Why don't we go through some of this and see where we are?"

"Okay," he said, breathing a sigh of relief, even as he seemed to brace himself for trauma.

"Hey." She curved her fingers under his and squeezed. "It's just a hot tub," she said, repeating his own words. "Nothing to be scared of."

His eyes crinkled. "Just a hot tub, huh? I'd be more comforted if I hadn't been lying my ass off when I said that."

If this were a real relationship, Olivia would circle the desk and give him a hug. She'd snuggle into his lap and tell him not to be worried, he'd be just as good at running a restaurant as he was at everything else. But they were only playing mentors. Granted, with a more delicious twist than usual. So Olivia only squeezed his hand one more time and let him go.

So far, the man had more than held up his end of the bargain. Now it was time for her to help make his dreams come true.

## CHAPTER TEN

JAMIE SLIPPED THE MEASURING TAPE from his pocket with one last look around the kitchen area of the brewery. There wasn't much equipment here: prep tables, a dishwasher, a fridge and a small oven and range used for the occasional catered events they hosted. There was definitely space for a pizza oven, but just how much space was the question.

He measured the empty wall of the kitchen for a start, then measured out the prep space. He thought there was more than enough usable prep area, but he'd have to ask Olivia about that. They'd need a much bigger fridge, but that stood on a wall by itself, so there was plenty of room to expand. The electrical needs he didn't know much about. He'd need to bring somebody in. But when? Electricians didn't work on Sundays, and his brother and sister were around the rest of the week. Maybe he could bring somebody at 8:00 a.m. before anyone else showed up.

"Hey!"

Jamie spun, fumbling the measuring tape before he registered that the voice wasn't Eric's.

"Where the hell is that spring barley I ordered last month?"

Jamie felt slightly dizzy with relief that it was only

Wallace, the brewmaster. And that was a hell of a lot
of relief, considering that Wallace's huge, bearded face
was crumpled into a scowl of fury.

"Well?" he boomed.

"Calm down. I told you when you ordered it that it
wouldn't be here for at least three months. It hadn't even
been harvested yet."

"How the hell am I supposed to work on the new IPA
when I don't have barley?"

Jamie shrugged, used to the man's temperamental
rages. "I thought you were working on the spicy chocolate stout."

"Yes! And the cranberry wheat and the dark ale. I
work on more than one batch at once, in case you've
never noticed, Mr. Donovan."

Oh, for Christ's sake. What the hell was up his ass
today?

"What are you doing?" Wallace suddenly asked, his
hot gaze dropping to the measuring tape lying on the
floor between them.

"What?" Jamie croaked.

The brewmaster gestured toward the object in question.

"Oh. Right." Jamie swooped down to grab the tape,
then stuffed it into his pocket. "Measuring things."

"I get that. But what—"

"Hey, is everything okay, man? You seem really
tense."

Wallace rolled his big shoulders and seemed to throw
off his question about the tape. "Eh. You know. Personal
shit."

"Girl troubles?" Jamie asked, but as soon as the

words left his mouth, he realized his mistake. "Or boy troubles?" He could never keep track of who Wallace was dating.

"Yes," the man answered, so Jamie just nodded.

Wallace put one of his giant hands on Jamie's shoulder and leaned closer. Jamie found himself staring up into fierce gray eyes. The guy had to be at least six-eight.

"You know how it is, Jamie. Everybody thinks it's all fun and games when you play the field. But I care about every single person I date. And sometimes…it gets complicated."

"Tell me about it."

"I knew you'd understand."

Jamie nodded, and Wallace's fingers squeezed his shoulder gently.

"I'm sorry I exploded. I'm just feeling tense. Maybe I need a good, hard workout." He winked.

"Um…Wallace?" Jamie cleared his throat.

"Yeah?"

"Are you coming on to me?"

"What?"

Jamie slid his eyes toward his shoulder and the big paw that engulfed it.

Wallace's bushy beard twitched. His grip loosened. "Good Christ, man," he barked, then threw his head back to howl with laughter.

"What?" Jamie demanded. His only answer was a hard slap on the back that nearly toppled him. "What's so funny?"

"You…You…"

Jamie crossed his arms. "What?"

"You're hardly my type, are you?"

"Well…" Jamie scowled. "I suppose not."

"I suppose not!" Wallace chuckled.

"Dude, it's not that funny," Jamie insisted.

"Oh, come on." Another slap on the back, but this time, Jamie was ready for it and only had to take the barest step forward. He scowled down at his crossed arms.

"You know what?" Wallace said. "Thanks for cheering me up. But even if I was attracted to you, it wouldn't be appropriate, since you're my boss."

"Well, sure—" Jamie started.

"Even more complicated than my normal love life. But thanks."

He was all the way across the room before Jamie registered what he'd said. *Thanks?* "Hey—"

Wallace just gave a friendly wave before he disappeared into the tank room, still chuckling as the door closed behind him.

"What the hell?" Jamie muttered, his skin still hot with embarrassment, though half of his embarrassment was because he wasn't sure what he was upset about: That he'd just been accused of inviting his brewmaster to come on to him, or that his brewmaster had rejected him out of hand? "Ridiculous," he scoffed. He was not upset that his nonexistent come-on had been batted away. That was crazy. And he should be glad he wasn't Wallace's type. The man dated people who were petite and soft, regardless of gender. Jamie didn't fall into either of those categories, thank God.

Totally thrown off by the conversation, Jamie turned in a slow circle, unsure, for a moment, why he was standing in the middle of the room with a pencil in his hand.

"Right. Measurements." Still, he looked around in confusion one more time before turning his attention back to the numbers. He had what he'd come in for, anyway. Now he needed to make some calls about a pizza oven.

Olivia had given him homework, of all things, so he'd given her some, as well. She'd looked more than a little doubtful at the idea of being ready to go to dinner at nine.

"Nine?" she'd pressed. "That's so…"

"Late?"

"Look, I've been out past ten before. You're being silly."

"All right. So it'll be silly. Nine o'clock."

Silly or not, she'd looked downright worried about it, and that made Jamie smile as he walked down the hallway that led to the brewery offices. He'd volunteered to take the smallest office, since he spent most of his time in the front, but he couldn't help but feel that it represented his share of the responsibilities, too. Hopefully his office would soon be too small for him, and he could sit in there and complain righteously about the lack of space. Someday. But right now, his few papers and files didn't come close to filling the available space.

"Jamie?"

Jamie froze in his tracks, then backed up a step to Eric's open door.

"I heard you arguing with Wallace. What are you doing here? You've got Tuesdays off."

"Just checking up on a few things." The tape felt like a lead weight in his pocket.

"Did Wallace settle down?"

Jamie narrowed his eyes, looking for a hint of mockery on his brother's face, but he didn't find any. Maybe that part of the conversation had been too quiet. "He's fine."

"Good. And you? You dealing with the rejection okay?"

"Fuck off."

"Hey!" Eric called as Jamie stalked toward his own office. "Wait a sec. I wanted to talk to you."

Gritting his teeth, he spun back toward his brother's door.

"I'm serious," Eric said. "It's about Tessa."

That wiped away all of Jamie's outrage. "Why? What's wrong?"

"Nothing's wrong. It's just… Do you think it'll be okay? Her living with Luke?"

"I don't know, man. You're the one who gave the go-ahead. I thought you were good with it."

"I'm not *good* with it. But she's twenty-seven and the house is hers. She can do what she wants."

"And she will anyway," Jamie grumbled. "No matter what we think."

"Exactly." The one thing they'd always been able to agree on was their little sister. And up until this year, they'd agreed that she was sweet and innocent and likely to stay that way for a long while. Boy, had they been wrong about that.

Jamie shrugged. "I guess. Anyway, you seem to have warmed up to Luke."

Eric didn't miss the accusation in Jamie's tone. Eric scowled and his hands fisted. "We were wrong about him. *You* were wrong about him."

"I'm telling you, he was a player in college—"

"Yeah, well, he grew up. And he makes her happy. Even you said that."

"Right. I guess."

Eric sighed. "She's with him, so we have to give him a real chance. Assuming, of course, that he treats her perfectly."

"Of course," Jamie agreed. "Did she say anything to you about when he would move in?"

"His lease is up in a month, so sometime before then, I'd guess. She was…a little vague."

"So next week?"

"Ha!" Even without being there, Tessa was the one happy link that joined them together.

Jamie left his brother laughing—a rare occurrence— and walked to his own office, pondering his resistance to his sister's new relationship. He and Luke had been friends in college. He liked the guy well enough. And while Luke had partied damn hard, he hadn't exactly been a dog. He'd hooked up with lots of girls, but he'd never been that asshole feeding women shots to loosen them up. He hadn't talked about them behind their backs.

And Eric was right. All indications were that Luke had left his days of drinking and dating behind. He'd grown up.

Maybe that was what pissed Jamie off. Luke's youthful indiscretions were accepted as just that, while Jamie was stuck with the label of slacker playboy for all eternity. But, hell, that was as much his fault as anyone else's. For a few years there, he'd thrown himself into that life with everything he'd had. Because…he'd believed that was all he was. A fuckup. A slacker. Way more of a disappointment than anyone else could even know.

So maybe that was what bugged him about his old friend Luke. Luke had long ago moved on from his youth, though he'd made other mistakes throughout the years. This was a possibility that Jamie needed to learn to accept: that he could put himself out there and fall flat on his face. And if that happened, it would be all right.

So he took a deep breath and fired up his computer. It was time to do a little homework. And then later… the fun.

## CHAPTER ELEVEN

OLIVIA GAVE JAMIE A KISS at the door and tried to pretend that the deepening dusk behind him wasn't distracting. But it was distracting. It was nine o'clock. If they went out now, they wouldn't get back here until after eleven. Assuming there were no post-dinner activities—and she didn't assume that at all—she wouldn't be asleep until midnight.

*And if you're lucky, you won't get to sleep until two or three.*

Olivia tamped down her anxiety. She could do this. If missing a few days of running was the price for a night with Jamie, she'd pay it. She'd pay the hell out of it.

He certainly looked worth it tonight. He wore jeans and a T-shirt, as usual, but he'd dressed it up with a green plaid button-down. The sleeves were rolled up, exposing his forearms, and the sight of them made her mouth water. They just looked so incredibly masculine, wide with muscle, rough with hair.

"Are you ready?" he asked, stepping back onto the porch to let her past.

"Where are we going?"

"It's a beautiful night. I thought we'd walk to a restaurant a few blocks over." He glanced down at her heels. "Are you up for that?"

"Sure." She paused to slip off her heels. "I can do that."

"Wow. That's extra credit, Ms. Bishop. Very impressive."

"I must have an inspiring teacher. I'm already more fun." When he took her hand, inspiration tingled up her arm and spread down from there. The sidewalk felt rough and cool beneath her feet. As the sun disappeared behind the mountains, the air nipped at her skin. And Olivia felt utterly, completely alive.

She tightened her fingers in his. "Tell me about the brewery."

"Hey, I'm done with my work for the day."

"No, I mean, who started it? How long has it been in your family?"

"My father started it twenty-five years ago. He had a brother who'd died in Vietnam, and he named the brewery in his honor."

"That's really lovely. Though I'm sorry about your uncle."

"Thanks."

"And your dad? I think you said he'd died…."

For a moment, Jamie's hold on her hand loosened. She thought he was letting go, that she'd stepped over a line. But then his fingers tightened again. "Yes, he died when I was sixteen."

"But you said your mom—"

"They died in a car accident."

Olivia pulled him to a stop, too shocked to go on. "I'm so sorry, Jamie. You were *sixteen?* That must have changed everything for you."

"It did, yes. But at least I was almost an adult. Tessa was only fourteen."

"So, what happened to you? Who did you live with?"

He tugged her until she started walking again. She could barely see his face now in the dark, but maybe he preferred it that way. "My brother, Eric, moved back in to take care of us. He took over the brewery until Tessa and I could do our part. Now all three of us run it."

"Is that why he has so much trouble letting you lead? Because he's done it for so long?"

"I'm sure that's a big part of it."

This was a sore subject. She didn't need to see his face to pick up on that. So Olivia dropped it. "Your sister seemed really nice."

"She is. Too smart for her own good, but she held us together as a family, even when she was young."

Olivia wondered what role that had left him, but she didn't ask. That seemed an awfully serious question for a fun night. She'd accidentally stumbled into something deep and sticky. "Well, I guess it's a good thing you have an affinity for beer. I wonder what would've happened if you didn't."

"Not possible. It's a gift passed through the blood."

She bumped him with her hip. "A gift, huh?"

"Some of us are born with it, but anyone can be taught."

"So there's hope for me?"

His thumb rubbed the sensitive skin of her hand. "Oh, there's hope. I know for a fact that you're a quick learner."

Maybe she was a quick learner, because she'd already dropped all her worries about the time, and she was just enjoying it. A barefoot stroll through the night with a sweet man. The nearly sure knowledge that they'd make love. The hot, heavy weight of anticipation low in her belly.

She'd experienced a lot of nervousness with Victor when she'd first started dating him. A lot of trembling, anxious want. But she'd never felt this languid melting. Not even close. This was a want so strong that she felt almost powerful with it.

Jamie took her to a restaurant she'd only been to once. They shared a bottle of wine and managed to avoid any more sticky subjects. He didn't ask about her divorce. She didn't ask about his family. Instead they spoke of music and university gossip. Then Jamie told her ridiculous stories of customers who'd had too much to drink or simply wanted free therapy from a friendly face. By the time they stumbled from the restaurant, Olivia was breathless from laughter, her sides on fire from the workout.

"Please tell me that isn't true," she gasped.

"It's true!" Jamie insisted. "She threw the ring back at him, dumped a bowl of peanuts over his head and walked out. And I'm not kidding about this—he turned to the woman sitting next to him at the bar and asked her to marry him. And she said yes."

"No!"

"The woman was her best friend. Apparently, she'd been waiting on the sidelines for the chance to get into the game."

"Oh, my God. Did they get married?"

"No idea. I never saw them after that. The other

woman—the *first* woman—she came in a few times, but I didn't think it would be appropriate to ask."

Olivia had to stop and lean against the wall of a bus stop, hands pressed to her stomach as she gasped for air. "That is the worst story ever!"

"Oh, I've got more where that came from, but I'll dole them out slowly—keep you on the hook."

She stood straight, grinning up at him, memorizing the sight of his face, blue in the night. The black sky behind him was full of stars, and they made her feel sparkly inside. Or maybe that was the brush of Jamie's fingertips down her cheek.

"You should take off your heels," he said. "It's a long walk home."

"I don't want to take off my heels," she answered, letting her head fall back against the glass. "I want to look *sexy.*"

His teeth gleamed when he smiled. "Oh, you look sexy regardless."

"Not true. I usually just look like a teacher."

"You do, actually, but—"

"Hey!" She gave him a little shove, but only his shoulder moved.

"I like that. I like watching you in your sweet little skirts and your cardigan sweaters and your glasses. You look so untouchable."

Olivia felt a sharp stab of regret, because that was the real her. She knew that, but she wanted something more. When she closed her eyes, Jamie's thumb touched her mouth, startling every nerve in her body.

"I like you like that, because when I look at you, so

buttoned-up and reserved, I picture you in the hot tub, naked, steam rising around you—"

"Jamie," she whispered, and the tip of his thumb eased between her lips.

"—your head thrown back as you ride me. Your lips parting as you come."

Lust crashed hard into her. She drew his thumb deep into her mouth and sucked at it, loving the way his breath broke into a groan.

"Olivia," he rasped. When she rubbed her tongue against the pad of his thumb, he growled and pressed his body to hers. He slid his thumb from between her lips, dragging the wetness down her chin as he kissed her hard. He plunged his tongue deep, letting her know he was just as aroused as she was.

The wine made her reckless enough to edge her feet apart so he could fit his knee between hers. His thigh pressed snug against her sex as she slid her fingers into his hair and kissed him deeper. Everything inside her burned for this, but when his hand covered her breast, her whimper was half in need and half alarmed. It was dark, but they were still in public, and Olivia hadn't had nearly enough wine for this.

When she turned her head away, Jamie's mouth slid to her neck as he dragged his fingers over her nipple.

"No," she whimpered, even as she pulled him closer. She edged one knee higher on his leg, and Jamie rocked his thigh into her until she moaned.

"We can't do this," she whispered.

"Do what?"

"This. We'll get into trouble."

"We're just kissing," he countered, nibbling his way along her jaw.

"No," she groaned. "This isn't just kissing. It's…"

"It's fun," he said, rocking against her again. "And no one can see."

God, he was right. It was fun, and they were all alone in the dark. Surely they'd hear footsteps first if anyone came near. His fingers plucked at her nipple. His mouth sucked at her pulse. Everything inside her tightened.

She sighed his name and let her head fall back as his hand found her neckline and snuck beneath. The moment his bare skin rasped against her breast, Olivia was lost. She'd never done anything like this, but she wanted to. She wanted to climax right here, with only the darkness hiding her from the rest of the world.

But she'd forgotten that darkness was a faulty shield. And, more importantly, that bus stops were always located on streets. Even from behind closed eyelids, she caught the glow of light and opened her eyes. "Car!" she gasped, scrambling to get her foot back on the ground and untangle her fingers from Jamie's hair.

He cursed and pulled his hand free of her dress just as the lights caught them head-on. Olivia held her breath and squeezed her eyes shut until the car whipped past and they were plunged back into darkness.

"I told you!" she cried.

"Crap."

She pushed him until his knee wasn't wedged between her thighs. "Jamie!"

"Okay, sorry. You were right. I just…*wanted* to."

In the face of that declaration, she could hardly muster the will to be outraged. "Let me be clear. I only want to have the kind of fun that *won't* get me arrested."

"You sure? That'd be a pretty wild experience."

She shoved him again, but he just chuckled and leaned in for one last kiss. She kept her lips tight together to prevent another disaster.

"All right," he sighed. "Even I'm not up for seeing the inside of a jail cell. And at this point, I'm not entirely sure my family would bail me out. Maybe we should head home."

"Maybe!" she said, but she couldn't hide her grin as they set out toward her place. "You're crazy, you know that?"

"Nah. I'm just horny. I don't know what your excuse is, though."

"Wine," she said dryly, as if she weren't still painfully aroused. As if she hadn't spent every waking hour looking forward to having him again. Her palm tingled when he took her hand and wove his fingers through hers.

"So, tell me what you used to do for fun."

Olivia frowned. "That's a silly question. I already told you I wasn't fun."

"I don't believe that. You're a natural."

"No, I'm not. For fun, I…I run. And I read. I go to museums."

"Whoa!" Jamie said. "You sprang that one on me too fast."

She elbowed him with as much dignity as she could manage.

"What I meant was…tell me what you did for fun when you were younger. *Before* Victor. Even you were a teenager once. You must have done something for fun. Music. Parties. Boys."

Boys. Olivia cleared her throat, because it was clogged with the secret that there hadn't been any boys. Not really. But he'd touched on something important. She had had a life before Victor, even if it had been a rather innocent one. "I used to Rollerblade. I liked country music. I played softball until I was fourteen. And…I loved amusement parks."

He looked at her.

"Roller coasters," she clarified.

"Roller coasters? Really?"

"Yes."

"Well," he said. "All right then. I think we know what our next assignment is going to be. Are you free on Sunday?"

"Why?" she asked warily.

"Because I don't have another full day off until then, and we can't do Elitch Gardens in two hours."

Olivia opened her mouth to protest, then realized she had no idea why she'd say no. She hadn't been on a roller coaster since college, and why not? Because Victor hadn't liked them. How pitiful was that? She'd seen the ads for the new coaster at Elitch Gardens. It looked amazing. "Okay. Yes. Sunday it is."

A streetlamp caught them in its glow, and Olivia glanced up to see Jamie's hair still mussed from her grip. She'd done that to him, and satisfaction filled her up at the thought.

Maybe she wasn't so boring, after all. She certainly wasn't boring around Jamie. So maybe his question was more significant than it seemed.

In the end, maybe Victor had been the one who wasn't any fun. He hadn't liked roller coasters, after all. Or country music. Or batting cages. Or board games. Or baseball stadiums. Or zoos.

Olivia had liked all those things when she was younger, and then… And then she'd met Victor.

But that wasn't fair. She'd been twenty-two. It had been time to grow up, hadn't it? She'd finished college. She'd been an adult. And adults did adult things like going to cocktail parties and attending the opera. Adults read important books and discussed politics and worked hard at supporting a spouse's career.

*Victor's* career.

So maybe she hadn't been boring. Maybe she'd just been so busy trying to be what Victor had needed that she'd been…less. Less than everyone else. Less than those girls who caught his eye and held his attention.

Screw him. All this fun she was having, all this time with Jamie… Olivia hoped she was becoming more like herself every day.

"I didn't want to teach," she blurted out, saying into the dark what she couldn't say in a brightly lit room. "I never even thought about being a teacher. I wanted to work on restaurant start-ups. I wanted to have my own business. The excitement of it. The risk. The challenge. That was how I wanted to have fun. Before."

Before Victor, she meant. Before she'd acted like every other stupid girl in the world.

Jamie nodded, not saying a word, and she was happy about that. Happy, because saying it had felt good and she didn't want to ruin it with figuring out why. She didn't want to delve into cloying regret tonight.

When they came to the sidewalk that wound through her apartment complex, Olivia began to worry about what would happen next. Not the sex. She'd acclimated to that pretty quickly. But this part, this awkward transition part, she didn't know how to deal with. Should she invite him in? Should she just assume he'd follow her? Did she have to make it clear she wanted him to stay? Would he spend the night?

Olivia couldn't believe people did this all the time.

"I'm impressed," Jamie said. "You haven't checked the time once."

"I don't want to know how late it is."

"It's late," he said as they stepped up to her door. "Very late."

Oh, God, did that mean he wanted to stay or go? How could she be so doubtful after they'd nearly had sex right on the street?

"Jamie," she said as she opened the door. "It's late, b—"

"Let me stay," he urged, curving his arm around her waist before she could even turn back to him. "Let me stay." He pressed against her back, his body fitting perfectly to hers.

"You're kidding, right? I was going to lure you in and lock the door behind you."

"Thank God," he murmured, his mouth already searching out her neck. "I can't keep my hands off you."

Olivia dropped her purse to the floor and turned into him, reaching for the buttons of his shirt as his mouth found hers. It seemed weeks since she'd been in his bed. Months. She pushed his plaid shirt off his shoulders, then slipped her hands under his T-shirt. His skin felt five times hotter than hers as she slid her arms around his ribs. When she dragged her nails along his back, he jumped.

Too impatient for slow exploration, she pushed his shirt up. "Are you ticklish?"

"A little," he said, his voice muffled by the cotton as he dragged the shirt the rest of the way off. She was busy tasting the heat of his chest. "Mmm," she hummed, making his skin jerk. "Just a little ticklish?"

"Maybe more like a medium amount."

"God, that's so cute. How did I not notice before?"

"You were busy mauling me?"

"Right," she whispered, distracted by the feel of the crisp hair on his chest. When she moved her hands down his sides, he shivered. "Sorry. I was only…" Olivia was too excited to keep speaking. Instead of explaining, she unbuckled his belt and popped open his button-fly jeans, one…slow…button at a time.

"Did I mention how cute you are?" she asked, eyeing the bulge in his black boxer briefs.

"You may have said— Oh, Christ."

She couldn't fit her fingers all the way around him past the fabric, so she gave up and slipped her hand beneath the band. "Ticklish?" she asked when he jumped.

"No," he answered. "Not one fucking bit."

"Mmm." Even now her fingers just barely met around his shaft. *Cute* didn't come close, not once you got below the belt. Below the belt, Jamie was glorious.

She stroked him, and he kissed her, his hands gliding along the neckline of her dress, easing the knit material over her shoulders and down her arms. She stroked him again, kissing him harder when she felt the slick wetness at the head of his cock, rubbing it down over his shaft and making him groan.

"Let's go to bed," she whispered. Jamie nodded and started dragging her backward. She couldn't believe she could manage to laugh and be so incredibly aroused at the same time, but she found herself giggling. "That's the kitchen," she said, sad that she had to let go of him so she could turn him in the right direction.

Jamie grabbed her hand and hauled her to the bedroom. "That's a tall bed," he muttered when he saw her big four-poster bed.

"I know. It's—"

"Perfect. Come here."

"What?"

He tugged her dress the rest of the way down, trapping her arms for a moment. She hadn't worn a bra tonight. In fact, she'd purposefully left it off, and now she was damn glad, because Jamie ducked down and drew her nipple into his mouth without any hesitation at all. Still trapped, all she could do was throw back her head and feel.

"You're so sensitive," he said softly, his breath whispering ice over her nipple. "I love that."

She shivered and wished, just for a moment, that her hands were free to cover herself. Her breasts were nothing to look at. Nothing at all. But he kissed her one more time as if he really did like them. Then he peeled her dress all the way off before turning her around.

She blinked in surprise, and her eyes widened in shock when he put a hand between her shoulder blades and gently bent her down. Her thighs were against the edge of the bed, and with his hand pushing her forward, she had no choice but to lean over.

Her hands touched the mattress, then her stomach. Then her cheek. She spread her fingers wide and held her breath, waiting. Finally, Jamie's hand smoothed down her back. He caught the edge of her panties and pulled them down in one easy motion.

She was completely exposed to him now. Naked, but for her heels. Open in front of him. Her heart beat so hard she could feel it like a drum in her ears. Beyond that pulsing rush of blood, she heard the faint shift of fabric, the soft thump of his shoes hitting the floor, the rustle of a condom wrapper. And then his hand gripped her hip.

Olivia closed her eyes and laid her cheek flat to the bed. This felt almost…impersonal, yet that somehow made it more intimate. She felt incredibly vulnerable, waiting for him to have her.

She expected him to simply push into her and braced herself for the shock of it, but apparently he had different ideas. She felt his fingers slide along her, tracing a slippery path to her clit. She gasped at the touch, her eyes fluttering open, then widening. She was stunned to find herself staring right at an erotic picture.

Not a picture. Her mirror.

And there she was, bent over and helpless, half her face hidden by the deep red comforter. Jamie stood behind her, totally nude, cock standing thick and proud. She expected to meet his gaze in the mirror, but apparently he hadn't noticed it. His head was bent, his eyes narrowed at the sight of her, as his hand— "Ah," she cried, watching her own face go tense as he slid two thick fingers inside her. His face went tight, too, as he slowly worked his fingers in and out, in and out. Olivia watched it like a movie, amazed to see her own face, her own body, being used like this. His fingers slid out, and Olivia held her breath as he reached for his cock. He wrapped his hand around it, pushing the condom farther down as he eased closer. She felt the nudge of his head as she watched his grip spread wider over her hip. He dragged himself along her sex, sliding against her clit in one slow, delicious stroke.

Olivia gripped the comforter, digging her fingers into the down, biting her lip until it went numb. He never once looked up. He was busy watching his shaft work against her. Her hips jerked when he pressed against her clit again, and she imagined what she must look like, so wet and swollen.

Finally, he notched the head against her and pushed in slowly. His jaw jumped with tension. The skin over his cheekbones was tight and flushed. Olivia let her breath slowly out, as if her body needed to make room for his. He stretched her until she was filled up with him, uncomfortable in the most perfect way. Long seconds later, his hips were snug against her ass, and she was panting against the pressure.

Olivia edged her feet a tiny bit wider. Jamie pulled her hips back, tilting them up, arching her back a little farther. He eased slowly out of her, then plunged deep. When she cried out, her eyelids fluttered shut, but she forced them back open. She didn't want to miss a second of this, so she bit her lip and clenched her hands and watched as Jamie Donovan fucked her.

He was a gorgeous machine, all tightening muscles

and tanned skin as he steadily drove himself deeper and deeper, each thrust turning his jaw to granite. And the whole time, his eyes blazed as he watched himself fuck her.

For Olivia, it was a like a movie. A filthy, pornographic movie, except that it was her starring in it. *Her.* And she could feel everything…every stroke, every thrust. She wanted to scream, but she only whimpered and held tighter and tighter.

His hands slid higher, shaping her waist for a moment before he steadied his grip on her hips again, his fingers digging harder as his movements grew more brutal.

"Oh, God," she whispered. "Oh, yes. Harder."

His gaze flickered up to her face, and his expression grew even fiercer. It was all too much. The sight of it so wrong and so arousing. Olivia felt everything inside her curl tighter and tighter, and her clit felt so hard it hurt. She'd never come like this, from just sex…no touching, hardly any foreplay, just her being used like a sex object.

"Jamie," she whimpered, as pleasure grew close to pain for one endless moment.

"Yes," he urged, his fingers digging in, adding to that pain until it all broke open with a wrenching shift that made her scream and scream until her voice turned to a rasp.

"Oh, God," she panted. "Jamie. Oh, my God."

"I can't…" he groaned. "Olivia, I…"

Her eyes cleared just in time to see his grimace of awful pleasure, and then he was coming, his muscles pressing against his skin as he drove himself into her.

Afterward, he held his body perfectly still, his grip easing by slow degrees. Olivia allowed her body to relax as she stared in stunned exhaustion at their reflections.

His eyes finally opened, and he watched her for a long while before his brow furrowed and he followed her gaze to the mirror. Their eyes locked and Jamie's jaw dropped.

"Holy shit," he breathed.

"Yeah," she whispered. "I know."

"How did you... What...?"

She raised her eyebrows.

He looked down at her body, then back at the mirror. "Why the hell didn't you tell me there was a show?"

Olivia began to laugh. She shook so hard that Jamie finally let her go so she could sink into the mattress. Her sex felt cold without him.

"Okay, we have to do that again. Not fair, Olivia."

"It looked like you had a pretty good view from where you were."

Surprise flashed over his face, chased by a cute pink blush. "Yeah, you're right."

He grabbed a tissue to ease off the condom, then collapsed onto his back next to her. "I don't give a damn about how much fun you are or aren't," he said. "Whatever you want to call it, you are fucking amazing."

She poked him with her elbow. "Shut up."

"I'm serious. That was... That was *hot*. For me, anyway."

Olivia turned toward him, easing her knee up his thigh, pressing her body to his side. Jamie tucked his arm beneath her head and she settled tight against him. His messy hair called to be touched, so she ran her fingers through it, smoothing it until it sprang back into wild waves. "You've changed everything for me. I mean that."

His eyes didn't hold a hint of laughter when he met her gaze. She realized then that his green eyes almost always danced with amusement, but now they were dark and serious.

"I haven't—" she started, then realized she'd been about to reveal too much. She didn't expect this to last, and she didn't want to scare him. "It's been a long time," she said instead. "And I wasn't sure…"

He caught her hand and brought it to his mouth for a careful kiss. "It's been a while for me, too," he said softly.

"It has not," she scoffed. "We're working on completely different time frames."

"I'm serious. I'm not that guy. Not really. Not now."

"Jamie. I've seen you. You practically glow when you get near women."

Keeping her hand tucked in his, he pressed her fingers to his chest. "I like women. I'm not denying that."

She didn't hold that against him. Oh, she felt a pure, hot coal of jealousy for everyone who'd experienced this pleasure with him, but she couldn't resent it. Who would ever turn him away? Who could have that strength? "Well, I'm not as experienced as you," she whispered. "And you've made this very easy. So, thank you."

He shot her a suspicious look. "You're not planning on giving me a plaque and sending me on my way, are you?"

"No!"

"That sounded a little like a farewell speech."

"No, it was just a celebration. I promise."

Jamie eased up, balancing himself on his elbow so he could look down at her. His gaze rose, and she turned to meet it in the mirror. They watched each other for a long moment. It seemed easier to let her feelings show at this distance, so she let him see how it felt to her when he dragged his fingers slowly down her throat, over her chest, to the faint rise of her naked breast. He traced her nipple, eyes locked with hers the whole time as she let the vulnerability rush over her. He made her feel warm and sexy and nervous and sad. All of it.

His touch trailed to her other breast, then down to circle her navel, then up to her shoulders. Finally, he touched her chin, turning her face toward him. He kissed her so softly that she hardly felt it at all.

"I know you get up early. Do you want me to leave?"

"No," she said too quickly, alarmed that he might go. Her fast reply made Jamie smile.

"Good. Let's cuddle."

She smacked his shoulder and rolled up to her feet. "I'll lock up. The bathroom's there." Though she started to reach for her robe, Olivia made herself stop and let her hand drop. Instead of covering up, she kicked off her heels and went to turn off the lights and check the door. It felt strange to wander naked through her living room. No one could see in—the blinds were all drawn—but still… She was nude, her skin cooling, her sex still swollen, and it felt daring. Maybe she'd do it more often. Maybe she'd become one of those people who cleaned house in the nude.

She smiled and snapped off the last light. When she returned to the bedroom, Jamie was already snug beneath the covers, tucked in on the wrong side of the bed. The opposite side of the bed her ex had slept in. Her smile stretched wider and she slipped beneath the comforter on the other side, enjoying even that moment of difference. He reached for her, pulling her close. Such a strange sensation being held from the left instead of the right.

"Wait," she said, lurching up.

"What's wrong?"

"Nothing. It's just the light." One long reach, and she plunged them into darkness.

She held herself stiff against him for a moment, but it was impossible to stay stiff with Jamie. He was warmth and relaxation, his body languid and sinking into the bed. By slow degrees, she melted into him. His hand stroked her hair. The scent of his skin filled her lungs. She could feel the press of her weight against him, and yet she was floating…suspended in the dark, anchored by him.

"Good night," he murmured, the words deep with sleep. His breathing slowed. His hand grew heavy on her back. And Olivia let herself pretend that he was hers. Truly hers.

A terrible idea, but it was two in the morning, she'd had half a bottle of wine, and she didn't give a damn about wisdom or prudence. Tonight she could pretend; tomorrow she'd get back to her responsible, grown-up life. For now, Jamie was all hers.

## CHAPTER TWELVE

"I'M WALKING IN RIGHT NOW," Olivia said into her cell. She pretended she was squinting against the sun, but in reality, she was grinning so hard that her eyes nearly disappeared.

"You'd better not be lying," Gwen said. "I tried calling you about ten times last night."

"I was busy," Olivia said, breezing into the building. The heels she'd worn were too high for work, but they made a satisfying riot against the marble floor.

"Oh, you were busy, were you? Filthy little witch. I hate you."

Olivia's laugh echoed down the hall, and she decided she'd better get off the phone before she disturbed the classes. "Are you busy right now?"

"No!"

"Okay, let me put my stuff in my office and then I'll—"

"That will take too long. You'll put your stuff down, check your email, check your inbox. Get up here right now or I'll explode."

"Fine. Okay. I'll be right there."

Gwen was still hooting when Olivia hung up and spun toward the hallway. Her progress was immediately interrupted by the hard shoulder she bumped into. "Oh, no," she yelped. "Sorry."

A man's hand closed over her elbow to steady her. "No, it's my fault," he said as she turned toward him. He was handsome and maybe a few years older than her. "I was trying to sneak by without disturbing your conversation."

"I hope that doesn't mean I've become one of those obnoxious cell phone users."

His smile made him look vaguely familiar, but she couldn't place him. "Absolutely not. Then again, my standards have plummeted. Last year I went on a blind date with a woman who carried on a full-fledged text conversation during dinner. I'm Paul, by the way. Paul Summers. We met a few months ago."

She must have still looked puzzled, because his smile faltered.

"I took over Johnson's classes when he retired."

"Oh, right! I'm so sorry. Every time a new group of students walks in, my memory for names sinks another notch. You came from Chicago, didn't you? How are you liking it here?"

"I love it. The winter was great. And, hey, no humidity."

Olivia smiled and ordered herself not to glance toward the stairs. She wanted to get up to Gwen's office so she could talk about Jamie. She was bubbling over with him. She needed to—

"So, this is probably a bad idea since you didn't remember me, but...would you like to grab coffee sometime? Or lunch?"

"I... What?"

"Coffee?" he repeated, his eyebrows rising. "Lunch? Maybe not?"

"Oh." She couldn't help but smile at his self-deprecating grimace. "Oh, I…"

"Hey, it's okay. I'll try again another time."

"No, it's not that. I'm not very good at this whole… thing."

"Are there people who are good at it?" he asked.

She thought immediately of Jamie, though she wasn't sure if she should be thinking of Jamie or not. They weren't dating really, they were just…having fun. It was temporary. They'd both been clear on that. Jamie was young, wild and, most important, he was free. This relationship would end in a week or two, and he'd move on. She'd have to move on, too.

And yet…

Olivia swallowed, trying to clear the dryness from her throat. "Honestly," she said carefully, "coffee might be nice. But I can't right now. Maybe another time?"

"Okay. I can live with that. I'll ask you again. Consider that a warning."

"I will."

"Nice to see you again, Olivia." He offered a friendly wink before he walked down the hall.

Paul was cute. Educated. And very solidly in his thirties. He was the kind of guy she would date if she was serious. But in this arena, being serious seemed much scarier than being fun.

She'd think about it later if he asked her out again. But right now her hands were full with Jamie.

Snickering at the unintentional pun, she hurried up the stairs to Gwen's office.

Gwen was standing in her doorway. "Holy crap, look at you," she said, then gave an old-fashioned wolf whistle.

Olivia glanced down at her shoes. "I know. I saw them in the closet, and—"

"Not the shoes, though those are hot. I mean the whole thing. The shoes. The extra button you left open on your sweater. The take-me look in your eyes."

"Gwen!" she gasped, nudging her into the office.

"It's true. That man must be just as miraculous as he looks. Did you make him wear the kilt?"

"I did not."

"Well, you should. And videotape the whole thing."

Olivia shut the door behind her and leaned against it. She tried to hold back her laughter and failed. "You're bad."

"Yes. And horribly, painfully jealous. I wish I was walking around with that look on my face."

"Do I really look different? Because a man just asked me out in the atrium."

Gwen collapsed into her chair, her shoulders shaking with laughter. "See? You're giving off a serious vibe, sister. Who asked you out?"

"Paul Summers."

"I don't know him."

"Probably because he's in International Business Law, two buildings over. But you should try to run into him. He's cute."

"Cute?" Gwen grabbed a pen and wrote down *Paul Summers.* "I'm sure I can think up a reason to run something over to his office. Although…" Gwen eyed her up and down. "We're not exactly the same type."

No, they definitely weren't. Gwen had blond curls and a gorgeous chest that she showed off with subtle skill. "Somehow I don't think he'll mind."

Gwen held up her hands. "Whatever! That is not why I called you here today. Sit down and tell me everything."

Olivia took the chair, then placed her hands firmly in her lap. "I don't know what to say, honestly. I don't want to violate Jamie's privacy, but I feel like I'm going to burst."

"Are you in love?" There was no missing the worry that flashed over Gwen's face.

"No, of course not. I'm not stupid. We're not even really dating."

Gwen raised a doubtful eyebrow.

"I'm serious. I told him I needed to learn how to relax and have fun, and…he just volunteered to help. Last night he made me stay out really late. On Sunday we're going to an amusement park. That kind of thing." She left off the hot tub skinny-dipping.

"Okay, that does sound fun, but there's more to it than that."

"I'll admit there are other things going on. Other *fun* things."

"Olivia, I can't believe you're doing this."

"I know. It's—"

"I am so proud of you! I wish I could do something like that. I'd like a little fun in my life, too."

That stopped Olivia in her tracks. "What are you talking about, Gwen? You're always having fun."

"Oh, I like to go out and have a good time, but I'd

never be brave enough to do what you're doing. With *Jamie Donovan?* Are you kidding?"

Olivia didn't know what to say. She'd been so surprised by Gwen's friendship—that a woman like Gwen would reach out to her.

Gwen shook her head. "I mean, can *you* believe you're doing this?"

"No! Even when I'm with him, it's like it's happening to someone else. He's just so…"

Gwen leaned forward. "Amazing?"

"Ha. Okay, yes. He's amazing. In bed and out." She ignored the groan of jealousy and shrugged. "He's just so simple and straightforward. I've never known anyone like that."

"Oh, sure, but back to the amazing part…"

"Gwen—"

"Come on," Gwen pleaded. "Just share something. A little crumb for a starving woman? Pleeease?"

Olivia took a deep breath. "Okay. One thing."

Gwen smiled and propped her chin on her hands.

"Last night we went to dinner, and we had a little too much wine. We walked home, but…we got distracted and we were almost caught messing around at a bus stop."

"No!" Gwen screeched. "What happened?"

"We were kissing and maybe a tiny bit more. It was dark and we weren't thinking straight. A car drove past and lit us up like a spotlight."

"So, what happened when you finally made it home?"

Olivia grinned. "We finished what we started, with no one watching this time." *No one but me.*

"You're my hero. You know that, right?"

"Heck, Gwen. I'm my own hero."

Gwen pointed at the door. "Get out. I don't even want to look at you anymore."

Olivia started to leave, then stopped with her hand on the doorknob. "Hey, do you want to see a movie on Saturday night?"

"What about Jamie?"

"He's not my boyfriend, Gwen."

Gwen's eyebrow rose. "So, he's working on Saturday?"

"Yeah."

After Gwen's laughter died down, she nodded. "Sure, let's see a movie. And dinner, too."

Olivia smiled all the way to her office.

Was she brave? She didn't feel brave. At first she'd felt terrified, then overwhelmed. Now she felt exhilarated and slightly bewildered. But she also felt happy. Happier than she could remember feeling in a very long time.

Sex with Jamie Donovan was a miracle elixir.

It was also physically exhausting. As Olivia sat down at her desk, her thighs protested the effort. Another tiny moment to make her happy. He'd taken her again that morning. Twice. Missing her morning run had been a joy. And the workout had been just as intense.

She'd only decided to come into the office because she'd been horrified with her own behavior. After he'd left, Olivia had lain about with a wide grin on her face. That was a little too close to lovesick.

So she'd showered and dressed and slipped on her highest heels. And now what was she going to do with herself? Something responsible, like planning or research. But considering the way her mind kept wandering back to Jamie's hands gripping her ass that morning, she thought maybe she'd better start with something simple like email.

Olivia fired up her computer and opened her email. There wasn't much traffic during the summer, so she noticed the letter from her department chair right away. He wanted to see her in his office as soon as she was able to stop in.

Her heart dropped, wondering what he might want. As an instructor, she had no permanent position with the university. She could be terminated at will, at any time, for any reason, even though she was a workhorse. She always had been, but since the divorce, she'd taken on four classes a semester, plus two summer seminars, determined to prove herself invaluable. She could not afford to lose this position, and with her husband out of the picture, the university would feel no pressure to keep her on.

Any desire to grin faded away as she read the message for a second time and then a third. The department chair gave no hint of what he wanted, and Olivia tried to convince herself it was something routine. Maybe he wanted to put her in charge of department birthdays. It wouldn't be the first time an instructor had been used as an assistant.

Suddenly wishing she'd worn more sensible shoes, Olivia walked down the long hallway toward his office.

Lewis Anderson had an office in the main suite of the department. The biggest office, of course, but that meant little enough in the Department of Applied Business. They were one of the least prestigious groups in the college and the size of the suite reflected that.

His door was already open, and when she knocked softly, he looked up, his eyes momentarily confused. When Lewis registered her presence, discomfort flashed over his features.

"Olivia. Good morning. Come in. And, um, could you close the door behind you?"

Oh, no. Not good. Not good at all. The blood left her head so quickly that she felt momentarily dizzy, but she offered him only a somber nod as she closed the door. "Is there something wrong?"

"I'm not sure." He gestured toward the chair, and she slowly lowered herself into it. "I've received some information that I need to present you with, though it's of a personal nature and I'd rather not."

She nodded as if she understood.

"There's been an allegation that you're inappropriately involved with a student."

"What?" she breathed. All the blood that had left her head rushed back with ruthless force, and her skin burned like fire.

"Have you become personally involved with one of your students?"

"Who told you that?"

"Olivia, that's not the issue. Is it true?"

"I… No… That is to say, there's a student…a man in my current class who's a friend of mine. But I knew him before the session started."

Lewis winced. "Which class is this?"

"The continuing education session on restaurant start-ups. It's not a credit course, Lewis. He's not a university student. He's a restaurant owner in the community. It's not… I'd never…"

Lewis held up a hand and exhaled slowly, before taking a deep breath. "Okay. This is good news. I worried it could have something to do with the group of students you're mentoring over the summer."

"No! Of course not!"

He managed a small smile. "Of course, I didn't think you'd actually be engaged in an inappropriate relationship with a student under your purview, but even an intimation of that kind of conduct must be immediately addressed."

"Of course. Of course!" Her throat thickened with tears created by the awful mix of fear and relief. "I'm so sorry you were even put in this position. I don't know why anyone would imply such a thing."

"I'm sure the person in question was only concerned about the ethical implications."

Oh, of course. When hell froze over. "If you could tell me who contacted you, I could address his…or her…concerns directly. I'm embarrassed that it even got to this point. Of course, I don't want the college's reputation darkened."

"I can't give you the person's name, Olivia. But I'll definitely pass on the information."

She nodded. "Is there anything else you need from me?"

"Just a moment." He typed something up on his computer and printed it out. "If you'll just sign this, acknowledging the conversation?"

She glared at the paper he handed to her. When she glanced at Lewis, he winced.

"I'm sorry. I have to leave a record. I'm not asking for his name. I've no wish to probe into your personal life, but I need you to sign that to show that we had this conversation."

This was going on her permanent record. This would come up when the department assigned classes in the fall. Her hand shook as she scrawled her name on the line.

Lewis wouldn't tell her who'd passed on this bit of nastiness, but Olivia didn't need a name. She knew exactly who'd done it, and she rushed outside to stalk to his building.

The Department of Economics was in a beautiful, traditional building with high ceilings and tall windows. Olivia rushed in as if she were storming a castle. She hadn't set foot in here for months, but she'd spent years walking up and down these stairs: meeting Victor for lunch when he'd asked her. Bringing him books he'd left at home. Rushing over a nicer shirt when he was called to talk to the dean. Speaking of instructors being used like assistants...

Olivia breezed past the department receptionist as the woman sputtered out an objection. Victor's door was closed, so she gave it a perfunctory bang before opening it. She half expected to find him humping a student on the desk, but the desk was empty. The whole office was empty.

"Mrs. Bishop!" the receptionist called as she jogged up.

"It's *Ms.* Bishop."

"Mr. Bishop isn't here today. He hasn't been here all week."

"Is he in town?"

"I don't know, but you can't just barge in here and—"

Olivia brushed past her, pulling out her cell phone as she walked. Her call went immediately to his voice mail, which could mean anything. One, he was on vacation with his twenty-three-year-old girlfriend. Two, he was at the racquetball court. Three, he was golfing with some important bigwigs from the university. Or four, he no longer had Olivia around to remind him to charge his phone.

Humiliated, mortified and violently enraged, Olivia knew there was no point in sitting down at her desk and trying to work. Her heart felt as if it would pound out of her chest.

How dare he? After everything he'd put her through, how dare Victor throw her to the dogs with such casual viciousness? She wasn't protected by her career, as he was. She didn't even have a contract, much less tenure. Given any doubt at all, the most prudent thing for the college to do would be to simply send her on her way.

By the time she gathered up her things and headed for her car, Olivia was near tears. If Victor made her cry at work, she'd ruin him. She'd destroy his world. And she could, which was why his pettiness was so shocking.

Luckily for Victor, she managed to hold her tears back until she got to the car, and by then the heat of her fury had burned out any desire to cry. The drive to Victor's house—*their* house—passed in a blur. She pulled into the driveway, satisfied to hear her tires squeal against the cement. That had only happened one other time.

Smiling bitterly, she threw her car into Park and descended upon his door like the angel of death. That was what she felt like, at any rate. She probably looked more like a mildly irritated college instructor in a dress and heels. The sound of the doorbell echoed through her pounding head.

When there was no answer, Olivia was sure he was gone. He'd put in one little phone call that could ruin her life, and then he'd blithely hopped on a plane to Hawaii. That arrogant, selfish, no-good… Olivia jabbed the doorbell over and over again, as if that could defuse her fury.

"Hold on, damn it!" a male voice called from inside.

Olivia froze, her finger poised above the doorbell.

The door whooshed open. "What the hell do—?" When Victor saw her, his words died.

Olivia automatically took a step back at the sight of Victor wearing nothing but a towel. His short brown hair dripped water down his temples. "Oh," she breathed.

"Olivia?" he gasped. "What's going on?"

She gathered up her outrage like a slipping shawl. "I need to speak to you."

"Right now?"

"Yes, *right now.*"

"Okay, fine. Come in. Is it all right if I put on some pants, or would you prefer me like this?"

She waved him away and stepped into the living room alone, aware of the horrid irony of being invited into her own home. She'd decorated this room, and every other room in the house. Now it felt strange to stand here with her arms crossed as if she were afraid to accidentally break something. And yet…there was no sadness. She might have decorated this house, but she'd done it according to Victor's desires, not hers. It had needed to be a home where he could host parties and serious dinners. The rooms were designed to impress, not for comfort.

She heard Victor's footsteps above her, and felt another wave of strange nostalgia. She'd lived in this house for so many years, and she knew all the sounds and quirks of it. But now she just wanted to leave.

Olivia crossed her arms tighter and felt a headache crawl up her neck and tighten around her skull. When she heard Victor's step on the stairway, she turned to face him.

He'd put on pants and a shirt, but he'd left the shirt unbuttoned. Was he taunting her? Trying to tempt her? Granted, she'd told him often enough that he had a nice chest, and she'd meant it, but her definition of "nice" had changed in the face of Jamie's body.

He dragged the towel across his hair one last time, then slung it over his shoulder. "What can I do for you, Olivia?"

"I can't believe you," she snarled.

"What?" His eyebrows floated high in innocence.

"Did you call my department chair?"

"Why would I do that?"

"To get me fired!"

Victor shrugged. "I have no idea what you're talking about."

What a damn liar. "Somebody called my department chair and told him I was sleeping with a student. Now, who do you think that could have been?"

"It wasn't me. Why would I do that?"

"Oh, come on. Don't pretend you weren't pissed about Jamie."

Victor smirked. "I wouldn't say I was 'pissed,' as you so delicately put it."

Another lie. She'd seen the outrage in his eyes. "Really, Victor? How would you describe your feelings, then?"

"You really want to know? Fine. I think it's embarrassing. A thirty-five-year-old woman hooking up with some stud muffin in his twenties. It looks desperate, and I feel sorry for you."

Olivia took a horrified step back. "I can't believe you'd say that to me. *You,* of all people."

"I'm the only one who'll tell you the truth, because I love you."

She felt her mouth fall open, but she couldn't make any words come out.

"You know I still love you. So why are you doing this?"

"You're insane," she finally managed to get out. "Completely certifiable. I should turn you in to *your* department chair."

"I didn't turn you in! Christ, you know I wouldn't do that. I'd be the first one you'd suspect, and I can't risk making you angry."

"You're damn right you can't," she snapped. "And how dare you call me an embarrassment. You chase after girls half your age like you're trying to relive your youth."

"I've never chased after any of them," he countered. "Not even you."

Olivia dug her nails into her arms and didn't let him

see anything but scorn on her face. He was right. He hadn't chased after her. He'd *groomed* her. He'd turned her into the one willing to risk everything to have him.

She raised her chin. "Maybe someday you should consider taking on a challenge."

"Oh, is that what you're doing?"

Actually, it kind of was, but not in the way he thought. "I didn't come here to rehash our problems. I just want to know why you did it."

"I didn't tell anyone your little secret, Olivia."

"Then who did?"

Victor threw up his hands, spreading his shirt wide. "How should I know?"

"No one came to you about it?"

"Plenty of people wanted to talk to me about it after the party, so thank you for that."

Olivia thought she felt a twinge of guilt, but it turned out to be the thrill of petty victory. "I'm pretty clear on how that feels, so I hope you're not trying to make me feel bad."

"There's a big difference, you know. I never wanted this."

"Victor—"

"I never wanted this and I still don't."

She wished she hadn't come over here now. "Victor, you're already on your second girlfriend. Give up the martyr act."

"One mistake, damn it. You—"

"No," Olivia said, turning her back on him to head for the door. "I'm not doing this. Goodbye. But if I find out that you were the one who called Lewis, so help me

God, I'll tell the dean everything I know." She yanked open the door and stepped out, slamming it behind her.

He pulled it open again. "Olivia—"

"And charge your damn phone!"

Backing out, she left him standing there on the top step, his frown fierce as he watched her pull away. He'd dropped the whole "I didn't want the divorce" crap a long time ago, so why was he resurrecting it now? It was sad, she supposed, wanting to have your cake and eat it, too, but she thought he'd moved on months ago.

Still, the state of Victor's heart was no longer her problem. She had real problems to figure out. Such as who'd turned her in. Victor had been right about that one small thing. He wouldn't have done it, not if he was in his right mind.

None of his coworkers knew the specifics behind the divorce: that he'd been sleeping with his teaching assistant. That Olivia had found out when she'd caught an early flight home from a trip to attend her grandfather's funeral.

She'd agreed to keep the truth quiet, her last concession to Victor's career. Still, she'd been shocked at how carefully he'd constructed his deception. That was when she'd realized how good he'd been at lying. As far as his colleagues knew, Olivia and Victor had broken up by mutual, civil agreement. Just a sad split of two people.

But if she told the truth, Victor's reputation would be tarnished. He wouldn't lose his position, but he'd no longer be the golden boy on a straight path to department chair. And there had been other women. Allison, for example, had once been in Victor's class. Olivia was sure it must have started then, as it had with Olivia so long before.

By God, she'd been an idiot, thinking she was the only one. That she'd been special. The truth was that certain men liked the worship of young women. They liked to be the wise mentor, the sexual teacher, the position of authority. And some girls liked that arrangement, too, or once had, long before.

Olivia shook off the memories. That wasn't her anymore, and hadn't been for a long while.

So, if Victor hadn't turned her in, then who? Who else knew? As far as Olivia could figure, Gwen was the only other person who knew both that Jamie was in the class and that Olivia was dating him. But it couldn't be her. No way. So maybe it was circumstantial. Maybe a fellow student had seen them out and been concerned about favoritism. But why? This wasn't a credit course. There wouldn't even be a grade assigned.

Maybe, in the end, Victor was the one who'd called, and he'd simply counted on his ability to lie his way out of any confrontation with her.

When she pulled into her garage, Olivia's mind was as muddled as it had been when she'd stepped out of Lewis's office. She couldn't think. Didn't want to think. And she only knew one way to stop her mind from working, so she changed into her running clothes and set out for the trail.

## CHAPTER THIRTEEN

"I DON'T HAVE TIME FOR THIS right now," Jamie muttered. "I have a bar to run." He hefted up the tray of clean glasses and headed for the swinging door, but Luke followed him all the way to the bar, wearing his official serious cop expression.

"There are only two people here. I think you can handle multitasking for a moment."

"I've already told you everything that happened with Monica. There's nothing else to tell."

"I'm not asking you for information. I just wanted to give you a heads-up."

Jamie tried to roll the tension from his shoulders. "What kind of heads-up?"

"She did it before."

"Jesus, do I have to drag it out of you? She did *what* before?"

"Monica slept with a man so her brother would have a chance to break into a business."

Jamie felt his hand tighten too hard around the glass he was holding, so he set it down before he cracked the damn thing. His stomach rolled, but he very calmly grabbed a towel and began polishing the bar. "Did she tell you that?"

"She hasn't admitted to it, but we don't need her to.

It happened. She slept with the owner of a construction company after a Christmas party at his office. Five hundred social security numbers were stolen from his office the same night."

Jamie polished harder. "Are you surprised?"

"I'm not. I just wanted to be sure you weren't blindsided by it if it comes out. We're using the information to pressure her to set her brother up. We've warned her if she doesn't cooperate the information could leak."

"That's a little harsh, isn't it?"

Luke laughed. "We finally untangled that mess of a so-called charity operation. Graham raised $435,000 with his last golf tournament. He donated exactly $12,275 to the cancer charity that was supposed to be the focus of the tournament. And that's just a drop in the bucket compared to all the people he screwed over with his identity theft scam. She was part of that."

"Yeah." Jamie finally gave up on the bar and carefully folded the towel into a perfect square. "Was she getting a cut?"

"That's the thing.… I don't think so. I think it was the thrill for her. The rebellion. That family is screwed up."

The thrill. Right. The *thrill.* Of deception. Of seduction. Of sex. Of power.

Jamie would've hated her if it had been worth it. Instead, he just hated himself a little more. "Well, thanks for the notification, but I'm fine."

"You'll tell Eric?"

"Sure." That would be a fun conversation. *Hey, remember that woman I had sex with who was only using me to get the alarm code? Good news. I'm not the only idiot who fell for it!* That would go a long way toward regaining his brother's trust.

"So, listen," Luke said. "About Tessa. And the house..."

"It's cool," Jamie said.

"I know you guys gave Tessa the house, but she doesn't think of it that way. She still thinks of it as the family home. I love her. I want to be with her. But I don't want to do something that will make her unhappy."

"Then don't make her unhappy."

"Jamie. You know what I mean. If you're pissed about me moving in, she'll be tortured about it."

Jamie was having trouble holding on to his distrust of Luke, and shit like this didn't help. "I'm willing to give you a chance, all right? I'll tell Tessa that, too, if it'll make her feel better. I'm happy for you."

"Really?"

"No, not really. But I'm happy for her."

Luke smiled. "Fair enough. I'll see you at Sunday dinner then."

"I can't go." He held up a hand to stop Luke's protest. "It's nothing to do with you. I have plans."

"I'll let Tessa know."

"Thanks."

Jamie was vaguely aware of the sounds that filtered from the back. He heard Tessa's squeal when she saw Luke. Conversation followed, then the alarm beeped as the back door opened. Tessa was gone for the day. Soon enough, Eric popped his head into the front room.

"I'm on my way out. You've got everything under control?"

It was Eric's standard line, but it made Jamie's hackles rise. "Don't I always?"

"You want a serious answer to that question?"

"Fuck off," Jamie muttered, hoping it was loud enough for Eric to hear without catching any customers' attention.

Eric stepped all the way in and crossed his arms. Apparently he'd heard it just fine. "Something going on that you want to talk about?"

"Nothing much. Did you see Luke?"

"He waved on his way out."

Jamie rubbed a hand over his tight neck. "He had some news. They're putting pressure on Monica Kendall to force her to help bring her brother in."

"Perfect. What kind of pressure?"

"Evidently she's acted as a diversion for him before." Jamie busied himself with tweaking the pressure on one of the kegs, but when his brother didn't answer, Jamie looked up.

Eric's mouth had taken on a familiar flatness. "A diversion, huh? Wow. You can really pick 'em."

Jamie's stomach clenched. "I didn't pick her, obviously. She picked me."

"Yeah, well…I think you're what's referred to as an easy mark."

"She did it on purpose. She came here, had a beer and asked me to drive her home. None of that had anything to do with my personality or my past."

"You really believe that?" Eric asked. "That it wasn't your fault? How do you think I would've responded if she'd come on to me?"

"Like an arrogant, self-righteous monk?"

Eric's hands fisted. "I would've responded like a god-damn adult," he growled.

Fury rolled through Jamie like fire, setting every muscle aflame with the need to lash out. But he only clenched his jaw. "I did respond like an adult," he ground out.

"You acted like a mindless teenage boy, just like you always do."

"You're the one who's in my bar right now, trying to start shit in front of the customers. Good job being the adult in the family."

Eric let his head fall back. He took a deep breath and glared at the ceiling for five seconds. "I'm sorry. It just sets me off when you seem unconcerned with what you did."

"I don't need you telling me what I should feel, Eric. And I don't need to prove *shit* to you, all right?" He caught the movement of someone approaching the bar and shot his brother a glare. "Now, get the hell out. I'm working."

"Jamie—" Eric started, but Jamie was already turning away, offering a smile for the grandmotherly woman approaching.

"Jamie." Eric tried again, but Jamie kept his focus on the customer.

"Are you ready to try the stout now, Maggie?"

"Oh, you," she giggled. "No, we just need some more pretzels."

Eric finally turned and left. A minute later, Jamie heard the beep of the back door and rolled his neck, trying to let the tension go.

Maybe his plan for this place was ridiculous. Eric

was never going to give him a chance. He'd never listen to Jamie's ideas. And in the end, Jamie was beginning to think he'd have to make some very different plans. He couldn't live like this for the rest of his life, like some kid under his big brother's thumb.

He'd give this brewery expansion idea a good try. He really would. He'd pour his heart into it. And then, if Eric chose to stomp all over Jamie's plans, Jamie would make new ones, and they'd have nothing to do with the other Donovans.

## CHAPTER FOURTEEN

OLIVIA HAD RUN FOR NEARLY TWO hours, and strangely, after that long run, she'd found it much easier to breathe. She was not going to let Victor or anyone else ruin her plans for fun. A few months ago—hell, a few days ago—she would've responded very differently to that call from her department chair. She would have cowered, retreated, turned a one-eighty and run far away from any hint of scandal.

But she hadn't done anything wrong, and the idea of running back to her safe existence pissed her off. She'd been safe, yes. But she'd also been lonely. And cold. And bored.

So when Jamie called and asked if she could stop by the brewery tonight to discuss his plans, she jumped in feetfirst. Still, her heart was fluttering like a bird when she stepped inside. It was busier than she'd expected for a weeknight, but she wasn't surprised to find that three quarters of the customers were women. So many book clubs; so little time.

She spotted Jamie at a corner table delivering a tray of beers to a large group of women. One of them jumped up and planted a kiss on his cheek. Jamie didn't even act surprised—he just smiled and handed her a pint glass, while the other ladies hooted their approval.

Olivia hurried toward an empty seat at the bar, not sure why she felt so nervous. He'd asked her to come, confessing that he was feeling a sudden urgency to get through the project.

*I'm brave,* she told herself as she scurried across the barroom like a mouse. Taking a seat, she folded her hands neatly in her lap and waited for Jamie to appear behind the bar. He was taking his sweet time, though. She dared a glance over her shoulder and saw him wiping down a table, his kilt rising up to show the backs of his knees.

His kilt.

Her face flashed hot. Other parts followed suit.

When Jamie finally came to the bar, he didn't notice her at first. He stacked the dirty glasses, wiped down his tray, then looked expectantly over the customers at the bar. His face was so open, as if he were anticipating happiness even under the most mundane circumstances. When his gaze touched her, he smiled.

"Hey, you're here!"

"I wasn't sure what I should bring…." She held up her notebook.

"Want a beer?"

"No," she said. "Absolutely not."

"I'll take that as a yes," Jamie said, reaching for a pint glass. "Try the hefeweizen."

"I won't like it!" she laughed. "I'm sorry, but I don't like beer."

"Everyone likes beer," he insisted, sliding her the glass. "Look, this one comes with a lemon slice."

"Is that to mask the awful taste?"

He slapped a hand to his chest as if covering a mortal wound. "Cruelty, thy name is Olivia Bishop."

She eyed the glass warily. "It looks thick."

"It's unfiltered. In fact, you can consider it a snack if you want to. Try it."

Bracing herself, she took a sip. It...wasn't awful. She shrugged and nodded. "All right, this one is my favorite so far. What is it, exactly?"

"It's an unfiltered wheat beer, less hoppy, which is probably what you prefer. Next month we'll have our Belgian version on tap, which has hints of orange. You might like that even more."

"We'll see," she said doubtfully, but she took another sip and didn't even grimace.

His eyes rose past her and he reached for a glass. "Hang on just a second. Someone needs a refill."

She watched his hands as he worked the tap, then turned to check out his calves when he walked to the table. Jamie had transformed her into a lecher. There wasn't even much skin to see between the hem of his kilt and the top of his work boots, but she looked anyway.

When he got to the table, the customer, a gorgeous blonde in incredibly tight jeans, stood up, threw her arms around his neck and planted a kiss on his cheek.

Olivia snapped back to face the bar, her cheeks flaming with an emotion she couldn't decipher. Embarrassment and jealousy and a creeping feeling that she was a damn fool. He could sleep with that girl tonight if he wanted to. Olivia had no doubt about that. Maybe he already had slept with her. She certainly hadn't hesitated to touch him. Women didn't just touch strangers like that, did they?

Then again, maybe Jamie had never met a stranger. He'd been kissed by two different women in the few minutes Olivia had been here.

If Olivia had come on her own, if Jamie hadn't invited her, she would've simply downed her beer and made an excuse to leave. She would've run like a coward, regardless of the words Gwen had said to her earlier. She didn't feel brave at all. She felt foolish and silly and *old*.

How in the world did men like Victor sustain their confidence in the face of hunky young undergrads and ex-boyfriends who were twenty years younger than they were?

Olivia took another big gulp of beer and wiped her clammy brow. Maybe that was why they couldn't stop. Maybe every young woman in their bed was a booster shot of arrogance.

She imagined herself moving on after Jamie, dating younger and younger men to prove to herself that she still had it. Choking back a laugh, she shook her head and told herself not to turn around again, especially when she heard a round of approving squeals, followed by Jamie's laughter. They all loved him, and she was so damn stupid.

"You already drank half your pint," Jamie said. She looked up to find him wiping his hands on a towel. "Is there an 'I told you so' in my future?"

"I was thirsty, that's all. And it's not awful."

He winked, his smile a warm secret. Probably the

same warm secret he'd shared a dozen times tonight. She cleared her throat. "It's busier than I expected."

His smile tightened a little. "Yeah. There's a Twitter special."

"A what?"

Yes, his smile was definitely losing its natural curve. "The brewery has a Twitter account, and we—I— announce nightly specials."

"So, what's the special tonight?"

Not only did his smile curve into a very unnatural line, but his cheeks took on a suspiciously pink hue. "It's 'Kiss me, I'm Irish.'"

"Oh." How many more kisses had there been? "I see."

His face fell into misery as he leaned across the bar, his voice dropping. "Listen, don't tell anyone this, but I'm not 'me' on the promo stuff. I mean, my name is on it, but it's my sister who's blogging and Twittering and Facebooking, or whatever it's called. Half the time, I don't even know what the hell's going on until women start showing up and smearing lipstick on me and asking for half-price pints."

"What?" Olivia glanced around at the nearly full barroom. "What are you talking about?"

"Like tonight, Tessa just waltzes out of here like she's sweet and innocent. Not a word to me. Not even a look. Then an hour later, she tweets, 'Kiss me, I'm Irish: half price on your first pint for a kiss on this Irishman's cheek.' I'd expect this for Saint Patrick's Day, but Jesus, it's not even March."

Olivia sat back a little, taking in his gorgeous shoulders and the hair that looked deliberately tousled for maximum sex appeal. She looked at that delicious mouth and those sparkling green eyes...then her eyes fell to the faint smear of red lipstick on his jaw. "Your sister uses you as a marketing ploy?"

"Yes."

She bit her lip and cleared her throat. "Half price on the first pint?"

"Yes."

"So what about that second round you just delivered?"

"Apparently that kiss was just a bonus in case the first one didn't take."

He did look a little miserable now, but he definitely hadn't earlier. "You don't seem to hate it."

"Well, they're all nice and everything. There's nothing *bad* about it. It's just that I'd like to decide when I'm up for women patting my ass, you know? I had a stressful day. My mind isn't on playing up the Scotch-Irish thing, you know?"

She dropped her gaze to his kilt.

"Okay, maybe I was up for it earlier, but after I argued with my brother...not so much."

She was trying very hard not to laugh, but relief was bubbling up inside her. That was why all these women found it so easy to touch him, because they'd been *invited* to. "So, let me be clear.... There are days when you're totally okay with strange women patting your ass."

"Over-the-kilt patting only. My reflexes have gotten pretty quick on the other kind. I can dodge damn fast, even with a tray of pints on my shoulder."

"That's a relief."

"Hey," he said, offering another wink. "I'm ticklish, you know."

She laughed as he moved down the bar to check on his customers. She was a fool, but not in the way she'd been thinking. She was a fool for even worrying about looking like a fool. Yes, Jamie truly liked her. He liked everyone. And the foolish part was worrying about his universal love of women. If it wasn't for that, she'd never have gotten even a taste, so what was the point in resenting it?

"Idiot," she muttered to herself. She'd take this fling for the gift it was, and she would not fall for him. She wouldn't. Not any more than she already had.

He took care of a bill before working his way back to her. "So…I was hoping you'd take a look around the brewery. Maybe check out the kitchen and the front room. I'd like to talk details tomorrow, and I really want your perspective."

Right. She was here to work. Of course. She picked up her notebook. "I should have brought a camera."

"You can use ours. Hold on one second." Jamie pushed through the swinging doors, then reappeared with a digital camera in his hands just five seconds later. He swept the room with his eyes, then motioned her back. "I'm sorry. I don't have time for even the flash tour. You mind looking around on your own?"

"Are you sure this is allowed?" she asked as she slipped past him.

"Olivia, I'm one of the owners. We could set up a tent and have a romantic evening back here if I wanted to. Do you want to?"

Eyes wide, she looked over the spartan kitchen and tile floors. "Um…"

"I'm just kidding. That wouldn't qualify as fun for *me*. Check it out, okay? I'll be back in a few."

When he pushed through the doors, a bright Van Morrison song swelled over her, fading away in fits as the door bobbed closed behind Jamie. Olivia took a few steps in with a feeling she was intruding on a private world.

The kitchen was as unremarkable as he'd described, but large enough to convert it to a restaurant kitchen, especially if they kept to the scale Jamie had described.

Olivia flipped open her notebook and started taking notes and pictures. There'd definitely need to be more ventilation and refrigeration, but actual physical remodeling would be minimal. She sketched out a few ideas, though she'd always been better with digital models than hand drawing. Half an hour later, she found herself standing in front of a glass wall, peering at the metal tanks beyond. They were larger than she'd expected and the room was utilitarian. Almost industrial. Hoses were coiled on the floor. Buckets lined a back wall, though she couldn't tell if they were empty or not. There were drains in the floor, spaced every ten feet or so, as if spills and runoff were just part of the job.

She tried the door and found it locked, which was a relief. It seemed like an area she shouldn't violate. Still, she took a few pictures of the wall, just to get an idea of it for the layout of the room.

Then she stepped quietly down the hallway that lay off the door to the front room.

Eric's name was on the first door. The office was large and well used. Neat, but a little cluttered, packed with filing cabinets and promotional material. Tessa's office was next, and it looked similar to her brother's, if slightly less neat. The last office was Jamie's. It was smaller than the other two, and Olivia's heart fell when she saw it. His desk was bare, completely bare but for a computer monitor. There were two small filing cabinets behind the desk, plus one larger cabinet that looked a bit like a small closet. That was it. Olivia backed out and hurried to the front room, trying not to think of his frustration when he talked about taking on more responsibility.

Two of the tables had cleared out, and the place was noticeably quieter, but Jamie seemed busier than ever as he served drinks and cleared tabs and cleaned tables. As soon as she saw his smile, Olivia felt relief uncoil inside her. It didn't matter how small and barren his desk was. It made sense, actually. This was where he worked. This was where he lived. A tiny office was no place for Jamie.

She took a few pictures of the front room, trying to stay inconspicuous. "Do you have the room measurements?" she asked when he passed her.

"I'll email them to you," he answered.

"Perfect. I think I'm almost done here. Do you want to email me the pictures, too?"

"No, those file sizes are huge. Just take the camera home with you. I'll get it tomorrow."

"If you're sure…" She didn't have any reason to stay now, and Olivia found herself standing awkwardly at the end of the bar, watching Jamie rinse glasses and stack them in the dishwashing tray. She didn't want to leave.

"Jamie…"

He shut off the water and wiped his hands.

She opened her mouth, but the wrong words came out. "You've got glitter lip gloss on your eyebrow."

"Oh. Hey, I bet you've never said that to a man before." He wiped at his eyebrow. "You look kind of horrified."

"No, it's not that."

"I meant what I said before. I haven't dated anyone in a while. Almost a year. It might seem like working here is a party, but…"

Almost a year? That shocked Olivia enough to push her into false courage. "What I meant to say was… would you come over again tonight?"

"With glitter or without?"

Olivia smiled in relief. "Either way."

"Lady's choice. I should be out of here by nine-thirty or so. Will you still be awake?"

"Oh, you're funny."

"I'll wake you up."

She shook her head, and started to move toward the front door, then changed her mind. Instead, she stepped over to Jamie and pressed a kiss to the cheek all those other women had kissed tonight. She let her hand linger on his jaw. "I'll see you in a little while. No glitter."

"You got it."

"And Jamie? Wear the kilt."

His eyes narrowed and the laughter left them. "Anything you want."

She'd have to press him for extra credit later. Having fun was one thing. Asking for it was surely a whole other level of accomplishment.

## CHAPTER FIFTEEN

"I MADE HIM WEAR THE KILT."

Gwen choked on her ice water. "Oh, God," she gasped, grabbing her napkin to wipe her chin. "You can't just spring that kind of thing on a girl. Does he go commando underneath?"

"No, he says that's an occupational hazard. I think he's talking about you and your friends."

"You bet your ass he is." Gwen clinked her glass against Olivia's. "Congratulations on breaking the kilt barrier."

"Thanks." Olivia sipped her water and waited impatiently for their martinis to arrive. "I feel guilty, talking about him this way."

"Do you really think he'd mind?"

She thought of him gamely offering kisses to every female customer. The only thing about his life he seemed to keep secret was his ambition. "I guess not."

"Anyway, I'm not going to tell anyone. And you can consider this a public service to your friend who isn't getting any."

"Why aren't you getting any, by the way?"

The waiter finally approached, bearing martini glasses. "Oh, thank God," Gwen groaned. "The topic of celibacy requires lubrication, don't you think? No pun intended."

"That was totally intended."

Gwen waggled her eyebrows in answer. "I don't know why I'm not getting any, honestly. Half the reason I started working at the university is because I thought it'd be a great place to meet good men."

"And is it?"

"Does it look like it is?" she asked, taking a swig of her green drink. "No, after seven years of working there, I've finally realized that I'm a second-class citizen. Nobody there wants to date someone with a GED."

"You didn't finish high school? What happened?"

"Oh, the usual stupidity. Shortsighted teenage rebellion. I've been taking two classes a year at the U for a while, but that's a long haul. I'm going to be the college secretary with no high school diploma for quite a while yet."

"Come on," Olivia said. "Surely not every guy cares so much about that."

Gwen frowned. "You know how it is. They start out focused so completely on tenure that they can't think of anything else. Then once they get it, they're competing for prestige. There's nothing prestigious about me."

"Your boobs are pretty prestigious."

"Christ, if you make me spit out this drink, you'll be in trouble. But…you're right. These men don't know what they're missing out on."

"Well, they know a little bit," Olivia said, gesturing toward Gwen's cleavage.

When Gwen laughed really, really hard, her cleavage bounced, and even Olivia found herself staring. She felt a brief moment of utter jealousy.

"Oh, don't glare at me that way," Gwen said. "I'd rather have Jamie Donovan than my awesome breasts."

"Yeah, but you get to keep your breasts forever. Jamie's just a loaner."

"Are you sure?"

Olivia rolled her eyes. "Come on. I'm not an idiot."

"You know who is an idiot? Victor."

"In some new way?" she asked.

Gwen nodded. "Yes! I talked to Lewis's assistant. I gather there was some sort of trouble."

"He did it, didn't he?" Olivia groaned. "I knew it. That bastard."

"So someone really did rat you out?"

"Yes! Victor, obviously. He called Lewis and told him I was sleeping with a student. The irony's so thick I can barely breathe."

"I don't think Victor's the one who did it."

"What do you mean? You just said he was being an idiot."

"Sure, but that's a constant, isn't it? What I meant was that Victor called Lewis *afterward*. From what his receptionist could gather, Victor called to assure Lewis that you'd never do anything inappropriate."

"Oh." Olivia shook her head in confusion. "Are you sure?"

"I'm sure, but that's not the crazy part. Victor told Lewis that this was all just a rough patch. That you two were going to reconcile."

"He did *what?*"

"I figured he was delusional, but I thought I'd better ask."

"It's… Of course it's delusional. Why would he say that? Our divorce was finalized a year ago!"

"Have you been nicer to him lately?"

"No! We've hardly even talked. I mean, when we first separated, he kept insisting that he didn't want a divorce, but he dropped that and seemed to move on."

Gwen nodded. "I've seen this happen with other friends before. Haven't you?"

Olivia had no idea what she was talking about and her confusion must have shown.

"Men can be totally reasonable about a divorce when they're getting the sudden chance to sow their oats. They feel free and young again. Sure, the divorce hurts, but there are nubile ways to soothe those wounds. So everything is steady and reasonable, going along just fine. Then the wife starts to date, and it all changes."

"But that's not fair."

"I'm sure it happens the other way around, too, but yeah, it's not fair. I had one friend who'd been getting along just fine with her ex for two years. They shared custody and they were a model for how divorced parents should behave. I was so impressed."

"And then?"

"And then she met someone and fell in love, and suddenly the ex was taking her back to court for stricter visitation rules and lower child support payments. He'd never give an inch on any scheduling compromises. It got ugly. The moment she stopped dating the new guy, things settled down again."

Olivia rubbed her forehead. "I just…I'm sure it's not that serious with Victor. I talked to him about Lewis. Maybe he was only trying to find a way to help me."

"Maybe."

But Olivia found it hard to believe her own words. Especially with the ugly things he'd said to her a few days ago. "So your friend said Victor definitely wasn't the one who'd called Lewis in the first place?"

"She didn't know anything about it. I can ask her to try to find out, but…"

"No, I don't want to get anyone in trouble. I suppose it wasn't Victor after all. Unless he created an elaborate plan to get me in trouble and then save my job."

"And then you'd fall at his feet in gratitude. It's possible."

"It is not!" Olivia laughed, picking up her glass for a much-needed drink. "Plus he wouldn't take the chance of looking like a crazy person to Lewis."

"Good point."

"Even if he has gone stark raving mad."

"I'll drink to that." Gwen finished her drink with a sigh. "If you don't mind my asking, why didn't you and Victor have kids?"

Olivia rearranged her silverware and considered the question. "I don't know. At first, I thought we'd have kids, but Victor wanted to wait until his career was more established. After a while, he seemed to want to just wait. I guess I just had to let the idea go. It was probably for the best. I'm an only child. Babies make me a little nervous."

"Is your family here?"

"No. They're in St. Paul. And my mom wouldn't

have been any help. She didn't quite know what to do with her own child. Anyway, now I'm too old."

"You are not."

"I'm thirty-five! Do you know how many years it would take for me to meet the right guy and get married?"

Gwen grinned. "Maybe you could have Jamie Donovan's love child."

It was Olivia's turn to choke on her drink. "Good Lord. Yes, that's just what I want to be is one of Jamie's baby mamas."

"Does he have more?"

"Not that I know of. He's certainly got protection handy no matter where we find ourselves. So what about you? Do you want kids?"

Gwen looked down at the table. "I don't know. I always thought…" She cleared her throat. "I always thought I'd get another chance, but…"

"Another chance?" Olivia sobered at the solemn sound of Gwen's words.

"I had a daughter when I was eighteen. I gave her up for adoption."

"Oh." She reached out to touch Gwen's hand. "I feel like I should say I'm sorry, but maybe those aren't the right words."

Gwen nodded and her gaze rose. "I made the right choice. I know I did. She has a great family. But the older I get… It's not that I'd make a different choice, but I feel like I should've been more aware that she might be my only child. I should've at least known that when I said goodbye to her."

"Oh, Gwen." Olivia squeezed her hand. "You're only

twenty-eight. You'll meet someone wonderful and have a family. I don't have any doubt. You're such a nice person."

"I've got a great personality, huh?"

"And a prestigious rack."

Even though it sounded a little watery, Gwen laughed and slapped Olivia's arm.

"Did you ever manage to drop into Paul's office?"

"I was just kidding. He asked you out, Olivia. I don't want to horn in on that."

She rolled her eyes. "Oh, sure, I'm used to keeping all the men for myself, but I can't be too selfish this time. I'm otherwise occupied."

Gwen shook her head.

"He's cute."

"I know," Gwen grumbled. "I Googled him."

"So talk to him."

"About what? My favorite new reality show? I've learned the hard way that I don't have anything in common with these tenured guys. I still eat ramen every Monday night."

"You do not."

Gwen winked. "Only when I'm too lazy to cook."

"We'll see," Olivia said, conceding nothing. If Gwen wasn't going to drop by Paul's office, then Olivia would arrange a meeting herself. He'd seemed nice. He was obviously smart and successful and looking to date. He was exactly what Gwen needed, and Olivia was finding him a little lacking in the kilt department.

"I've never told anyone about the adoption, by the way. So…"

"I won't betray your confidence," Olivia promised. "You hold one of my secrets, too."

"Are you talking about Jamie or Victor?"

"Okay, two secrets, I guess, but one of them seems to be getting around pretty fast. I was talking about Victor's little indiscretion."

"I still say you should've busted his ass."

"It wouldn't have changed anything. And in the end, he would've kept his job and made sure I lost mine. Then it would've been easier to make me come back to him."

Gwen's eyes fell for a moment. "I'm sorry I never said anything to you. We weren't close then, and I wasn't a hundred percent sure he was cheating. And sometimes people don't want to know the truth."

"I know that. Believe me. It was all there for me to see if I'd wanted to. I realize now that it happened before, but I didn't want to look too closely. You don't need to feel guilty about that. And you're right—if you'd been the one to tell me, we wouldn't be friends right now. It would've been weird."

"Screw it then. Want another drink?"

"Absolutely."

Their food finally arrived, and Gwen ordered another round. Her eyes stayed on Olivia as she took her first bite of salmon.

"What?" Olivia asked.

"I kind of thought you'd leave after the divorce. Go work for a school in Denver."

Olivia found it hard to swallow. "Mmm."

"Did you think about it?"

"Sure," she lied, trying to hide the fact that the idea terrified her.

"I mean, you could go anywhere, not just Denver. Anywhere. There's nothing keeping you here. In fact, you should find out if they have any openings at Hawaii State."

She *could* go anywhere. She knew that. And she didn't understand why the thought made her want to cry. She was free now. There had to be a school somewhere that was looking for knowledge like hers. All this tension and awkwardness with her ex would be gone in an instant.

But the very idea hurt her deep inside, like acid gnawing through the core of her. "Hawaii," she murmured. "I'll have to check that out."

"Do it. Then find out if they're hiring any administrative assistants."

Olivia raised her new drink and even managed a smile, but she knew she'd never look into it.

Was she that afraid of change? Was she so weak that she couldn't imagine going somewhere new, trying something different? She was trying to stretch her wings and take more chances. But the idea of searching out a position at a new school made her feel sick.

*Baby steps,* she told herself, hoping that was all it would take. But maybe she wasn't brave. Maybe Jamie Donovan made everything so easy that it didn't take any courage at all.

# CHAPTER SIXTEEN

"Oh, God," Olivia screamed. "Oh, no."

"Hold on," Jamie urged.

She wrapped her hands tighter around the bar and squeezed her eyes shut as the coaster crested the hill. "Why am I doing this?"

"You know why!" He laughed.

"This isn't fun!" she cried just as the world dropped from beneath them and gravity disappeared. Olivia didn't scream. She pressed her teeth tight together and held her breath as if she were plunging into water.

When they swung into the bottom curve, she finally gasped for air.

"Are you okay?" Jamie asked, his big hand closing over her knee.

She nodded, still trying to catch her breath. But by the time they hit the next hill, Olivia was laughing. Hard. She couldn't manage to stop, even when the coaster flew into its last long stretch and Jamie pulled her in for a kiss.

"You look exactly the same way you do after sex," he said.

"Because I'm laughing?" She collapsed into giggles again at his look of outrage.

"I was thinking more of the breathless screams."

"I bet you were."

He kissed her one more time before helping her out of the car. "Where to now?"

"I can't take any more. My voice is almost gone."

"Come on. One more ride."

Exhausted as she was, she was having a great time. "Okay, but something small. The merry-go-round."

"God, no. Not unless you want to see me puke."

Olivia stopped in her tracks. "You're kidding. The merry-go-round makes you sick?"

Jamie glared. "What? It's the spinning. Not, like, the gently bobbing horses."

"First, you're ticklish, and now this?"

"Just keep it quiet, all right? I'll lose my man card."

"Oh, I'm pretty sure you've got a permanent membership, Mr. Donovan. No one can ever take that away from you."

He pulled her out of the flow of traffic, tugging her hips into his. "Ms. Bishop, you're not implying something vulgar, are you?"

She leaned closer and let her breath chase over his ear, knowing that he'd shiver at the feeling. "Absolutely not. It's not vulgar." She brushed her lips against his ear. "It's gorgeous."

Jamie growled before he let her go. "How about the Ferris wheel?"

"Can you handle that, big guy?"

"Stop trying to flatter me."

Olivia grinned at him over her shoulder and set off toward the Ferris wheel. "That wasn't supposed to be flattery."

"Sorry. You said 'big guy.' That's all I heard."

When they reached the Ferris wheel ten minutes later, her cheeks ached from laughing. What was it like to be Jamie, so carefree and easy? So confident and cheerful? She relaxed into the rocking seat with a sigh of happy relief.

The first high turn was a frightening thrill, but after that the ride turned peaceful. She laid her head on his shoulder and watched the city rise and fall before her. At the very top, the breeze was brisk and cool, but Jamie's arm was pure heat draped around her. She felt as if she could simply curl into him and fall asleep.

On their fourth rise to the top, the wheel slowed to a stop, leaving them stranded in the sky as more passengers boarded. Silence settled over Olivia and Jamie, as if time had stopped and left them rocking.

"This is nice," he said, his thumb stroking her shoulder. "It's beautiful."

It was. The setting sun had dipped behind a bank of clouds, leaving them with a perfect view. Olivia looked out over the city, to the mountains beyond, and she thought of leaving it behind. She could simply get in her car and drive. Through the mountains, across the desert, all the way to the ocean. And that didn't scare her. Not at all.

The night before, she'd lain in bed for hours, poking and prodding at her psyche, trying to puzzle out her fears. And it had finally hit her.

"Jamie," she said softly.

"Hmm?"

"I told you I never wanted to be a teacher."

"You're good at it, though."

"Maybe, but I never *wanted* it. Ever."

The wheel began to turn again, pushing them toward the mountains, then sinking them to the ground.

"You wanted to work at restaurants?" he asked.

"Yes. I grew up around restaurants. My parents were investors, and over the years, they were partners in several places. We went out to eat constantly. But the part I always liked best was before the restaurant opened. The excitement of the new idea. The brainstorming and planning. Watching as an empty space was made into something beautiful. The thrill of opening day, all of it sizzling with the risk of failure. That was what I wanted."

"So, what happened?"

She shrugged. "I went to school in Virginia, just to get away from my parents. Typical teenage stuff. 'They don't understand me. They never will.' I just wanted to be far, far away. I worked at restaurants to support myself, trying my best to get jobs with places that were just starting up. Six years later, I'd finished my master's and fallen head over heels in love."

"With Victor."

"Yes." The wheel reached the top again, and they fell in a slow circle. "And he didn't need a wife who worked fourteen-hour days, seven days a week. His career was important. He needed support. So, instead of sinking money into a small business, we bought a house, and I took a job teaching."

"You gave it up."

"I did. All of it."

"You can start over," he said. "That's what I'm doing. Trying to get to what I really want. Trying to make up for...other things."

"Do you ever feel trapped? Like there would've been something better for you if you weren't obligated to your family?"

Jamie let his head fall back. He stared up into the tangle of metal spokes above them. "No. Mostly I just wish things were different for us. I wish my brother could tone it down. I wish I'd gotten my shit together earlier. I wish I hadn't... I wish my parents hadn't died. But I like what I do. I don't feel trapped." He lifted his head and looked at her. "You don't have to feel trapped, either. You're *not* trapped."

"I've spent so many years teaching. I've invested my whole professional life in it. How can I walk away from that?"

"You just do. That's what walking away means, doesn't it? Leaving something important behind?"

"It would take years to start again." She managed a smile. "Gwen thinks I should just move to Hawaii and find work at a school there. I have to admit, it's a good idea."

"Really? I kind of thought you'd hang around here."

"Don't worry. I wouldn't dream of leaving until we finish your plans."

"Oh." He flashed a quick smile. "Thanks."

The earth rose more slowly toward them this time. They were coming to a stop. "I'm sorry," Olivia said. "I don't know why I dumped all that on you."

"I don't mind."

"There's nothing fun about playing therapist though, is there?" She felt his gaze on her, but when she turned her head, he looked away.

"It's no big deal."

Olivia shifted, uncomfortable with his sudden silence. "Hey, do you want to talk about your competitive research now?"

"No. But thanks."

Olivia was relieved when they rocked to a stop and an attendant opened the door. She hadn't experienced Jamie unhappy before, and she wasn't sure what had happened. The talk about his family and his parents, probably.

"Are you ready to go?" he asked once they were back on solid ground.

"Yes." She touched his arm as he turned away. "Are you okay?"

"I'm fine," he answered. He winked and took her hand, and Olivia breathed a sigh of relief.

"Ferris wheel too much for you, after all?"

"I'm a little shaken up."

They strolled down a walkway, heading for the blank spot past the trees that signaled the acres of parking lots. "Thanks for listening, Jamie."

"I'm good at it," he said, but he was still a little distant, and discomfort prickled over her skin.

"I'm sorry I brought up your family."

He let her go, his hand sliding free, and Olivia felt as if she was going to be swept away, back to her old life, where she jogged every morning at six and never, ever had dirty sex in front of a mirror. Jamie folded his arms and looked out over the rows of cars. "It doesn't have to only be fun all the time."

"What doesn't?"

"This. You can talk to me about your life. We can

discuss things that have nothing to do with the brewery or sex."

"I know that. It's just that…our arrangement—"

*"Arrangement?"*

"You know." Her face burned. She didn't want to say aloud that he was giving her sex in exchange for help with the brewery.

"Olivia, I know you're buttoned up and business-oriented, but I'm not. This isn't an *arrangement.*"

"You said you'd help me with—"

"I meant as friends or lovers or whatever you want to call it."

"It's semantics, Jamie. I'm not saying you don't like me at all, but I'm not the kind of woman you'd normally date."

"What the hell do you know about who I normally date?"

"Oh, come on. How many thirty-five-year-old strait-laced divorcées have you dated? You're a twentysomething bartender. Women travel from all over town just to *pay* for the chance to flirt with you. Hot women. College girls. Women with breasts who wear low-cut jeans and go skinny-dipping every week." She glanced down the walk to be sure no one was near and lowered her voice. "Tell me I'm wrong."

She wasn't wrong, she knew that, but Jamie looked furious. His mouth was so flat and hard that it looked like it had never cracked a smile, much less a grin. His jaw jumped in a tense rhythm. And his eyes…all the warmth had left them, and the green now looked like pine in the dead of winter.

Olivia sighed. "I'm sorry, I didn't mean that as an insult."

"You didn't mean it as an *insult?* What was it? A compliment?"

"Neither. It's just…true."

"That I'm an immature, womanizing, beer-slinging kid who sleeps with any drunk college girl who flashes her cleavage at me?"

"That is not what I said."

"What about the part where I agreed to sleep with you if you pay me in restaurant-planning help? Is that what's true?"

She reached toward him. "Jamie——" He started to pull away. A shriek of laughter stopped her movement, and Olivia stepped back as a herd of teenagers tumbled past them. Jamie glared at the cement beneath his feet while Olivia just stood there helplessly, wondering why it had seemed like a good idea to have this conversation. And now she could feel that current growing stronger, pulling her away from him, back to what she'd been before. She'd ruined it.

The last teenager finally sprinted past, trying to catch up to the others.

Olivia's heart had dropped and pressed all the air from her chest, but Jamie's whole body seemed to expand when he breathed in. After a few moments, he blew all the air out on a slow sigh. "I'm sorry," he finally said. "I shouldn't have gotten so worked up."

"I didn't mean that," she whispered, "not that way." She couldn't believe how quickly he'd calmed down. He looked almost like the old Jamie now, though his mouth was still solemn. Still, all the tension had vanished from his jaw, and his eyes shifted from cold to sad.

"It's no big deal. I'm used to it. Hell, I deserve it."

"No, you don't. And I only meant that I'm not an ideal date for you. For anyone. And that's okay. I don't need to be that."

"How about you let me decide who's ideal?"

She almost agreed. That would end the argument. He'd tell her that she was exactly who he wanted to date. She'd be reassured. She'd feel attractive and wanted and flattered. But it wouldn't be true. She didn't want to be told any more lies. So instead of agreeing, she shook her head. "I like that you're sweet and flirtatious and charming. I love it. Everyone does. But I don't want you to charm me by pretending there's more to this than there is."

Jamie threw his hands up in exasperation. "Did I do something to offend you?"

"No. You've been great. You're always great. That's why I can't let my guard down."

He dropped his hands. His frown softened. "Hey," he said, "you don't have to have your guard up with me."

"Oh, Jamie. You are so wrong about that."

Stepping closer, he took her hand and glared at her. "I don't have my guard up with you."

"Yeah, and look at you. You're fine. But you're the first man I've dated since my divorce, and I can't risk not being fine. Not so soon. And not with you."

His fingers slid between hers. "What is it you think I'm going to do to you?"

*Just that,* she thought. Just the touches and sweet looks and perfect sex. She'd let her guard down and she'd be gone. Broken. Destroyed. There'd be a few months of sweet, hot sex and then she'd be relegated to that list of "good friends" he no doubt had. Women he held a vague, remembered affection for. Women he was totally at ease around, because in his world they'd been wonderful friends, while in each woman's world, he'd been a man she loved fiercely. Christ, that would be worse than being an ex.

Olivia shook her head and moved toward the parking lot, her hand snug within his. He was still frowning when he opened the car door for her. Still frowning when he got in and started the engine. He deserved honesty after the rude things she'd thrown at him.

When he reached to put the car in gear, she touched his hand to stop him. "It's less complicated for you if I don't throw myself into this."

"How do you know that?"

She cleared her throat and pulled her hand back, pressing it to her knee. She stared at her fingers as if there was something interesting to see there. But there was nothing but the still-strange blankness of her ring finger. "Victor was my first lover. I'd never done more than kiss another man."

He was quiet for a moment. She could almost hear the blank question in his mind. Four heartbeats passed before he drew a sharp breath. Realization heated the air inside the car and burned her skin. "Oh. So I'm…"

"Yes. I wasn't going to say anything. I know it's weird. But it's why I can't just…give in to you."

"Olivia." His hand covered hers, so much larger and darker that it made her heart skip. "I don't want you to surrender anything. Not to me."

He really had no idea. He was so damn *easy.* Easy to be around. Easy to want. Easy to love. And because he was easy, he could never understand how hard life was for other people. "I just want you to understand why I have to be on guard."

His hand tightened on hers. "Okay. I think I get it."

"Thank you."

He inhaled as if he'd say more, but in the end, he simply put the car in gear and pulled out. Olivia watched the Ferris wheel turn above them, the white metal on fire with the sunset, and she wished they'd never come down.

## CHAPTER SEVENTEEN

JAMIE TRIED HIS BEST not to look as freaked out as he was. There was no reason to panic. Nothing had changed. Not really. Except that he now realized all the naughtiness he'd been coaxing from her...that hesitance hadn't been simple modesty but true inexperience.

No, not inexperience, he assured himself. She'd been married for a decade. She was totally experienced. *Totally.*

Except that he didn't think he'd ever been with a woman who'd only been with one guy. Not that he'd known of. Certainly not after high school. He definitely hadn't expected it from Olivia Bishop, she of sophisticated older woman fame.

He slid a look toward her, watching her out of the corner of his eye. She seemed tired, crumpled a little in her seat. He'd originally planned on one more adventure this evening, but she definitely wasn't up for a trip to the local erotic boutique. Hell, he wasn't up for it, either. He couldn't believe he'd done her outside in his hot tub. And bent her over a bed for a hard ride.

Blood crept up his face. He should've romanced her, not screwed her within an inch of her life. "I assume you're too tired to go out for dinner?"

"Tired and messy. I think there's dust stuck to my sunscreen."

"How about dinner at my place?"

"You said you didn't cook dinner."

"Well, I'm not exactly a chef, but I do have an amazing list of take-out places tacked to the fridge door." He finally dared a look at her just in time to catch her yawn. "I also have a very comfortable bed with fluffy pillows."

"I remember. Would you let me borrow your shower? And maybe a T-shirt?"

Jamie kept his mind blank, afraid to think of her damp and clean and half-dressed. "Sure. Absolutely. Anything you want."

"Then I'd love to."

*Romance,* he told himself. Hopefully he still had a bottle of wine in the pantry. Maybe he should buy some flowers or something.

When they got to his place, Jamie grabbed two dozen takeout menus and piled them on the kitchen table. "Choose anything you want. I'm going to jump in the shower really quick, and then it's all yours."

He showered in record time, then toweled off and yanked on clean underwear and jeans. His bedroom door opened as he was reaching for a T-shirt.

"Oh, you're out," Olivia said. "I was suddenly worried I was supposed to join you. Shower initiation."

She'd never done it in a shower? Jamie fumbled the shirt, but managed to catch it before it hit the floor. He dragged it over his head as quickly as he could. "Ha! No. I'm in charge of food, remember? Did you make a decision?"

Olivia cocked her head. "Are you okay?"

"Sure. Why?"

"You seem stressed. Are you still angry?"

"Nope. No way. I just felt rude leaving you out there. And I didn't want to use all the hot water. And I'm starving."

She shrugged. "Okay. How about Vietnamese?"

"Absolutely. Anything you want."

"Anything?" she asked, her gaze dipping down his body.

Jamie was surprised by the hard twist of lust in his gut. He still felt nervous, but just the stroke of her gaze down his body, and blood rushed to his dick. There was some chemistry between them that had nothing to do with him teaching her how to have fun. It got stronger every time he saw her, as if each round of sex layered another degree of heat between them.

He suddenly didn't give a damn about his nervousness. He was just glad she was here. By the time he'd ordered the food and grabbed his keys, Jamie had a new reason for rushing. Olivia was strolling back toward his bedroom, and he knew that if he heard her turn the shower on, he wouldn't make it out the door. Shower initiation, indeed.

Yeah, his nervousness was definitely gone. The meaning of her revelation had finally sunk in. The things they'd done together, the things they would do... it was all new for her. She'd only ever been with her husband, in a serious relationship. Jamie was only the second man to touch her, to slide into her body. He couldn't say that those sorts of things mattered to him, but he also couldn't deny the wild grip of possession he felt.

"Fucking caveman," he muttered, but his body didn't offer even a twinge of regret. His role as mentor had just gained an unimaginable new intensity, and now that he'd shaken off his nerves, he couldn't wait.

Half an hour later, as he unlocked his front door, he realized he'd never left a woman alone in his house before. It felt strange, walking in and knowing someone else was there. Someone who might be naked in his shower. Or maybe she'd changed her mind and decided on a long bubble bath. Maybe—

"Hey."

Jamie spun to see her standing next to the couch, her long legs bare and smooth. His chest tightened at the sight of her in his dogs-playing-poker T-shirt. She wore her glasses with no makeup, and her hair was slightly wavy with damp. In short, she looked perfect. His gaze fell to the tiny hem of black fabric that covered her just past the bottom of the shirt. They looked like very short shorts. He squinted. "Are you wearing my underwear?"

She spread her hand as if to cover them. "I hope that's okay. I didn't have anything else."

"Oh, I'm perfectly fine with that." He held up the bag and gestured in the direction of the kitchen. "Hungry?" She hurried ahead of him, offering the view he'd been looking for. Just as he'd expected, her small ass looked perfect in the soft cotton, especially when she leaned forward to clear a space on the table. "I got some plates and silverware out. What do you want to drink?"

*You.* He cleared his throat and handed her the sack. "Here. I'll get the drinks."

He filled two glasses with ice water, then opened the bottle of red wine from the pantry. All the while, he could hear her behind him. The paper rustle of the bag. The clink of silverware.

His neck went warm with awareness. Jamie ignored the strange feeling and carried the glasses to the table. "So, tell me where you grew up," he said as he waited for her to serve herself.

"St. Paul."

"Sounds cold."

A smile flitted over her face. "It was all right. I lived in a nice neighborhood, went to a nice school."

"But?" There was no mistaking the weight in her voice.

"But…my dad was an investment broker. My mom was a real estate agent. They spent their free time investing in businesses. And I was a latchkey kid. A big house, but just me in it most of the time." She shrugged. "That's all. No abuse. No movie-of-the-week trouble. It was just quiet. And they expected a lot of me."

"They're still alive?"

"Yes, I just don't see them very often. There's no point, especially now that Victor is gone. They approved of him, so I was successful in their eyes. Now…back to disappointing. I'm sorry…I know you must miss your parents terribly.…"

"I do, but that doesn't mean you have to get along with yours."

"That's a relief."

"So were you an overachiever in school?"

"Oh, boy. Was I ever. I was too busy for parties and boys. Being involved in a dozen after-school clubs tends to suck up a lot of time. What about you? What were you like?"

"Exactly what you'd expect I was like."

"Hmm." She studied him as if she really had to think hard about it. "I think you skated by with C's. You were popular. Really popular. You went to all the parties. Got drunk a lot. Went to school late. But you were always respectful of your teachers. Always polite."

He inclined his head in acknowledgement. "All true, except for the drinking. I didn't do that very often." He said it as if it meant nothing, and Olivia took it that way.

"You? The heir to a brewery throne?"

"Well, beer is more like food. As long as you're not doing keg stands."

"Keg stands?"

He waved his hand. "Never mind."

"And your brother took care of you?"

"Yeah. There was tension, though. Needless to say, I didn't think I needed taking care of. I thought I'd be fine on my own. Of course, I wouldn't have. We lived in my parents' house. My sister still lives there."

"When did you buy this place?"

He told her all about his house. The changes he'd made. The plans he still had. He loved this place. It belonged to him in a way nothing else in his life did. Hell, even his family was growing apart. He fought with Eric more than ever, and Tessa was in love and moving on.

"I've always been fascinated by siblings," she murmured, pushing some noodles around on her plate.

"Yeah? You can borrow mine if you like."

She laughed. "You know you love them."

"I do, yeah. But the relationships are insanely complicated. The thing is…you think you know each other better than anyone else in the world. You grew up with these people, so you should, right? But it's not that simple. Sometimes they know less about you than anyone else."

Olivia set down her fork. "Like what?"

Oh, no. He wasn't going to go there. He shook his head. "Nothing. Just little things. Like how I thought my sister was a sweet, innocent girl and now she's shacking up with a jaded cop."

"Really?"

"Yeah, really."

"You thought she was sweet and innocent? Why?"

Jamie groaned. "I don't want to talk about it. As far as I know, they're sleeping in separate bedrooms every night."

"Oh, my God, you're so cute. How old is she?"

"Twenty-seven."

Olivia shrieked with laughter.

"Hey. She's my baby sister."

"Did I mention how cute you are?" she asked, bumping her knee into his.

"Eat your dinner," he grumbled, tilting his wineglass toward her to urge her on.

Olivia leaned back with her glass, a big smile on her face as she propped her leg on his knee. Jamie tugged it higher, until her heel was snug against his hip and his fingers were wrapped around her ankle. Her skin was impossibly soft and warm. There was something about a woman's skin…the feel of it so much more delicate than his own. He slid his hand up until his fingers brushed the back of her knee, and she sighed and leaned in to kiss him.

Somehow, she ended up in his lap, but Jamie kept the kiss soft and slow, letting her feel every movement as he slid his hand higher. Over her thigh until his fingers brushed the underwear she wore. He loved that she was wearing his clothes, and that would scare him if he wasn't enjoying the feel of her so much. But Olivia was curving closer and his hand was sliding even higher on her tight thigh, and what the hell could it possibly matter if he felt possessive?

"Mmm," she sighed, her hand slipping beneath his shirt. "I'm so glad we made up."

"Not as glad as I am." Her fingers brushed his nipple and he hissed.

"I love your body." The words teased along his jaw. "I really, really love it."

He groaned as her tongue traced along the edge of his ear. She'd never been so aggressive before. "Are you tipsy?"

"Maybe a little. Where do you want me tonight?"

"Where?"

Her husky laugh cooled the skin she'd licked. "In the shower? The hot tub? Right here on the table? I've never done that."

She'd never done any of it, damn it, and the thought of it made him hard as a rock. "I kind of thought maybe we'd do it in the bed. I want it slow. And thorough."

"Just a bed?"

"Yes. Unless you'd be disappointed."

She laughed and slipped both her hands around to his back. Her nails pressed into his skin. "Never." She began to suck at the perfect spot on his neck, waking every nerve in his body to glittering life. But just as he started to sigh, her mouth left his and she sat straight up.

"Wait a minute. This whole 'slow in the bed' thing isn't because of what I told you, is it?"

He was sure that the guilt flashing over his face must glow like neon, but he tried to keep his expression blank. "Huh?"

"I made this weird, didn't I? I knew that was going to happen!"

"Hey." He took her hand before she could scoot off him. "What are you talking about?"

"You know…"

He tried his best for a confused look. "That? Come on. It takes more than that to throw me off."

His lie had the exact effect he'd hoped for. The anxiety clouding her eyes cleared and he could see the awful vulnerability beneath. "Really?"

"I'm a bartender, remember? I've heard it all."

She hesitated for one more doubtful moment before breaking into a smile. "Right. I forgot that you've heard everything already."

He had. Everything from every type of person she could imagine. But that didn't change how much this meant to him. "Listen," he said, spreading his hands over both of her thighs. "If you want me to dress you in a French maid's outfit and fuck you on this table, I will. But what I'd really like to do is carry you into my bedroom and have sex on a bed. Not because of what you told me earlier, but because it's been a long day and you're tired and my bed is really comfortable. And there's nothing *not* exciting about horizontal sex with you. Um, not for me, anyway."

Olivia closed her eyes and snuggled close again, laying her head on his shoulder with a sigh. "That sounds perfect." After a quiet moment, she raised her head. "Do you have a French maid outfit just lying around?"

"No, it's pressed and neatly folded." He stood, picking her up as she threw her arms around his neck with a shriek. "Shh. I'm just trying to liven up this boring sex for you."

"It's not boring!" she cried, her words tumbling over themselves in laughter.

"Well, not now." He carried her into the bedroom and tossed her onto his bed. She was still trying to catch a breath, so he took off his shirt and grabbed her ankle to pull her closer. His T-shirt rode up her body, exposing her flat stomach and cute little belly button. His black underwear hugged her hips like a glove.

"Shit, you look good," he murmured.

She put a bare foot to his chest and nudged him. "Do you have any idea how much you turn me on?" Yeah, she was definitely drunk. Not that he was complaining.

"Why don't you tell me?"

"Just looking at you makes me wet."

He'd thought he was turned on already, but her words struck him like lightning.

"I didn't even know that was possible," she said, her eyes devouring his chest. "To look at a man's body and want it so much I'd do anything."

His hand followed her leg up to her thigh. She let her knee fall to the side. She was still fully covered, but he could see that hollow at the inside of her thigh. If he tucked his fingers beneath the fabric right there, he'd find her wet and ready.

"I think about you all the time, Jamie," she confessed, her words falling to a whisper. "I think about your mouth on me. Your cock inside me..."

"Christ," he breathed, lowering himself slowly over her, loving the way her hands touched him as her legs wrapped around his hips. When he kissed her, he bumped her glasses and she reached to take them off and toss them toward the table.

Jamie kissed her hard, and she sucked at his tongue as if she needed this as much as he did. Framing her face in his hands, he kissed her for a long, long minute, then dragged his open mouth down her neck. She smelled like him. His soap, his shampoo. She wore his clothes and his scent and she was in his bed. He wanted to snarl with satisfaction.

When she pulled his hand to her lips and sucked two fingers into her mouth, he did snarl. The heat...the wet suction...Jamie forgot all his intentions to be slow and gentle. Instead he pushed his fingers deeper into her mouth, feeling the strong muscle of her tongue work against him.

He tugged her shirt up and returned the favor by drawing her nipple between his teeth, making her cry out against his hand.

She hadn't even touched his cock and he was already harder than he'd ever been, his skin so tight it hurt. He imagined her opening her lips over him, taking him in, sucking hard. He imagined thrusting against her tongue, opening her throat.

Jesus Christ, he could come just from the way she drew at his fingers.

Jamie shuddered and slipped lower down her body, determined that this would last longer than his body thought it could. He dipped his tongue into her belly button. Pressed his teeth to her hipbone. But when he moved lower, he had to slide his fingers free of the hot fantasy of her mouth. Her teeth nipped him in protest, but he was intent. He needed both his hands to drag the underwear off her hips and down her legs. He needed both hands to spread her thighs wide.

She was as wet as she'd promised.

Jamie's mouth watered as he slipped his thumbs along the hollows of her thighs. When he brushed her sex, Olivia's muscles jumped and her knees fell farther open, urging him on, as if he would deny her anything.

He kissed one thigh, then the other, then he traced his tongue along her folds, sighing as the taste of her flooded his mouth. She bucked when he touched her clit, so Jamie curled his arms around her hips and held her down so he could close his lips over the tight bud of nerves.

"Oh, God," she moaned. "That feels so good." He pressed his tongue to her and she moaned louder. So began another game of seeing what noises he could coax from her. He teased and suckled and gently bit. He licked and nibbled then plunged his tongue deep into her pussy. When he worked his way back up to her clit, Olivia cried out, her hips fighting his hands. Jamie tightened his grip and got serious, concentrating all his attention on the strokes that made her shake and scream. Her clit was a tight, hard bud against his tongue, her thighs trembled, her screams turned to a choked gasp. It was over too soon. She moaned as the last spasms shook through her.

"Oh, God, Jamie…"

He stood and unbuttoned his jeans, his gaze on her fingers against her sex, her tight thighs still trembling. He felt strange. Not himself. Not charming and easy and smooth, but mindless and rough. He wanted to find out everything she'd never done, just so he could be the first. He wanted to take her so thoroughly that she'd have no inclination to move on to a third lover, or a fourth. Jamie pulled a condom from his pocket, then unzipped his jeans.

Olivia's eyes opened. Her gaze slid to his zipper, then to the wrapper in his hand. "Wait," she murmured as she pushed herself up. "Wait."

What the hell could waiting accomplish? He set his jaw and did as she asked, and when she put her feet to the floor and slid off the bed, he was damn glad he had.

"Olivia," he said as she went to her knees, forcing him back a step. "You don't have to…" His body ordered his throat to close before he could finish the sentence.

Thank God Olivia ignored him and edged his jeans down. "I know. But I want to."

She did. Hell, he knew she did by the way she'd sucked his fingers like a damn Popsicle earlier. Just the thought made his heart beat so hard that his vision blurred for a moment. But when Olivia reached for his briefs, Jamie blinked his vision clear.

His cock sprang free, and she immediately wrapped her hand around the base with a little sigh. He would have sighed, too, if he could only catch his breath. Then she licked her lips and there was no hope of that.

"You're really big, you know that?"

He felt really fucking big right now, that was for sure.

Olivia slowly stroked all the way up his shaft, then down again. "I love the way it feels when you fuck me. Like I can just barely take it."

Jamie heard himself breathing now, and he could feel the oxygen surging through his blood, making everything brighter, including her touch.

She drew her hand up again, and this time, she slipped her thumb over the head, smearing the drop of liquid across the ridge. His pulse rose to a frightening pace.

Jamie was just reaching out a hand to stop her when she carefully touched her tongue to his cock. He dropped his hand and watched as her pink tongue tasted him again. This time it swirled around his head, and lights flashed through his brain, blinding him for a moment.

"Mmm," she murmured, and then he felt her lips slide over him.

"Oh, Christ," he groaned.

She smiled against him, her eyes flashing up to watch him through her lashes.

*Oh, Christ.*

Her mouth closed over just the head, her tongue teasing against the ridge before she slid deeper. There was nothing hotter than this and there never would be. Olivia taking him in for the first time, her lips stretching around him.... Then she began to suck, and he forgot everything except how to feel.

His world became heat and slickness and suction. Her hand tightened at the base of his shaft as her mouth worked him.

He realized then that he'd been so focused on showing her pleasure that he hadn't expected this. That only made it sweeter as she took him deep. He closed his eyes and let his head fall back, then changed his mind and looked again.

Pleasure weighed heavy at the base of his cock and grew heavier with each draw of her hot mouth. "Olivia," he murmured, wanting to speak her name.

She dipped her head deeper, and he felt her choke.

"Don't," he said, setting his hand to her hair. "Don't do that. Just… You feel so good." He didn't need her to perform. He just needed *her.*

She shifted her hand and Jamie gasped.

Olivia slid her mouth from him and looked up. "You like that?" She stroked him again.

"Yes," he answered with the last of his breath. "I like that."

She smiled. "Good," she said, before she slid her mouth down him again.

He lost his ability to speak at that point. She worked her hand and mouth in a slow rhythm that pulled him under and drugged him with pleasure. He felt like coming already, and he didn't want to. Not yet. Not when she was taking him deeper, her tongue a firm stroke against his shaft. Her mouth pure white heat.

Only sheer willpower helped him hold on. This first time with Olivia would never happen again. Hell, it might never happen again at all. So he forced the pleasure down as far as he could. He watched her mouth against his wet shaft and felt the tiny hum of her voice against his skin. And finally it was too much.

He slipped his fingers into her hair. "I'm going to come," he ground out past clenched teeth.

Her sigh whispered over his cock.

"Olivia," he warned, trying to ease her back, but she didn't budge, and he wasn't inclined to force her. Instead he let himself feel everything build inside him, the pleasure growing, building to an impossible weight. "Ah, shit," he growled, then let it crash over him, breaking him down.

She squeezed him, milking him, her mouth still tight over the head. He knew she was swallowing him down, he could feel himself pulsing into her, and that made the climax so much sweeter.

When she finally let him go, Jamie spun on his heel and collapsed to the bed. He heard Olivia's laugh and waved her up. "Come here."

She collapsed beside him, and he realized they were both still half-dressed.

"You're pretty good at that yourself," he murmured.

"Liar."

"Liar, my ass," he countered.

He felt her rise up on her elbow. "You know what? I really, really *liked* that."

He cracked one eye open to check her out. "You sound surprised."

"I wanted it. With you. I *wanted* it."

"That's a first?" he asked lightly, pretending he wasn't dying to hear her answer.

"Definitely."

His heart flipped. "I told you I make everything fun."

She slapped him before collapsing against his chest with laughter. But of course, it was a lie. She was the one making this great.

"Take off your shirt," he said. "Take off *my* shirt." She snuggled closer, and Jamie felt his heart flip again.

"Why?"

"Because I'm going to give you two choices and neither works with a shirt."

She smiled and he felt the movement against his skin. "What are the choices?"

"Sleep…or shower."

"Are you kidding me? I'm exhausted. Sleep!"

"Come on. One of those ledges in the shower will make a good bench."

"No." She rubbed her cheek against his shoulder.

"You can lean on it. Sit on it, whatever you like."

"Sleep."

"You don't have to do anything. Just sit there."

She began to laugh again. "You just came. What do you even want with me?"

"Mmm. It involves soap. And nudity."

"Jamie—"

He shoved off the bed and scooped her up. "Come on."

"You're crazy!"

"I'm a young man, Ms. Bishop. I bounce back. Isn't that why you seduced me in the first place?" Her outraged shriek of laughter echoed against the bathroom tiles until Jamie stopped it with a kiss. And water. And soapy, soapy hands.

## CHAPTER EIGHTEEN

THERE MIGHT HAVE BEEN a bounce in Olivia's step the last time she'd set foot on campus, but now she was practically flying. She didn't care who found out. She didn't care who knew. Let them all see she was getting great sex and lots of it. Compared to being invisible, it was a nice way to walk through the world.

And it wasn't just Jamie making her glow. She'd made a decision this morning. She was only thirty-five. Not even halfway through her working years. She couldn't just give up and decide to do something she hated for the rest of her life.

To be fair, she didn't actually *hate* it. Teaching was simply…nothing to her. Nothing good or fulfilling or happy. She'd taught because Victor had arranged a position for her. It was as simple as that. And every year she taught kids who moved on and graduated and went out into the world to do what *she* wanted to do. That was the awful part of it. That was the part that made her stomach churn and clench.

Walking across the grass—or maybe floating over it—Olivia headed straight for her office. She wasn't foolish enough to think she could simply quit her job and make her dreams come true. This was real life, not a Hollywood production. But she could work toward it every day. She could start crunching numbers and making plans and sketching out logos. In a year or two, maybe she'd be ready to start up her business part-time. The college would—

"Olivia!" The voice was distant enough that she had no idea who to expect when she turned around. Jamie or Victor or one of her colleagues. She tried not to let hope bubble up inside her as she scanned the lawn. A man raised his hand then, jogging toward her, and she bit back a smile at the sight of Paul. Did he have some sort of sixth sense for satisfied women?

"Hey," he panted when he drew near.

"Good morning."

"Just one second," he said, holding up a finger as she drew in a few deep breaths. "Haven't had my coffee yet."

"No stamina?"

He frowned at that, and Olivia wished she could pull the words back. Probably not what a man liked to hear.

"So, I wondered if it was another time yet."

"Another time?" she asked.

"You said I should ask you another time, and I *do* need coffee."

She grinned at him, still thrilled with this new attention. And he was cute. He seemed to have spent the weekend outside as his skin had lost a little of its academic pallor. His pale gray eyes were now a striking contrast to his skin.

He raised a hopeful eyebrow at her study.

"I'm actually seeing someone right now," Olivia said. His face fell. "But would you consider another blind date?"

"Oh." A look of mild terror flashed in his eyes.

"I promise I've got good taste. She not only has a great personality, but she's got a smokin' bod."

"A smokin' bod?" he laughed.

"Yep."

"Okay," he admitted. "I'm intrigued."

"Her name is Gwen. She works here at the university. But before this goes any further, let me be clear. Gwen's in administration. She doesn't have a degree, but she's smart and determined. If you have a problem with that, tell me now."

He looked genuinely confused. "What do you mean?"

"Tenured professor? Rising star? I need you to ask yourself whether you're an arrogant ass."

"An arrogant…" Paul burst into deep, rich laughter, and she had her answer. An arrogant ass would never laugh like that at himself. "I don't think I am," he said. "Do you want me to ask around?"

She grinned and shook her head. "No, you seem all right. So, what do you think? Are you interested?" Olivia leaned a little closer. "She already looked up your picture. She thinks you're cute."

His cheeks went slightly pink. "Oh, yeah? Well, I can hardly walk away from that, can I?"

Olivia suppressed the urge to clap her hands and bounce. "Okay. I'll talk to Gwen." She drew a business card from her purse and wrote Gwen's phone number on the back. "Will you call her?"

He handed over one of his cards. "I'm putting my life in your hands. Can you live with that responsibility?"

"I'll try."

"Okay. I'll trust you then. If you're sure you're already taken."

"Not taken," she corrected. "But definitely occupied."

Olivia waved goodbye and continued on her path, but she detoured toward the hallway that led to Gwen's office. Gwen was on the phone, so Olivia tossed the card on her desk and smiled.

"Absolutely," Gwen said, picking up the card with a frown. "Monday at the latest. Yes. Uh-huh. Listen, a student just walked in, so I'll have to talk to you next week. Thanks, again." She set the phone in the cradle and pointed the card at Olivia. "What's this about?"

"Paul is interested in a date. With you. He's going to call."

"What?"

"You're welcome." Olivia spun to walk away, but Gwen snagged her shirt.

"What do you mean he's interested?"

"I told him about you and he's going to call to ask you out."

"Sight unseen?" she scoffed.

"Kind of. I told him you had a smokin' bod."

Gwen gasped. "You did not!"

"I did, too."

"I haven't done a sit-up in weeks!"

Olivia rolled her eyes. "I was talking about your boobs and you know it. Your taut abs didn't enter into the equation."

"Olivia..." she started, puffing up in outrage, but a smile escaped her control. Then a laugh. "Oh, all right. I suppose.... Do you think he'll call?"

"Definitely. I told him you thought his picture was cute and he blushed."

Her eyebrows flew up. "He blushed? Really? That's kind of adorable."

"You should see it in person."

"Maybe I will."

Olivia left Gwen staring down at the card. It felt good to spread the joy around. And if Gwen started getting lucky they could go out and gloat together. That would be way more fun than a book club.

She floated through three hours of work in her office, using most of her time to begin a plan. By lunch she hadn't actually built anything yet, but she'd assembled some pieces, she'd made some lists. She was just opening her online bank statement for the fourth time when the phone rang. She reached for it, her eyes touching on the numbers on the computer screen, hoping they'd ticked up since the last time she'd looked. She hadn't been vicious enough with Victor over the settlement. She hadn't wanted the fight.

"Olivia Bishop," she said into the phone.

"Olivia," her mother said. She always sounded vaguely disapproving. Always. Olivia had learned not to take it personally.

"Hello, Mom."

"I was just calling to tell you that your father and I are off to Vancouver for two weeks. We're leaving tomorrow evening."

"Oh, I'm glad you called. I'd totally forgotten. Have a great time."

"We will. Or at least your father will. You know how much he loves being on the water." Her voice suggested that there was something indefinably distasteful about that. Olivia had gotten through her teenage years by pretending her mom had a speech impediment that made her sound critical no matter the place or situation.

"Well," she said brightly, hoping to cut her mom off. "Call me when you—"

"What are you up to this summer? Dating anyone?"

Good Lord. Not this again. "Mom—"

"It's time to get back in the game, darling. Nobody likes a quitter."

"Thanks," she muttered. "I'll keep that in mind."

"I'm not trying to be cruel, but you're thirty-five. You don't have the luxury of nursing your wounds for years. You—"

"Mom, I'm a little busy for dating."

"Doing what? Working? You university people don't work nearly as hard as your father and I did, and we always had time to socialize."

Yes, they certainly had. Half their weeknights had been spent at dinners with VIPs. "I'm busy. I'm supporting myself. And…I'm working on a side project, too." She thought immediately of Jamie and pushed that thought away. "I'm thinking of starting my own business." For a split second, she wondered if her mom might perk up at that. Maybe she wouldn't reach approval, but she might possibly crest neutral. Her mother admired nothing more than entrepreneurs.

"Your own business?" she asked. Her voice crackled with doubt, sinking Olivia's expectations. "What kind of business?"

"Do you remember what my plans were when I went to school? What I wanted to do?"

"Oh, darling. Not that again. That's not the life for you."

"What do you mean?"

"Well, you're not a shark, are you?"

Olivia leaned back in her chair and closed her eyes. "Mom…what are you talking about?"

"You're not a predator, Olivia. You need someone."

"Someone for what?" she snapped.

"Someone to take care of you. Your father and I felt Victor was a little old for a girl your age, but at least we knew he'd support you."

Olivia felt the hair rise on the back of her neck. The chill spread from there, easing down her back and along her arms. This was what her mom had been trying to tell her for the past year. All the hints. All the disapproving comments and worried warnings. She'd never said it outright before, but this had been the crux of it all. *You're weak.*

"Why would you say that to me?"

"Oh, sweetheart, don't take it the wrong way. There's nothing wrong with that. You've always been serious and quiet and smart. You always did what we asked you to."

"I was trying to be a good daughter."

"And you were! That's what I mean. You've always been a lovely girl. Always."

"I'm not a girl anymore. I'm a grown woman."

"Of course you are, sweetheart."

The condescension in her mother's voice made Olivia's hands tremble. "I have to go. I'll talk to you in a few weeks." She hung up before her mom could object. If Olivia stayed on one more moment, she'd start screaming.

Unbelievable.

On one hand, she was shocked. On the other, she wasn't surprised at all. It had all been right there for so many years. *Sit down and be nice so somebody will put up with you.*

Be good. Be quiet. Don't cause trouble.

"Jesus Christ," she whispered, pressing her trembling hands to her face. They'd taught her to be an obedient daughter who didn't cause trouble, and now her mother held it up as a fatal flaw.

Though Olivia watched the phone nervously, her mom didn't call her back. She didn't want to have a deep, difficult conversation any more than Olivia did. So Olivia turned her eyes to the charts she'd printed out. The tables and graphs and lists. The future she wanted to build out of nothing.

*You're not a shark.*

Maybe she wasn't. She'd certainly given up all her dreams easily enough before. And hadn't it been a bit of a relief? Hadn't it felt like a burden had been lifted when she'd finally given in to Victor's plans?

The numbers blurred for a moment, turning into columns of sooty, shifting liquid. *Don't let her under your skin,* she told herself. That's what those chills had been. It had been her mother's doubt slipping beneath the surface of Olivia's body, *infecting* her.

Olivia pushed to her feet and walked out to the hallway to make her way to the little galley kitchen. She poured herself a cup of coffee that was alarmingly black, but steam coiled up from it, and that was all that mattered. She didn't add sugar or cream, she simply cradled the cup in her hands to warm them. When she got back to her seat, she took one sip and then another. She drank the whole cup, and by the time the coffee was gone, the chills had passed and Olivia felt better. Much better. She wasn't floating, but she wasn't stumbling, either.

She closed the online bank statement without looking at it again. It didn't matter how small her savings were. She'd build them up. She'd make a way.

Even the most docile pet could turn dangerous when it needed to survive, and everything inside her was filling up with the instinct to fight.

## CHAPTER NINETEEN

OLIVIA COULDN'T REMEMBER much of class although it had ended only half an hour before. She'd managed a halfway decent presentation on staffing and hiring practices, but she'd been distracted by her frantically working brain. An urgency had overtaken her, a need to turn her plans into action. But as she'd broken the class into groups to work on a mock budget, she'd managed a few spare thoughts for Jamie.

A few X-rated thoughts, despite her fractured mind. She loved the way he moved. The way his hands shaped ideas as he brainstormed with the group. The way his mouth stretched into a smile when someone cracked a joke. His shoulders were so wide and straight. His stance so confident. Watching him made her sigh, and when Jamie caught her looking, she didn't even blush. She just stared straight at him and let him see her lust.

She wasn't going to be weak anymore, not if she could help it.

Their lunch plans took them to a restaurant that would serve as a good comparison for Jamie's ideas. But Olivia couldn't stop herself from floating an idea of her own. "I have a proposal," she said firmly.

Jamie looked up from the menu he was studying.

"I'd like to frame this in a different way. I'd like you to be my client instead of my student."

"You want me to be your…client?"

"For the restaurant! Not the…other stuff?"

He waggled his eyebrows. "Other stuff?"

She wanted to blush and stammer, but instead she held his gaze. "The sex will continue to be free."

He smiled so widely she could see his back teeth.

"What I mean is that I'm moving forward with my plans. I'm going to start this business, consulting with restaurateurs. Helping them with start-ups."

"Wow! That's great, Olivia."

"I'm moving slowly, but what I'd like to do is use you as a test client. At no charge, of course."

"I thought I already was. Isn't that why we're doing reconnaissance at this fancy Italian place?"

"Yes, but I've been *teaching* you. Helping you figure it out on your own. What I'm proposing is that I work it up for you, as if you were a client who'd hired me to do just that."

"Isn't that cheating?"

She rolled her eyes. "I'm not helping you with a class project. I want to help you make this real. I want to help *me* make this real."

He took her hand. "Absolutely. If you want to do this, it'd be a godsend for me. What do you need?"

"All your files. Everything you've put together. I'll turn it into a portfolio. A really glossy one with photographic mockups of the interior and exterior. Finished menus. Profit and loss reports. Budgets. All of it."

"And what will I do?"

"Work with me, of course. And maybe allow me to

use your brewery portfolio as a selling tool for my consulting firm?"

"Absolutely."

Relief swept over her. "Thank you. This will be great. And it'll save you from having to do reconnaissance on the other brewpubs. I know you were uncomfortable with it, but now you won't have to do it. I will."

"That would be amazing. Although I'm not sure how I feel about you flirting with other bartenders."

She tapped his foot with hers. "I won't flirt with them."

"Promise?"

"Well…only if it means getting more information."

"But you're not going to give them some sob story about how you don't know how to have fun, are you? I still can't believe I fell for that."

"Hush," she scolded, holding back a laugh. "You know that was all true."

"Yeah, well, no one else ever managed to break the towel bar in my shower."

Instead of giving his foot another tap, she kicked him. "That was you!" she whispered.

"I was trying to brace myself against the force of your—"

She lunged for him and pressed her fingers to his lips. "Stop!" she gasped, laughing too hard to put any strength into the words. His warm eyes told her he was thinking of exactly what they'd done in the shower. How he'd pressed her against the tile. How she'd— His mouth opened and she jerked back from the feel of that heat.

"Naughty," she scolded.

Their pizzas arrived while Olivia was still blushing.

They were supposed to be individual size, and they'd ordered three of them to get a good feel for the variety, but her eyes widened at the sight of them. "These are individual portions?" she sputtered.

The waiter laughed. "They're maybe a little more than one serving."

"We can handle it," Jamie assured her, sliding the first slice onto her plate before he served himself.

"You can take the leftovers home," she said. "I don't need the calories."

"That works out perfectly because I'm a growing boy."

She descended into laughter again. He certainly was a growing boy. He grew and grew every time she asked him to.

While she was still thinking dreamily about his body, Jamie turned serious. "Too much cheese," he said, pointing at his slice. "Now, normally, that's not a phrase I'd utter, but it's overwhelming the thin crust."

She took a bite. "Yes, it needs better balance."

"Too greasy. But it's good. I really like the crust."

"What do you think about having different kinds of crust?"

He nodded as he swallowed another bite. "We'll definitely need a whole wheat crust in Boulder. Maybe even a gluten-free." He frowned. "I'll have to find out what that means."

"You'll have to bring in a chef fairly early on," Olivia suggested. "He'll be able to provide a lot of input to the menu. You've got a great start, but keep an open mind for a chef's suggestions."

"Absolutely. I'm no expert. I just know what I like to eat."

"On that note…try the one with artichoke."

Jamie groaned—the veggie pizza had been Olivia's choice—but he agreed that the strong flavors were intriguing. By the end of the meal, she could see the way his mind was turning, ideas tumbling through his head. His eyes looked far away, so when her phone rang, she didn't feel guilty about slipping it from her purse.

"Do you mind if I get this? It's Gwen, and—"

"No problem."

Olivia walked toward the front door, already smiling as she put the phone to her ear. "Well?" she asked. Gwen could only be calling about one thing…lunch with Paul.

"Well…" Gwen drawled coyly.

"How did it go?"

"Okay, he's just as cute as you said he was. And I'm so glad we went to lunch, because if it had been dinner, I would've taken him home afterward and broken the first-date rule."

"Really?" Olivia squealed, pacing along the sidewalk.

"He was so funny! I swear I was laughing the whole time. Who would've thought a business-law guy could be goofy?"

"You mean goofy in a good way? Because I've known some who were fantastically nerdy."

"Yes, goofy in a good way. He's so smart, but he likes bad television and scary movies and great music. And his socks matched. And he smelled really, really good."

"Oh, yeah? Just how close did you get?"

"Not close enough. But he asked if I'd like to go out again, and he said he'd call...."

Olivia smiled down at a rosebush that was just starting to show buds. "Do you think he will?"

"God, I hope so. I think he will, but who can tell? Men are such teases sometimes."

"I bet he'll call. Men love it when women laugh at their jokes, right? You probably made him feel manly and powerful."

"Yeah? Well, let's hope he is manly and powerful. I could use a little of that in my life."

"Do you want me to call him and see what he thought?"

Gwen sighed. "I do, but you'd better not. Not until next week when he hasn't called."

"Got it. I've got to get back to my date now, but congratulations. I'm glad it worked out."

This was a novel feeling, playing Cupid. She'd never done it before, and she grinned like the Cheshire cat as she walked back into the restaurant. She liked Paul, and despite her new aversion to dating professors, he seemed like a truly nice guy. Just the fact that he was asking out grown women instead of students... Maybe Olivia's standards were low, but that seemed like a good place to start.

For herself, though...she wasn't even sure she wanted a nice guy. Jamie was a truly nice guy, and that was part of the problem. Everyone liked him. And he liked so many. Maybe she needed somebody grumpy. Somebody who would never cheat on her because he didn't have an ounce of charm in his body.

She was weaving her way through the tables when her neck prickled with awareness. She looked toward Jamie, certain he was staring at her, but he was making notes on a napkin. Curious, she glanced around at the other tables. When she caught sight of the person staring at her, Olivia jumped in surprise. It was Victor, seated at a table in the far corner. His eyes burned into her, until he was distracted by the movement of the woman with him. Allison stood, her movements jerky with anger as she tossed her napkin down and grabbed her purse. Victor made a halfhearted effort to reach toward her, but she pulled back and stalked away from him. Away from Victor, but straight toward Olivia.

Olivia tensed up, expecting a confrontation, but the girl only glared for a moment before storming past, her cheeks streaked with tears.

"Oh," Olivia murmured, at a complete loss. She looked helplessly around and caught Jamie's wide-eyed gaze. He grimaced in sympathy as she walked toward him. She did her best not to look in Victor's direction.

"Yikes," Jamie said. "What was that about?"

"I'm not sure. I guess we chose the wrong restaurant."

"I don't want to start anything, but did you notice—"

"Crap! He's coming over here."

"Victor?" Jamie glanced over his shoulder, then rolled his eyes. "Speak of the devil."

Olivia watched him approach, keeping her face as neutral as she could. There was no denying the small glimmer of satisfaction after witnessing that scene. The girl might be young, but she wasn't malleable, apparently. *Not like you were,* the voice of Olivia's mom whispered in her ear. She scowled.

"Victor," she said. "You remember Jamie."

Victor's smile was all false joviality. "Nice to see you again. Olivia, how have you been?"

"Wonderful. And you?"

"Great," he answered, as if his girlfriend hadn't just raced out in tears. "I've never seen you here before. I thought you weren't crazy about Italian."

"It's not my favorite, but I'm trying new things. Getting out of my comfort zone."

His eyes slid to Jamie, and she tried not to smirk. Yeah, she was trying all sorts of new things with Jamie.

"The pizza was wonderful," she said, trying not to ooze too much satisfaction onto Victor's expensive loafers.

"How's the summer semester going?" he asked. His words were always meant as blades, she realized now. Sometimes they were used to shape the situation around him, and sometimes—such as now—they were meant to cut. He was either reminding her that she was forced to work more hours because she'd left him, or he was pointing out that Jamie was, technically, her student. On second thought, it was likely a double-edged sword, meant to wound on both sides.

"Great," she answered brightly. "It's laid-back. Everything is very quiet."

"Good." He stood for another uncomfortable moment. When it stretched on too long, Jamie gestured at their to-go boxes.

"Can I offer you a slice of pizza?"

The fact that Jamie had spoken seemed to jolt Victor

back to reality. "No. Thank you. I just wanted to say hello. Have a good afternoon."

Olivia held her breath as he walked away. After a few seconds had passed, she let it out slowly. "I'm sorry. That must be weird."

Jamie shrugged one shoulder. "It's fine. But I know it's upsetting for you. Seeing her…"

Olivia frowned. Actually, it hadn't been upsetting. Not this time. In the past she'd always burned with a terrible mix of betrayal and discomfort and hatred, but now… Now she just felt vaguely ashamed of him. And of how much she'd given up for him. "No," she said. "It was just…*fine*. I didn't feel much at all."

"Mmm," he said, his eyes darting toward the pizza boxes, then toward the front door. He didn't meet Olivia's gaze.

"Jamie? What's wrong?"

"Nothing. I already paid, I just need to sign the slip."

"Okay, but, why are you being all shifty? Are you having a fling with my ex-husband?"

He barely cracked a smile at that, so Olivia reached to touch his wrist as the hair stood up on her arms. She didn't like this feeling. He was lying, and this kind of obvious lying foretold disaster when it came to charming men.

"What's going on? The truth."

He sighed and set down the pizza box he'd been rearranging on the table. "This is just a theory. I shouldn't even say anything." His gaze was soft with worry when he finally looked her in the eye.

"What kind of theory?" Olivia asked, easing her body back into her chair to brace herself. "About what?"

"Did you notice…?"

"What?"

Jamie cleared his throat, and his eyes darted around one last time. He slumped a little and sighed in defeat. "When Allison walked past, she was moving so quickly that her dress sort of blew back into her body, and her stomach looked…" He gestured toward his belly, forming a little round bump with his hands.

Shock slammed into Olivia so hard that she gasped. "No fucking way." She hadn't meant to curse, and she hoped the words had run together enough that she didn't offend the couple next to them. "I mean…are you sure?"

"No, I'm not sure, but…let's put it this way. If I saw you looking like that about five months from now, I'd shit myself."

"Holy crap," Olivia breathed. She racked her brain for the memory of what Allison had worn to that last party. A red dress. Gorgeous and low cut, but it had been rather flowy from the bust down. "Oh, my God, do you think it's possible?"

"It depends on whether they've consummated their courtship or not, I guess."

Olivia couldn't believe it, but she managed a smile at that. Jamie really was an amazing man.

"If it's true…will you be okay? I mean, were you two trying…?"

"What? *Us?* No, we weren't." Olivia was a bit lost, trying to figure out the answer to his first question. Would she be okay? Did she have a choice? If Victor had a child with another woman… If he remarried… In the end, all she could find within herself was a feeling of pity for everyone involved.

"You know what? I think I would be okay. But the

question is, will Victor be okay? We weren't trying to have kids because he didn't want them."

"Do you?"

She wasn't sure if that was an honest question or a test, but she chose to tell the truth. "If I could, then yes, I'd like kids. But I'm not a man, and I'm about to run into a big brick wall."

"Are you talking about your age? Thirty-five is still pretty young for starting a family these days."

"It might be young society-wise, but it's not young to Mother Nature." Once she'd realized her marriage was over, she'd done a little reading. "I'd need to know where I stood. What my future would look like, long term."

"And what does it look like?" Jamie asked softly.

She took a deep breath and set her shoulders. "It looks like I'm going to be a successful businesswoman."

He answered her smile. She looked for relief in his eyes, but found none. "What about you? I never asked. Do you have any kids?"

"Me?" That one loud word echoed incredulity through the restaurant. "No. No kids. I suppose I'll have some one day, but I haven't thought much about it. I feel like I'm still raising my little sister, though she'd strongly disagree."

"Because she's twenty-seven?"

"Whatever."

"I think you'd make a great dad."

"Hell, who knows. I've never even been in a long-term relationship."

Another shocking revelation. Olivia wasn't sure why she felt a sharp stab of pain at that. Had she begun to fantasize that he'd be her boyfriend and they'd fall in love and go steady forever? Pitiful. "Not one?" she managed to ask lightly.

"Yeah, I know. I've just…" He shrugged, his eyes sliding away again. He offered a distracted smile to the waiter when he brought the credit card slip.

"Well, at least you weren't living a lie," she said. "Most men want to have their cake and eat it, too."

"I watch those guys at the brewery. It looks exhausting to me. Who has the energy to lie to so many people at once?"

That was the biggest difference between Jamie's charm and Victor's. Jamie promised nothing but pleasure and a smile. If a girl fell for him, it was her own damn fault. Olivia would do well to remember that.

Victor, on the other hand… "I bet that's why he's been so…"

"So what?" Jamie asked.

"He's been in touch. Bothering me."

His open face snapped to a frown. "How so?"

"Nothing scary. He came by to yell at me after the party. And I think he might have told my department chair that I was sleeping with a student."

"Me? Oh, shit. I'm sorry. Are you in trouble?"

"No, you're not under my purview. You don't get a grade, so there can't be favoritism or manipulation. It was just embarrassing."

"I'm sorry," he said again.

"Come on. I was the one who asked you out, remember?"

"The last time, yes. I'll give you that. So, what does her possible pregnancy have to do with all this?"

She shook her head. "I don't know. If she's pregnant, I'm sure he wants out."

"What a dick," Jamie murmured. Then, "Sorry."

Olivia laughed at his apology. "Well, it doesn't matter what the hell he's doing. It's none of my business anymore. So, back to what is my business. Can I stop by and pick up your notes on my way home?"

"Stop by?" The briefest frown flashed over his face. Did he not want her dropping in on his place? What did that mean? But then he smiled. "Yeah, of course."

"Great. I've got to grab a few things from my office, and then I'll drive over. Unless you had other plans?"

Another brief twist of displeasure took his mouth, but he vanquished it with a smile. "Great," he said again.

He was lying about something, and her heart lurched. But Olivia told herself she didn't care. She didn't have to trust him for this, whatever it was. She'd take what she needed from him. He'd take from her. And this time, nobody would get hurt.

BARE FEET PLANTED against the warm wooden planks of his deck, Jamie glared at the closest forsythia bush. He'd tried everything, but the plant refused to grow. Last year, he'd told himself it was still in shock from being transferred, but this spring it looked worse than ever. It didn't like it here. Neither did Olivia, apparently.

He was pouting. He knew he was pouting, but that didn't stop the urge. He'd started the day assuming he'd spend it with Olivia, as he'd spent his last four days off with Olivia. He'd opened his eyes this morning with a damned smile on his face.

He liked her way more than was healthy. There was

enough chemistry between them to light a city, but it wasn't just that. He liked the way she took things too seriously. He liked that he was the one who could make her face melt from serious to soft. He liked the way she laughed as if she was trying not to.

But best of all was the way she made him want to try. He'd given up trying long before. The night his parents died had taught him a brutal lesson and he'd learned it well. Sometimes the bad did outweigh the good. Sometimes you were just a fuckup who ruined everything. Everything. Even when you were trying to fix your mistake, you only made it worse.

After that night, he'd accepted that about himself. He wasn't a good, upstanding son who always gave his best. He was the one who screwed up no matter how hard he tried. So why try? Why be responsible and committed and serious? He was a party guy and a clown whose irresponsibility had killed his parents. The fact that he'd been *trying* had only made it worse.

So he'd given up. At sixteen he'd thrown in the towel and accepted what he was. But now it was time to try again. Not just with the brewery, but with his siblings. And with Olivia.

She didn't see him any differently than he'd seen himself. She thought he was a young, happy-go-lucky bartender with only a few simple things on his mind. She thought of him as a boy. But he was a man and it was time to show her that.

Which would've been much easier if she were here.

He stretched out his bare feet and crossed his legs at the ankles. That damned forsythia bush was still in his line of vision and he knew right then that he'd have to get rid of it. It was the only thing about the backyard that he didn't love. If he moved it to a quiet corner with less sun, maybe it would take off.

Originally, he'd started working on the yard out of necessity. The lot was large enough, but it was separated down the middle by a high fence. The right side belonged to the resident of the second floor. The left side belonged to Jamie. After the construction of the house, he'd been looking at a deep, narrow rectangle of packed dirt, with only an ancient oak at the back and a few sprigs of wild grass. He'd sketched out a few halfhearted ideas for grass and bushes and a deck, but the trip to the garden center had inspired him.

Somehow, Jamie Donovan, playboy bartender extraordinaire, had found himself studying landscaping books and outdoor design magazines. A plan to sod his backyard had been transformed into a xeriscaping design, complete with walkways and water features and a two-tiered deck with an enclosed hot tub.

It had changed something for him. Maybe it had changed everything. He'd done every bit of it by himself, with his own two hands. He'd finished it. He'd *tried.* And it was beautiful. Peaceful. Damn near perfect.

And yet, he hadn't shown it to anyone. Oh, some people had seen it. His sister had come over a few weeks ago and noticed the garden for the first time, but for some reason, instead of giving her a tour and showing off his accomplishments, Jamie had downplayed it. After a few minutes of unresponsiveness on his part, she'd stopped asking questions and dropped the subject.

Relief had swelled through him, though he hadn't

known why. Now he understood. It had been the *try-ing.* The vulnerability of that. He hadn't wanted Tessa to know that he'd cared enough about this place to put everything he had into it.

His gaze slid to the hot tub nestled behind trellised walls, and he found himself smiling. He'd done another great thing with his own two hands. Olivia. And he was pretty sure he cared enough about her to try his very best.

Pushing to his feet, he started toward the small shed to grab a shovel. He'd move the bush today and get it over with. He could run over to the garden store and get a new one, and he wouldn't have to think about it anymore.

As he opened the metal door, the faintest female voice touched his ear. Freezing, he tilted his head.

"Jamie?" the woman called. It might be Olivia. If it was, maybe she'd like to help him. They could dig and replant and head out to the store together. He could walk her around the yard and show her everything he'd done.

"I'm in back," he called out, slamming the shed door and stepping toward the side gate. It started to open and he smiled in welcome. But his sister was the woman who walked through.

"Oh, jeez," she said. "At least pretend to be happy to see me."

"I'm busy," he snapped.

"Is someone here?"

"No." He was proud that he kept the petulance out of his voice.

Tessa looked around as she walked toward him. "You don't look busy. What are you doing?"

He was about to lie and say, "Nothing." He wanted her to go away, mainly because she wasn't Olivia. But he also wanted her to leave because of that old desire to keep this place to himself. But there was no reason to do that. She was his sister. She loved him. He could let her see what mattered to him.

"I've got to dig up a plant. It's not doing well and it's screwing up the look of the yard."

"Oh." She looked confused.

"Want to help?"

"Um." Tessa glanced around, still confused, but then she nodded. "Okay. Sure. I've never done much to Mom's old garden, though. I'm not sure how much help I'll be."

"It's simple. Come on. I'll show you."

He found a new spot for the bush, and explained to Tessa how to dig the hole. How deep to make it, how much improved soil to add. He showed her the drip system and explained how it worked with the xeriscaping as he added a small line to the new location.

"Maybe I should have you come over to my place," she said. "With all those huge bushes, I must be using a ton of water."

"No, Mom's garden is established, and those trees are fifty years old. The roots are deep and they don't need nearly as much water. The grass gets a lot of shade from the mature trees. If you installed all that landscaping today, you use ten times as much water to keep it alive."

She paused in her digging to wipe a hand across her sweaty forehead. "How do you know all this stuff? Is this from when you mowed lawns that summer in high school?"

"No."

Tessa rolled her eyes. "No? Just no?"

Jamie stared hard at the narrow black tube he was trimming to just the right size. He cleared his throat. "I taught myself a lot while I was working back here."

That seemed to satisfy her. She stared out at the garden before beaming a smile in his direction. "This is really neat, Jamie. I can't believe you have this…" a wave of her hand took in the whole yard "…this secret life I know nothing about. You never said a word. Heck, I didn't even know you were buying this house until you had to take time off for the closing."

"Yeah, well…" Blood heated his face at the thought of all the secrets he'd kept. "We all have things we keep private. You certainly do."

"That's different. I kept my love life private because you didn't want to know about it."

"I never said that."

"Oh, come on, Jamie. When I was fifteen you told me that any boy who touched me would be thrown in prison for statutory rape! That's not exactly an opening for honest conversation."

"I didn't want to have a conversation! I wanted you to be scared shitless."

"Yeah, I know. So how could I ever have been honest with you?"

"Maybe when you were older…?" he started, but Tessa was already shaking her head.

"Do you remember that sit-down talk before I started

college? You told me if I ever got drunk at a party, I'd be kidnapped and raped and sold into white slavery."

"Hey, it happens."

"Does it, Jamie? Does it really?"

He cleared his throat and got back to work. "Parts of it."

"My point is that I couldn't talk to you about sex, but I don't understand why you'd keep things like this to yourself."

"I don't know," he said. Though he tried to think of something more to add, the only thing that popped into his head was the truth. "I don't know," he repeated dumbly.

Tessa put down her shovel and eased down to sit on the dirt, seemingly unconcerned about the damage to her shorts. She just put her chin on her knees and watched him work. "I miss you," she murmured, and Jamie's heart twisted.

"I'm right here."

"Jamie, you— Actually, you are here right now. Right at this moment. But usually you're not. Usually, you're being charming with customers or you're busy with the bar. Occasionally you stop by my place for Sunday dinner because I cornered you at work and made you promise. But then…then you're just gone. You're busy. You're off to a life we know nothing about. And I *miss* you."

Her words sunk deep, slicing through flesh and bone because they were true. "I'm sorry. You know how tense things are at work."

"I know it's tense, but we're not just your job, Jamie. We're your family."

He set down the tube he'd been uselessly clutching for the past minute. He'd squeezed it so hard that his hand ached.

"You know…I sometimes think you were hit hardest by Mom and Dad's deaths."

"What?" he asked, the word barely audible even to his ears.

"It was almost like…like you lost part of yourself."

He stood up so quickly that his head spun. "Of course I did. We all did."

"I know that." He didn't understand how she could stay so relaxed, talking about something so awful. But she just looked up at him, eyes sad and mouth serious, her chin still perched on her knees.

He walked away, but he heard the scrape of her shoes as she got up to follow. Bending down to avoid her eyes, Jamie worked the offending bush out of its spot with a hand shovel. It came up easily, letting him know the roots had hardly grown at all.

"You were so angry that first year," Tessa said softly.

He glanced up but pretended the sun was in his eyes so he wouldn't have to meet her gaze. "I wasn't."

"It's normal, you know. The anger. It's okay to be mad at them for dying. For being out on that road late at night. It had been raining for so long, and with all the snowmelt, maybe they should've known. There'd been landslides…"

Jamie surged up and rushed away as if transferring this damn bush was a life-or-death matter. "I wasn't mad," he ground out past his tight jaw.

"You were, Jamie. You were furious. You lashed out

at Eric all the time. You skipped school to party with your friends. You even cursed out the principal."

"He was an ass."

"Maybe he was. But that wasn't like you. You might've been a little irresponsible before. You might've been lax about your schoolwork, but you were never bad. But after they died, for a while there, you didn't care about anything."

"You don't understand," he said, dropping the bush into the hollow of dirt so he could press a hand to his tight neck.

"I do understand," Tessa whispered. Her hand touched his shoulder. "I was mad at them, too."

"No, you don't get it. I wasn't mad at them. I was mad at *myself.*"

Her hand slid down his arm. "Why?"

A confession spun through him like the blades of the barley grinder, chewing up his insides and turning them to meal. He couldn't do this. He didn't want to do this. Bile rose in his throat and he swallowed it back. "I wasn't the son they deserved," he said simply. And it was the truth, but not even close to all of it.

"Oh, Jamie." Her hand moved down his arm as if she meant to take his hand, but Jamie pulled away to grab the shovel and start filling in the hole with black soil. "They loved you so much," Tessa whispered.

"I know."

"Even when you got into trouble…they'd put so much effort into lecturing you, grounding you, try-ing to break you down. But afterward, I'd hear them laughing in their room, because it was so hard to keep a straight face when you were being a smart-ass. They loved everything about you, Jamie."

Jesus, she was trying to make him feel better, but she didn't realize she was only driving the blade deeper. "I know they did, damn it."

If he'd been looking, he could've avoided her, but since he was glaring at the shovel, Tessa was able to sneak her arms around him and squeeze. He heard her sniffle, and he cursed.

"Come on, Tessa."

She sniffed again. He couldn't ignore a crying Tessa, so he dropped the shovel and turned toward her. Her arms held him more tightly as he pressed his hands to her back. "Don't cry."

"You've felt like this all this time? That's awful."

She had no idea. But he deserved to feel like this. He deserved to feel much worse.

"I want you to start talking to us again, Jamie. I want to know you better than all those strangers you spend so much time talking to."

He rested his chin on her head and didn't answer. It was easier talking to strangers. He didn't owe them anything. He hadn't taken anything from them by being a stupid, selfish kid.

"Please?"

"Yeah," he answered. "Sure."

"Jamie." He felt her shake her head, her hair sliding against his chin. "I'm serious. Please don't say yes just to make me shut up. I love you."

His throat thickened, so he let her go, closing his eyes against a sudden dampness as he turned away. He'd decided he wanted to try again, and here was Tessa asking for something difficult and it was so much harder than he'd imagined. Shit.

"I just want you to talk to me."

He grabbed the shovel, just to have something to do. But after he finished tamping down the soil, Jamie decided the drip line could wait. "Do you want a Coke or some water or something?"

"Sure." Tessa followed him to the house. They sat down at his kitchen table with two glasses of ice water and a bubble of uncomfortable silence lodged between them.

"So, what have you been up to?" she asked carefully.

*Try,* he ordered himself. "I...I've been seeing that woman."

"Which woman?"

"The woman who came to see me. Olivia."

"Really?" She leaned forward. "Is it serious?"

"I don't know yet. Maybe. Yes." When Tessa laughed, he felt the bubble of awkwardness burst and there was clear, bright space between them.

"Your ambiguity makes me think it might be serious, after all. Jamie Donovan stuttering over a girl?"

"I didn't stutter."

"No, but you practically said, 'Aw, shucks,' when I asked about her. Are those stars in your eyes?"

"No."

"Maybe you're just overwhelmed with the novelty of dating a genuine grown-up."

His first instinct was to take offense, but instead he smiled. Damned if his little sister wasn't right again.

"So, what else are you up to?" she asked. "Or are you spending all your time with this Olivia?"

He'd thought he had been, actually, but here he was alone on his day off. Then again, it was probably a blessing. If Tessa had walked in on him and Olivia in the hot tub… Heck, there was no telling what she might've posted on Twitter.

Jamie cleared his throat. "Not all my time, no. Just some of it. The rest of it, I…" Her smile was all warm encouragement, but he wasn't ready to reveal his plans yet. They were too new. Too raw. Still, he could share something.

"I've been thinking a lot about Donovan Brothers. About becoming more active. More plugged-in."

"You should," Tessa said brightly. "Absolutely."

"I know you think I should, but Eric doesn't. It's going to be a fight."

"So fight him."

"Don't worry. I plan to."

Tessa's eyes widened when she belatedly realized what she was encouraging. "Well, don't fight. Just talk to him like you're talking to me. He has no idea you've changed, Jamie. Neither did I, because you've kept it from us. As far as I knew, you spent all your free time throwing hot tub parties."

"How do you know I don't?"

"Because this place isn't a college party house, Jamie. It's a home. I bet you've even got real food in the fridge."

Jamie flushed, thinking of the steaks and vegetables he'd bought at the grocery store that morning. He'd anticipated Olivia staying over, and on the off chance she might become hungry while naked in his bed, he wanted to be able to feed her without bothering with dressing and going out. He wasn't sure if that put him in the party house camp or the real home camp, but he kept his mouth shut.

"Just talk to him," Tessa repeated. "It would be so nice if you two could be friends like you used to be."

"We were never friends," he corrected. "He was my big brother, not my buddy."

"He was your hero! You looked up to him. I don't understand how you can go from that to barely tolerating each other."

He understood why. Sometimes it felt as if he hated Eric. Hated the way he always did the right thing. Hated the way he was always responsible. Always the good one. But the truth was...Jamie knew full well that the person he really hated was himself.

"We clash," he muttered. "It's just that simple."

"So *don't* clash. Get along. Talk. Everything doesn't have to be a battle between you two."

Try. Just try. That's what she was asking, and he now knew he could do that. Jamie took a deep breath. "Okay."

"Okay?" She looked stunned.

When he nodded, Tessa squealed and jumped up from her chair to throw herself at him.

Wrapping his arms around her, he managed a laugh past her bone-crushing hug. He kissed the top of her head before shoving her off his lap. "You're not as little as you used to be."

"Hey!" The hard slap to his arm signaled that everything was back to normal. Everything was fine. The only difference was that Jamie was finally starting to find his footing after having been knocked off his feet so many years before.

"Are you already off work?" he asked. "You wanna grab dinner later or—" His phone beeped, and Jamie snatched it up so quickly that Tessa jumped.

"What is it?"

"Shit," he cursed, viciously disappointed that it wasn't from Olivia. "It's from the new part-time guy, Zach. His car broke down in Colorado Springs. He can't make it in tonight."

"Oh, no. I can go in, if you want."

"No," he sighed. "He's my bartender. I'll cover it."

"Okay," Tessa said. "But if you're going in, wear the kilt. I'll put it on Twitter."

"Tessa—" he started, but she'd already whipped out her phone and started typing. What the hell. Olivia might call, and it never hurt to be prepared.

## CHAPTER TWENTY

"WE'VE GOT A PROBLEM," Tessa's voice said into his ear.

Phone clutched loosely in his hand, Jamie settled back into his mattress. "Hmm?" he asked sleepily. Tessa got upset about a lot of stuff, and an early-morning phone call from her wasn't exactly something to get worked up about.

"Jamie, are you awake?"

"Kind of," he grumbled, eyes still closed. "What time is it?"

"It's nine."

Nine o'clock on a Thursday morning. He opened his eyes and stared at the ceiling. He'd only talked to Olivia once since Tuesday. Concentrating in class today would be challenging. He hoped she wore heels again. And maybe that innocent little button-down dress she'd worn the first day of—

"Jamie! Wake up!"

He forced his eyes open. "I'm awake. I swear. What's wrong?"

"I know you normally come in late on Thursdays, but Chester just called and he can't make it."

"Are you kidding me? I already filled in on Tuesday, and I had to get in at eight yesterday to meet the plumber."

"I'm sorry. I'd do it myself, but I've got an appointment with the accountant and I have to stop in and do a press check at the printer for the new coasters. Eric's supposed to leave at two for—"

"Do not ask Eric. Crap. What the hell's wrong with Chester, anyway?"

"His girlfriend's really sick with the flu. He's taking her to the emergency room."

Great. Now Jamie couldn't even be grouchy about it. Well, not publicly. But privately he was going to be grouchy as hell about missing class. And Olivia. She'd gotten all caught up in her work on the brewery expansion, and she seemed to have forgotten the other side of the coin. She was supposed to be having fun. With *him*.

"All right," Jamie growled. "I'll be in before eleven."

"Okay. Great. Wear the kilt."

"No. I'm not in the mood."

"Just wear it. Come on. It's great for business."

"I don't want to wear the damn kilt, okay?" He heard a suspicious clicking sound in the background. "Tessa—"

"Too late. I already tweeted it."

"Goddamn it! You'd better—" The phone went dead in his ear. Jamie shot it an incredulous glare, then threw it as hard as he could into the mattress. It landed with an unsatisfying, soft plop and barely even bounced.

This damn social networking thing had gone far enough. Jamie stormed to his bathroom and turned on the shower. Not even the sight of the broken towel rack cheered him up today, and he showered as quickly as he could.

He didn't feel up to the kilt today. Didn't feel up to the flirtatious comments and outright ogling, but it would be worse if he didn't wear it after the announcement on Twitter. Fielding disappointment would take twice as much charm, even if most of the women were feigning it.

He pulled on his dark brown kilt, and added a plain black T-shirt as a protest. A damned ineffectual protest, but the black reflected his mood, at least.

Aside from his irritation with Tessa, he wasn't quite sure what was wrong with him. He felt restless. Impatient. He wanted to move forward with his plans, but he expected a fight and that weighed heavy on his shoulders. He was off balance. Uncertain. He didn't know what was coming with his family, his work. And he had no idea what the hell was happening with Olivia.

Jamie grabbed a bagel on the way out the door. He was tired already, and he had a twelve-hour day ahead.

Mist wet his skin as he walked to his truck, but it felt good, cooling him down a little. A little. But his neck was still tight as hell when he walked through the back door of the brewery. Ignoring the sounds of activity coming from the office area, Jamie grabbed an apron and started loading the stacks of dirty glasses into the dishwasher. Thank God the front room didn't open for another hour.

Henry came out of the tank room, rolling a bucket and a mop in front of him. "Oh, hey, Jamie. I'll get those. Next on my list."

Nodding, Jamie started up the wash he'd loaded, then headed to the front. The doors were still swinging behind him when Tessa pushed through. "Hey, Jamie."

"Give me the password to the Twitter account."

"What?" She stopped dead. "Why?"

"Because I'm taking it over."

"Jamie, no! I'm sorry about the kilt thing, all right? I shouldn't have done that."

He shook his head. "I'm done with it. Tomorrow morning I'll go buy a smartphone. Customer service is part of my job and I need to take care of it. The password, please."

"You don't even know how to use Twitter."

"Give me a little credit, will you? I can figure it out."

Tessa frowned down at the phone in her hand. "But I like it."

"Sorry."

Tessa stomped over and grabbed a slip of paper from under the register. She scrawled out the Twitter account name and the password and handed it over with no grace at all.

"Gee, thanks."

"You have to be entertaining, all right? You can't just put dry stuff out there. You need to respond to people's messages and—"

"I can handle it," he interrupted. "I'm not a complete imbecile."

"Why are you so grumpy?"

"Because I'm supposed to be off until four!"

"So, what's so important?" she asked, now as irritated as he was.

"I—" Crap. Jamie shook his head and bit back the words he'd been about to say. "Nothing. I'm just tired."

"I don't know. I think you're up to something."

Jamie snarled. "Whatever it is, it can't be anything important, right?"

"You've got a chip on your shoulder. I'll be in my office if you cheer up, all right?"

Ignoring her, he started wiping down the taps. By the time the whole bar was shined to a polish, Jamie felt slightly calmer and almost sorry he'd snapped at his sister. But really, her little Twitter jokes were getting to be too much. He had a right to be pissed.

But when Henry brought in a crate of still-steaming glasses, Jamie forced himself to give a small smile. "Thanks, Henry."

"Hey, I can fill in for you for a couple of hours if you want. I helped Eric at that trade show a few weeks ago."

"Naw, I'm good. But thanks."

Henry nodded and headed back to the kitchen.

"Wait. If you want to start training, let's set up a schedule."

The back of the kid's neck reddened and he nodded eagerly. "That'd be great. I think I could be good at it."

Jamie wasn't so sure. Henry was twenty-one, but he looked sixteen and he was still as awkward and gangly as a teenager. Still, he deserved a shot, and his eagerness was a good sign. It actually went a long way toward cheering Jamie up, and he was whistling as he grabbed the vacuum and turned it on. He'd finished half the room when he realized the growl behind him wasn't the vacuum. He glanced over his shoulder and saw Eric standing there, arms crossed and mouth turned down in disapproval.

Goddamn it. Jamie did not need this now. He kept vacuuming.

"Jamie!"

Jamie took a deep breath and turned off the vacuum. "What?"

"I said, what are you doing here?"

"I'm filling in for Chester." He left off, *What the heck does it look like?* in an effort to be civil.

"Why?"

"He couldn't make it."

Eric's jaw ticced. "What the hell is wrong with your bartenders? This is the second time this week."

"Ease up, man. Chester had to take his girlfriend to the hospital. Did you want me to say no to that?"

"And what about Tuesday?"

Jamie's shoulders tightened to steel. "What about it?"

"New guy, right? Some friend of yours? Decided to drive to Las Vegas instead of come in to work?"

"That is not what happened. His car broke down. He—"

"I am sick and tired of these losers you keep hiring. I'm going to start sitting in on the interviews."

"The fuck you will," Jamie growled.

Eric growled right back. "You obviously need some help."

"I don't need help! When have I ever asked you to pick up the slack?"

"Boulder Business Expo a couple months ago? Sound familiar? Wait, maybe it doesn't it, because you never showed up. You were too busy filling in for a bartender who took off for Mexico for spring break!"

*I'm not going to hit him,* Jamie chanted in his head. *I'm not going to punch him in his smug mouth.* "Look," he ground out, trying to keep his tone reasonable. "Hiring servers and bartenders isn't like hiring an office person. The wages suck, and it's not the kind of job you take when you're ready to settle down. So, yeah, there's going to be some turnover, but Chester is a good—"

"This isn't up for discussion."

Jamie's patience snapped, and he slammed his hand into a table. "You don't get to decide that, damn it. We're all equal partners here."

"Yeah? You really think you're pulling your weight around here, Jamie?"

He'd said it. Eric had finally said exactly what he'd always thought. That unspoken sneer that lurked behind his words. Jamie heard a strange rushing sound and realized it was his blood surging through his veins. His pulse beat in his temples. Everything in his body tightened until he thought he'd either explode or simply snap in half.

Eric seemed to recognize that he'd gone too far. He dropped his head, and his shoulders rose on a breath. "Look—"

"I pull my fucking weight," Jamie ground out past clenched teeth. "I do my job, and it's a job you couldn't do in a million years."

"You—"

Jamie shoved away the arm that Eric reached toward him. "I'd love to see you try it, brother. I'd love to see you be charming and interesting and approachable. I'd love to see you make small talk with grumpy old men and washed-up sports stars who talk about themselves for two hours and women who think it's okay to touch your ass because you're nice to them."

"Listen—"

"I'd like to see you clean up a spilled pitcher of beer with a goddamn smile even though you're exhausted because you've already been on your feet for ten hours and you know you've got another hour to go, because if everything's not perfect in the morning your own brother will call you an irresponsible, idiot asshole who can't do anything right."

Eric's face paled as if Jamie had punched him right in the gut.

Good.

"Guys?" Tessa whispered. She stood in the doorway, her purse clutched in one hand, the doors to the kitchen still swinging behind her.

Jamie reached for the vacuum again.

"Jamie," Eric said. His hand touched Jamie's arm and it felt like an electric shock that connected directly to all his rage.

He shoved Eric. Hard. *"Don't touch me."*

"Hey!" Eric shouted, catching himself on a table.

"Jamie," Tessa said, rushing forward. "Stop it."

"Stop what? You're the one who told me to stand up to him."

"Not like this!"

"I was in here minding my own business. Doing my job. And he came in looking for a fight. Didn't you, Eric?"

"I just wanted to talk about—"

"You didn't want to talk about shit. You wanted to

tell me what I was doing wrong. You wanted to let me know what a fuckup I am, just like always."

"All right," Eric snapped. "That's enough. I'm sorry if I stepped over the line, but you have to admit that you contribute to the problem. You were late last week. Your brand-new bartender has already called in. And you keep saying you want to take on more responsibility, but you never do anything about it."

"That's not true." Jamie felt his nails cutting into his palms, and considering how short his nails were, that wasn't a good sign. He tried to relax his grip, if only because Tessa's eyes were welling with tears. "It doesn't matter what I do. You're not ever going to give me a chance, are you?"

"A chance at what? If you're trying to do more, I sure as hell haven't seen any sign of it."

Tessa elbowed him, but Eric just shot her an annoyed scowl.

Jamie had wanted to wait for the perfect moment. He'd wanted to call a meeting and sit down with his siblings as if they were only business partners and not a family with baggage and fears and long-simmering anger. But he could see now that there wasn't any use. His chest felt empty with it.

He looked his brother in the eye and felt nothing. "I've wanted to make some changes around here. Start serving food."

"We talked about that last year," Eric said, brushing away Jamie's words as if he were a fly buzzing around the room. "We decided it would pose too many problems."

"You decided," Jamie said. He wasn't even mad anymore. He was just tired. "I talked about it, and you decided."

"I am not the bad guy here," Eric said, stabbing his thumb at his chest. "I'm not the bad guy because you woke up one morning thinking you'd like to start serving hamburgers and I said no. This isn't a restaurant, it's a brewery."

Tessa put her hand on Eric's arm. "You've been wanting to expand, Eric. Just listen to him."

"I want to expand our business, and our business is beer, not food."

Jamie decided to give it one shot. One last shot, because what did he have to lose? He'd already lost it all in those years of running from his own potential. "Our business isn't beer. Our business is this brewery. This place right here. You're the one who wants to expand beyond that, and that's fine. That's great. But I'd like to focus my work inward."

Eric put his fists on his hips and dropped his head. "A restaurant isn't something you just jump into, Jamie. Do you know anything about it? We'd have to expand. There'd be more insurance, more employees. Think about it, for God's sake. This would be a completely different place."

"I'm not just throwing this out there."

Eric's laugh held no humor. "What was it you said? 'Burgers and stuff'?"

"That was last year. I've actually put some work into this, Eric."

His brother tossed a dismissive look around the taproom. "Yeah?"

"Yeah, I have. I've been taking a class…"

Tessa's head popped up and her eyes slowly widened.

"A cooking class?" Eric asked.

"No, a restaurant development class. I have an idea. A real idea. I want to—"

"Jamie." Eric sighed. "This kind of thing could take years to develop. We'd have to expand, and—"

"No, we wouldn't. If you'll just listen to me—"

"Fine!" his brother snapped. "You write down your ideas, and we'll talk about it sometime." Tessa started to speak, but Eric held up a hand. "But not this year. This year has been crazy enough, and I've got my hands full."

"Eric," Jamie said wearily. "I'm not asking your permission to bring this to the table. I'm not begging for your approval. I'm telling you that I have a good idea, and I'm going to move forward with it."

"You're not making changes to the brewery unless we all agree."

"Fair enough," Jamie conceded. "But there are a hell of a lot of other changes I can make without consulting you. If you need to run this place on your own, then go ahead and run it, Eric."

"No," Tessa said, shaking her head in a quick staccato. "No, Jamie. What are you saying?"

He hated the fear in Tessa's eyes, but he was done. He'd defined himself by his family for so long, but he was never going to be the good one, not even in his own mind. "Don't worry, sis. I'm not going anywhere."

Tears spilled over her eyes, but Jamie could only shake his head. He had to do what was best for himself. Not just what he *wanted* to do, but what was best, for once.

"Jamie, please don't do this," she said, her voice trembling with tears.

"The brewery is my home just as much as it is yours, Tessa. I'm not walking away from it. I'm just going to spread my wings a little."

Eric frowned and crossed his arms again. "What are you talking about?"

Jamie met his brother's eyes, and for the first time in a long while, he truly looked at him. The intensity in his blue gaze. The lines of stress around his eyes. The hard set of his mouth. Eric had carried the responsibility of this place since he was twenty-four years old. He'd carried his siblings as well, and it wasn't good for any of them.

"I'm growing up, Eric. Just like you always wanted. And I can't prove myself here."

"You don't need to prove yourself to me," Eric muttered.

"You know what? It's not really about you."

Eric threw his hands up in disgust. "This is ridiculous. We open in five minutes. We'll discuss this later."

"Sure," Jamie agreed. It didn't matter when they discussed it. He wasn't going to get anywhere with Eric. Tessa was right; Eric still saw them as kids. If Jamie wanted to stop being the little brother, he had to get out of here.

Eric walked out without another word, but Tessa stayed and another tear leaked from her eye, tracing a slow path down her face.

"Cut it out, Tessa."

"You cut it out!" she yelled. "You shouldn't say things like that. You're just mad."

"I'm not mad," he said quietly.

She nodded, her eyes glinting with fear. "Yes, you are."

"Look at me. Do I look mad?" He knew he didn't, because it had all drained out of him. He'd screwed up one too many times. That night with Monica Kendall had been the last straw. Another moment of bad judgment on top of so many others. Not the worst mistake he'd ever made, though. Not by far.

Tessa must have seen the truth in his face, because she stepped closer and grabbed his arm. "What are you doing, Jamie? What are you talking about?"

"I'm growing up, Tessa."

She lunged and wrapped her arms around him, pressing her cheek to his chest. "Please don't."

"Grow up?"

"No, don't go. Please, Jamie. Don't do this to us."

He held his arms up, hoping she might let go. "I'm not doing anything to you."

"Yes, you are!" she sobbed, and Jamie gave up any hope that she'd back off.

He lowered his arms and wrapped them slowly around his sister, sick at the way her back trembled.

"I don't want to lose you, Jamie," she whispered. "I can't."

"I'm not going anywhere. I'm still a Donovan Brother, just like you." Instead of laughing at his pitiful joke, Tessa sobbed again, and he tightened his hold. "Tessa, I need a chance to stand up on my own."

"You can stand up here. I'll back you up, Jamie, I swear. Tell me your plans. What do you want to do?"

He wanted to reassure her. He really did. All Tessa

had ever asked for was happiness for her brothers. But he didn't have the energy to lie, and he could no longer see a way through this mess. Eric didn't trust him, and Jamie couldn't set aside his resentment long enough to be calm. In the end, he was saved by Henry.

"Um… Sorry to interrupt…" Henry's eyebrows were nearly to his hairline as he eased one of the swinging doors open. "It's eleven. Should I go ahead and unlock the doors?"

"Yes," Jamie said quickly. "Thank you."

Tessa squeezed him harder.

"We'll talk about this later, Tessa. I've got to finish prepping."

"No! I'm not going to—"

"I'm not going anywhere. I'm going to be here all day, and I'll be in tomorrow and the day after that. Nobody's running off, all right? Even if I decide to open another place, I'm not planning on breaking up the partnership."

"You promise?" She eased back, swiping a sleeve over her face as she looked up at him.

"I promise."

She was still a mess when she left, but Jamie felt fine. A little too fine, actually. The calm was a welcome change, but letting all that anger out had left a hollow place inside him, like something important had been scooped out.

"It's fine," he murmured as he wound the cord around the vacuum. There was no time to finish sweeping the carpet. He hadn't even taken the chairs off the tables yet.

Jamie raced through the rest of the cleaning, taking

down chairs and wiping tables with such speed that sweat trickled down his neck. The thought of half the room being unvacuumed nagged at him. It nibbled at his calm.

There were few things in life he was good at, and the hollow place in his chest was like an echo chamber, reminding him that he'd left this job undone.

Jamie glanced at the doors one last time. If a customer walked in, they'd hardly find it welcoming to be hit by the roar of a vacuum, but there was a crushed pretzel in the far corner that he'd just noticed.

"Shit." Jamie unwound the cord in record time and made a few frantic passes over the rest of the room. Just before he'd finished, a square of light burst across the floor as the front door open. Jamie flipped the switch and let silence fall over the room. Crap, he'd forgotten to turn on the music.

"Sorry, I'm running a little late today. If—" The rectangle shrunk as the door closed, and he could finally make out the customer as the glare subsided. The words died in Jamie's throat. "You," he breathed.

"Hello, Jamie," Monica Kendall said. A million sparks sizzled through his brain at that moment. Shock. Shame. Anger. And worry. Worry blazed brighter than the others for a moment, and Jamie's eyes fell to her stomach as he remembered the conversation he'd had with Olivia the other day. *If I saw you looking like that a few months from now...*

But, no. No, thank God, she was as slim and sleek as ever. The thought came and went with such suddenness that he felt dizzy. He hadn't even wanted the briefest connection with her, much less a lifetime. "What are you doing here?" he managed to get out on a rasp.

"I wanted to say hi, see how you're doing."

"You can't be serious."

The brittle smile slipped for a moment. "I saw your tweet and I was in the area.…"

What the fuck was she talking about? He watched her as if she were a scorpion about to strike.

"I wanted to apologize for my brother."

"For your *brother?*" he laughed. "Are you kidding me?"

Her eyes flashed with some hard emotion. She was as beautiful as ever, but she'd always had that icy edge. She practically glittered with it. "Jamie, I didn't mean for that to happen. You have to believe me."

"I don't have to believe anything," he scoffed, unplugging the vacuum and walking it to the small closet next to the bar. When he turned around, she was right there behind him.

"Jamie—"

The door opened again, and two bikers walked in, their clip shoes clicking against the tile. "Hey," one of the guys said, raising a hand in greeting. "Two IPAs."

"You got it," Jamie said in relief, heading for the tap. But Monica didn't leave. She started to step behind the bar with him, but when he shot her red high heel a look of warning, she moved back behind the line and waited impatiently.

He drew two pints and delivered them to the bikers, but when he tried to ease past Monica again, she grabbed his wrist. "Can we just talk for a minute?"

"The last time I gave you a minute, you took ten

hours." That wasn't all she'd taken. He would've jerked his hand away, but he didn't want Monica to know how much she affected him.

"I didn't know—"

"Bullshit," he said quietly. "You were the one to give him the code. While you were hanging on me, rubbing your tits against my arm, you were watching me enter the code. So don't tell me you didn't know."

"Okay, I knew he wanted to get inside, but I swear, I thought he only wanted information. He said my father needed more data on—"

"Why are you here?"

She finally let go of his wrist. Jamie wanted to massage the feeling of her fingers off his skin, but she was watching him, so he only swiped his arm against his apron and stepped back behind the bar.

"The police are trying to make this into something it's not. I liked you. That was why I came by that night. It wasn't some premeditated crime. I told Graham I was stopping by and he asked if I'd…"

"Be an accessory?"

"No!"

"Did you get a cut? Did he pay you to take me home and screw me?"

"No!" she yelled, her voice loud enough that the two customers stopped talking to watch them.

"You need to go," Jamie said. "Now."

"It wasn't like that. I wanted you."

"Yeah," he muttered. "I remember. Whether I wanted it or not, right?"

Her mouth became a red slash of anger as her cheeks went pink. "Don't pretend you didn't want it. You're a man. If you hadn't wanted it, there wouldn't have been much to work with. And if I remember correctly, there was plenty."

"Get out," he ordered.

She seemed to realize she'd gone too far. Her sneer disappeared and she shook her head. "I'm sorry. Really. I swear, I had no idea what he had planned."

"What is it that you want, Monica?"

Her gaze flickered down. She shook her head.

"Just say it so you can leave."

She reached for him, drawing one finger down his arm, her lower lip edging out a little as if she were a young girl in trouble. "They're trying to set me up, Jamie. If you would only tell them it wasn't like that. We had a connection, and I'd never have done anything to hurt you. Just tell them that. I know your sister is dating the lead detective. He'll listen to you."

Monica Kendall looked ridiculous playing this part. There was nothing soft and vulnerable about her, which was exactly why he hadn't been the least bit attracted to her. It was why he'd said no until he hadn't had a choice.

"I really care about you, Jamie."

He pulled his arm out of her reach and shook his head. "You're a lying, ice-cold bitch. I'm not the only man you played this way. There was that construction company Christmas party, right? Is that the only way you can get a decent guy to sleep with you? By tricking him?"

She reacted as if he'd just set a live wire to her nervous system. First her spine snapped straight, then her eyes went wide. Her lips parted, but no sound came out.

He hated her with a fury that would've surprised him

if he hadn't recognized the phenomenon. It was hate for her mixed up with hate for himself. "You're beautiful, Monica. There's no denying that. But there's something wrong inside you. I could see it right away."

This time when her mouth opened, plenty of sound came out. She screamed, "Fuck you!" and lunged for him, her bright red nails swiping toward his face. He pulled back just in time, but she kept coming.

"Hey!" he yelled, grabbing at her wrists to stop her attack.

"You loved it!" she screamed. "You loved every minute of it."

"Get out now before I call the cops."

The swinging doors burst open and Eric stormed in. "What's going on?" His eyes narrowed on Monica. "What the hell is she doing here?"

"She was just leaving," Jamie growled, straining to keep her hands away.

Monica was still raging, her lips pulled back from her perfectly white teeth. "You suck in bed, you know that? You didn't even make me come."

Yet another lie. The girl had screamed so loudly in bed she'd made his ears ring. "Yeah, sorry. I wasn't really into it."

She pulled her chin in, took a deep breath and spit right into his face. He let go of her in shock and one of her nails caught his cheek.

"Shit."

Suddenly the tornado of nails and screams was gone. Eric had wrapped his arms around her from behind and he dragged her toward the door. Jamie grabbed a rag and wiped his face before sprinting toward the door to open it. Eric pushed her out and Jamie closed the door as quickly as he could.

"Holy crap," one of the bikers said.

"Makes me glad I'm married," the other one muttered.

Jamie ignored them and wiped his face again, his hand feeling distinctly shaky. He noticed a smear of blood against the rag and pressed it to the spot on his cheek, which burned like acid.

"Sorry about that, guys," Eric was saying. "Those pints are on the house."

The men whooped, clearly untraumatized by the soap opera moment they'd witnessed. Jamie, on the other hand, felt on fire with adrenaline, and his lungs burned as if he'd just run five miles.

Eric turned on him. "Could I speak with you in the back for a moment?"

Jamie nodded, but on his way to the back, he stopped, drew himself a pint of pilsner and downed half of it in one gulp.

When he pushed through the swinging doors, Eric was waiting with arms crossed and eyes blazing. "What the hell was that about?"

Jamie dabbed at the scratch. "I have no idea."

"You'd better come up with an idea. You just had a brawl with a woman in front of the customers."

"That wasn't my fault."

Eric raised an eyebrow. "Is there someone else to blame for the fact that you slept with her?"

"That's not the—"

"Is there someone else to blame for you leaving her alone in front so she could unlock the door? How about the fact that she got the alarm code because you were distracted by her tits. Who should I blame for that?"

Jamie slammed the glass down on the counter. "I've already apologized for that."

"A lot of good it does."

"Right." Jamie picked up the glass and finished the beer before setting it carefully back down on the metal table. "Right."

"I'll cover the bar," Eric said, his voice low and rough.

"No," Jamie answered. "You don't get to tell me that. I'm covering this shift and I'll work it whether you like it or not."

Eric paced away and then back. "What was she doing here? Did you call her?"

"No, I didn't call her," Jamie said dully. "She wanted me to tell Luke that she hadn't been playing me that night. I guess he's got her running scared."

They'd never really talked about that night, but Jamie could see all the disgust in his brother's face now. That was fine. Jamie was pretty damn disgusted himself. "I'm going to get back to work," he muttered. He didn't want to hear one more word about it. If he could take it back, he would, but there was never a chance to take back mistakes, no matter how much you regretted them.

But as he pushed open the doors, Eric's soft voice stopped him.

"Why can't you ever do the right thing?" his brother murmured.

Jamie looked at his own hand spread against the wooden door. He remembered how large his father's hands had seemed to him when he was a child. Now he had the same hands: large and wide and touching this same door in the same building where his father had worked. The worst kind of irony. He was nothing like his father. Nothing at all.

He pushed through the door without giving an answer. There wasn't one.

## CHAPTER TWENTY-ONE

SHE OPENED HER APARTMENT DOOR so quickly that her hair whooshed forward. "Jamie! What happened to you?"

Hands in his pockets, Jamie grimaced. "Oh, nothing." One hand rose to touch a scratch on his cheek. "Just banged into something when I was tapping a keg."

"No, I meant, where were you today?"

"Sorry. I got called in to the brewery."

Though she'd been rushing around for days now, time slowed for a moment. Jamie filled her doorway, his shoulders wide, even when they curved down in weariness. His forearms were sculpted muscle. His mouth a wry quirk as he waited for her to say more.

God, she'd missed him, but she'd been too busy to realize it until this moment.

His gaze fell to his feet just as a breeze shook the night behind him. As his wild hair ruffled in the wind, he looked up, past his dark lashes, and the light from the entry caught the green beauty of his eyes.

"Come in," she urged, but before he could get past the threshold, she put her arms around him. "It feels like it's been weeks."

"You were too busy for me."

His arms came around her and she tried not to recognize how good it felt, even as she closed her eyes and breathed in his scent. "I'm sorry," she said. Had he missed her? She flinched away from the foolish thought and let him go.

"But," she said, "all my time was spent on you."

"Odd. I didn't even notice you around."

She smiled and kissed his cheek just to have another chance to touch him. "Your plans for the brewery, silly. I've been working on them day and night, and I wanted to show them to you right after class. Oh, I've been so excited, Jamie. I didn't realize until I started just how much work you'd already done. All those napkins add up."

He offered a brief smile at her joke, but nothing more.

"You're not honestly angry, are you?"

Jamie sighed. "No, of course not. I'm just tired."

"You're too tired to look, then?" She tried not to sound crushingly disappointed.

"Tonight?" He cringed a little, so she kept her expression neutral as she nodded. "Sure," he finally said. "But is there something I can steal from your fridge for dinner first?"

"Of course." She started to turn away, but changed her mind. "Hey, are you okay?"

"Yeah. It's nothing. Just another argument with my brother."

"I'm sorry."

He managed a more sincere smile this time. "I'm fine. Just hungry and tired."

"I can make you a salad and a chicken sandwich."

"How about if you just put the lettuce on the sandwich and we call it good?"

Olivia rolled her eyes. "You're such a boy."

"I'm glad you noticed."

He seemed easier then. Lighter. Olivia found herself smiling as she made him a sandwich with extra lettuce and sat down at her small table to watch him eat.

"You don't have to look at the plans tonight. Let's just go to bed. I mean…if you were planning on staying."

"No," he said and her heart shook. "I mean, yes, I was hoping to stay. But no, I'm not so tired that you need to tuck me in. Not right away."

Thank God. Now that she'd finally come up for air, she wanted him close. Wanted his hands on her. If he was too tired, she didn't know how she'd survive it.

Maybe she was the one who wanted to head straight to bed.

"All right," Jamie said, dusting off his hands. The sandwich seemed to have disappeared in three bites. "Let's see your plans."

Thoughts of going to bed burned off in a flash of excitement, and Olivia had to fight the urge to clap her hands in giddy anticipation. "Okay," she said. "Come on. I set up a chair for you in my office."

"Yeah? Can I start calling you Ms. Bishop again?"

She rushed ahead to arrange the chairs and tidy up the desk before he walked in. Then she sat down and put both her hands flat on the folder as she waited for him to get settled.

Her blood felt like it was shivering in her veins.

"Um, are you ready?" he asked after a few moments.

She took a deep breath and turned on the monitor. "We'll start with something exciting first. I worked with the photos you sent me. I'm no designer, but…" Olivia

clicked open the first photo, which showed the front of
the brewery as it was now, a white sidewalk laid along
the base of a plain brick wall. "This is what the front
looks like now. And this is what I was thinking for an
outdoor eating space.…" She pulled the next picture up,
her eyes darting over all the details. The long wooden
deck, the dark green table umbrellas, complete with
Donovan Brothers logos, the casual tables and chairs
that would allow Boulderites to relax with a beer in
their favorite place: the outdoors.

"Outdoor space?" Jamie murmured.

"I know we didn't talk about that, but I thought it
would be a great way to add more eating area during
your busiest months. Not only does it give you room
for six more tables, but it's like a living advertisement
for the brewery."

"It's really nice," he said, nodding.

"Okay, let's go inside." She clicked to the photo of
the interior. "Per your request, I didn't want to change
much here, but…" She opened the mock-up picture of
the front room. "I think square tables will let you add a
few more seats, not to mention that it will offer the option of pushing tables together to make space for larger
parties. But we can use the same chairs you have now,
which will save money."

"Mmm. Good."

She dared a sideways look at him, trying to read his
face, but for once, she couldn't tell what he was thinking. "Here's the menu. It's only a draft, of course. And I
had to guess at the beer pairings, but…" She loved this
menu. It had been so much fun. Who wouldn't have fun
developing a pizza menu?

She'd used Jamie's ideas, and created some pies of her own. As he'd suggested, she'd added some salads, plus the option of a French onion soup. The soup could simmer on the stove all day, then the chef could simply add bread and cheese and run it through the pizza oven to toast it up.

After a few moments of grinning at her own creation, she realized Jamie hadn't said anything yet. She cleared her throat. "The menu is simple and small, so you can leave it right at the table with your beer menus. Or you could incorporate the two. Either way, your customers can sit where they like. You won't need a hostess."

"Good. That's great. I really like it."

Did he? She could hardly tell. Olivia's heart sank as she opened the next picture. "The kitchen," she said simply.

He grunted in response.

Now her heart had sunk low enough to ache. "Is there something wrong? Is it not what you wanted?"

"No. No, it's exactly what I wanted. I'm only tired. I'm sorry."

"It's okay," she said, but she couldn't keep the confusion from her voice.

"I'm sorry," Jamie repeated. He did sound sorry, but was it only regret that he couldn't compliment her plans?

She slumped in her seat, staring at the layout of the new kitchen. "I chose a midrange model pizza oven," she said dully. "I think it will serve your needs."

"Maybe we should go to bed," he interrupted. "I'm insulting your hard work, and I don't want to do that. I never want to do that. It's just…"

"What?"

He turned to meet her gaze, and Olivia finally found the emotion she'd been searching for in him. But it wasn't the right one. It was...*despair*.

"Jamie? What's wrong?"

He stared at her, lips parted as if he'd speak, but in the end, he only shook his head and looked away. "I'm tired. And the fight…"

"Let's go to bed, then. The rest will wait until morning. It's all budgets and schedules and boring numbers."

There was something more. Something he wasn't telling her, but she couldn't be surprised by that. She wasn't his girlfriend. She wasn't even his friend.

So she took him to bed and tucked him in. The sex was slow and soft and perfect, and Olivia told herself that she was satisfied.

But the ache stayed lodged in her chest, and she didn't sleep for a long time.

THE ROOM WAS DARK and Olivia was warm against him, but Jamie couldn't find comfort. His mind kept turning. It was only 5:00 a.m., but he was wide awake and staring into the dark.

He tried to fall asleep for another thirty minutes, but his eyes kept opening, his pulse too fast to let him rest. In the end, he slipped from the warmth of Olivia's arms and tugged on his shorts and T-shirt.

Feeling like an intruder, he wandered through Olivia's apartment, too restless to settle in one place. When he idly opened her fridge, he saw a six-pack of Donovan Brothers Hefeweizen and managed a smile. Had she bought that for him, or for herself?

Though he was tempted, he bypassed the beer and got a glass of water instead, then headed for Olivia's office. Her computer still glowed with welcome, and when he nudged the mouse, her monitor blazed back to life.

Earlier, he'd been too tired to feel anything when she'd shown him the plans, but now his heart lurched at the sight of the picture. He clicked back through, noticing details he hadn't seen the first time, and he felt… grief.

He wanted this. He still wanted it. But Eric would fight him. Jamie might be able to convince him—actually, he was certain he could. But every step of the implementation would be a test. Every misstep an opportunity for Eric to shake his head and look disgusted. Nothing would have really changed.

Jamie needed a clean start. Maybe he didn't deserve it, but he needed it.

He opened the manila folder on the desk and looked over the numbers Olivia had assembled in a remarkably short amount of time. Pages of numbers that meant something different now. If he were really going to branch out on his own, it would be a very expensive endeavor. He wasn't sure he had the skills to pull it off.

He dropped his head to his hands and closed his eyes.

"You really don't like it, do you?"

His shoulders stiffened at the sound of Olivia's voice. He shook his head.

"I don't know what I did wrong. I thought it was what you wanted."

"It's not that," he whispered.

"Well, what could it be? You look like…like I've crushed all your dreams or kicked your puppy or…"

"I'm not going to be doing the expansion," he said, pushing his fingers against his skull.

"What?" she breathed. "Why?"

"I told my brother about my idea. He laughed it off. Told me I was ridiculous."

"Jamie…" She came closer, her footsteps whispering over the carpet. "I thought you were going to wait. Present it to him with the portfolio. I—"

"It wouldn't have mattered."

"You don't know that!" Her hand spread over his back as she knelt beside him. "You have to try again."

"It's too late for that, Olivia. It was already too late, and I didn't realize it. My brother doesn't trust me."

"Why?" she cried, her fingers digging into his back.

Jamie sighed and lifted his head. "Because I've never done anything to earn his trust. My misspent youth lasted a little too long."

"Doing *what?*"

He shook his head. He couldn't explain it. There were so many little things. Classes skipped. Curfews broken. Tickets for underage drinking. And once he'd taken his place at the brewery, he hadn't cared about a damn thing except having fun. Oh, he'd done his job, but no more. Those first few years, Eric had tried to teach him things, tried to turn over some responsibilities. Jamie had refused them.

"Things add up," he said, hoping it would make sense to her. "You said you don't get along with your mother."

"I don't."

"But there's no one thing you can point to, is there?

With family, it's a thousand moments. A million. And there's no undoing a million small mistakes. It's impossible."

"So…what? You're just going to give up? You can't do that!"

Jamie met her gaze. "Why?" he asked, honestly wanting an answer.

Olivia's eyes fell. She pushed up to her feet and paced away from him, her arms crossed as if she were cold. "I admit that when I met you, I thought you were just… I don't know. Just a bartender. No plans. No goals. And I thought that was what you wanted."

He tried not to feel insulted. It was the image he'd constructed, after all. Olivia had seen what he'd wanted her to see.

"But that's not all you are, Jamie, and you have to let your brother see that. You can't just go back to wiping tables and drawing beers. You won't be happy."

He hadn't realized it, but that was exactly the answer he'd wanted to hear. "You're right. I can't."

Olivia's brown eyes lit up. She took a deep breath and smiled. "So you'll try again?"

"Not with Eric. I've already decided to branch out."

*"What?"*

He actually smiled at the shock on her face. "I think I'd like to open my own place."

She blinked, her mouth still round as a cherry.

"I know this will mean something very different in terms of planning—"

"Different," Olivia gasped. "It'll be… Jamie, this will be much, much harder. You'll have to raise funds.

There'll be long-term commitments in leasing space and equipment. You can't… You…"

"I understand."

"But, Jamie! Listen to me. You'll be starting from scratch. Everything that Eric and Tessa do—all the stuff that's eye-blurringly boring—you'll have to do that on your own."

"Maybe not," he said, the words taking all his breath with them as they left his mouth.

"With your background and name, I'm sure you can find investors, but it's such a big risk. And every single investor will want to have his finger in the pot. Believe me, I know."

"That's not what I meant, Olivia." His heart beat too fast, and every second that passed only increased the speed of his pulse.

She shook her head and her hair fell over her eyes until she shoved it back. "I don't understand."

"I thought…you could help me."

"Well, I will! Of course, I will."

She didn't understand what he was trying to say, and Jamie felt a little panicky. "Just…" He stood and swung her around to sit in his chair. "Sit down for a second and listen to me."

"Sure. Okay." But now she looked almost as lost as he felt.

Jamie pulled up the second chair and faced her. "What I meant was that I thought we could do this together."

"Together?"

"You could be the manager. We could start the restaurant together." He expected a reaction on her part.

Any reaction. But her face stayed blank. The idea had first occurred to him just an hour before. He'd awakened from a deep sleep and the thought had been there. Something hopeful to grab on to. And with every minute that passed, it seemed like a better idea.

Maybe he needed to give Olivia a few minutes, because it wasn't sinking in.

"Manager?" she whispered.

"It doesn't matter what the title is. Director. Anything you want. What I mean is…we're good together."

"We are?"

He laughed. "Don't you think so?"

"Jamie…I don't… This is crazy."

"I know. But we're good for each other. And this is what you wanted. This is your dream, helping to start up a place. We can do it together."

She blinked several times. Jamie understood her shock, but he was feeling great now that he'd gotten it off his chest. Now that he'd said it, it sounded even better. It sounded perfect. He relaxed and smiled. This was going to be all right.

"Yeah," he said. "This could be really, really good, Olivia. For both of us."

OLIVIA DIDN'T KNOW what to say. Her mind spun and swooped, leaving her heart stammering.

On one hand, people were offered jobs every day. Every single day. Sometimes from complete strangers. She shouldn't be so taken aback.

On the other hand, this was *crazy*.

"We get along," she whispered. "Of course. As friends. As people who…*see* each other."

He took her hand. "It's more than that. You bring out something better in me."

Her heart leapt at his words, but it quickly fell back down again, thumping in fear. Was he saying he loved her? That couldn't be right. "Have you been drinking?" she blurted.

"No," he said on a laugh. "I'm sober. And sincere. When I'm with you, I feel mature. Responsible. It's what I liked about you from the start. You're so serious—" When she gasped, he held up a hand. "I know that's not what you want me to say, but it's true. You're serious and smart, and I like that. You make me want to be more."

"More," she whispered, but the breath had been knocked from her. She made him feel *mature?*

"Don't look at me like that. I like you serious. It's who you are."

"But I don't want to be that person. Not just so you can feel *mature*." What the hell was she to him? A mother figure? Her face burned with humiliation, but when she tried to draw her hand away, Jamie's fingers tightened around hers.

"Think about it, Olivia. This would be your answer, too. Instead of working at the university and saving for years to start a business, you could do it now. With me. You wouldn't have to work for years toward it. You wouldn't have to risk everything all on your own. You said yourself how hard it would be."

"It will be hard," she murmured. Hard, yes. Just as her mother had warned her years ago. Just as her mother had said this week. *You are not strong. You need some-*

*one to take care of you.* And Victor had said the same thing. And now Jamie.

For a moment, everything inside her went numb. And for a moment, she actually considered it. He had a good idea. He had the name and the personality to pull it off. He only needed someone…someone *serious* behind him. Someone mature.

Someone who couldn't do it on her own but would happily support him.

She tried again to pull her hand free, and when Jamie resisted, she yanked hard. "Let me go."

"What's wrong?" he asked, bewildered.

"I can't make you more serious."

"I know—"

"I can't make you *mature.* My dullness doesn't rub off."

"Oh, come on. That's not what I meant."

She stood and backed away. "I know what you *meant.* You have dreams. I can understand that, because I have dreams, too, and I don't intend to set them aside."

"I wouldn't ask you to."

"You just did! I know the sound when I hear it, because I've heard it before!"

Jamie's hands curved around the armrests until his knuckles showed through the skin. "I'm not your ex-husband," he growled.

"No," she said quietly. Then louder. "No. You aren't. But you are *just like him.*"

"That's ridiculous," he snapped, shoving up from the chair.

"You're charming and clever and handsome. You tell people what they want to hear so that they'll like you.

And you want to use me for what it will bring *you*. You want me to give up my dreams to make yours happen."

"I don't want you to give up anything! It'd be just what you wanted. I thought you'd *like* the idea!"

"Why? Because it would be easier for me?"

"Yes!"

She scoffed. "Easier than coming up with my own plans? Easier than saving my own money? Easier than risking everything to do what I want?"

"Jesus Christ!" he shouted. "It's just an offer. I'm not trying to steal your future. Shouldn't you be flattered that I respect you enough to want to go into business with you?"

"Flattered that I make you feel *mature?* Let me tell you something, Jamie. If you need someone to help you grow up, you wouldn't exactly make an ideal business partner."

"Oh, yeah?"

Despite her anger, the hard smile on his face pricked her conscience, but she wasn't going to lie. "Yeah."

"Well." His laugh was rough as rock. "I'm sure that's exactly how my brother feels. I'll let him know you concur."

"If this is about you growing up and standing on your own, you can't lean on me."

"I wasn't planning to lean on you, damn it. I wanted to hire you, just like I'd hire a chef or an architect or a designer. Why the hell are you turning this into proof of my weakness?"

"You're the one who said I made you want to be *better*. As if I were your crutch. But I'm not that woman,

Jamie. I'm not the woman who wants to dedicate herself to you until you don't need her anymore."

"I am not your ex-husband," he snarled again.

"Fine. But I'm still his ex-wife. And if you think I'm going to sign up to be a man's helpmate again, you're a fool." She took a deep breath and made herself see him as Jamie and not just another man asking her to give something up. "You helped me, too," she said softly. "You helped me see something more inside myself. But it's time for us to move on."

His angry pacing stopped and his head came up to meet her gaze. "You're breaking up with me? Right now?"

"Jamie…it's not a breakup. We had an agreement—"

"Fuck you," he said. Instead of anger, the curse was filled with disbelief.

She tamped down another jolt of guilt. "If you decide to go through with this, I'll still do the portfolio for you. I want to help, Jamie."

"I wouldn't want to use you as a crutch," he snapped. She started to deny his words, but it was too late. Jamie spun around and disappeared into the hallway.

Olivia followed, but she moved slowly. She had no idea what to say to him. She couldn't make this better. How could she? He'd admitted that his attraction to her was tied in with his desire to grow up. Part of the reason he liked her was the thing she hadn't even wanted him to notice. That she was older. That she was half-used-up already by a man who'd seen her as too serious, just as Jamie did.

A serious woman whose attributes could be reliably broken down on a spreadsheet. A woman whose body was an afterthought compared to what she brought to the business table. Next time, she'd demand a man who needed *nothing* from her. Then she'd know she was *wanted.*

When she reached her bedroom, Jamie was already dressed and lacing up his boots. "I meant what I said," she whispered. "Let me help you with the planning."

"I don't need your help," he lied, yanking the laces one last time before he tied them. He rose and brushed right past her as if she weren't quite real. "I'll see you around, Olivia."

"Jamie, wait." She hurried after him and reached for his arm. "I'm sorry, but—"

"This isn't a breakup, so save the drawn-out good-bye."

When she tried to put her arm around him, he stepped away.

"See you in two weeks," he muttered.

"Two weeks?"

"Book club. I'll be sure to wear my kilt, since you like it so much." He paused at the door and when his eyes touched hers they seemed armored with ice. "You…and all the others."

He left quietly, the door closing with only a whisper as he stepped into the blank dark.

Olivia stood there for a hundred heartbeats. A thousand. She stood and stared until the curtains began to glow with the sunrise. Then she took a deep breath and walked to the office. She closed the file and shut down the computer and turned off the lights. Then she stripped down her bed and loaded the sheets into the washer.

By 6:00 a.m. she was dressed and out the door for her daily run, right on schedule. Things were back to the way they used to be, and she tried not to hate the thought.

## *CHAPTER TWENTY-TWO*

HE SHOWED UP FOR CLASS.

Olivia couldn't believe it. She'd thought he would avoid her, thought he wouldn't want to see her. But there he was, typing away as he always did. Although now, when she stole looks at him, he wasn't looking back. Maybe her first instinct had been right. He didn't want to see her, so he didn't bother looking.

But she couldn't stop herself. He might be smiling a little less today, but he was no less handsome. And ironically…today, without that mischievous grin and flirtatious sparkle in his eyes, he looked older. More mature. Just as he'd wanted. But it hurt Olivia's heart to see him like this, as serious and boxed-in as everyone else.

By the end of the class, she was staring at the clock with the strong suspicion that it was deliberately dragging its hands.

"Ms. Bishop?"

She looked past the student in front of her to steal another glance at Jamie. He was talking with the girl sitting next to him. "Hmm?"

"The numbers?"

Olivia forced her attention to the boy leaning over her table. "I'm sorry. Yes, you've done a great job. How many sources did you check?" She made herself concentrate on the student and his project, but the shuffling of papers around her spoke of impatience. She glanced up at the clock.

"All right. You may—" But her eyes found Jamie again and she stuttered. He was already moving up the stairs, his back a wide wall against her. "If you haven't finished your estimates, please do so before the next class. And be sure to review the new information I've posted online. You'll need to know it before Thursday."

Several students moved toward her with questions, but Jamie didn't even look back. The door closed behind him and she had to swallow a heavy lump in her throat.

She didn't know what this grief was. She couldn't love him, not so quickly. She couldn't feel betrayed; he'd never promised her anything. So what was this awful ache? And why did she feel so guilty? He'd spoken just as carelessly as she had. Though it was possible she'd been more than careless. He'd wounded and shocked her, and she'd lashed out.

Olivia faked enough enthusiasm to get through the students' questions, but she breathed a huge sigh of relief when the last one left. She quickly packed up her papers and her computer and hurried toward her office.

If she just kept moving forward, she'd leave this behind. There had never been a future for them. It had only been temporary. And in all honesty, they'd both gotten what they'd wanted. Olivia had discovered her fun side, and Jamie had gotten his plans. He just hadn't wanted her.

That was fine. She was keeping busy. She just hadn't expected to *see* him.

Now she wanted to go home and hide, but after her divorce she'd never allowed herself to spend any time wallowing and she wasn't going to start now. There were plans to be made. *Her* plans.

Setting her mouth in a determined line, Olivia opened her office door, but the sight of the man sitting there made her yelp in shock.

"Hell of a way to greet me," Victor said.

"I wasn't expecting you." She narrowed her eyes. "And I wasn't expecting anyone to be waiting in my private office."

He winked. "I thought tongues would wag if I waited outside."

She shoved the last of her shock away and sat down as if his presence didn't bother her. "What do you want?"

"I just wanted to see how you were doing."

"I'm great."

"Are you still seeing your young man?"

Olivia nearly growled at him. "Why are you here, Victor?"

"Your mother called me."

She almost dropped the book she was sliding back onto the bookshelf. "My mother? She's on vacation."

"I know, but she decided she couldn't wait until she got back. You upset her."

"Well, the sentiment was returned." She was trying her best to sound bored, but she hated this. Whenever her mom called Victor it felt like a conspiracy against Olivia. A strategy to turn her into what they wanted. Probably because that's exactly what it was. "Spit it out," Olivia said. "What is she disappointed about now?"

"Not disappointed. Worried."

She rolled her eyes as she slipped her laptop from the case and set it squarely on the desk pad. "Fine. *Worried.* Just get to the point."

"She said you're thinking of starting your own business."

Olivia stiffened and had to bite back a snarl, but she met his gaze and let him see her anger. "I'm not *thinking* of it. I'm going to do it."

His mouth quirked up in that familiar, pitying smile. "Olivia…"

"Don't."

The smile stayed but the edges of his eyes tightened. "You're going to quit your job and risk everything on a fifteen-year-old dream?"

"I'm not a fool, Victor, whatever you might think."

"Are you sure? Because it seems like you haven't read the news in the past few years. This isn't the time to start a business, O."

"I asked you to stop calling me that a year ago."

"Sorry." He flashed a charming smile. "Force of habit."

She clasped her hands together to help fight the temptation to slap him. He'd no doubt call the police and press charges for domestic violence…with, of course, an offer to drop all charges if she'd only be reasonable about a reunion. Still, it might be worth it, just to feel the hot sting of his skin under her palm. But it wouldn't be worth losing her job.

"Seriously, Olivia, don't do this. You'll lose everything. Your mother is frantic."

"I thought you wanted me to lose everything."

"I told you I wasn't the one who called. I don't want you ruined, which is exactly what you'll be if you chase after this dream."

She sighed in exasperation. "Do you know nothing about me? I'm not going to throw everything at this like an idiot. I'm saving money. I'll take on four classes in the fall."

"If Lewis can give you four."

"Regardless, this is a long-term goal. A really long-term goal, considering I gave it up for you."

Victor put on his sympathetic face. "I know I asked a lot of you. I've been selfish."

Well, this was a new admission. In the past, he'd only tried to convince her *she'd* been mistaken. Mistaken about his motives and his feelings and his actions.

"I'm going to do this, Victor, no matter what my mother wants. No matter what you think. I don't need to be protected from myself."

His head cocked, and he studied her, his lovely gray eyes warm with affection. She'd always loved his eyes. It hadn't occurred to her until much too late that he knew their effect on women. They looked so damn sincere. "You really want this, don't you?"

"Yes," she said wearily. "I really do."

He sat back in his chair and gazed upon her as if she were a child ready to leave the nest. "Then I'll support you any way I can."

"Gee, thanks," she muttered, feeling churlish and self-righteous all at the same time.

When Victor leaned forward, his eyes grew even more sincere. He opened his hands on the desk, palms up, as if he were offering the world. "What can I do to help make this happen?"

"For God's sake, Victor. I don't need your help. I'm totally capable."

"You might not need me, but I want to help. I love you, Olivia."

Her stomach burned with sudden rage. "You know who I think needs your help? And your love? Your pregnant girlfriend."

His face changed color so quickly she almost reached forward to make sure he didn't fall face-first onto her desk. "What are you talking about?" he breathed.

"I saw her at the restaurant. She's pregnant."

The grayness of his skin slowly warmed to pink. The tips of his ears turned red as he scrubbed his hands over his face. "God," he groaned.

"Why do you keep telling me that you love me when you're having a baby with Allison?"

"I don't want this." He dragged his fingers through his hair. "*I don't want this.* Listen—" When he reached for her, she jerked away. "Please, Olivia. I never stopped loving you. I know I screwed up, and I couldn't figure out how to fix it—"

"There's no way to fix it! You betrayed me!"

"I know, but I thought…I thought if I just gave it time, you'd realize how much you need me."

She sprang to her feet, pressing her fists against the desktop. *"I don't need you!"*

"Okay. Okay, fine." He held up both hands and

smiled gently. "I get it. I meant that I thought you'd realize how much you love me. I was waiting for you."

"You certainly managed to occupy yourself in the meantime."

"Did I think you might get jealous? Yes. I thought the women would work to my advantage. But I've never loved any of them. And now… Shit." He crumpled, collapsing back into his chair as if his bones had turned to mush. "I don't want her, O. I want *you*."

Her outrage drained away, and Olivia carefully lowered herself down to her chair. "Victor…she's having your child. You're going to have to try to love her."

"Maybe it's not mine," he muttered.

"Was she dating anyone else?"

The way his eyes slid away made it clear he was only grasping at straws. "I don't even want kids."

It didn't matter that she'd known that—her heart still wrenched at the words. He'd never said it so bluntly, never admitted it to her. There had always been excuses, reasons to delay, but he'd never admitted the bare truth…and now it was probably too late for her.

"I don't love you, Victor. I haven't loved you for a long time. And you owe it to this child to try. You can't just pretend it doesn't exist. You can't treat her mother like crap. This will probably be your only child."

"I can be a good father to it whether I'm with Allison or not. In fact—" his eyes glinted with a flash of sudden thought "—I'd probably be a much better father if I were with you. I'd be happy. I'd want to make you proud. And you'd be a wonderful stepmother. You've always wanted a baby."

That blow fell so hard that Olivia felt numb from the force of it. "You bastard," she whispered.

"What?"

"You *bastard*. I blamed myself, you know that? I thought maybe I hadn't been straightforward enough. Maybe you didn't realize that I wanted to be a mom. But you knew. You knew and you didn't give a damn."

"That's not true. We were so busy, I just kept thinking we'd put it off, and then—"

"You're a liar, Victor. And I'd never be with a man who could sneer about his own child the way you have with Allison's baby. Get out of my office. Get out of my *life*."

He stood but didn't move away. "This has been a shock to you."

She laughed in disgust.

"I'll call you when you've had a chance to cool down."

"Get out right now, or I swear to God I'll call campus security and tell them you're refusing to leave."

"Fine," he said. "I'll go. But think about what I said."

She picked up the phone, and she must have looked serious, because he scurried toward the door like the rat he was.

What the hell was wrong with him? What the hell was wrong with *her?* She wasn't one of those women who'd spent years paging through catalogs, wistfully lingering over the baby furniture. Sure, she'd thought they'd have kids, but she hadn't ached at the thought. She took a deep breath, and already felt better. It wasn't that he hadn't given her kids. It was just some phantom jealousy that he'd denied her something that he was now giving to another woman.

Well, not of his own free will, but…

"What a mess," she murmured. He'd really dug himself a deep hole this time. Whatever antipathy she'd had toward Allison was quickly transforming itself to pity.

Still, Allison wasn't her concern and neither was Victor. Olivia's only concern now was her new business. Victor's idiotic words had made her more determined than ever. More determined. And more impatient.

Olivia spread all her plans out on the desk and opened the spreadsheets on the computer. Maybe she wouldn't have to save for years. Maybe she wouldn't have to take on four sessions next semester. Instead, she could scale back to two sessions if she could find one paying project. Just one. That would be a start.

## CHAPTER TWENTY-THREE

FRIDAY NIGHT BROUGHT a big crowd and Jamie's favorite local Irish rock band. Everyone was in a great mood, tapping their feet to the music and roaring with applause after each song.

Jamie was having a great time, too. Why wouldn't he? He was back in his place, behind the bar, slinging beers and smiling. Tessa was serving tonight, and though she kept shooting him questioning looks, he made sure he was grinning every time.

"Do you want to talk?" Eric had asked warily when Jamie had stalked in at 2:00 p.m. Jamie had asked, "About what?" and that had been the end of it.

What the hell were they supposed to talk about? They could spend days hashing out their problems and nothing would be solved. Eric might grudgingly give some concession, throwing his little brother a few scraps to keep him happy, but Jamie would be damned if he'd be treated like a dog. Any plans he made, he'd make on his own.

But at the moment, he couldn't imagine what they might be. He felt lost again, but this time he was determined to find his way out of it.

"Hey, Jamie!" a woman called from a table. "Where's your kilt?"

"At the dry cleaners!" he shouted back. The damn kilt made him think of Olivia, and how she'd stroked her hand up his thigh, easing the kilt higher until her hand had closed over his cock. Then she'd climbed atop him, completely naked, while he'd been fully clothed, his boots still laced. She'd—

He shook off the thought. No more thoughts of Olivia. He'd gone to class on Tuesday just to prove a point, but that point had nearly killed him. He'd done a damn good job of not looking at Olivia, but he hadn't been able to will her voice away. Hadn't been able to make himself deaf. He didn't want to give up the class and the information he needed, but he'd felt sick to his stomach by the time he'd left. On Thursday, he'd fabricated a reason to skip. He had the notes and the information she posted online. He'd have to make do with that.

"Jamie?"

He looked up to find Tessa watching him with a worried frown. "What?"

"Did you hear the order?"

He cleared his throat. "The music was too loud. Give it to me again."

She stared for a long moment, but he ignored her, busying himself with drawing a stout for the guy at the end of the bar who'd signaled for a refill. Tessa finally gave in and repeated the order before hurrying away.

Tired of thinking about Olivia, Jamie tried to distract himself by singing along with the band, but he'd missed the chance. The chorus ended with a flourish and a crash of cymbals. The last note of the fiddle faded away. "All right, folks!" the lead singer said in an Irish brogue that got considerably thicker when he was onstage. "We're going to go spend a little quality time with a pint, but cease your lament! We'll be back in ten."

Wincing at the quiet that fell in the momentary lull, Jamie turned up the piped-in music and delivered a pitcher to the band.

"Hey, bartender!" a man called when Jamie got back to the bar. He held up a finger and grabbed the bowl of pretzels he'd promised the band. A few seconds later, he was back.

"Sorry about that. What can I—?" The words turned to gravel in his mouth when he saw who'd spoken. *Him.* Victor. What the *fuck?*

"Jamie," the guy said, smiling as if they were old friends. "Good to see you again."

"Okay," he responded, warily accepting the hand Victor offered. As usual, the guy's fingers tried to crush Jamie's. Not likely.

"I'll take a pint of your best."

"It's all the best," Jamie said flatly.

"All right, then…" He picked up a menu and looked it over as if he were reading an important treatise. Jamie tried not to let his violent irritation show. He'd never been jealous of this bastard, but now something dark and hot rose up in Jamie's chest. Had he come here just to force Jamie to wait on him?

"I'll try the brown ale," Victor finally said. Jamie grabbed a pint glass without responding.

"How's Olivia been?"

Jamie shot him a glare. "If you want to know how Olivia is, I suggest you ask her."

"Sure, sure. I just wanted to know if you're treating her right."

He handed Victor the glass, wiped his hands and went to serve another customer. What a smarmy creep that guy was. A powerless, pitiful creep. Which was exactly why Jamie shouldn't be bothered by him.

But Jamie wasn't in Olivia's bed anymore—he wasn't in her life anymore—and suddenly this bastard seemed like the enemy. Not competition, exactly. It was just that…Jamie was no longer the winner. He was in the same boat of losers with this creep. Rejected. No longer wanted. A pitiful club of two.

When was the damn band going to start playing again? The music would at least drown out Victor trying to make conversation.

"Why do you look so grumpy tonight, Jamie?" A girl looped her arm around his waist and pulled him to a halt.

Jamie gave her a grin. "I'm not grumpy, darlin'."

"Then why haven't you been smiling at me?"

He recognized her now. A pretty brunette who came in a couple of times a month with her friend. They were too young and giggly for his taste, but harmless otherwise. "I'm smiling at you now, aren't I?"

"You sure are."

"You need another beer?" he asked, then he swept an eye over the table, noticing that the pitcher was nearly empty and there were only two of them. "Or a cab?"

She laughed uproariously at that, her hand slipping lower on his back. "A friend's picking us up," she said, beaming up at him. "But it's awfully sweet of you to care."

Sweet. Sure. Also, he didn't want to lose his license. But he winked at her before he slid away from the friendly hand. He stopped at another table, but Tessa shooed him away with a look of outrage. His responsibilities lay at the bar, and he had no choice but to return there.

Victor's glass was empty, and he pushed it toward Jamie. "Another," he said with a superior smile.

"Yes, sir," Jamie muttered under his breath. He managed not to look at the guy once as he drew his beer and handed it over. Just to be clear on the matter, he printed out Victor's bill and slid that over, as well.

Despite a good five minutes spent avoiding the guy as he chatted with other customers, in the end, Jamie had no choice but to get close to grab his credit card. Victor had set the bill and card on his side of the bar, and Jamie had to reach for it.

Before Jamie could grab the card, Victor's hand closed over his wrist. "You know she's just using you, right?" Victor said, his voice still dripping with friendliness.

Jamie tensed and glanced toward the band again. The drummer had stood up, but the rest of them were taking their sweet time with the last drops of beer.

"She's trying to teach me a lesson. Make me jealous. You're just a prop."

Jamie clenched his teeth together and jerked free of the hold. Yes, he knew he'd been used. That had been the whole point of it. Fun for all.

"I'm going to get her back," Victor said. "And you'll just be an embarrassing memory. Something she wishes no one knew about."

"Back off," Jamie growled. He stalked to the computer to close out the bill, noting with a snarl that Victor had given him a fifty-cent tip.

He practically threw the final receipt at Victor, but he didn't miss the man's next words. "She needs someone who'll take care of her, not the other way around."

Jamie's face burned with anger, but he walked away. Distracting himself with other customers wouldn't help this time, so he walked straight for the end of the bar and the double doors that led to the back. The band finally rattled a few instruments, as if they could be any help now. Next time their free pitcher would be slightly less generous.

"Hey," a voice barked. "You didn't thank me for my patronage."

Jamie glanced back just as Victor's hand closed over his arm. "Get off me," Jamie warned, breaking away from Victor's attempt to stop him. "And get out of my bar." He pushed through the doors, and the cool air of the kitchen was an immediate relief. Until the loud bang of a hand catching the closing doors echoed through his bones.

"She's my wife," Victor said, his fake smile finally slipping to reveal lips tight with rage. "And she's *nothing* to you."

"You're wrong."

"She needs a man, Jamie. Not a boy like you."

Jamie's vision went dark at the edges, but Victor's face grew sharper.

"And I have exactly what she needs," Victor whispered. "A juicy bank account to fund her little business dreams."

"Get out of here before I pick you up and throw you out."

Victor's next words were drowned out by the band as they finally came back to life. Jamie pointed at the door, but Victor just sneered and took one step closer. "I can only hope you taught her a few new tricks in the bedroom," he shouted.

The whine of the violin seemed to drag across Jamie's nerves, and they snapped with a pop he felt through his whole body.

Victor bared his teeth. "God knows, if anyone could use a little livening up in bed, it's Olivia."

Jamie didn't even feel his arm pull back. His first awareness of it was the feel of Victor's chin as it ricocheted off Jamie's knuckles and snapped away. Victor's body snapped with it, and he flew backward, his shoulders parting the doors as if they were weightless.

Before the doors swung closed again, Jamie saw him bounce along the floor. The whole room seemed to gasp at the same time, with a few screams as punctuation. The music died an ugly death as each player lost momentum. Jamie pushed through the doors and grabbed Victor by the collar to haul him toward the front door. A few people assumed Jamie was the good guy and cheered, but Tessa rushed forward like a streak of blond fear.

"Jamie!" she cried.

"Stay here."

Victor moaned and tried to scramble to his feet, so Jamie gave him a helpful tug. Before the man could regain his balance, Jamie opened the door and pulled Victor out.

"You bastard!" Victor huffed. "You *hit* me!"

"Yeah, I did." His knuckles ached and his stomach had sunk as if he was still on a roller coaster with Olivia. He knew what was coming next. He pushed Victor toward the parking lot. "This is a bar, you asshole, not the dean's office."

"I'm calling the cops!" Victor shouted, digging his phone from his pocket.

Damn it. Jamie tried to look as unconcerned as possible. "Go ahead. But keep in mind, I'm going to recount every single detail to the police. And the paper."

Victor's eyebrows twitched, but he pushed the nine.

"And remember, I'm a bartender. An arrest for a minor assault isn't really going to affect my career much. But a story in the *Daily Camera* about a professor in a bar brawl over his ex-wife? That should be exciting for your department."

The man's finger hovered over the one.

"And there's a whole barroom full of people who saw you being a dick. You grabbed me twice. Followed me into the back room… Who knows what happened back there?"

Victor's hand wavered, and Jamie smiled. "If you've still got all your teeth, you should probably cut your losses."

As if he needed to check, Victor raised a hand to gingerly touch his jaw.

"All there?"

Despite the fact that Victor tucked the phone back into his pocket, he still smirked as if he'd won the argument. "Wait until Olivia hears you attacked me. Do you really think mindless thugs are her type?"

"We're not even dating anymore, you stupid asshole. Do whatever you want." Jamie spun to stalk back into the bar, but he was faced with a wall of people piled into the doorway. Front and center was Tessa, her expression caught somewhere between worry and outrage.

She grabbed his shirt. "What happened?"

"You're ruining my grand exit. Excuse me."

The crowd backed into the building, and he managed to slide past the bodies and the hands that reached out to pat him on the back. "Good job," some of them called. They had no idea who Victor was, but the man who served them their beers was an automatic hero, apparently.

Tessa was less biased in his favor, ironically. Her hand closed over his sleeve and when he tried to slip behind the bar, she hauled him toward the back. "Excuse us, folks. We'll be right back."

A small cheer of support went up from the tables, but Jamie didn't feel encouraged. His heart was still beating hard enough to keep a small army supplied with blood. What if Victor had called the cops? What would've happened then?

*"Jamie,"* his sister growled.

"I know." He held up his hands before he even turned to face her. "I *know.*"

"What the hell was that?"

"He grabbed me twice, Tessa. I tried to walk away from it, but he followed me back here."

"Who is he?" she yelled.

"Olivia's ex-husband."

Tessa's eyes went wide.

"He came in here to talk trash. Then he said something about her that set me off. I shouldn't have hit him, but—"

"No shit!"

"Jesus, if the cops had been called… Listen, let me talk to Eric tomorrow. I'll try to…" The words faded from his mouth when Tessa's face shifted to guilt. "What?"

"I already called him."

"Christ, Tessa, what are you trying to do to me?"

"I'm sorry," she cried. "I thought you were going to be arrested or something! I just told him to get over here. I didn't have time to explain."

Jamie slammed his hand down on one of the tables. "Damn it! Okay, let me handle this. I'll tell him my side of the—"

The doors swung open and Eric stepped through, his face drawn into fury.

"Eric." Jamie sighed.

"You got into another fight?" Eric asked, the words barely making it past his clenched teeth.

Apparently he'd heard the story as soon as he'd stepped through the front door. Crap. "It wasn't a fight," Jamie argued. "The guy wouldn't back off. He followed me back here and pissed me off."

"So you punched him?"

Jamie shifted and crossed his arms.

"Do you know the guy?"

Jamie slid a look to Tessa, but he knew there was no hope for help. "He's the ex-husband of a woman I dated."

Surprisingly, Eric didn't say anything. He stared at

Jamie for a long moment, then jerked his head toward
the door.

"Go home. I'll take care of the bar."

"I'm fine," Jamie said. "I talked him out of calling
the cops."

"You're not anything close to being fine," Eric
snarled. "What you do in your personal life is your
business, no matter how thin you spread yourself. But
now it's affecting the brewery."

"I tried to walk away from him. It's not my fault
he—"

"Of course it's your fault. Jesus, this is the second
time in a week. First you fight with Monica Kendall,
and now you knock out a jealous ex-husband?"

"I didn't—" Jamie made himself stop the explanation. That wasn't the point. "I acknowledge that I
shouldn't have hit the guy. It was a mistake. I'm sorry.
But I don't have to answer to you for every—"

Eric snorted in disgust. "You know what? I'm sick
of playing this role."

"What role?"

"The mean boss. The asshole brother. You want out
of here, then get out. You've become a liability."

"What?" Jamie's head was spinning, his pulse still
racing from the fight.

"You want to grow up, get out there and do it, because I'm tired of waiting."

"Jesus Christ, Eric, Monica came in here and attacked me! And that asshole was insulting a woman
who doesn't deserve to be insulted. I didn't instigate
anything."

Eric flashed a bitter smile. "You bring this on yourself, Jamie. You always have. After all, I've never sunk a business deal with my dick, and no crazed woman or jealous husband has ever come in here and attacked me in front of the customers."

That hollow place inside him was filling up now with pain that felt like cement. He was reeling, and the worst part was, he had no one to turn to. His family was part of the problem, and Olivia was gone.

"Go home," Eric said. "We'll talk about this tomorrow."

"You don't get to send me home, Eric. You don't get to chastise me or tell me I'm not welcome here. But you know what? I'll save you the trouble of trying. I quit."

*"What?"* Tessa yelped.

"I quit. It shouldn't be a problem since you'll be better off without me." He untied his apron and tossed it to Eric, who caught it with a steady hand. His eyes narrowed, but he didn't try to stop Jamie. Why would he?

"Jamie, just calm down," Tessa said. "You're still upset about the fight."

"This has been coming for years, Tessa. Just leave it alone." Unable to face the bright, crowded cheer of the front room, Jamie headed for the back door.

"You promised me!" she yelled. "You promised you wouldn't leave."

"I don't have any choice," he muttered.

Then he was out in the night, the cool air rushing into his lungs. He sucked in a few deep breaths, hoping to loosen the tight bands around his chest. Amazingly, it actually worked. He stood a little straighter, his shoulders pressed back. It had been coming for a long time, after all. And he was ready to get the hell out there and do something on his own. Maybe he should thank Victor for setting this in motion. If he hadn't been pushed, Jamie would've stayed for months. Maybe years.

"Yeah," he muttered with a smile. "I'll thank that bastard when hell freezes over."

He pulled his keys from his pocket and walked to the car, still smiling. But when he drove away from the brewery, he made sure not to glance in the mirror. He didn't want to see his dad's place growing smaller and smaller as he drove away.

## *CHAPTER TWENTY-FOUR*

HE DIDN'T WORK on Tuesdays, so Olivia wasn't taking too much of a chance by coming to the brewery. She didn't know if she'd see him in class today, but she definitely didn't want to see him here. And there was no reason to think he'd show up. Still, she sat in her car with both hands wrapped around the steering wheel, peering carefully at every car that looked as if it might turn into the parking lot.

There were only three cars here right now, and none of them were Jamie's. She could safely go inside.

The portfolio sitting on the passenger seat seemed to pulse beside her, so she only glanced at it before closing her eyes. This felt like the right thing to do, but she couldn't be sure.

She understood what it was like to want to walk away. She'd walked away from her parents with a deep sigh of relief. But Jamie deserved a shot with his brother. He deserved the chance to make his mark on the brewery, but pride would keep him from taking it.

But did she have the right to take the chance for him?

"No," she said weakly. She didn't have the right, but she was still going to do it. Jamie wouldn't thank her for it. If he ever spoke to her again, it would probably only be to yell at her, but that was okay. She could handle it.

That is, if she could ever manage getting out of the car.

She'd spent the whole weekend strategizing a more accelerated business plan for starting up her own company. Every list she made, every column she balanced added another ounce of certainty to her mind. She could do this. She would do this. Every cell inside her was coming alive with excitement.

If she could find one client, one person to work with at a seriously discounted rate, then she'd be on her way. One success would lead to another. She'd charge a little more each time. And pretty soon, her dreams would be real. Her fingertips tingled with the sensation that it was just within her reach.

But something was weighing down her happiness, and there was no doubt what it was. Every time she'd glimpsed the Donovan Brothers folder on her desktop, her heart had twitched.

So on Sunday night she'd set aside her own work and opened the Donovan folder again. She'd added her last-minute touches, the details she hadn't quite finished. She'd had the menu laminated, and printed out the plans and mock-ups on glossy paper. And then she'd taken everything into the local copy place and had it professionally bound.

It was gorgeous. It deserved to be seen.

Olivia took a deep breath, picked up the portfolio and looked around the parking lot one last time.

It was just after eleven, and when Olivia walked into the brewery, there was only one person in the whole room. She sighed with relief when she realized he was someone she didn't recognize.

"Good morning," the young redheaded boy said. He couldn't be more than twenty-one. He looked a lot younger.

"Hi."

"Are you here for the tour? You're a little early."

"Oh, I… No. Is Eric Donovan here?"

"Sure. Want me to get him?"

Olivia managed a smile, but she felt it wobble. "That would be great. Thank you." He was here. Oh, God, Eric was here, and she'd have to go through with this. The boy disappeared into the back, and Olivia had to stop herself from chasing after him to stop this.

"Calm down," she whispered. She couldn't present this to Eric Donovan as a proposal from a frantic psycho.

For the first time in her life, Olivia wished for beer, and the humor in that thought gave her the chance to catch her breath and calm her nerves. "Okay," she whispered. And then the doors swung open.

If this was Eric Donovan, he looked nothing like his brother. He was dark haired and pale eyed, and the lines on his face marked him as a man who carried a lot on his broad shoulders.

"I'm Eric," he said. "Can I help you?"

"Hi," she thrust her hand at him. "I'm Olivia Bishop."

Not even a glimmer of recognition crossed his face as he shook her hand. She told herself she wasn't insulted.

"Do you have a moment? I wanted to speak to you about a proposal."

The faint friendliness in his face disappeared in an

instant, and Olivia winced. "You're a vendor? I set aside time each week to meet with vendors. If you could—"

"No! I'm not a vendor. I'm… If you could just give me a moment to explain…"

He narrowed his eyes and studied her for a few seconds, then shrugged. "Fine. My office is in back."

She followed him into the office she'd already seen once, then slipped into a chair before he could change his mind.

"What can I do for you, Ms. Bishop?"

"I…" She had to swallow hard to clear the nervousness from her voice. "I'm an instructor at the university. I teach classes on retail business. Restaurants and hospitality, to be specific."

He inclined his head warily.

"I've been working with your brother, helping him develop some new ideas for the brewery."

Now he let all his wariness show, and his shoulders grew stiff. "We don't need new ideas, Ms. Bishop."

"Still, it wouldn't hurt you to look at them, would it? We've been working on a portfolio—" she put it on his desk and slid it toward him "—if you'd be willing to—"

"Does Jamie know you're here?"

"He…" Good Lord, this man really was intimidating. She felt as if she'd been called to the dean's office. "No. He has no idea."

"That makes sense, because Jamie quit last Friday."

*"What?"* she gasped. He quit? She scrambled back through her thoughts, trying to remember exactly what he'd said. He hadn't meant to quit, had he? "How can he quit? He's an owner."

"He's still an owner, but he's no longer working here."

"But…" Oh, poor Jamie. Something awful must have happened. "But you can't let him do that. He loves this place so much. If you'll just look at what he's done…" She moved a shaky hand toward the portfolio.

"Ms. Bishop, I appreciate your concern. But it's really none of your business."

He was right, damn him. And now Olivia felt like the younger sibling called to task by this man. He looked simultaneously disappointed and unmoved. She squirmed, but she didn't concede. Whatever had happened, Jamie must be heartbroken. She wished they hadn't ended it so badly and she could call and find out how he was.

Olivia looked down at her hands and took a deep breath. "I'm sure you think it's none of my business, but I've been working with Jamie for weeks on this. I admit that in the beginning I may not have taken him seriously, but he's passionate about this place. And thoughtful. He has what it takes to turn the front room into a true gathering place. A destination."

"It's already a gathering place," Eric snapped. He shoved the portfolio back at her. "And I'm sorry to ruin your admirable portrait of Jamie, but he's not as adorable as you think he is."

Adorable? A flush climbed up her neck at the implication of his words. "I didn't say he was adorable. He really stepped up to the plate, and if you'd bother looking over his work, I promise you'll be impressed. Whatever mistakes he's made in the past—"

"In the past? Is that how he sold it to you? *In the past?*"

Aware of all of her own mistakes she'd stumbled over in the past few years, Olivia glared. "We all make mistakes. That doesn't mean we're not still valuable."

His gaze rose to the ceiling as if he were praying for patience. "Look, I don't know what your investment is here, but your argument is moot. Jamie didn't get what he wanted, so he left."

"Because you wouldn't give him a chance?" she challenged.

"A chance?" His mouth curved into a bitter smile. "You're saying I didn't give him a chance?"

"Um…" Olivia found herself squeezing her fingers tighter and tighter together. "I'm sure you—"

"This isn't a matter of a few late arrivals or entering credit card totals incorrectly. This isn't about me being an asshole who holds every order error against him."

"Maybe…"

She cringed when Eric set his hands on his desk and leaned closer. "Do you know what his last little innocent mistake was, Ms. Bishop?"

She shook her head as the tips of her fingers went numb.

"Two months ago, he tanked a business deal I'd been working on for months. I have plans for this place, too, you know. And my plans included a new distribution deal that Jamie destroyed by sleeping with the daughter of the distributor."

Olivia's heart stopped. It just stopped. And for a long moment, she was stuck there in complete silence while those awful words sunk into her skin.

"He made the *mistake* of throwing everything away for a chance at meaningless sex. Do you want to know what he's done since then?"

"No," she croaked, but he was already speaking.

"Just last week, that woman came in and they argued. And by *argued,* I mean I had to haul her off of him, in my goddamn bar. Oh, and on Friday, he got into a fist-fight over a woman. A *different* woman."

Oh, Jesus. Olivia bit the inside of her lip until that pain overtook her horror.

"So I don't want to hear about giving him a *chance,* Ms. Bishop. He's had plenty, and I. Am. Done."

Olivia blinked slowly and tried to think how to exit this place gracefully. Jamie had slept with someone else just two months before? And maybe more women since then. He'd told her it had been a year. He'd lied about something he hadn't even needed to lie about. Why would he do that?

Eric frowned, his gaze slipping down to Olivia's hands. She couldn't feel them at all now.

"Um…" For the first time since she'd met him, Eric looked uncomfortable. He darted a worried look toward the door, then back to her. "I'm afraid I've… Perhaps I misunderstood the nature of your relationship with my brother."

"No," she managed.

"I shouldn't have said what I did. I'm sorry. I hope you—"

She stood up so quickly that Eric jerked back.

"Thank you for your time. I appreciate it." She started to reach for the portfolio, but when her fingers touched it, she paused, then drew her hand away. Jamie might be a lying, cheating asshole, but the plans for the brewery were his work. She left the portfolio where it was and stood straight. "It was nice to meet you," she managed in a raspy voice.

"Listen—" he started, but she was already out the door, already rushing as quickly as she could down the hall.

*It doesn't matter. It doesn't matter.*

"Olivia?" a woman's voice said from behind her.

As Olivia pushed through the swinging doors, she glanced back to see Tessa Donovan watching her with complete confusion written on her face. Olivia didn't respond, she just raced for the front door and the parking lot beyond.

Thank God she hadn't fallen in love with him. She couldn't handle being broken like that again. What had she done to deserve so many lies in her life?

She'd been the good girl, done the right things. She'd saved herself for love once and given in to passion the next time, and both had turned out the same way. With lies. And platitudes. And stupid, false reassurances that she was special and desirable and sexy.

Swiping tears from her eyes so she could see well enough to drive, Olivia started the car and pulled out. She drove deliberately, not speeding away, not trying to escape. She had nothing to escape from, after all. It was over with him.

It was over with *all* of them. She wasn't getting involved again, not with anyone. In a few years, once she'd established her business and made her own dreams come true, *maybe* she'd think about dating again. After she had everything she wanted for *herself,* she'd consider seeing a nice man. Someone smart and shy. Someone who'd never offer sweet lies about other women just because the act of lying gave him some misguided thrill.

"I got what I wanted," she said aloud, the words broken with tears. And she had. She just didn't like feeling like a fool again. A stupid, blind, helpless fool.

Even though she was almost home, Olivia could no longer drive. She turned onto the very next street and pulled to the curb. One sob escaped her control, and then another. Olivia put her forehead to the steering wheel and let the tears come.

She'd wanted it to be special for Jamie, because it had been special for her. She'd wanted it to *mean* something to him, because for a few days, he'd meant the world to her.

And instead he'd taken her heart and—

But, no. No, Jamie hadn't taken anything.

She swallowed another sob and shook her head. He hadn't taken anything, because Olivia had given herself, and there was power in that. She was going to take that power and turn it into something amazing. She was going to emerge from this smarter and stronger.

But first she was going to cry like a baby and let herself mourn what she'd never had.

## CHAPTER TWENTY-FIVE

THE TREES FLEW PAST HIM in a blur of cool green. Jamie steered around a sharp rock and balanced his weight on the balls of his feet as the bike dropped down a shallow ledge.

For a third time, he felt the vibration of the phone in his pack. For the third time, he ignored it. He was fifteen miles into a twenty-mile ride, and he'd come out here to *not* think about his family. Damned if he was going to invite them to join him. And who else could it be, calling over and over as if there was an emergency?

Shit. What if there was an emergency?

Jamie pushed on, splashing through a stream that tossed ice water against his legs. He popped over a disintegrating log and slid around a curve. A few yards later, the trail emerged from the trees into a wide turnout that seemed to hang in the air above the town. The sky went on forever above him, miles and miles of blue. Jamie propped his bike against a tree and dug the phone out. Three missed calls from Tessa. Before he could call her back, the phone buzzed again.

"What's wrong?" he asked as soon as he answered.

"Nothing," she said. "What are you doing?"

Jamie let his head fall back and he sighed his exasperation into the sky. "I'm on a ride. Why the hell did you call me three times—*four* times—in a row?"

"I just wanted to talk."

"Well, I'm busy."

"Every time I call you you're busy!"

Jamie paced to the edge of the cliff and back. When he didn't acknowledge her complaint, Tessa pressed again.

"Can you come in today?"

"No. I'm busy."

"Please, Jamie. I want to talk to you. And Eric wants to talk to you."

Jamie took a deep breath. He paced to the edge a few more times, then sat down on a boulder that eased out even farther into the air.

They wanted to talk. A few days ago, he would've said no. He was done talking. He was done pleading for a chance.

But after his first days of outrage and fury had worn off, Jamie had felt a hundred different things. Determined, yes. And self-righteous. And scared. And hopeful. But at night, those feelings had slowly fallen away and revealed the one true emotion pulsing beneath it all. Grief. Grief for what he'd lost.

"Jamie?" his sister whispered. "Will you please come talk to us?"

He closed his eyes and listened to the silence around him. The peace. It sounded nothing like what was going on inside his head. "Tessa...I don't want to talk anymore."

"I mean, we really want to talk. Not argue. And not lecture."

"Why?" he asked wearily.

"Because you're a part of this place!" she yelled. "And we don't want to do this without you." Jamie heard Eric's voice in the background before Tessa snapped, "Shut up. You're on my shit list, Eric, so zip it."

Jamie's eyes popped open. Eric was never on Tessa's shit list.

Tessa cleared her throat. "Please come in, Jamie." Her voice was all sweet vulnerability again. "You've already quit, so what can it hurt?"

Crap. His pride told him not to go, but the truth was that he missed the place. He'd only been gone a few days, but the distance was there. He missed the brewery. He missed his place there. He missed his sister. For now he was leaving Eric out of it.

He'd tried to turn his mind to the future. This morning, he'd even gone to look at a few available properties, but it felt strange. It wasn't the exhilarating passion he'd felt before. Jamie rolled his shoulders, trying to shake the feeling off, but even after fifteen miles on the trail, it was still there.

"Fine," he bit out. "I'll try to be there in an hour or so."

"Thank you!" she gasped. "I'll see you in an hour."

*"Or so,"* he clarified, unwilling to leave an opening for Eric's criticism. The phone clicked off. He got back on the bike and headed downhill. None of his worry had left, but at least he felt as if he was heading in the right direction.

Exactly one hour later, he stepped through the front door of the brewery. His timing was no accident. He hadn't even bothered to dry his hair after the shower.

He wasn't going to give Eric the chance to aim that familiar look in Jamie's direction.

"I'm here," he said flatly as he stepped into Tessa's office.

She jumped up from her chair and shooed him out. "Eric's office."

"Fine." He stalked into his brother's office and dropped into a chair. Eric looked exactly the same—stern. Jamie met his eyes and said nothing. If Eric wanted to talk, let him talk.

The door behind him closed with a snap, and Tessa dropped into the last chair. "Okay," she said, taking his hand into her smaller one.

"Okay, *what?*" Jamie asked.

Her hand squeezed his, and for one heartbeat, everything was quiet inside him. Then Eric pushed something across the desk.

Jamie looked at it but didn't understand. This meant nothing to him. At first it was just a flat brown rectangle with a white square in the middle of it. Then he saw the Donovan Brothers logo inside the square. Then the black stripe of fabric that ran up one edge of the book.

Jamie raised an eyebrow and shrugged.

Eric looked...surprised? "I understood that this was yours."

"I've never seen it before," Jamie said.

Yes, he definitely looked surprised. "You're sure?"

Tessa reached for it. "Look." She opened the book and laid it back down.

Jamie's heart jumped so hard that he nearly choked on it. It was the menu. *Olivia's* menu. "Where the hell did you get this?"

"Olivia brought it in," Tessa said softly.

His head jerked toward her. "What?"

"Ow!" Tessa complained, wriggling her fingers free of his. "That hurt."

"What do you mean? She gave this to you?"

"She gave it to Eric," Tessa answered.

Jamie couldn't believe his ears. He shook his head to try to clear them. "What the hell are you talking about?"

"She came in today," Eric said. "She brought me this. Told me I needed to give you a chance."

"Well, I didn't know a damn thing about it!" His eyes were drawn to the laminated menu, which stood out in contrast to the thinner pages behind it. "She had no right to give you this."

"You didn't recognize it," Eric said. "She told me it was your work."

"It is my work, and that's why it's none of your business." He started to reach for it, but Eric slid it back. "Hey!"

"We need to talk about this," Eric insisted.

"Like hell we do." Jamie surged forward and snagged the book from his brother's hand. When he stood, Tessa stood too.

"We like it, Jamie."

He glared at her.

"We *like* it."

"Oh, yeah?" he snarled. "*We* like it?"

She nodded. "Eric. Tell him."

"I was...surprised."

"Eric!" Tessa snapped.

Jamie rolled his eyes. "Look, I'm not interested in watching you twist his arm, Tessa. Just let it go."

"I was surprised," Eric repeated, "because it's really, really good."

"Gee, thanks." But even as Jamie fell back on his normal tone with his brother, his pulse sped with something far less cynical.

"If we were going to serve food here—*if*—then this would be a good idea."

He didn't like the way his pulse leapt with hope, so he tamped it down with a snarl. "Let's not pretend you can change your mind that quickly, Eric. Let's not pretend you could take one look at this portfolio and see the light."

Eric arched an eyebrow, but Tessa was the one who answered. "We want to talk about it, Jamie. If you can give me some time to go through the numbers, if you can let Eric and I have some input, then—"

"No. I'm not going to let you lure me back here with scraps like a damn pet. You're right. This is a good idea. It's my good idea. And I'm not interested in having Eric smash it down until it's safe enough for him. I'm not interested in giving up bits and pieces of it while you orchestrate a negotiation between us, Tessa."

"We're partners," Eric snarled. "We all get a say."

"You mean *you* get a say. You always get a say. When have you ever asked for my advice or permission?"

"I always run things by you—"

"Don't pretend you don't know the difference, Eric. You run things by me and Tessa on a fast train with no brakes. You keep us notified for courtesy's sake. You don't ask us shit."

Eric leaned forward, his mouth opening on a response, but Jamie cut his hand through the air to stop him.

"If you deny it, brother, you're a goddamn liar and we both know it."

He watched the anger creep up Eric's face in a tide of red. His hands turned to fists. But he didn't deny it. He was too honest for that.

"If I come back—*if*—then this is going to happen." He slapped his palm against the cover. "It's going to happen my way, and I'll be in charge of it. All of it."

"Jamie," Tessa cautioned.

"No, Tessa. No. I'm not going along this time. I'm not worried about keeping the peace. This idea is solid. It hardly requires any investment at all, and there's no significant remodel. It's a goddamn gift, is what it is."

Eric huffed. "You can't really expect us to make a decision like this on the spot."

"Of course not. And the same goes for you. I meant it when I left here. If I'm coming back, then I have to be sure."

Eric's eyes slid to Tessa. They stared at each other for a long time. Finally, Tessa's hand curved over his arm. "You're serious? You'll think seriously about coming back?"

"I will."

"All right. Then Eric and I will go through this line by line. We'll need at least a few days to consider it."

Jamie recognized that tone. He heard it every day while Tessa was on the phone with suppliers or distributors. It was the voice she used when she meant business.

Suddenly, this was real. It wasn't another family argument. There was a deal on the table. His deal.

"All right," he said quietly. "Call me when you want to meet."

Tessa reached for the portfolio and Jamie stepped back, nearly falling back into the chair.

"We'll need to review it."

"Oh, right." His hands tightened on the rough texture of the cover. He hadn't even seen it yet. Olivia had done this. His mind couldn't figure out what he felt about that. "Would you mind if I take it to my office for a minute? I haven't seen it like this yet. There were only loose pages before."

"Sure. Of course."

Jamie walked slowly to his sparsely furnished office and closed the door behind him. He collapsed into his chair before he finally let out a shaky breath. He'd stepped into a rabbit hole. None of this made any sense. Maybe he'd been thrown from his bike and was still lying up there on the mountain with a giant lump on his head.

Watching his own hands carefully, he slowly opened the cover of the portfolio and began to review it. She'd done an amazing job. That night at her apartment he'd barely been paying attention, but now every page stood out in vivid detail. It was all here, every idea he'd gathered. Every number he'd researched, plus some of the things he hadn't gotten to yet. It was all there in full color on glossy pages. By the time he turned the last page, his hands shook.

Why had she finished it? More important, why had she given it to Eric instead of Jamie?

Before he could overthink it, Jamie pulled out his phone and dialed her number. The phone rang five times before it went to voice mail. Jamie hung up. He had no idea what to say. Was he thankful or pissed? Had she violated his trust and privacy or had she done something amazing?

Jamie had no idea. But when he stood up, he felt stronger than he had in years. He felt...proud.

Tessa was waiting for him when he stepped into the hallway. He handed over the book without a twinge of reluctance. "Let me know if you have any questions. I'll be in touch in a few days."

This time when he walked out, he didn't look back because he knew he'd return. It was a good idea, and they'd be fools not to go with it. They might drive him up the wall 365 days a year, but his brother and sister weren't fools.

In a few months, Jamie would be running a restaurant.

## CHAPTER TWENTY-SIX

WHEN THE DOOR OF HIS OFFICE opened, Jamie held up a finger and pressed the phone harder to his ear. "Well, I'm glad you're doing well enough to be busy, but I need you out here to give me an estimate tomorrow. If you can't do it, I'll find someone else."

The electrician sighed. "How late are you guys there?"

"It's a brewery, man. If you can make it before nine, we're good."

"All right. Let's say six-thirty."

"Perfect. And another guy is coming at one, so if you want the job, you'll be sure the estimate is competitive." He hung up, glad he'd overheard so many of Eric's phone calls over the years. Jamie was damn good at being the nice guy, but nice didn't get you anywhere in the world of electricians and plumbers and equipment salesmen.

Someone cleared his throat, and Jamie glanced up to see Henry standing there. "Oh, hey. Thanks for coming in, man." He stood up to shake Henry's hand, which seemed to make the young guy nervous. "Sit down. I heard you filled in at the bar a couple of times while I was gone."

"Yeah."

"Did you like it?"

"Sure."

"I want an honest answer about that, Henry. Enjoying what you do is really the number one qualification for tending here. There are no mixed drinks to remember. There aren't a lot of complicated bills. You've just got to be friendly and happy to be here. Did you really like being at the tap?"

Henry's Adam's apple bobbed up and down when he swallowed. "I was a little nervous, but I liked it."

"Okay. You can work with Chester tonight. Close down with him. See how it feels. If Chester give you the thumbs-up, I'll give you a couple of day shifts this week so I can keep an eye on you. How does that sound?"

"Great!"

Henry scrambled up from his seat and headed back out the door. "Hey, I'm glad you're back," he added before he slipped away.

Yeah, Jamie was, too. It felt good. It felt great.

Before he could forget, Jamie opened the Twitter application on his phone and began to type. We've got a new guy behind the bar. Come meet Henry tonight. But be gentle. He's just a pup. He retweeted a couple of kind posts about the new wheat beer, then tweeted that the new apricot hefeweizen would debut next month.

He was actually having a good time, getting things done. In fact, he would've been in heaven if thoughts of Olivia hadn't been niggling at the back of his mind. She hadn't returned his calls for five days. She hadn't come to book club. It seemed she hadn't even been home for the past week. According to the school, she'd canceled class on Thursday due to "an unexpected personal development," and she wasn't expected back until tomorrow.

Unexpected personal development. What the hell did that mean? He refused to believe it could have anything to do with Victor. Whatever that man wanted from Olivia, she'd been clear that she wanted nothing from him. Hadn't she?

Jamie cracked his neck. He just wanted to see her. Any sense of betrayal over what she'd done had disappeared. It'd been pretty half-assed in the first place. Now he was back at the brewery and it seemed like last Tuesday was a hundred years ago.

Still, he couldn't do anything more than drive by her place each evening to see if she'd returned. Jamie forced his mind back to the tasks at hand.

They were still scrambling for more bartending coverage as Jamie would be spending a lot more time behind the scenes for a while, so the next thing he did was pull out his list of fill-in bartenders and the file of applicants he'd never brought in. Most of them were probably out of the job search by now, but you never knew.

"Anthony," he said when the first guy answered the phone. "It's Jamie Donovan. I know it's been a few months since you filled in, but I wondered if you were looking for any work this month."

A soft knock on the door distracted him from writing down the days Anthony could work. Jamie looked up to see Eric leaning against the doorjamb, his arms crossed. Jamie held up one finger. "Sorry, Anthony, did you say Friday night, too? Great. Why don't you come in Thursday and Friday from four to close? I'll see you then."

He hung up and raised his eyebrows at Eric. "What's wrong?"

"Nothing. I can hear you working in here and it's distracting."

"Oh. The door's closed. Do you—?"

"I'm just kidding, man." Eric dropped into the chair and leaned back as if he were settling in.

"Are you gonna watch me like a movie or something?"

"Maybe. I'm on the edge of my seat waiting to see what you do next."

Jamie finally smiled. "The cliffhanger of the season?"

"Yeah." Eric's mouth turned up the tiniest bit. "I'm glad you're back. No one wants to be alone with me sixty hours a week. Not even me. I think my arm is bruised from Tessa punching me in the same spot a thousand times."

"That bad, were you?"

"I was pretty fucking grumpy."

"Yeah?" Jamie asked. "Just because you missed me?"

Now Eric really smiled. "Something like that. And Tessa didn't let me forget for one second that it was my fault."

"I'm pretty clear on what that's like."

Eric nodded and reached idly for the catalog of restaurant supplies on the corner of Jamie's desk. He paged through, his eyes sweeping over the marked pages.

Jamie took a deep breath and braced himself for suggestions, critiques, helpful pointers about what he was doing wrong. That was fine. He could handle it.

When Eric set the catalog down, he cleared his throat and met Jamie's gaze. "You're doing a good job," he said, his mouth stiff around the strange words.

"Thanks."

"I'm a little worried you two won't need me anymore."

Jamie laughed, but Eric wasn't laughing.

His eyes tightened. "I don't really have any sort of gift, you know. I don't bring any specific skills. It's all just hard work."

"That's a skill in itself," Jamie answered.

"I suppose. But what I'm trying to say is…you can do this. All of it. You've got that same special thing Dad had. You put people at ease. You make them smile. And if you add in working your ass off, you've got it all."

"That's not true, man. I can do the front room stuff, sure. But I can't do what Tessa does with numbers and schedules. And I could never do what you do, day in and day out."

"Sure you could."

He seemed serious, but Jamie couldn't figure out what the hell was weighing on him. "Eric, the big picture means nothing to me. I can't see it. You're the only one here who can do that. And all my hard work is done on things I enjoy. You can't convince me that you enjoy dealing with those beer show guys all the time. And I know you hate managing the bottling and shipping. So spare me the pity party."

That seemed to snap Eric out of it. He managed another smile and slapped his hand down on Jamie's desk. "All right. I just wanted you to know I'm proud of you. And Dad would be, too. Not just today, either. I should've said it before."

Jamie didn't like the heat rushing to his face, so he just muttered a foul word and ordered Eric out of his office. "I've got work to do. God knows you'd better not take a chance of interrupting my rhythm."

"Good point." Eric was halfway out the door when he stopped and turned back. "Um, listen. I may have screwed something up."

"You?" Jamie scoffed.

"When Olivia Bishop came to see me, she said she was with the college. You'd said you were taking a class, and…"

"Don't worry, man. She was my teacher, but it was all on the up-and-up." Jamie winked, still a little thrilled with the idea. Or a lot.

"Right. But I didn't realize… I wasn't under the impression that you were dating her. But you were?"

"We saw each other for a little while, yes."

Eric ducked his head and let out a long breath.

"What did you do? Come on to her?" Jamie smiled at the idea. When Eric swallowed so hard Jamie could hear it, his smile faded. "What's wrong?"

"She came in here to tell me I should give you a chance. I was defensive. I said I'd already given you plenty of chances. When she pressed me, I threw your last mistake in her face."

"Which one was that?"

Eric met his gaze. "Monica Kendall."

It felt like all the blood drained from Jamie's body in an instant. His heart beat, but there was nothing for it to grasp on to. "What did you tell her?"

"The truth."

Shit. His mind spun like a tornado. Olivia must think… "Shit," he breathed. "What did she say?"

"She didn't say anything. But I could see she was upset. That was when I realized… Christ, Jamie. I'm sorry. Even if you hadn't been dating her, I had no right to say that."

"No, you didn't," Jamie said, but he didn't even feel angry. He didn't feel anything except panic. He'd made it very clear to Olivia that he hadn't been with another woman in a long time. And he'd meant it. Nobody understood. But now that she knew he'd lied, she must think the worst. That he'd been screwing with her. Playing with her feelings. She must think he was exactly like her ex-husband, just as she'd suspected.

Jamie scrubbed a hand over his face.

"I'm sorry," Eric said again. "I let my temper get the better of me."

"It's all right. I need to try to—" He looked around at all the work on his desk. He couldn't leave now. And hell, he had no idea where she might be anyway. But it had been *six days.* Six days of cursing him and hating him and telling herself that all men were cut from the same evil cloth. Jesus.

He shifted his hand and found himself looking at the pile of applications. "It's okay, Eric. I'll talk to her tonight."

"Good. I hope I didn't screw anything up for you."

"No, it's fine." What the hell had there been to screw up, anyway?

Jamie picked up the phone and got back to work, but his stomach burned with dread.

HER COFFEE STEAMED into the thin air, the wisps trailing slowly up until the breeze caught them and swirled them into the sky. At this altitude, it was cold in the shade of the balcony, even in the middle of summer, and Olivia had wrapped herself in a blanket so she could enjoy the morning view.

It had been a foolish trip, maybe. Certainly, she should be saving her money instead of spending it. But she'd needed to get away. Just away. From everyone and everything.

After she'd left the brewery, Victor had called. When she hadn't answered, he'd come to her house, and she'd been forced to hunker down in her chair and listen to him ring the doorbell for five minutes. Jamie would've come soon, too. And she'd realized that it was all too much.

Olivia had packed a small bag, and after class she'd set off in her car. She'd taken the back roads to Winter Park, the long, windy, narrow roads that added an extra hour to her drive. Once there, she'd found a little studio room right on the ski slopes that went for next to nothing in the summer. It was quiet here and nearly deserted, and she'd done nothing but sit. Sit and drink coffee. Sit and eat lunch. Sit and watch movies at night.

It was what she should have done when she'd left Victor. She should have sat and turned her thoughts inward. But there'd been so much to do. All the horrible tedious work of a divorce. The sorting out of possessions, the search for a new place to live, the panic of bank accounts and insurance and retirement plans. But what she'd really needed to do was think.

"Better late than never," she sighed, propping her feet up on the balcony railing.

She had to go back to her real life today, and that would be fine. She hadn't suffered a change of heart about anything. She was glad she'd left Victor. She was glad she'd had those days with Jamie. And she couldn't wait to start her real work. The work she'd always wanted to do.

So, these days of quiet hadn't changed anything, but they had been so worth it. She felt… My God, she felt like a grown-up, and how ironic was that?

Smiling, she finished her coffee and then went to pack her bag for the drive home. When the phone rang, she knew who it was. Her cell phone was off as it had been since she'd driven away from her apartment, and the only person who had the hotel number was Gwen.

"Good morning, Gwen," she said when she answered.

"You sound chipper. Are you going to find your way back home today?"

"Yes, but only because I have class tomorrow. What have you been up to?"

"I was hoping you'd ask. *Because I totally made out with Paul last night.* It was awesome!"

Olivia laughed. "I thought you made out with Paul last week."

"No, we kissed last week. Granted, it was for a long time, but this was waaaay more than that. Like, making out on the couch until half our clothes were off. Oh, my God, I feel like a teenager again, with the notable exception that I actually had an orgasm."

"You naughty little witch," Olivia said, echoing exactly what Gwen had said to her a few weeks ago.

"Hell, yes," Gwen growled. "I plan on being even naughtier tonight when I let him have his way with me."

"Or vice versa."

"Semantics," Gwen insisted. "However you say it, I am finally going to get laid."

Olivia's cheeks already hurt from smiling too hard. "I'm so glad you two hit it off. Do you really like him? Not just physically?"

"He's just… a regular guy. He's a real *person*."

"I think most of the faculty are actual people, you know."

"Yeah, well, you don't read their email."

"And you do?" Olivia asked.

"Ugh. Some of them make me sort it for them. Some of them even make me print it out. I know way too much. Speaking of…"

Uh-oh. Back to the real world. "What?"

"There's a rumor going around. I'm only going to tell you because I don't want you to hear it from someone else. But it might not be true."

"Just tell me," Olivia said, bracing herself for the worst. Her mind was already turning, figuring out what she'd do if she lost her job or—

"People are saying Victor's girlfriend is pregnant."

"Oh." Olivia frowned. "Is that gossip-worthy? That a man knocked up his girlfriend?"

Gwen was quiet for a minute. "My God, you already knew."

"Yes," Olivia admitted. "I did."

"So it's true?"

Olivia sighed. "Why is everyone talking about it?"

"Well, the rumor came from the dean's office, as far as I can tell. There's maybe some question about when he started seeing her."

"Ah." Here it was. Exactly what Victor had feared. He wouldn't be fired for it. He was tenured and Allison was a grown woman, not some starry-eyed undergrad. But it would hurt his reputation and his ever-important campaign for department chair.

"I wanted to tell you so it wouldn't be a blow. Especially after our talk about having children. I'm so sorry, Olivia. This must be really hard to take."

Olivia took the phone out to the balcony and leaned against the railing. The sun slanted past the roof now, and it felt like golden fire on her arms. "I was shocked, but that's it. I've been thinking about this. Poking at my feelings a little. And I'm so glad I didn't have kids with him. So thankful. And…I'm not even sure I wanted to. I think it was just one more thing to hold against him. One more thing to call unfair. I'd given up a lot and it was easy to say I gave that up, too."

"Screw him," Gwen muttered. "He deserves to be blamed."

"He does. But I own a lot of it, too. And I'm doing great, aren't I?"

"Damn right you are."

"Thanks for telling me. You're a good friend. I'll see you tomorrow, all right?"

"Be careful," Gwen admonished.

"You, too. Condoms are your friend." She hung up on Gwen's hysterical giggles and glanced at her purse. Her cell phone was there, probably full to bursting with messages. She didn't know what the hell had happened with Victor, but she didn't want to find out yet. His problems could wait. She had a drive home to enjoy.

Somehow she managed to slip back into town with no one the wiser. Her peace lasted as she unpacked and showered and washed clothes. But she still hadn't turned on her phone. And soon enough, she found herself standing in front of her kitchen table, staring down at the dark screen.

"You suck," she told the phone, but she picked it up and hit the power button. It finally blinked to life with its ridiculous message. "Twenty-two missed calls," she muttered. "Good God." Fifteen of them were from Victor. He'd really gone off the deep end, poor guy. She only had four messages, though. And three of those were from Jamie.

Her heart lurched at the thought of hearing his voice again. She missed his late-night phone calls, and she wanted to know if anything good had come of her underhandedness. And...and sadly, she just wanted to hear his voice.

Disgusted with her own stupid heart, she steeled herself against the thrill and started the first message. Her whole body tightened at his voice. "Olivia," he said. Just her name hanging in the air. She heard him sigh and had to stop herself from answering in kind. "I saw the portfolio. I don't know what to say. Just call me, okay?"

Another call from Jamie asking her to get in touch.

Then another. "I'm worried about you. Hope everything's okay."

She saved it, hating herself as she did it.

The last message had been left on her phone late last night. "Did you call the dean?" Victor demanded. "Did you tell him about Allison? Jesus, I never thought you'd really do this, Olivia. This is it now. It's over for me. I guess you don't have to worry about me bothering you anymore. I won't have the fucking time."

Well, that was mysterious, but she wasn't even curious. Their lives were no longer intertwined. Heck, they weren't even walking on parallel paths. She'd veered far off and every step took her farther away from him.

Olivia deleted his message and blocked his number. She blocked his home number, as well. She wished him luck in his new life, but she couldn't involve herself anymore.

After opening all her windows to an evening breeze, Olivia poured herself a glass of wine and turned on her laptop. The email she was looking for was right there, amazingly, unburied by junk mail. As if it were a sign.

Bracing herself for disappointment, Olivia clicked on the email from the graphic designer. There was a large file attached. It had to be the logo she'd commissioned two weeks before. Olivia crossed her fingers and opened the file. Still, it was hard to see the image with her eyes clenched shut, so she forced her eyes open just a crack, and then she gasped.

"It's perfect," she breathed. "Oh, my God, it's perfect."

*Good Table Consulting* stood out in a clean, friendly font. The letters were orange against the pale yellow oval of the background. She'd chosen to forgo any images except for a modern, stylized white plate behind the *G* of *Good Table*.

Her eyes filled with tears, and Olivia pressed a hand to her mouth to stop herself from crying. This was real now. It was real and it was hers.

She immediately typed out a gushing thank-you to the designer, then opened her website development application. She knew exactly how she wanted the website to look. Clean, modern and friendly, just like her logo. She'd already written down headers and content ideas. Tonight, she was going to build herself a website.

Olivia sipped her wine, but she didn't need it. She was dizzy with triumph and confidence and joy. She whipped through design details and layouts, her mind buzzing. Buzzing so loudly that it took her a moment to register the sound of someone knocking on her door. She frowned at being interrupted, then her eyes flew wide at who it might be.

*Jamie, Jamie, Jamie,* her stupid heart pattered. She hadn't called him back, and he wanted to talk. It could be him. Or it could be anyone. Victor or a neighbor or just the UPS guy. But she smoothed down her hair and licked her lips and hoped to God she didn't look crosseyed from staring at the computer for so long.

Not that it mattered. He meant nothing to her. As little as she'd meant to him.

She looked through the peephole and her heart flipped before beating even faster. It was him. She braced herself for the sight of him and opened the door. And just like that, all her triumph was gone and all she felt was yearning.

"You're okay," he said immediately.

"Yes." Her eyes disobeyed her, dipping down to take him in. It didn't matter that he'd hurt her. He'd also inspired the greatest pleasures she'd ever felt, and her nerves seemed to ripple at the sight of him, like rings of warm water spreading through her.

"We need to talk," Jamie said. He didn't seem to have any trouble holding her gaze. Apparently he wasn't quite as afflicted as she was.

Olivia opened her door wide. "Come in."

He stopped a few feet into her living room, seeming to have no idea where he should go.

"Would you like a drink?"

"No, thanks. I'm fine. I just…" Hands in his pockets, he swept a lost look over the room. "Were you out of town?"

"Yes."

He waited for her to say more, but if he wanted to talk, he needed to get to it. She didn't want to pretend they were still friends. Friends didn't lie to each other.

Jamie cleared his throat. "I don't quite know where to start."

"I'll start," she said softly. "I'm sorry. I shouldn't have done what I did."

His shoulder rose on a deep breath before he turned to face her. "You probably shouldn't have, but that's okay."

"I wanted to help, and…" She held up her hands. "And I just wanted to help."

"It did help."

"Yeah?" Relief bloomed inside her.

"We talked. Me and Eric and Tessa. In fact, I'm back at the brewery. We're making it happen."

"You're doing it? Seriously? That's great." She started to move toward him, then realized that she shouldn't.

"I wanted to tell you, but you never answered, and..."

"I was out of town," she said, as if cell phones didn't function at a distance. They stood there awkwardly, just staring at each other. She didn't think she'd ever seen Jamie look awkward before. "Well, I'm truly glad it worked out. I hope you'll... I hope you'll keep in touch."

His eyes flickered to the door, but he didn't move. "I know what my brother told you," he said. "And I wanted to explain."

That snapped her from her awkward hovering. Olivia shook her head and retrieved her wineglass from the table. "There's no need. Really."

"No, I want to be—"

"I mean it," she snapped as she opened her fridge and grabbed the wine. "I don't want an explanation or... whatever you want to call it. It's done. I'm over it."

"You're *over* it? Just like that?"

"What do you want me to say, Jamie? We had a thing. We had fun. And if you want it to mean something to me, then that would mean your lies meant something, too. And I *need* them not to mean anything."

"Olivia, please listen. It's—"

"I don't want to listen! What could you possibly say? 'It isn't what you think? It meant nothing? I only told you that to make you feel better about yourself?' I've heard it all before, Jamie. And believe me, none of it makes it better. Do you know what it's like to be lied to? To be made a fool of?"

"*Yes.* In fact, I do know what it's like to be made a fool of. That woman—" He looked up at the ceiling as if it could help guide him through this minefield of manipulation. But apparently the ceiling offered no answers, because Jamie closed his eyes, his brow furrowing.

"Even if she screwed you over, Jamie, that doesn't mean she doesn't count. How many other women have you slept with that you don't count? Jesus, were there others while you were seeing *me?*"

"No. And that's not why I don't count her."

"Did you have sex with her?"

"Yes," he growled.

"Then why are we having this conversation? You made a damned *point* of telling me you hadn't slept with anyone in over a year. You didn't even have to say it! I wasn't asking!"

"I wanted you to understand that you meant something to me."

"Jamie…" Olivia threw her hands up. "I feel like I'm in the twilight zone! It doesn't mean *anything* if you're lying."

"I'm not lying!" he shouted. "I don't count her, because I didn't want it."

"Oh, for God's sake. I give up."

Jamie paced to the dining room table and put both his hands flat on the wood. His head dropped, the muscles in his neck standing sharp against the skin. "My brother had been working this deal for months. He didn't want to involve me, but I insisted on coming to dinner with Roland Kendall."

"Roland Kendall?" She tried to figure out how she knew the name.

"He's a real bigwig. The owner of High West Air."

Oh, right. He was a huge name in Colorado business. She waved an impatient hand.

"We struck a deal to become the sole provider of beer for High West. It was a big deal. Our biggest ever. It would get our beer into the hands of a national audience. And I wanted to be involved. Wanted to prove myself. So I went to dinner with Eric and Roland Kendall and the VP of High West…who just happened to be Kendall's daughter."

When her eyes widened, he laughed bitterly. "Yeah. Exactly. But I'm not an idiot. I'm honestly not. A few weeks later, she came into the brewery. Wanted to try some of the beer. I gave her the VIP treatment, of course."

He laughed again, and goose bumps spread over Olivia's skin at the sound. Bitterness sounded completely wrong coming from Jamie.

"By closing time, she said she was too drunk to drive. I was playing the part, you know? Friendly, helpful. I offered to give her a ride. That's all I offered. In fact, I very pointedly said that I'd drive her car and take a taxi back to the brewery. She was all over me in the fucking car. What was I supposed to do? I pulled up to her place, and she asked me to walk her in.…"

"And you had sex?"

"Yeah, we had sex. After I told her I wasn't interested. Said I didn't want to complicate things since we were going to have a working relationship. She didn't like that at all. Monica is pretty. She's rich. Used to getting what she wants. She said if I was going to be rude about it, maybe we shouldn't have a working relationship at all."

Olivia had told herself she was only listening so he'd get it over with and leave. There was nothing he could possibly say that would make a difference. But her frown edged from scorn to concern. "She said that?"

"Yeah. 'What will my father say when he finds out I asked you to drive me home and you wouldn't keep your hands off me?'"

When Olivia gasped, Jamie laughed that awful laugh again. "I realized I was going to ruin the deal. The damn irony almost killed me. It was all my brother had talked about for months. He insisted it was the future of the brewery. And this bitch was going to kick it aside like garbage if I didn't stay. So I stayed."

"Oh, Jamie…"

"I spent the night, and then I went home in the morning, and I'd ruined everything anyway."

"What do you mean?"

"Her father saw me leaving. But in the end, it didn't matter. Because while Monica Kendall was, literally, fucking me over, her brother used my absence to break into the brewery in an attempt to steal credit card information."

When Olivia's forehead wrinkled in confusion, Jamie waved a hand. "It's a long, screwed-up story. The deal fell through, and my brother had yet more proof that I was the ultimate fuckup."

"He didn't understand why you did it?"

"I didn't tell him."

"Why?" she cried.

"First of all, I didn't particularly want to talk about it. Second, what could it possibly matter? Was Eric going to explain to her father that his little girl had forced me into her bed? No, it wouldn't have changed anything."

"It would've changed how your brother felt."

"No, it's going to take a lot more than that to change how he feels about me, but I'm doing it."

"Jamie…" She didn't know what to say. "I'm so sorry."

He shrugged. "I wouldn't have told you, either, but… That's why I don't count her, Olivia."

She had no fight against this. She couldn't stop herself from walking to him, putting her arms around him. "I'm sorry," she whispered. Tears choked her voice at the thought of what that woman had done to him. "I'm so sorry."

His arms were so warm when they curved around her back. He tucked his face against her hair and breathed in. "Don't say it like she…like I… It would've been over and done if nobody had found out. I'm fine."

But she wasn't sure he was fine. He sounded more than angry. He sounded *hurt*.

"So, there hasn't been anyone, Olivia. Not until you. And it did mean something to me. It *does*."

"God, I'm so sorry." She hugged him, wanting to hold on forever. But there was more. "But…your brother said you also got into a fight with a jealous husband."

He eased away, holding her in front of him so he could meet her eyes. "Olivia, that was *your* jealous husband."

"What?" Her hands curled, grabbing on to his T-shirt. "Please tell me you're kidding."

"I'm not. He came into the brewery last Friday night, looking for a fight. Unfortunately, I gave it to him."

"Oh, no." She let go of him and covered her mouth in horror. "I'm sorry. That was when you left. He's the one who—"

"It's no big deal. I shouldn't have punched him."

"Are you okay?" Reaching for his face, she stroked his jaw. "Did he hit you?"

"Hell, no, he didn't hit me. Hard to reach my face from the floor."

"Oh, my God." She tried to look serious, but her lips kept curving up. "I'm so sorry."

"Are you? You look a little bit thrilled."

"Shut up!" she said, laughing despite her best attempts to stop it.

Jamie's face softened. "Does that mean you forgive me?"

"For hitting Victor? No forgiveness necessary."

"No, I mean for lying. About Monica."

Olivia forgot her amusement and slipped back into his arms. "Of course, I do. Of course. And I'm so sorry if I caused you any trouble."

"Never. You made everything better."

Olivia closed her eyes, but she felt a tear escape and slip a jagged path down her face until it disappeared into the warm cotton beneath her cheek. He felt so good. He smelled so familiar. And she had no idea what this meant. He wasn't her boyfriend. He wasn't her lover. Yet she wanted him so much. So much that it hurt like a coal inside her chest, burning through everything.

"Christ, I've missed you," he whispered.

She couldn't respond or she'd cry all over him and beg him to stay. Just stay. Olivia tightened her hold on his shirt and pulled him even closer. His heart thundered at first. She held him until it started to slow. Then she held him some more. All of his tension was gone. She should really let him go.

After a few minutes, she was strong enough to ease her hold and draw back. "Will you tell me what you've been—?"

Her words were cut off by his mouth on hers, his tongue sliding in to taste her. Lust slammed through her so hard that she whimpered and sank her fingernails into his back. The same urgency seemed to take him over. His hands were everywhere, shaping her body as if he needed to remember everything about it.

She was panting, whimpering, immediately desperate. She wanted closer. Impossibly close. When he lifted her, she wrapped her legs around him just to feel more of him. Jamie swung her around and set her on the dining room table.

"Yes," she urged, drawing back to shove his shirt over his head. She kissed his chest, licked his nipple, while Jamie struggled to lift her shirt, as well.

"Your arms," he ordered, and she raised them to help. She took her glasses off and heard them fall to the floor, but Jamie was unhooking her bra so she didn't give a damn. Instead of scrambling for her glasses, she reached to unbutton his jeans. Jamie pressed his palms to her breasts with a sigh of pleasure.

But she didn't have time for this. The last button of his jeans had given way and she stroked her hand down the ridge of his shaft. "I want you inside me," she rasped. "Now."

He groaned and kissed her again. She felt the sharp catch in his breath when she slipped her hand inside his underwear and touched the bare heat of him.

Turning her face away, she begged, "Please. I need you." And she did. Desperation clawed through her, hurting her heart with its brutality. "Please."

His hands reached for her jeans. One heartbeat later and he was tugging them down, taking her underwear with them, and she was totally naked, her knees spread around his hips. Jamie's eyes glittered as he pulled his wallet free and slipped a condom out before tossing the wallet to the floor.

She licked her lips as she watched him roll the condom down his thick shaft, and then he took himself in hand and rubbed the head against her. He slid and slipped until she moaned. Finally, he pressed forward and Olivia sobbed in relief as his shaft stretched her pussy. "Yes," she said, watching him disappear into her body. "God, yes." When he'd finally sunk as deep as he could go, she sighed.

"Shh," Jamie whispered, his thumb wiping a tear from her face.

She shook her head, but more tears came.

"Don't cry, sweetie."

"I'm sorry," she murmured, but when he tried to pull her gently against him, she refused to let him comfort her. Comfort wasn't what she needed. Instead she surged up to kiss him, rolling her hips into him.

He thrust and kissed her back, so she rolled her hips again, sucking at his tongue until he moaned and stroked deep into her mouth at the same time he thrust deep into her sex.

For a while it was slow and good and hot as he primed her body, easing her toward a climax, but that desperation was back, clawing through her. Olivia put her hands to the table and eased back until she was flat against the cold wood. "Fuck me," she ordered, bending her knees to slide them higher up his body.

He looped his hands behind her legs and pulled them even higher. This time when he thrust, she cried out at the strength of it. She was totally open to him, totally vulnerable, and he slid deeper than ever with every thrust.

Olivia spread her arms and curved her fingers over the table edges, holding tight as he began to pound into her. She'd wanted this. Wanted him to take her just like this on a table, as if she'd been served up for his pleasure.

His hands tightened their grip and eased her legs wider. He was a glorious work of art as he worked himself inside her, his muscles flexing beneath his skin like an animal's. Olivia couldn't look away. Instead she watched him as she forced one hand to let go of its death grip on the table. She slid that hand down her body, and stroked her fingers over her clit.

"Yes," he snarled. "I want to see you come."

Oh, he would. Her body was already humming. Her nerves already pulling tighter around her clit as she rubbed it. She wanted to come for him. Wanted him to see what he did to her.

His teeth bared in a snarl, Jamie let go of any restraint. His thrusts became brutal as he watched her touch herself.

"Oh, God," she whispered as her body seemed to draw itself in. She felt nothing but his relentless invasion and her circling fingers. She was nothing but this in that moment. Nothing but an animal act. "God," she prayed. "Jamie."

Her body seemed to shiver and float up for a split second, and then it crashed hard back into her. She threw her head back and screamed, and Jamie growled his pleasure like an animal as her hips bucked against him.

Her body was numb by his last thrust. She couldn't even open her eyes as the last tremor shook through his body. She'd wanted to watch him, but she couldn't summon the will to be sorry.

Her skin was slick against the table. Jamie's hands eased their hold on her legs. But she couldn't open her eyes.

"Come 'ere," he muttered, bending down to ease one arm behind her back. When he lifted her, she managed a frown of displeasure and tightened her legs around him, so he wouldn't slip free of her body. She wasn't ready for that. But when he collapsed onto the couch, he was still deep inside her. Olivia snuggled close with a happy sigh.

"I don't want this to just be fun," Jamie said, his breath sliding over her shoulder. "I want it to be everything."

The last horrible remnants of that desperation stirred inside her. It dug its claws into her throat and pulled itself higher. She let it free on a sob. Her tears fell down her cheeks and slid over his skin. "I'm so sorry," she sobbed. "I'm sorry for what I said to you."

"Shh. It doesn't matter. And you were right. I did need to grow up."

She shook her head. "So did I."

"I think I'm in love with you, Olivia."

Her eyes popped open. She must have tensed, because she felt him chuckle. "I know it's harder for you. There's the divorce, and… I don't expect you to return the feeling. Yet. But I've never said it before, and I wanted to say it to you. Now you can tell me I don't know what I'm talking about."

She leaned back and framed his face in her hands. "You don't know what you're talking about."

"Screw you."

Her gaze slipped down to their laps.

"Exactly."

"Jamie…" She tried hard to think what to say. How to dissuade him or herself or—

"Hush," he ordered. So she closed her mouth and just looked at him. His gaze slipped to a place past her shoulder.

"What's this?"

She tried to look without moving too much, but Jamie was easing her up. She closed her eyes as he slid out of her.

"Good Table Consulting," he said, and her eyes popped open.

"Oh," she said, twisting around to sit beside him. "That's… That's me."

"Are you kidding?" His face lit up. For her. He grinned and touched the logo on the screen. "That's you?"

"It is." She ducked her head when he looked at her, but his finger eased her chin up.

"You're doing it."

"I am." She couldn't help but answer his smile.

"You're amazing, you know that?"

"I'm just doing something I should've done a long time ago."

"I guess we're just a couple of late bloomers, huh?"

She kissed his sweet smile. "Some of us later than others?"

"Just a little, Ms. Bishop."

"I…" She couldn't say it. Not yet.

"I know," he whispered.

## CHAPTER TWENTY-SEVEN

OLIVIA BURST FROM HER FRONT door as if she were breaking out of a starting gate. She was late. *Late.*

Well, she wasn't quite late, but she wasn't early, either,
and she couldn't stand the idea of being late for her first
dinner with Jamie's family. She was driving to Jamie's
place first, so she could spend the night and still leave
early enough to make it to Denver on Monday morning for an eight-o'clock meeting with a commercial real
estate agent. She didn't need new space herself, but she
needed to keep up with what was available on the local
market.

Rushing for the parking lot while she balanced her
bag and the chocolate cake she'd made for dinner with
his family, Olivia didn't notice the girl standing next to
her car. In fact, she'd already hit the locks and reached
for the door when she caught movement close by and
jumped with a little yelp. The cake slipped, but she held
on to it.

"Allison?" she gasped as the girl stepped away from
the bumper. "Good Lord, you scared me."

Allison set her jaw and didn't say anything.

Olivia blinked in shock at the sight of her. Not just
because her presence was unexpected—and it was—but
because she'd changed completely in the three weeks

since Olivia had last seen her. Gone was the girl with the long ponytail and slightly bohemian dress. She'd cut her hair into a shaggy, trendy bob and she was wearing dark jeans and a black maternity top that was clearly designed to emphasize her pregnancy rather than hide it.

"Um. Were you waiting for me?" Olivia asked. The cake started to slip again, so she opened the door and set it carefully down.

When she straightened, Allison was glaring. She put her hands on her hips. "We're getting married," she said, each letter deliberately crisp.

"Oh. Well. Congratulations."

"I want you to stay away from him."

"Allison," she sighed. "That really won't be a problem. We've been living separate lives for quite a while now."

The girl smirked. "Yeah, right."

Good Lord. "Listen, I don't know what he's told you, but—"

"What he's *told* me is that he's still in love with you and that you're going to get back together."

"That's not true."

"Oh, I know it's not true now. I took care of that."

She looked so proud, the stupid girl. As if she'd won herself a prize. As if she'd trapped some valuable animal who— Olivia blinked and stared at Allison's smirk. "Oh, my God, you called the dean, didn't you?"

Her smirk wavered for a split second, but then she smiled as if she'd wanted Olivia to figure it out. "I had no choice. Victor was obsessed with you. He claimed I tried to trap him by getting pregnant, as if he had nothing to do with it."

"Did you?"

"No! But once I found out I was pregnant… He just wanted to walk away."

"I'm sorry. That's…" Olivia could understand how terrifying that must be, but, then again… "Did you ever think about letting him walk?"

"I'm not going to be like my mom. Kids by three different men, none of whom ever stuck around for more than two years. I didn't work my ass off in college to end up back where I started. I wasn't going to let him walk away."

"So you told the dean."

"You don't understand," she snapped, pointing her finger in Olivia's face. "After you started dating that guy, Victor couldn't stop thinking about it. It was driving him crazy. I kept telling him that he had me, but he just… Do you know what he did when I told him we were having twins?"

Olivia's eyes flew to the girl's belly in shock. She watched Allison curl a protective hand around her stomach.

"He went to your boyfriend's bar and got drunk and started a fight with him! As if that was going to change anything! He was panicking, so I did what I had to do."

"How does getting him in trouble fix anything?"

Allison shrugged. "It's not much of a scandal if we're married when the girls are born, is it?"

Oh, she was smart. Olivia could just imagine Victor's conversation with the dean. *This isn't sordid, sir.*

*In fact we're getting married in a month. Everything here is on the up-and-up. Not a scandal in sight.*

Olivia crossed her arms and looked down at her feet. She wanted to tell Allison she was making a terrible mistake. Why would she want to marry a man who didn't want to marry her? But anything she said would be shadowed by the specter of the jealous ex-wife. The spurned woman. She—

"Oh, my God," Olivia breathed. "You're the one who called Lewis, aren't you?"

Allison shrugged again. "I figured things would be easier if you had to leave. Then Victor wouldn't see you every day at the U."

"You know what? You deserve him. Congratulations."

"Just stay away from him," Allison repeated, her eyes glowing with triumph.

"You got it, girl."

Olivia got in her car and tried not to gloat as she pulled out. After all, she was on her way to see her cute boyfriend. The one who wanted her around and wasn't in love with another woman. But as she drove away, Allison grew tiny in the rearview mirror and Olivia's smile faded. Ten years from now, maybe Allison would wake up and realize she had bigger dreams than Victor Bishop. Olivia took a deep breath and wished her luck. The girl was going to need it.

All thoughts of Allison and her reluctant fiancé disappeared like a popped bubble when Olivia pulled up to Jamie's house and found him sitting on the porch waiting for her. "Am I late?" she asked as she scrambled out of her car.

"Nope." He leaned in for a kiss as he stole the cake from her hands.

"I'm sorry. We'd better hurry. I don't want to make you late."

"Oh, I doubt anybody would be shocked."

"Don't say that."

"It's true." He transferred the cake to his truck and dropped her bag inside the house before locking up.

Once they'd pulled out onto the street, she took his hand and squeezed it. "Everything's going well now, right? With your family?"

"Everything's great, but it'll take a while to build up trust. I spent a lot of years breaking it down."

"I don't understand. From what I've heard, you didn't do anything too awful."

"I think it was more quantity than quality. When I was a teenager, I was always skipping school and blowing off assignments and hanging out where I shouldn't have been hanging out. Sometimes I'd take off for a couple of days, then just waltz back home like nothing had happened. But mostly, I just blew them off. I wanted them to leave me alone. I didn't want to owe them more than I already did."

She frowned at him, trying to figure out what he meant.

"But that was in high school," he said. "I mostly screwed around in college like any other kid at a notorious party school. Since then, I've just…gotten by."

"Why did you feel like you owed them?"

His eyes flew to hers before sliding away again. He shrugged. Traffic stalled out as a huge crowd of bicyclists passed in front of them. A police officer held up his hand when the light turned green. More bikes passed. They must have accidentally cut through a race route.

"What did you owe them?" she pressed.

He shook his head. "Everything."

"You mean Eric? He took care of you guys, right?"

"Yeah. It's complicated."

"By what?"

The last of the bicycles appeared to have passed, but the light had turned red again. Jamie shifted in his seat.

"I'm sure it's perfectly normal for a teenage boy to act out after his parents die, Jamie. Anyone would. You can't blame yourself for that."

"That's not what I blame myself for."

"Then what is it?"

He set his jaw and didn't answer, and Olivia decided to let it go. He'd talk about it when he wanted to, and she didn't want to start a fight. They'd only made up a week ago and they were on their way to see his family. Now was not the time for tension.

She took his hand and squeezed it. "All that matters is that you're getting along now. I thought you were happy when I first met you, but now it's almost like you've found peace."

"Yeah," he said, squeezing his hand again. "It's something like that."

The traffic jam finally gave way, and Jamie seemed to sigh with relief.

"We're late, aren't we?"

He laughed. "We're not late. I told them we'd be there around six."

"You told me five-thirty. I've been so worried!"

He leaned in and stole a quick kiss. "You know how hot it gets me when you're responsible."

"Jamie!" She shoved him back to his side of the car. "Why did you say five-thirty?"

His smile faded and he cleared his throat. "I thought we might stop somewhere else real quick."

The nervous way his fingers tightened on the steering wheel confused her, but she nodded. "Of course."

They drove down the street, then took a few more turns until they were in a part of town she didn't think she'd ever driven through. Jamie pulled into an entry gate that made her sit up straighter. It was a cemetery.

He eased slowly down the narrow lane before he stopped and cut the engine. "I wanted to bring you here because…my parents are buried here." He gestured up a hill dotted with large trees.

Olivia gasped and reached for the door handle. "Do you want to go up? We can. I don't really care about being late, Jamie."

His hand closed over her wrist. "No. I don't want to. I…I don't go up there."

"Ever?"

"Only when Tessa insists."

She settled back into her seat and watched Jamie as he stared out the window.

"They were really great parents," he said.

"I'm sure they were. Do you look like your dad?"

His lips turned up for a moment. "Yeah. My mom used to complain that she did all the work of having babies, and we got all of his genes."

She didn't know what to say. That she was sorry he'd lost them? Those words seemed so paltry in the face of what had been taken from him. "I'm so sorry," she said helplessly.

"Me, too. I wasn't…I wasn't the son they deserved."

"Oh, Jamie—"

"It was my fault, Olivia."

"What was?"

"The accident."

Her heart clenched and her lungs seemed to freeze. "What do you mean? You were there?"

"No. None of us were there. Tessa was spending the night at a friend's house. Eric was already living in Denver. And I was out doing what I always did— getting into trouble."

"So how could it have been your fault?"

Jamie closed his eyes for a moment and swallowed hard, but when he opened his eyes they were dry. "I told my parents I was going to a school dance, but there was no dance. Some rich girl was having a party at her house up in the mountains. I had a car, so I volunteered to be the designated driver. I wanted to do the right thing. But I didn't. When we got to the party, I started drinking along with everyone else. But then we had to go. My friend had to be home by midnight or he'd be grounded. I was drunk. Everyone was drunk. So I called my parents. I told them I'd had a drink and I needed a ride home. Of course, Mom and Dad jumped in the car. But they never made it. It'd been raining for three days. There was a rockslide. They drove right into a boulder. Never even hit the brakes."

He let Olivia take his hand, but he didn't look at her. She tried to swallow her tears. My God. He'd been six-teen. He must have felt… "It was an accident, Jamie."

"It wasn't an accident. It was me being irresponsible. 'Oh, sure, I'll drive. I'll just have one beer.'"

"You called them because that was the right thing to do!"

"No," he said firmly. "The right thing to do would've been to not lie and go to the party. Or stay sober when I told my friends I would."

"You did the right thing by not getting in the car with your friends and driving home drunk. Then *you* would've been dead."

"I know. But at least my little sister would've been raised by a mom and dad instead of two clueless brothers. At least—"

"Stop. Jamie, you can't blame yourself for an accident. Your family doesn't blame you, do they?"

He finally looked at her then. "You're the only one I've ever told."

Oh, God. She saw it in his face then. The reason he'd pushed his brother and sister away. The reason he felt he owed them so much.

"I couldn't tell them. I didn't want them to hate me as much as I hated myself."

"Jamie, no." She reached for him, getting as close as she could in his car. "Don't say that."

"It's true. I was a coward. I never wanted them to know how worthless I was."

"Don't say that," she managed to say past her tears. "It's not true, Jamie."

"It's okay," he whispered into her hair. "I'm finally figuring it out. I think I deserve something better than how I've been living. At the very least, I want to live in a way that would have made them proud. I owe them that. My parents and my siblings."

"Jamie, you don't owe anybody anything. You were sixteen. You made a stupid mistake, but then you did exactly what they would've wanted you to." Tears spilled down her cheeks, but she kept her face against his shoulder so he wouldn't see. "And no matter how hard you tried to throw your life away, you couldn't do it, because you're a good man. You took care of your sister and graduated from college and you worked with your family every day. I've never seen you be unkind to anyone. Ever."

She felt his cheek rise in a smile. "What about that time I punched Victor?"

"That was an act of mercy. For me, anyway. I'm just saying that you were trying to do the right thing. And you're no more at fault than your sister would've been if she'd asked them to pick her up at the mall. You wouldn't have blamed her, because it was an accident."

"I can't see it that way, but I've started learning to forgive myself." He took a deep breath. She watched his chest expand and felt his breath tease over her hair. "I told you about this so you could understand. I'm working on it. I'm trying. And I know I said the wrong things that day we fought, but…"

"It's okay."

"Olivia, I don't like you because I think you'll make me a better person. Or because you're smart and mature and I need that in my life. I like you because I think there's a chance I might actually deserve you. Just a chance."

Forgetting her vow to hide her crying, Olivia burst into tears.

"Come on. I'm not that bad, am I?"

"Shut up," she sobbed. "I love you."

"Yeah?" He eased her away so he could see her face, though she tried to hide her blubbering. "Really?"

"Really," she gasped, tucking her face back into his shirt so she could cry freely. She loved him so much that she should be scared, but somehow she wasn't. Whatever would happen would happen, and she was strong enough to bear heartbreak if she had to. But maybe she wouldn't have to.

"Thank you for telling me what happened," she whispered. She couldn't believe he'd lived with that for so long. No wonder he'd been so lost. "You have to tell your family, Jamie."

He shook his head. "Maybe someday. Not today. I need time. I need to think."

She let it go. It was his secret. His truth.

"Are you done crying?" he finally asked.

"Maybe."

"Should we go see my family?"

"Yes." She sniffled a few times, trying to stop her tears. "Okay. Just give me a minute." Olivia snapped down the passenger-side mirror to look at her face. "Oh, no. I look terrible."

"You're just a little moist. Here." He stuffed a Dairy Queen napkin into her hand.

She dabbed carefully at her cheeks and told herself it didn't matter. So she'd be late and blotchy, and it didn't matter. She'd be with Jamie, and things were good with him, and getting better every day.

Jamie put the car in gear, but for a long moment his foot stayed pressed to the brake. "Next time," he said, "maybe we'll go up the hill."

When she took his hand, his fingers squeezed hers hard. "I think that's a great idea."

JAMIE GAVE A PERFUNCTORY knock on the front door before opening it wide. He gestured to Olivia and watched as she stepped inside and glanced around the front rooms.

His chest felt suddenly tight. What did she see? It just looked like home to him. Dark wood floors, a big fireplace, the front window where his mom had always put the Christmas tree. It all looked the same to Jamie, but as he followed Olivia in, he realized he was different now.

He didn't feel like a kid coming home. And he didn't feel like someone stealing into a place where he didn't deserve to be. Instead, he felt…good. Peaceful. Happy to have Olivia here. Thrilled to see her smile and reach for his hand.

"It's beautiful. You must miss living here."

"No. This house has too many memories. But I'm glad to be here now. With you."

She always blushed when he said things like that, and she was still blushing when the sound of Tessa's quick footsteps echoed down the hall.

"Are you ready?" he whispered.

"No!" Olivia answered, her eyes wide with trepidation. "I'm not ready."

"Too late." He took the cake from her hands as Tessa

rushed into the entry, a wide grin already spreading across her face. "Hello!"

"Hi." Olivia stepped back as if she were alarmed by Tessa's mad rush, but Tessa just opened her arms and caught Olivia in a hug.

"It's so good to finally meet you!"

"Um." Olivia tentatively patted his sister's back. "We already met at the brewery."

"Yes, but not like this. This is *official*."

Jamie grinned until Olivia finally smiled at him past his sister's shoulder. "First girl I've ever brought home," he said with a wink.

Tessa snorted. "First girl whose name we even learned," she clarified.

Olivia eased out of the hug and laughed. "I feel kind of like I'm your prom date, Jamie."

"Don't worry," Tessa whispered. "I'll only make you pose for a few pictures."

"Um. Okay." Olivia clearly couldn't tell whether or not Tessa was joking. Actually, Jamie wasn't sure, either.

"Luke will be here in a few minutes. He had to work—"

Tessa was interrupted when the front door opened on a loud whoosh, but it wasn't Luke.

"Oh," Eric said, his eyes flying to Olivia as he stepped inside. "Hello."

"Olivia, you've already met Eric," Jamie said dryly.

"I have. It's nice to see you again."

"Yeah," Eric said. "Nice to see you, too. And, um… I'm sorry about the last time." Eric was actually squirming. That was something Jamie had never seen before.

He was pretty sure he was enjoying it, so he didn't bother to step into the awkward silence. Instead, he just smiled. Let Eric be the one left swinging in the wind.

"So," Eric said, his eyes sliding away.

Tessa jumped into the pause. "You brought a cake!" She snatched it from Jamie's hands. "It looks delicious. Dinner's not quite ready yet, so Jamie, why don't you show Olivia the house. I'll put this in the kitchen."

"Thank you!" Olivia called as Tessa hurried away.

Laughing at the dazed expression on Olivia's face, Jamie took her hand and led her on the grand tour. He started upstairs, pointing out the window in his old room that he'd used as a frequent escape route as a teenager. Then the banister where he'd broken his arm trying to slide down it as if he was grinding on a skateboard. In the hallway, there were pictures of his family. He'd always wondered how Tessa could stand to live with the pictures of Mom and Dad on constant display, but now he was glad they were here.

"You really do look like him." Olivia touched a finger to his dad's cheek. "He looks happy like you."

"He was."

"And what's this?" she asked, pointing at the senior picture Tessa had forced him to sit for.

He shook his head, but Olivia didn't drop it. "Look at that smile. Was every girl in your school in love with you?"

"No."

"Liar. It doesn't matter. You're mine now."

"I am." He glanced toward the kitchen, and when he didn't see his sister, he pulled Olivia into his arms. "You know my favorite thing about you? All my family can see is my new responsible girlfriend. They have no idea what you're really like underneath that cardigan."

"Jamie," she warned, her eyes widening as she glanced around. But he noticed the way her neck arched when he kissed it, giving him better access to that spot just beneath her ear.... She sighed when his mouth closed over it.

By the time he drew back, her eyes had gone soft and dreamy. God, he loved her like crazy. "All right, I won't molest you in the hallway. But I'm giving you a heads-up. Your final exam is after dinner."

"What?"

"We never finished your training."

"What training?" she asked.

"In fun and adventure. On our way home, we're going to stop at a store."

She shook her head in confusion.

"I've got a crisp hundred in my pocket. We're going to stop at The White Orchid, and you have to spend every penny."

"The White Orchid!" Olivia yelped.

Tessa stuck her head around the corner. "Oh, my God, have you guys been there lately?"

Jamie laughed, but Olivia looked like she might be stroking out as she slapped a hand over her mouth. She shook her head in frantic denial. Jamie tugged her into the kitchen, although she seemed to be trying to dig her heels into the wood.

"I'm sure you've never been there," Jamie said to his little sister. "Right?"

"Ha! I'm on a first-name basis with the manager."

He hadn't noticed Eric leaning against the wall, but

Jamie damn sure noticed when his brother started choking. Eric's face turned beet-red, and he banged a fist
against his own chest as he coughed.

"Jesus, man. Are you okay?"

Eric shook his head, but the coughing subsided.

Tessa rolled her eyes. "Oh, come on, Eric. It's not a
seedy sex shop. It's really pretty inside. Not one X-rated
video booth to be found." She turned her smile on
Jamie. "Are you guys going in for a class?"

"A class?" he scoffed. "Hardly."

Eric cleared his throat. "What do you mean? What
class?"

"The last time I was there, the manager was giving
a class on…" She glanced at each of them in turn, then
waggled her eyebrows. "*Fellatio.* I almost died. There
were cucumbers on the table. I think maybe she gave
demonstrations."

Eric's face went from red to ghost-white in the space
of one breath.

"Jeez," Tessa said. "Calm down. I didn't sit in on it.
I just overheard it as I was leaving."

Eric's lips were pressed so tightly together that Jamie
had to roll his eyes. Sure, he was horrified that Tessa
was so familiar with The White Orchid, but Eric was
taking the uptight act to a new level. "Maybe you should
stop in and ask if they offer any classes on loosening
up, Eric. I don't think you've had fun since 1997. Maybe
that woman could teach you something."

Eric's eyes went wide. *"What?"*

"I'm just saying—" But before Jamie could finish his
sentence, Eric spun on his heel and stalked out of the

kitchen. The sound of the back door slamming echoed through the whole house.

"Wow," Jamie muttered. "What's wrong with him?"

Tessa shrugged. "He probably just thinks he hasn't raised us right if we're hanging out at The White Orchid. Speaking of which…" She pointed a spatula at Olivia. "Check out the pretty lingerie from France. It's amazing."

When Tessa disappeared into the pantry, Olivia poked Jamie hard in the ribs. "I hate you," she whispered.

"Uh-uh," he said, turning so he could put his arms around her. "Too late for that, darlin'. You already confessed your love. You're stuck with me now."

"But now your family thinks I'm…"

"Sexy? Hot? Perfect? You are."

"Jamie…" Her frown melted as she shook her head. "God, why is it so hard to stay mad at you?"

He leaned in and pressed one soft kiss to her mouth. "Because I'm a really good, decent guy?"

Her lips turned up in a smile. "You say that like you mean it."

"Yeah." Something warm and sweet filled the last of that hollow space inside his chest. "I'm pretty sure I do."

\* \* \* \* \*